Keep Them Close

Sophie Flynn is a Cotswolds based psychological thriller author with an MA in Creative Writing from Oxford Brookes. Alongside writing, Sophie is the Head of Marketing at Jericho Writers. After being awarded a place at Swanwick Writers' Summer School on the TopWrite scheme for young writers in 2017, Sophie began writing short fiction. She has since had many stories published and placed in competitions with organisations such as Writing Magazine and The Cheltenham Literature Festival.

D1100702

keep them close

SOPHIE FLYNN

hera

First published in the United Kingdom in 2022 by

Hera Books
Unit 9 (Canelo), 5th Floor
Cargo Works, 1–2 Hatfields
London, SE1 9PG
United Kingdom

A CIP catalogue record for this book is available from the British Library.

Print ISBN 978 1 80436 029 3
Ebook ISBN 978 1 80436 916 6

Look for more great books at www.herabooks.com

Printed and bound in Great Britain by Clays Ltd, Elcograf S.p.A.

1

For my mum, who is the best in every way

Prologue

One day, someone will find everything I ever wrote and they will judge me for it, hate me for it, blame me for it. They'll pull apart my sentences, look for meaning where there is none and miss it where it hides in plain sight. They'll call me terrible things.

A bitch. A bad mother. A killer.

They'll dissect my every move. Could they have seen it coming? Was there something someone could have done to stop it? To save her?

But the answer is no. Nothing could have stopped it.

No one could have saved her.

My daughter was doomed from the beginning.

And no matter what I wrote, no matter what I said or did before it happened, I was doomed too. Nothing I could do was ever going to be good enough. Nothing any of us does ever is. We mop up the piss, wipe the sick, feed them, clothe them, care for them, love them – all silently, all without glory. But when it goes wrong, when we turn our backs for a second, everyone is watching us then.

So you can read my words and hate me for them. But you were always going to hate me. No matter what I did.

It's always the mother who gets the blame.

One

Now

My finger hovers over the 'delete profile' button. I hesitate, only for a second, then click. The screen changes to a bright white message box: *We're sorry to see you go, MotherOfTwins! If you change your mind, your profile will be available for 30 days. After that, all data from MumsOnline will be deleted. Hope to see you again soon!* My stomach churns; I don't want the option to go back so easily. I thought deleting my profile would be the end of it. It would be gone forever. I sigh. It doesn't matter, not really. I'm not going back. I've made my decision. Thirty days is nothing, I can wait. And then everything I ever wrote on this stupid site will disappear forever.

'Em, girls?' My husband, Mark, calls for us from the hallway, announcing his arrival home. 'Where are my little horrors?'

I smile as the girls shout 'Daddy!' from the living room, the familiar soundtrack of our evening routine beginning. Each night at around six fifteen when Mark walks through the door, the girls stop whatever they're doing to jump into his arms. Hearing their squeals, I shut my laptop screen and walk from the kitchen to the hallway to watch the display.

Sure enough, the girls are already clambering over Mark; Ella giggles excitedly as he picks her up in one arm and Lara in the other. Mark calls me over to join the family hug and my heart tugs, desperate to block out any thoughts of MumsOnline.

'Hello, darling,' he whispers in my ear before kissing the top of my head. 'Which one do you want?' He jiggles the girls in each arm, offering them up to me. Their squeals are piercing but the noise no longer grates on my ears. Now, it fills me with the kind of happiness I was starting to forget could exist at all.

'Mummy! Me, Mummy!' Lara squeals, reaching her chubby arms out to me.

They say parents shouldn't have favourites, but I can't deny that if we could, Lara would be mine. She is the youngest, technically, though only by ten minutes as both girls were born by Caesarean. But even if Lara hadn't joined the world after her sister, she'd still be the baby. It's in every element of her character. Though they only recently turned four, their personalities are already deeply ingrained. Ella is more like Mark. Commanding, sure of herself, defiant at her worst, brilliant at her best.

'Come on then,' I tell Lara, taking her from Mark. She wraps her arms around my neck as I carry her into the kitchen. Mark follows with Ella who loudly chatters to him about her day.

'And we went to the park and we saw a dog and a duck and—'

'Wow, a dog AND a duck? That is impressive,' Mark replies. He's always been much better at keeping up with Ella's incessant chatter than me. Lara and I are much quieter souls.

We sit the girls down at their highchairs and Mark moves towards the fridge.

'Wine?' he asks.

'Absolutely,' I say. 'I put the bottle of Bordeaux in earlier.'

He raises his eyebrows. 'Oh? Thought you were saving that for a special occasion?'

I shrug and give him a little smile. 'A Friday night with you is special enough for me.'

He laughs sceptically, not used to such sweet words, but then shrugs and pulls out the bottle. Mark is not a suspicious person by nature, even after everything I've done he'd still rather take my words at face value. A tiny stab of guilt tugs at my stomach as he pours me a glass, but I ignore it. What's done is done, I can't take it back. I can only move on. And that's what today is about. Putting the bad stuff behind us and moving on. Even if Mark doesn't know it.

'Cheers!' Mark says, clinking my glass.

'Cheers!' the girls shout in reply, holding up their empty sippy cups.

Mark and I share the sort of smile that only parents can; a smile that says 'look what we have; look what we made,' and I let myself take it all in and try to ignore the voice in my head that tells me I don't deserve this. Not any of it.

After the girls have had their bath and been put to bed, Mark and I curl up on the sofa and put on trashy Friday night TV as we wait for our Thai takeaway to be delivered. We've drunk most of the bottle of Bordeaux and my cheeks are pleasantly warmed.

'So,' Mark says, 'last Friday at home for a while. How's it feel?'

I bite my lip and pull the blanket further over my body. 'Exciting, I guess.'

'You guess?' He lowers the volume on the TV and looks at me uncertainly. 'You don't have to go back, you know, if—'

I shake my head quickly. 'No, I want to. I do.'

Mark frowns and searches my eyes, as if trying to catch me in a lie.

'I promise,' I say. 'It's just going to be different, that's all.' I smile and add, 'But good different. Less cheese sandwiches and ducks in the park, and more Pret salads and conference calls.'

He laughs, my words giving him the reassurance I know he needs.

The decision to go back to work was not taken lightly. I always thought I would, before we had the girls; it didn't occur to me that I would join the ranks of women who got to the top of their PR career only to have a baby and disappear forever. But after the girls were here, I didn't really have much choice. Twins take over every aspect of your life. I already knew they would, but I thought I'd be able to handle it. It turned out I overestimated my coping ability.

But that's over now. It's not something I want to think about. We're back on track. I'm ready to join the world again. Things are finally back to where they should have always been. This time, it will be better. We're settling into the new house back in town, and though I sometimes miss the silence of the countryside, I don't miss the feeling I would get stuck inside with the twins as if we were the last people on earth. We were in the centre of Cheltenham before, happy in our two-up, two-down townhouse but as my belly grew, the rooms turned from cosy to claustrophobic and so we made the stupid decision to move out of town. As if more space was what would make us a real family. Sometimes I wonder if things would have gone so badly wrong if we'd not done that, but I can't dwell on our bad decisions. We're back where we belong now, surrounded by people and noise, just the four of us. Like life was always supposed to be.

'It's only three days,' I say. 'It's not like I'll be gone all the time.'

Mark nods, his eyes firmly planted back on the television. We've had this conversation so many times; me adding up all the hours I'll be away from the girls, counting each last penny of what will be spent on child-care versus what I'll be bringing in. I've always presented it in the most positive light I can for Mark, wanting to give him no reason to not support my decision to return to work. The idea of being back in the office again does sometimes fill me with dread. But I know it's what I want. What I need.

The doorbell rings and Mark jumps up to answer it. I hear him speaking to the delivery driver from the Thai restaurant in town that we know so well after ordering from them most Friday nights in the year since we've moved here. They've only ever known us as parents of twins. That bothers me sometimes. But I'm not going to let myself go down this path. I've found the best way to cope with the thoughts that trouble me is to block them out altogether.

We ordered from them on our very first night in this house. It was so noisy compared to where we'd been. The girls were in bed by the time the food arrived. I was still feeling more than a little shell-shocked from everything; the move, all of it. I don't know how Mark knew where to order from, I don't remember much about the day of the move at all but I do remember sitting amongst the unpacked boxes and eating the sweet, nutty Pad Thai from the container, Mark by my side, and feeling like perhaps things might one day be okay again in this house.

As Mark brings the food through the hallway, that same sweet, nutty smell fills the room and the same feeling of hope washes over me.

'Come on!' He shouts from the kitchen.

I reluctantly pull off the blanket from my lap and walk through to join him. I take a seat at the breakfast bar and watch him move around the room pulling out plates from the cupboards, whistling as he goes.

'Feeling confident?' he asks, holding up the chopsticks to me with his eyebrows raised. I laugh and shake my head.

I'm terrible at using chopsticks, despite trying my hardest. Mark knows this but never gives up on trying to teach me. Growing up in the centre of Cheltenham with two incredibly busy working parents, he spent many nights eating Chinese food at the restaurant close to home in place of a good, home-cooked meal. We didn't have anything quite so cosmopolitan in rural Oxfordshire, and I've never managed to master the art of chopsticks since.

Mark sets the table, kindly putting a knife and fork alongside my chopsticks, and pours me another glass of wine.

'Dead!' he says, holding up the empty bottle. He raises his eyebrows as if we're naughty teenagers, then gets himself a bottle of beer.

We sit across from each other and eat in easy silence. It's funny how quickly you fall back into a comfortable routine. It's only in the last few months that Mark and I have been able to feel like a couple again, instead of just parents. Well, that's true for me at least. Mark has never struggled to be both husband, friend, employee, son, and father. It's only me who could only manage the 'mother' label when I had nothing else.

'Food okay?' Mark asks, noticing that I've stopped eating.

'Yep, lovely,' I say, pushing thoughts of the last few years away.

This is a fresh start, I remind myself. No more berating myself, no more raking up the past, no more bloody MumsOnline. I think of my profile disappearing in thirty days – all the secrets I've shared on the site, soon to be hidden from view. A pang of anxiety rumbles in my stomach as I imagine Mark, or anyone I know, discovering my words before then. But they won't. I've managed to keep everything I wrote on there secret for years; another thirty days is nothing.

When we finish eating, Mark offers to wash up and ushers me back into the living room. I cosy myself up on the couch again and pull out my phone. I took the most gorgeous photo of the girls at the park today and suddenly I have the urge to share it with the world, perhaps all too aware that soon my Fridays won't include the girls at all.

I open Facebook and start writing a post *Final Friday with these two terrors before going back to work!* I add the screaming emoji and heart eyes and click post. Almost instantly, the likes start coming in. *You're going to be great!* An old colleague writes. *Good luck, babe!* A woman from my NCT class that I've not spoken to since we moved adds. I start to type a reply but find everything I write sounds wrong, so flick through the TV channels looking for something to watch instead, but am drawn back to refreshing my page to see if anyone else has wished me well.

A red notification at the top right of the screen brings the hit of validation I've been waiting for. A new inbox message. I open it, expecting it to be the love eyes emoji from Mark's mum who's recently joined the world of social media, or perhaps even an old colleague asking about my return next week, though I have very few of them left as friends on Facebook. But it's neither. There's no profile picture but the name of the account makes the hairs on the back of my neck stand up. TwoIsTrouble.

Hi, Emily.

My heart bashes in my chest as I read the words. How has she found me? I've always been completely anonymous on MumsOnline, using only the cringey username I chose years ago to identify myself, 'MotherOfTwins'. We never shared names. Not ours, not our children's, not our partners'. Nothing. It was the beauty, and the downfall, of the site. An anonymous place we could go to and share our deepest, darkest secrets. Where we'd write down the sorts of things that we'd never say aloud. It always felt so safe to share there. I know it wasn't. I realised that already. It's why I deleted my account; I'd given up too many of my secrets there to ever be safe staying and TwoIsTrouble reminded me of that. I didn't want to be in that world any longer, where women gathered to bare their souls on a moment by moment basis. Most of all, I wanted to be away from TwoIsTrouble. And now, here she is. On my personal, private, Facebook page.

Threatening to ruin everything.

Two

Then

What have I done?

This is my first entry and I don't know how to start. At the beginning would be the most logical but how do you know where that is? Was it the day I brought my twins home? The day I got pregnant with them? Or even before that?

I don't know if writing this will help but I have to do something; to get these thoughts out of my head and down somewhere so that they can't torment me in the middle of the night. Is this how everyone feels? My husband says it is. We'll call him H. I can't bear to write down their real names. It feels too personal. Too revealing. And my daughters, I'll give them other names too. All three of them. Daughter One. Daughter Two. Daughter Three. That looks so wrong.

Really, it's more like Daughter One.

Then, Daughters Two and Three.

The twins are only ever together. Separating them into Two and Three is almost unthinkable, they are connected in every way. But for sake of clarity, I will.

It's Daughter One (perhaps D1 is simpler?) that I'm worried about. Ever since I brought the girls home, I've been gripped by this absolute fear that something isn't right with her. The way she looked at them, at me, when we walked through the door, two tiny bundles of warm, soft, innocent joy. She curled her nose up and told me they smelled. H laughed and said something about nappies, but I know she didn't mean that. She looked me dead in the eyes and glared. It felt like she was warning me, telling me that my babies were rotten.

So, why am I writing this? Well, in the hope that I'll discover these thoughts aren't totally insane. That it's normal to feel like this. That I'm not totally alone.

Does that make sense?

Three

Now

I joined MumsOnline six weeks after the girls were born. I was sitting in the living room, surrounded by plates, cups, and babygros when the day's post came. By that point, any break from the never-ending routine of trying to get the girls to sleep, or to feed, or to be changed, was a welcome excitement. The cards had mostly stopped by then, as had the visits. No one tells you that when you're pregnant, how quickly people tire of baby visits. When the girls were first born, I couldn't keep people away. And I tried. The last thing in the world I wanted was visitors; my sister, Mark's parents, friends from work, I couldn't stand seeing anyone in those early days. Remembering how I'd force myself to smile through their visits then break down into fits of tears when they were gone still makes my chest tighten with shame. I was awful. I had no idea that I was suffering from what so many women before me had also suffered, post-natal depression. That diagnosis came much later and instead, I hated myself and everyone around me for what I was feeling. Perhaps that was why, six weeks in, I no longer had any visitors. So I remember that day well, because alongside the usual crap from takeaways, the local paper, and bills, the postman brought a letter from Mark's mum.

She'd been worried about me since the girls arrived. She told me she understood what those early days were like, but I wouldn't talk to her about it. I didn't want to equate anything to do with her experience to mine – she could never understand the fears I had. But she kept trying. She'd sent me a pack of leaflets she'd obviously spent time collecting from various places that offered help to new mums. A cheaply stapled NHS booklet about coping with post-natal depression, something I was far from being able to recognise in myself, some brightly coloured flyers for local baby groups, and then an article ripped out from *Prima* magazine about MumsOnline. I shoved the NHS booklet and too-cheerful flyers into the bin but was drawn in by the article. *How MumsOnline Saved One Mum from Herself.* I read the words hungrily; the story of a previously successful, together woman in her thirties who couldn't get through the day without crying after she had her first baby was so similar to my own that it made my stomach twist. She told the interviewer how the online forum, full of mums just like her, had seen her through her darkest days, been there for her in ways that no one in her real life was able to. Mark's mum had attached a handwritten note to the article: *If you don't want to talk to me about what you're going through, I thought you might like to try this.*

I didn't go on the site for a few days. But as soon as I did, it felt like a lifeline. Opening my laptop to a world of women just like me, sharing their constant worries, gripes, frustrations. Anonymously. That was always the most appealing part. I could be anyone there. There was no need to wrap my frustrations in cloths of gratitude, to temper my anger with assurances of love. It was addictive. It still is. But now it's the kind of addiction that I recognise for what it is: dangerous. But at first, it didn't feel like that at all. At first, it just felt like I was being saved.

Mark encouraged it at first. He was so worried about me all the time – that I wasn't bonding with the girls, wasn't cooing over their every move the way he'd been led to believe women did – that he was happy to know I was spending time talking to other mums. He'd smile when I'd mention a tip I'd picked up from the forums. I think he liked the idea of having a wife who would spend her days happily sharing baby-rearing techniques with fellow mums. And I did use the forums for that at first; I'd look up tips on how to get a good nap schedule going, or what the best type of vegetable to puree was. But after a few months of relentlessly trying to be so outwardly perfect all the time while the washing piled up and the girls never slept and Mark was always working, I started to use the site for what it was really designed for. And I began sharing the darkest parts of myself with anonymous strangers.

The thought is like ice down my spine as I read TwoIs-Trouble's message on Facebook again. These worlds are not meant to collide. How the hell has she found me?

People on MumsOnline often talked about being outed. You'd read stories about women recognising each other through their posts; tiny details they'd let slip which connected the dots and unmasked them. But I thought I'd been careful. And more to the point, why would anyone ever want to out me? The idea always felt so dramatic, like anyone would want to waste hours of their life trawling the depressing threads of MumsOnline, looking for people they knew. Because the threads are a depressing place. That's what I know now. I couldn't see it before, when I was knee-deep in physical and emotional chaos.

No, back then, MumsOnline felt like the only thing that kept me going.

In the last year, TwoIsTrouble became a friend. More than that. She went from being a username that occasionally commented on my posts about the twins to the first person I turned to, no matter what. The only person who was always there when I needed her. In the dark of night, when words felt impossible to say aloud, I'd type them to her like a confession. We've shared thousands of direct messages with each other; away from the prying eyes of the forum, we laid bare our souls even more than usual. I read her message again, *Hi, Emily.* There's something so menacing about saying so little. My stomach flips beneath me as I try to convince myself she means no harm. But I'm not going to take any chances; she's crossed a line by contacting me outside of the site. She must know that. We all knew no matter how strong the friendships we formed within the forums were, they never crossed over into the real world. Where our families, friends, colleagues lived. Where our dirty secrets do not belong.

I move my fingers across the screen and click 'BLOCK' then delete her message. That will be enough, I tell myself. She'll give up.

Over the rest of the weekend, I don't have time to think about anything except my imminent return to work.

'What time did your mum say she can pick the girls up from nursery tomorrow?'

It's Sunday evening and Mark is ironing his shirts in the kitchen, ready for the week, as I hover anxiously behind him.

He sighs as the iron puffs out steam. 'Still three o'clock, Em.'

I drum my nails on the kitchen counter and try to smile back in reply. He puts the iron down.

'It'll be fine,' he says as he holds up my empty wine glass and raises his eyebrows, his way of asking if I want a refill. I nod.

'I know. I know it will. It's just a long time for them to be away from me, isn't it?'

Mark turns his back on me and pours the wine, the reassuring glug of the liquid momentarily calming me.

'What time will you finish?'

I shrug. 'It's supposed to be five, but, you know...'

No matter how much I tell myself going back to work will be good for me, I can't stop worrying about the nights when a client plays up and I have to stay late. Before I took maternity leave with the girls, I'd worked my way up to Account Director at the PR agency where I started as a Junior Account Executive in my early twenties. It's where Mark and I met; he was the Business Development Manager and seemed so much older and more mature than I was. We didn't work together very long and only started dating after he'd left to work for a big banking client. Much more his speed. He never really enjoyed the agency culture; he always said he wanted to leave work at work. We were never like that at Whiteley; strategy meetings would often spill over into the pub next door and only end when the company credit card begged for relief. Late nights were the norm, not so much encouraged as simply expected. I didn't mind. I loved that lifestyle, I loved my job. I'll love it again. I know I will, even if I can't take part in the late night binge sessions any more.

I'm lucky they're taking me back at all. There aren't many places that would after their six-month agreed maternity leave stretched to four years. Not that I've been paid by them in that period, of course, but the fact that Daniel has let me come back to my old position and part-time is frankly more than I deserve. Especially given everything he knows about what happened in the years since I've been gone.

Mark places my glass down and squeezes my shoulder. 'Right, I'll give the girls their dinner, you sit here, drink your wine, and take a breath.' He smiles, trying his best to be casual, but I know he's worried.

Mark doesn't wear worry well. He's not built for it; he likes things to be easy, simple. I had no idea he had any interest in me when we worked together and the way he asked me out was so nonchalant – a throwaway comment about grabbing a drink after his leaving do – I didn't realise it was actually a date until I turned up in jeans and a T-shirt and saw him standing on the street holding a bunch of flowers. I smile at the memory, though the carefree man and woman who turned up that night are far from the couple we've now become.

As I'm sipping my wine, a high-pitched wailing scream comes from the living room and I run in, expecting the worst.

Mark has Lara in his arms, her face buried in his shoulder as she sobs. Ella is sitting in the middle of the living room floor, clutching a doll and scowling.

'What's going on?' I ask.

Mark frowns and I know straight away that Ella has done something.

'Mummy,' Lara cries, reaching her arms out to me. I take her from Mark and tell her it's okay, that Mummy's here.

Mark takes a seat on the floor next to Ella whose face is scrunched up in anger. A kick of anxiety rumbles in my stomach; the look on her face is so enraging that I have to stop to remind myself that she's my daughter and I love her. My tiny, four-year-old daughter who cannot control herself yet. Guilt replaces the anger as I remind myself not to ever feel that angry at my daughter. It's not right.

'Els, remember what we said about sharing?' Mark says in his most patient fatherly tone. Ella pushes out her bottom lip and holds her doll tighter, as if Mark might rip it from her arms.

'Pushed me,' Lara whispers into my ear. I sigh and close my eyes. This is the last thing we need tonight.

'Did you push your sister, Ella?' I ask. Mark glares at me; my tone is harsher than I'd intended. I try again, this time softer, more patient, more like Mark. 'Els, you can't push your sister. Or anyone. Okay? It's not nice.'

Ella's face starts to crumble and tears pool in her big, beautiful blue eyes. Any irritation I felt at her drains away. I give Lara a kiss and pop her down on the floor next to her sister.

Side-by-side, my girls are amazing. Though to the outsider, they're completely identical, to me they are so very different.

'I sorry Lala,' Ella says, reaching out to her sister. Lara's face breaks into a huge smile; she's always been the easier one. She can go from devastated to brimming with happiness in a second; she doesn't hold grudges. Not like her mother. Lara hands Ella the doll and Mark smiles at me, his look saying, 'See? We're good parents!'.

'Good girls. Now, I think it's time for dinner, don't you, Daddy?'

He nods. 'What do you think, girls? Today on the menu we have…' He rolls up his sleeves and mime's reading from a huge menu. The girls giggle manically, tears long-forgotten. 'Tender corn-flaked grass-fed chicken, alongside a hand-picked selection of garden vegetables, and the finest of fine, sweetest corn.' What he means is homemade chicken nuggets, sweetcorn and green beans.

Mark takes the girls into the kitchen to eat their dinner and I stay in the living room, checking the to-do list I wrote yesterday on my Notes app. I have lunch packed and ready in the fridge, my outfit is chosen, ironed and hung up on the back of our bedroom door, my car has petrol. I have everything done. And yet I still feel so incredibly anxious. It will be fine. I can do this. Everyone else manages it. As I pull out my phone, I have to stop myself when my fingers start to navigate towards MumsOnline. I'm not doing that any more, I remind myself. But that's the problem with addictions, isn't it? They're very hard to break. Especially when you're at your worst.

Right now, all I want to do is start a thread about going back to work. I know there would be tens of comments within minutes if I asked how people had managed it. Some would be good, cheering me on, telling me not to worry about it, that everything would be fine. But inevitably there would be the horror stories; women whose children got sick on their first day and they had to leave, only to be forever known from then on as unreliable; women who turned up perfectly presentable only to find their pockets stuffed with wet wipes, ready to wipe the faces of the children they'd left behind. No, I won't do it. I don't need these stories. I don't need the confidence of strangers any more.

—

'Excuse me…' Mark says from the side of the bed. 'Is that…'

I laugh and hide my phone under the covers like a schoolgirl. 'I know – just five more minutes and I'll put it away.'

Mark raises his eyebrows and gets back to his book. It's one of the things my therapist advised, to sleep with my phone out of the bedroom, but I have a hard time doing it. When I'm particularly anxious it gets worse. I know my phone feeds the anxiety but it's a loop sometimes I just get stuck in. I close Twitter and open Instagram, telling myself I'll scroll for five minutes then put my phone on the landing where it will stay all night.

As I open Instagram, the red dot in the right of the screen indicates I've got a new direct message, giving me the kick of satisfaction I'm searching for. Expecting it to be the love heart emoji from one of the NCT mums that I've not spoken to since we moved in reacting to my latest Insta story of the girls, my stomach flips when I see the name. TwoIsTrouble.

'What's wrong?' Mark says.

'Nothing,' I lie. 'Just something on Instagram.'

'For god's sake, Em, put it away.'

I ignore him and turn on my side, so he can't see my screen. I open the message. *Hi.* My body itches with worry which quickly turns to anger. How dare she do this? She knows MumsOnline is anonymous. Why can't she respect my decision to leave? I go onto her Insta profile; it's completely empty. No personal name under her username, no followers, in fact I'm the only person she's following. What is she playing at? Has she made this account purely to message me again since I blocked her on Facebook? Furious now, I type back. *Leave me alone.* And then hit BLOCK.

'Enough now,' Mark says, leaning over and taking my phone from my hand. He gets out of bed. 'Tomorrow is a big day, you need to sleep,' he calls from the landing.

I lie back and stare at the ceiling, my heart pumping violently in my chest; work tomorrow the last thing on my mind.

Four

Then

JaneyElainey222: After reading your latest post I have to say… get some help? Sorry OP but you sound like you're losing it.

NothingButAMum: Eurgh, really, JE? That's not what we're here for. If you want to judge, piss off to Facebook. We're here to help each other. OP, ignore her.

JaneyElainey222: LOL. Supporting means blindly clapping for each other now does it? Oooookay.

NothingButAMum: I've reported JE to admin! Just going to ignore her now. This isn't the place for b*tches. Anyway, lol. OP, honestly babe don't feel bad. No one copes well with multiples and it sounds like you've got SO much going on in ur life right now.

MotherOfTwins: Thank you, @NothingButAMum. Also have to say your username couldn't sum up my feelings any better right now!

NothingButAMum: Ha, glad you like it! If you ever wanna chat, DM me. Don't have to deal with b*thez like JE there!!

MotherOfTwins: Thank you, I will.

ALittleLonely: Just going back to the original thread…
Have you tried talking to anyone IRL about how
you're feeling @MotherOfTwins? It can be so lonely
but your DH sounds like he's a good egg! Maybe try
opening up to him?

Jill27: I don't think you should just assume that the
OP has a supportive husband????

ALittleLonely: I wasn't assuming – I've read her posts
and it seems that way to me!

Jill27: Yeah well you can't actually tell what's really
going on in a marriage unless your in it though can
you. Especially not online!!!

MotherOfTwins: H is supportive, as much as he
can be. And before the twins, I really did tell him
everything! But don't you think it changes once you
go from being a couple to parents? I don't know,
maybe it's just me. But sometimes I feel like the
only people who can really understand what I'm
going through are MumsOnliners… Is that horribly
desperate?

ALittleLonely: No babe, not at all. Its why we're all
here!! Everything changes when you have babies.

NothingButAMum: Absolutely with you @Mother-
OfTwins – this place is my total lifeline! And not all
of us have a DH anyway…

Jill27: My DH used to be great but now… It's just not
the same for men is it?

MotherOfTwins: No. I don't think it is.

ALittleLonely: At least we have each other.

NothingButAMum: 100%!!!!

MotherOfTwins: Yeah, thank god for that.

Five

Now

I arrive at the office feeling absolutely terrible. My blow-dried hair from this morning has been viciously windswept on my short walk from the car park to the office and I can feel sweat spotting my upper lip; my body's reaction to the sudden temperature change from outside to indoors. I passed our old house on the drive in, where we lived before the girls. A young woman was walking out of the door, coffee in hand, looking just like I used to before my bag contained nothing but baby apparel and it took an hour to leave the house to do the simplest thing. I watched her walk down the street I used to walk down, a smile on her face as she put in her ear buds. How different our mornings have been.

'Emily!' I hear my name being squealed from behind the reception desk and I spot Louise looking perfect as ever with a massive smile on her face. 'You're back!'

'Morning,' I say, brushing down my hair.

'They said you were coming in today,' Louise says, her smile spreading wider across her beautiful face. 'So glad to have you back. Can I get you a coffee?'

'That would be great, thanks.' I smile, gratefully. We stayed in touch at first, Louise and I, but like any friendship, when one of you checks out the other soon abandons it. I think back to the many unanswered WhatsApps she's sent me over the years – '*just checking in!*' – and feel my cheeks redden.

To avoid examining the feeling too long, I look around the reception area. It's so different than when I left four years ago that it almost feels like a totally new office. They've added a wooden pallet wall behind the desk with *WHITELEY PR* lit up in pink neon writing. It's the sort of sign that screams to be on Instagram and I reach for my phone instinctively before pulling my hand back as I remember last night's message. No social media for today. I'm not going to let anything distract me.

'Here you go,' Louise says, returning with my coffee. 'Daniel's on his way in but sit down, we can have a gossip while we wait.' She nods and walks towards what can only be described as a pod across the other side of the office. I follow behind her, feeling more and more uncomfortable in what should be familiar surroundings.

Inside the pod, Louise laughs as we sit down.

'I know,' she says, raising her eyebrows at the strange structure. 'Bonkers, isn't it? But you know what Daniel's like, always easily led and apparently pods are the latest trend in "break out" spaces.' She laughs and blows on her too-hot coffee. 'I said to him, we wouldn't need pods if you hadn't turned the whole bloody place open plan!'

Louise isn't much older than me, but suddenly it feels like we're the two old women moaning about how times have changed. I don't like it.

'Whose idea was all of this, then?'

Louise rolls her eyes. 'Alyssa's, you'll meet her. She's great, don't get me wrong. Reminds me of you, actually. Very full on.'

I try to laugh but it comes out awkward. I'm so unused to holding adult conversations like this that the easy banter I used to share with Louise is stilted.

'I'm not sure anyone would describe me as "full on" any more...'

Louise smiles and reaches across the table to squeeze my hand. 'Don't worry, Em, you'll be back to your old self in no time. I promise.'

I make non-committal noises and take a sip of the strong coffee, avoiding an answer. God, I've missed proper, scalding hot coffee. No matter how hard I try, I can never manage to drink a hot cup of coffee at home. By the time I get to it, it's always stone cold. Here, I'll be able to drink hot coffee every other day. The thought amazes me, like I've been given a gift that I don't deserve.

'Em?'

'Sorry, I was just thinking...'

'It's so hard the first time you leave them. But it will get easier, trust me. The morning of my first day back, I walked into the office in tears.' She laughs at the memory. 'Honestly, Daniel was so good about it. I know it's not the same, after what you've been through—'

A knock on the pod door stops Louise mid-sentence and saves me from getting into the topic of conversation that I'm desperate to avoid. A face appears at the door; a young, pretty face that smiles with perfectly white teeth.

'Hi, sorry to interrupt. Emily?'

I nod.

'I'm Alyssa, nice to meet you. Daniel's looking for you, when you're ready.'

I stand up, eager to leave the conversation with Louise and follow Alyssa across the office, my eyes glued to her childlike figure. My own black trousers suddenly feel ridiculously formal and old-fashioned as I watch her confidently stride past the desks wearing high-waisted denim jeans and a sheer black blouse. I can see her lace bralette through it, but she's got the type of figure that somehow makes it totally reasonable to have your underwear on show. Model-like. Almost androgynous. I feel my own chest bulging through my bra and wish I'd tried harder to diet before coming back here. My body feels frankly ridiculous next to hers.

'Emily!' Daniel's booming voice stops me in my tracks and I feel every face in the office turn to me. Daniel puts his arms out and shouts 'She's back!' like I'm an old Hollywood star making her triumphant return to the movies – except half the people in this office have absolutely no idea who I am, having joined after I left, and the half that do would probably quite like to get through today without having to acknowledge my existence at all. Avoiding the curious glances from the faces I don't recognise, I follow Daniel into his office, which I notice has conveniently escaped his 'make it all open plan' rule.

'Em,' he says, sitting down and nodding at me to close the door. 'So good to have you back, but listen, I've got a call first thing so I can't chat now. Sorry – but we'll do lunch, yeah? Go get Louise to set you up at a desk; she's sorted all your access out and you'll see we've got a meeting together at eleven anyway. Client thing.' His words feel like an avalanche. Desk. Meeting. Clients. I can't take it all in, but before I have a chance to say anything, he's ushering me out of the door.

–

By midday, I'm so hungry that I have to hold my fist against my stomach to quieten its rumblings.

'Sorry,' I say, noticing the young, pretty account manager from earlier – whose name now escapes me – glancing over. She smiles tightly, almost like she's stifling a laugh, then turns her attention back to Daniel.

'Okay, so we've got a great chance to pitch here. I think we all feel really strong about the team, right?' He looks around the room and everyone nods in return. 'And we've got something none of the other agencies have… we've got Emily.' Daniel beams at me and my cheeks get hot. The account manager turns to look at me again, this time with what I decide is thinly veiled resentment.

Half an hour later, when everyone's agreed the strategy for the pitch, we're finally free to leave the conference room and grab some lunch. I walk out feeling like I'm escaping a prison cell; the air in the room felt like it was getting more stifling the longer Daniel talked about consumer reach, influencers and outreach. Words that have been so far from my life for years that I can't be totally sure if I even remember their meanings. Trying to quell the sense of rising panic, I check my phone hoping to see a message from Mark but my screen is empty.

'Em,' Daniel calls after me. 'Wait up.'

I hang in the doorway as he finishes chatting to the account manager, whose name suddenly comes back to me: Alyssa. She can't be more than twenty-five, but she gives off the air of someone who is absolutely certain of herself. As Daniel talks to her, there's no sense that he is the CEO and she a junior employee. They're talking like equals. I watch in awe as Alyssa nods curtly and repeats back what Daniel says as if confirming she understands. Watching them makes me feel old and flustered. Was I ever that confident? Though I'm sure the age gap between us can't be more than ten years at most, it feels a lifetime.

A memory of one of the managers snakily telling the rest of the team that they always knew when I was in a meeting with Daniel as they *could hear my high-pitched laughter down the corridor* flashes into my mind. I feel a flash of embarrassment for my younger self. I bet Alyssa never loudly laughs in Daniel's presence. Watching her, I wonder if she ever laughs at all.

'Sorry,' Daniel says as Alyssa finally leaves and we walk out together. 'Japanese okay?' he asks, referring to the small Japanese cafe at the end of the road.

'Oh god, yes. I've been dreaming of their dumplings since the day I left,' I laugh.

We walk the five-minute journey to the cafe chattering away about everything except work: Daniel's grown-up children who are around my age; his wife who I've spent many an awards dinner with downing prosecco at the back of the room, and of course, the girls.

As we reach the cafe, Daniel holds the door open for me and the waitress rushes to greet us like we're old friends. We order a bowl of edamame covered in salt and soy sauce and talk in between ripping open the pods with our teeth. It's hard to believe that this life has been going on regardless as I've been hidden away with the girls.

'I want you to lead on the Browngate pitch,' Daniel says.

'Oh. But isn't that next week? I—'

He holds up his hand and smiles. 'Come on, don't give me all that "first week" crap. You're not new – you're one of our best.'

'But it's been years since I've pitched. God, it's been years since I've worn high heels for more than a few hours at a time.'

Daniel laughs, but he's insistent. 'You're leading it, no arguments. You're perfect for it.' He puts another pea pod in his mouth and I let his compliment sink in. I'm glad that he's not treating me carefully or easing me back into work slowly like the frail, damaged woman people so often see me as now.

Yes, it's been difficult today trying to keep up with all the new techniques and systems (don't even start me on that new version of Gorkana – the bloody thing's impossible). But the general idea of my job hasn't changed and Daniel's right; I was one of the agency's best. Why wouldn't I still be? Perhaps I haven't lost all my talent in the years I've been away. Before I can convince myself otherwise, I feel a smile pulling at my lips and I hear myself telling him that I'll do it.

'Great. I mean, you're the perfect fit.' Daniel stops to rip open another pea pod and I let his confidence in me fill me up, my body sitting up straighter, less embarrassed by myself. I'd forgotten what this felt like, to be seen as good at something other than just being a mother.

'Thanks, Daniel. I really appreciate you giving me the opportunity.'

He waves away my words. 'Their marketing director's not long had another baby. It's all she talks about.' He rolls his eyes. 'Make sure to bring up the girls with her. Hell, you can even tell her it's your first week back – that's good, actually, you should mention that in the pitch. I know how you women like to stick together over things like this. There's no way we'll lose it!'

His words are like a gut punch and the edamame beans sit lodged in my throat. Daniel doesn't want me because I'm good at my job. He doesn't see me like that any more. To Daniel, to everyone, all I am is a mother.

The afternoon sours after that. I can't get Daniel's comment out of my head. Everyone I speak to at the agency makes me feel like a fraud; like I've been taken back out of pity rather than for my talent. Mark would tell me it's all in my head, that I'm letting my imposter syndrome get the better of me. I know that's probably true, but it doesn't make it any easier and I can't get Gorkana (or whatever it's called now) to save this stupid media monitoring report Daniel's had me pull, like I'm an assistant.

By the time the clock hits five o'clock I'm desperate to leave. I look around the office for signs that someone else might also be thinking of home, but everyone remains where they are, staring at their laptop screens and diligently clicking away. My leg twitches beneath me. I wait another five minutes but there's still no sign of movement. Don't they have homes to go to? Oh god, I realise, I have turned into one of those people. I never used to be a clock-watcher. I didn't stay late because I felt I had to, I just always had so much to do and I loved it. Things are different now. I sigh and get up from my desk.

'I'm going to make a move,' I announce to no-one in particular.

Alyssa looks up and smiles. 'No worries. Bet you can't wait to see your girls.'

I breathe out and feel my shoulders drop from the hunched position I've carried all day. 'Mark's picking them up tonight, so by the time I get home they'll be fed and ready for their bath.'

She makes 'aww' noises that I'm convinced are totally insincere as I collect up my stuff and leave. First day done.

As I walk the ten minutes to my car, I can't ignore the urge any more and take out my phone. I check Facebook first. Three notifications. My heart drums as I wait for the names to load. Friends. Just friends leaving heart symbols on my status from last night. Twitter next. Nothing at all there. And, finally, Instagram. I let out a deep breath; TwoIsTrouble is nowhere to be seen. I put my phone back in my bag and whisper *thank god*. Perhaps I overreacted to her contacting me; I do have a tendency to do that.

I walk through the front door to home and try to shake off any last worry about her, or anything else. Things are going to be better now.

Six

Then

Something and Nothing

I'm quite embarrassed reading my words from last time back. D1 is just a little girl. What was I thinking? She doesn't hate her sisters. She doesn't hate me. Sometimes, it feels like there's another me writing these things; like I've totally lost my mind since the twins. You're not supposed to say that any more, are you? The point is, as usual, I'm overreacting to everything that happens lately. I was just like this when I had D1 but it feels even worse this time around. Twice the babies, twice the hormones, perhaps?

My midwife came by this week and I should have asked her about it. To check in, she said. I had completely forgotten, though H had marked it on the kitchen wall calendar with a red circle. He's gone back to work now. It felt like he was hardly here at all, though he assures me he took as long as he could. It's just not the same for them though, is it? They make the transition from man to dad with a barely perceptible nod. Maybe a beer with some mates to celebrate the occasion. Wet the baby's head. The girls' heads must have been positively soaked.

I'm trying not to compare how things were with D1's dad. This situation is nothing like that one; we were barely more than babies ourselves. We didn't even live together and I went back to work within months, I had to! I hated it at the time, was so jealous of the women swanning around on maternity leaves that you knew would stretch to forever. Yet now that I have that, all I want is to have my old life back.

Which is ridiculous. Things were much worse when I had D1. And her dad was absolutely not better than H. We weren't even properly together. But when he would come to see D1, his face would light up like I'd never seen before. It never lit up like that for me. Not once. Even before I got pregnant. Is it terrible of me to compare him to H? H is good. He's solid, respectable, reliable. Nothing like D1's dad. Nothing at all.

Anyway. The midwife asked me how I was getting on earlier and I lied. I can be honest here. But I couldn't be honest with her. It's my own stupid fault for forgetting the appointment; I wasn't ready for her. The house was in total chaos; I was in total chaos. Aren't we always, now? It just didn't feel like the right time to admit that perhaps yes, like she said, I might need some extra help. For some reason, hearing those words enraged me. Like I said, I overreact. So, instead of admitting that I was finding things more than a little difficult, I lied. Told her everything was great. The girls were sleeping. D1 was being the perfect big sister. H was even getting up in the night to help with the feeds.

As if.

Great. The girls are crying, again. I have to go.

D1 is hiding away in her room, sulking because I wouldn't take her to the park this morning. She doesn't understand that things are different now. It's not just me and her any more. She's so bloody jealous. See? I'm doing it again.

Overreacting.

I'm not going to keep thinking like this. There's no need. Everything is going to be fine.

Seven

Now

'Park! Park! Park!' The girls are chanting incessantly at me as I try and glug down a lukewarm coffee.

I feel dead on my feet this morning and am silently thanking god that I took Daniel up on his offer to go back three days a week instead of the five I felt I should. I'm doing one day working, one day off and right now I literally can't imagine how I ever thought I could do anything more. Is it normal to be this tired after a single day of work? I remind myself again that I once longed for this return to normality; I have no right to moan.

'Yes, we're going. Go and put on your shoes,' I tell the girls.

They run down the hallway, their tiny feet banging against the oak floor. They've just started to be able to do their own shoes – not laces of course; Mark's mum bought them the cutest Velcro trainers from the Disney store when she went to London for the day with a friend. The girls love them and I love watching them wrestle with the Velcro straps. I place my cup in the sink and suppress a sigh at the washing up already piled up below it. I should do it before we go, I hate coming back to stacked up plates, but I really just can't be bothered. Mark's always telling me that it doesn't matter; that leaving dirty dishes in the sink or laundry in the basket for a few hours really isn't the end of the world but I can't shake the feeling of failure when the house looks a mess. As if gleaming counters and an empty sink are somehow proof that I'm okay; that I'm doing a good job.

I shake my head and turn my back on the dishes. I'm going to leave them and take my daughters to the park. That's being a good mother too, I tell myself.

In the hallway, the girls sit side-by-side on the bottom step struggling with their trainers. Well, Lara does. Ella has her trainers on with the Velcro strapped up so tight I have to reach down and loosen it or she'll cut off her circulation. She's helping Lara who has yet to master the art of sticking one side of the Velcro to the other. Ella presses the straps down on Lara's trainer and smiles, then rips it open again and says 'See?' as she places it back down, trying to show Lara how it works. Lara nods but I can tell she doesn't really see, she just wants to keep her sister happy.

'Coats on,' I say, pulling their matching blue Cath Kidston coats from the rack and wrapping them both up.

–

The park is busy this morning, despite the chilly weather. It's a nice day, the sun is out and a few of the other mothers are even wearing sunglasses. I squint through the sunshine, wishing I had mine. I sit on a cold metal bench on the side of the playground while the girls run around hand-in-hand. Other children come up to them occasionally to play but they totally ignore them. It does worry me sometimes, how completely reliant they are on each other, not letting anyone else into their world, but I try and ignore the feeling. There's nothing wrong with my girls. I did take them to baby classes in the village for a while but I got sick of the comments from the other mums about how anti-social they were. They'd say it like a compliment: *your two just love each other, don't they? Our poor babies can't get a look in!* and then they'd giggle with each other as the girls continued to totally ignore everyone except each other. It made me paranoid. I'd leap on Mark the second he got home asking him if he thought they'd never make friends, if there was something wrong with them for only caring about each other. Eventually, I stopped going to the baby groups altogether, desperate to avoid their judgement and egged on by other stories of bitchy mums' groups by users on MumsOnline. Now, I realise the women I met probably really were only joking, or perhaps jealous that I had two beautiful girls that loved each other so much. If I'd been able to see that then, I may have made some real-life mum friends and not spent quite so much time alone online sniping about them instead. Maybe I can do that now. Perhaps I'll be one of those women who starts conversations with other mums in the park and ends up back at their houses for cups of tea that end up in a bottles of wine and ever-lasting friendships.

I look around the park, hopefully. Across from me, a woman around my age is sitting with an older woman, watching a little boy in a red coat. They've got takeaway coffees from the cafe nearby and the steam floats out of their paper cups as they chat. The younger woman rolls her eyes at something the other says and shakes her head, then laughs. They barely take a breath in their conversation until the little boy runs across the playground and launches himself into the older woman's arms shouting 'Nanna, look!' as he shows her a very special stone he's found. I wrap my coat around me, and turn my gaze back to the girls.

They never really knew my mum like that. She was never a proper nanna to them; she died last year before they turned three and despite telling myself if she'd lived longer we could have spent days in the park together like this, I know we never would have. We didn't have that kind of relationship. I watch the mother and daughter across the park with the kind of longing I thought I had left behind. Is the grief finally hitting me? Her death didn't register with me all that well last year. I wasn't coping with things anyway, we had our own more immediate loss to deal with, so I had very little involvement in any of it. My sister, Allie, begged me to come and clear out the house with her, but I couldn't face it. I should have been there for my sister; but I just couldn't be. My feelings for my mum are so complicated it felt like the very worst thing I could do would be to delve headfirst into playing the perfect grieving daughter while what I was really feeling over her death was relief. The memory stirs a deep feeling of sadness and guilt in me but I shut it down before it threatens to take hold.

Unable to explain my feelings to Mark, I turned to MumsOnline to share my outpourings of guilt. That was when TwoIsTrouble and I started talking, now that I think about it. I had been using the site for a while by then, but only the forums – posting publicly with various different women about all sorts of topics. TwoIsTrouble had lost her mum around the same time, if I remember rightly, and after sharing a few public messages on the forums, she got in touch privately through my direct messages and we started talking like that more and more. I think that's why I opened up to her even more than the others. There's safety in the privacy of a stranger. We treated our posts on that horrible site like a diary; writing down words that we'd never say in public.

'Mummy, look!' Ella shouts. She's pointing at something on the floor, her eyes wide.

'What is it?' I ask, getting up from the bench. The girls don't reply, just stare down at the floor then back at me with their mouths open. I see what they're looking at then, a piece of paper with writing on it.

In the seconds it takes to walk from the bench to them, my mind goes into overdrive. There's something bad on that paper. There's something that the girls shouldn't see. I imagine all the words the paper could hold and feel my stomach twist beneath me. It's from her. I know it is. TwoIsTrouble.

When I reach them, I grab the paper from the floor in one swift movement and the girls gasp.

'What is this?' I snap, hearing too late the harshness of my tone. My eyes fly over the paper, scouring it for evidence of what has made the girls' faces look like this. I read it once, then again.

It's nothing.

A shopping list, discarded from someone's pocket. Ingredients for dinner – a chicken casserole, by the sounds of it. I look back at the girls who are now looking up at me with frowns.

'It's just a shopping list,' I tell him. They nod, solemnly. 'I'm sorry that I snapped… I thought it was something bad,' I say.

'Why bad?' Lara says, looking even more upset than before.

I shake my head and close my eyes, wishing more than anything that I hadn't reacted like that. 'Sorry, lovelies.

Mummy is being silly.' I scrunch the note in my fist and give them a big smile. 'Shall we go and feed the ducks?'

This finally shakes the look of fear from their faces and they graciously agree, taking each other's hands and following me out of the playground. I hold onto Ella's hand as she holds onto Lara's and we walk like that, the three of us side-by-side, as we make our way to the duck pond. They chatter in their twin-speak as I try to calm myself down. That reaction was totally ridiculous. What was I thinking? Why would I jump to the most insane conclusion about a note on the floor?

TwoIsTrouble hasn't contacted me since the other night, but I can't shake the feeling that she isn't done with me yet. Perhaps it's the thoughts of my mum that have rattled me.

As we reach the duck pond, I'm surprised to find it empty. This is a popular spot with mums looking to find cheap entertainment for their kids. Usually, we'd be one of at least two other groups standing here eagerly awaiting the ducks. You can't feed them bread any more; apparently it expands in their stomach and kills them. I'm doubtful of that, to be quite honest. I think of the pond in our garden growing up, filled with ducks that we would chuck bread to all year round. I don't remember any of them being found dead, their bellies full of expanded bread. The image makes me wince.

'What's wrong, Mummy?' Lara asks, gripping my hand.

'Nothing, darling. Here you go,' I say, handing her some duck food from my bag.

It's amazing the things you learn to carry in your handbag once you're a parent. Once upon a time, my bag would be full of make-up, receipts, the odd shopping list.

But now it's jam-packed with baby wipes, dried fruit (for the times when they need a snack and there are no other options), tissues, hair bobbles, everything and anything that the girls could ever need. Duck food is a recent addition. They sell it at the charity shop on the corner of the park for fifty pence a bag (to stop you blowing up the ducks' bellies with bread, I assume) and after one incident where they were closed and we couldn't get any duck food which led to more than a bit of a strop from Ella, I decide to stock up the next time I went past. So now, I walk around with a seemingly endless supply of duck food in my bag. Like that's totally normal.

Ella lobs great handfuls of the brown pellets into the water and the ducks crowd around the water in front of us. The girls squeal with delight as the ducks bob their heads under water, desperate to get to the soggy lumps. Lara is more conservative with her offerings, waiting until the ducks are finished with what's in front of them before scattering a few pellets in one by one. Ella gets impatient and grabs a handful and chucks it in, making the water ripple. I watch the water for a few seconds, mesmerised, before something in the corner of my eye catches my attention. I look up, across the pond to the trees opposite us. I'm sure I saw movement there, but now there's nothing. I flick my eyes across the trees, searching for what it could have been but the leaves barely move in the breeze.

'I'm cold,' Lara says, tugging at my sleeve.

'I'm hungry,' Ella adds dramatically. As I look down to reply, I'm sure I see movement again but it's gone by the time I look back up.

'Come on, then, let's go home.'

The morning's sunshine has disappeared and the air has turned cold as rain starts to patter lightly on our coats. By the time we reach the playground, all the families from before have gone and suddenly the park feels deserted. The girls skip in front of me, totally unaware of the turn in weather and atmosphere as they sing an indecipherable song between them. I speed up, desperate to be back in the warmth of the house. There's something incredibly eerie about an empty park when the swings are left to swing alone in the wind; everyone else must have realised the weather was turning before us and already made their way into the warmth. I see a lone figure standing on the other side of the park in a black coat and realise we aren't the last ones out just as the rain really begins to pour. I grab the girls' hands and tell them to hurry up as the rain lashes down in front of us. They giggle madly; they think the rain is great fun, too young to care about their clothes being ruined or hair getting wet. Across the park, I notice the figure in black isn't moving at all. Just standing by the trees, the rain pouring.

'Come on, Mummy!' Ella squeals as I slow down to get a better look. What are they doing? I squint through the rain, but we're too far away to get a good look at them. 'Mummy!' she cries again, tugging at my hand.

I shake my head and ignore the feeling of unease that rushes through me as I turn my back on the figure and walk on.

–

'Wait! Take off your shoes—' I shout after the girls as they run straight through the house as soon as I open the front door. Useless. Their footprints leave puddles through the hallway as they squeal in delight. Everything makes them laugh so much at the moment I feel like I'm the permanent black cloud looming over them, telling them to stop this, stop that. Today, I'm going to just let it go. The mess can be mopped up. As I'm shaking my own wet coat off, a red postcard on the doormat catches my eye. Probably marketing junk mail; no one I know sends postcards any more. But as I lean forward to pick it up, I realise I'm only half wrong. While I don't know the sender, they certainly know me.

> *There are no strangers here. Only friends you haven't yet met.*

The words are handwritten in thick black marker on a bright red postcard. I flip it over. There's nothing on the other side. No address, no stamp. I shiver runs down my spine; she must have hand-delivered it. I can't think where I know the quote from at first but then I realise; it's the tagline of the website. Stolen from some long dead poet, or writer, I suspect. It was MumsOnline's way of luring us into a false sense of security. Telling us it was fine to tell total strangers our secrets. But they were wrong. Nothing about this is fine.

'What's that?' Ella asks.

'Nothing.' I shove the postcard in my pocket and try to smile. 'Just junk mail. Let's get you two out of your wet clothes.'

She's not going to go away. Not if I don't do something about it.

Eight

Now

> Would you like to reinstate your account, Mother-
> OfTwins?

My stomach churns as the words flash up on the screen.
I hover over the YES button, then click. Within seconds,
my profile is live again, as if I was never away. I instantly
feel the pull of the site as I force myself away from
checking the latest threads. I don't need anyone else's bad
news stories right now. And this isn't something I can ask
for advice on. I came here for one reason: to work out
who the hell TwoIsTrouble really is. My hands shake as I
open the private message thread between us and begin to
read the last messages we exchanged.

> TwoIsTrouble: What will you do about the girls
> though?
>
> MotherOfTwins: I've got them into a nursery. And MIL
> will help out.
>
> TwoIsTrouble: And DH doesn't mind?
>
> MotherOfTwins: No. He wants me to be happy.

I squirm reading it back. When I first joined the site, the
acronyms threw me. I couldn't work out what anyone

was talking about it. But I soon picked it up after a few botched attempts at making up my own versions. I eventually learn that 'DD' stands for darling daughter. 'DH' means darling husband. 'MIL' is short for mother-in-law. Darling husband sounds ridiculous when you write it out like that, but it was just the way everyone wrote. It kept your anonymity, stopped you from accidentally slipping in the names of your nearest and dearest. Obviously, it didn't work for me.

> TwoIsTrouble: I'm sure he does!!! I'm just worried that it isn't going to be worth it. You'll be away from the girls all day, and when you get back you'll be exhausted.
>
> MotherOfTwins: I'll be fine
>
> TwoIsTrouble: Just looking out for you, babe!!

Things started to sour between us when I told her I was going back to work. I thought she would cheer me on – they're very good at cheering on MumsOnline – but she did the opposite. Spent all her time sending me messages like this, putting doubt into my mind. I thought she was jealous. I got the impression her husband wasn't all that supportive; she didn't mention him very often, usually only when I'd complain about Mark and then she'd agree how awful he was being and usually offer up some equally annoying thing her own husband had done. I feel my cheeks redden as I think about it; all the intimate stories I've shared with this woman. I can barely look at the message she sent me that finally convinced me to come off the site for good. Away from this total stranger who knows everything about me, and yet is still a mystery to me.

Well, not for long. If she's been able to find me, I can find her.

I rummage in my work bag for a notepad and pen; I do my best thinking when I can write things down physically. I start by listing out the things I do know about her that I've picked up over the year of anonymously messaging.

Woman. Mother to identical twin boys. Lives in South West. Married. Stay-at-home mum.

Looking at this list, a chill runs through me. That could be thousands of people. Anyone. I press my fingers into the bridge of my nose and take a deep breath. There must be more. I can't have been the only one giving away clues about my real identity. When I think about going through all of our old conversations to look for something that will help me, I'm overcome by a feeling of unease. This whole thing feels so utterly ridiculous. This woman, despite all of the weirdness of the last few days, has been the first person I've turned to for over a year. She knows details of my life that no one, not even Mark, knows. My very worst secrets. Yet I know nothing about her. How have I let this happen? Surely I can't have been telling her all my secrets for so long and not gaining any of hers? But the more I think about it, the more I realise that's exactly what I've been doing. We always talk about me. A hot wave of something I can't name sweeps over me. Shame? Embarrassment?

I open my laptop again and decisively scroll up through our conversation history. The worst things are in here. The forums are bad, yes, but what's hidden in my private messages is far worse. When I first joined the site, I posted longer, almost blog-like posts. As though it was my own personal diary space. I was so happy to just have somewhere to vent. Then I started replying to other people's posts on the forums, and then last year, not long after everything went so wrong, I met TwoIsTrouble and we held most of our conversations in private. Though we would both still regularly comment on other people's posts, too. That makes me think that before I delve into the hours of conversations between the two of us, I should check what she's been doing on the site since I left. There must be a reason that she's gone from being a normal, functioning person, to sending creepy postcards to my house.

I navigate to her profile and look for the feed of recent comments.

Nothing. Not a single comment. I'm not sure what to think. I'm relieved, in a way, that she hasn't spent her time lurking in the dark corners of the forums, yet rattled at what else could have been occupying her time. I imagine her sitting at her laptop right now, in a nondescript, modern kitchen, perhaps a glass of wine on the counter as she looks through my social media accounts. I've blocked her, but how can I be sure that's stopping her? She obviously has her mind made up that she's going to track me down; it's not exactly difficult to get into someone's social media accounts if you know how.

But this isn't helping. I need to find solid answers about her identity, not spend time imagining what she's doing.

Back on her MumsOnline profile, I click through to our DMs. I scroll through the messages then realise I can arrange them in reverse order. Suddenly, my screen reloads to the very first message we ever exchanged, over one year ago now.

TwoIsTrouble: Hi, I'm sorry to read about your mum. I lost mine recently, too. Did I see you say you have twins?

MotherOfTwins: Hello. Sorry to hear that, but yes I do. Two girls. You?

TwoIsTrouble: I have two boys. Been desperate to find someone on here in the same boat! How old are yours?

MotherOfTwins: Two months off turning three... Yours?

TwoIsTrouble: 2 years 9 months! Wow. So you're a whole month ahead of me and can tell me everything I need to know, right :) :) ?

I remember this exchange. I'd been on the site for hours that day, desperate for a distraction from what was going on at home. I'd been lurking silently on other people's threads, but that morning I'd replied to a few things on the grief forum before moving back to the parenting ones. There was a thread about twins, I don't remember exactly what it was. Someone asking who else had twins under five in the South West. Why were they asking? I really can't remember now, but I remember feeling desperate to find other women who might understand what I was going through. The lack of sleep, the hatred of your own body, the absolutely terrifying thoughts that came to you every moment of every day that something bad might happen to your babies. Mostly in my case, the fear that the bad thing was me.

Then, she messaged me. And I thought I'd found someone to help.

At first, I didn't really like her. Though I'd grown used to the excessive use of words like 'hun' and 'babe' from the other women online, the overly familiar language never became natural to me and I squirmed when I found myself using it in reply. But I was desperate for a friend and when you're desperate, you do all sorts of uncharacteristic things.

The next few messages I read through offer little in the way of clues as to who this woman really is. We exchange details about how little sleep we've had, how everyone around us is so quick to praise our husbands for 'helping out', how much we wish someone had told us this is how it would be. It's hard reading my own words back; I seem so bitter, so totally ungrateful for what I had. I take a deep breath and remind myself that this wasn't me talking, it was the post-natal depression. I didn't know it then, of course. That diagnosis came months later after I finally started taking therapy seriously and opened my eyes to what had been causing me to act the way I had; then everything started to get better. I close my eyes and take a deep breath, needing some relief from my own angry words. I don't want to be dragged back into all of this. Anger flares up in me at TwoIsTrouble, this stranger dragging me back into a world I want to be out of.

I keep reading, jotting down little notes as I go in the hope that knowing things like how much she 'bloody loves crumpets dripping in butter with a bit of salt on top' is going to somehow help me track her down. I scroll until I get to the message I can't bear to read again. Even knowing it's coming up makes my palms slick with sweat. I remember the exact day I confessed my very worst secret to her. The very hour. It was not long after the accident, the other day that is forever implanted in my head, and those two dates haunt me. The first, the worst thing I ever did to my family. The second, the day I told someone the truth about it. Despite that, a small grain of hope still exists inside me that her stalking me now has nothing to do with the confession about the accident. That my guilt is amplifying what I said; to her, it may have meant nothing at all. But deep down, I think I know that somehow this is all connected. It's the reason I had to leave MumsOnline; I realised she hadn't forgotten what I told her and had simply been waiting for the most damning time to bring it back up. She's the only person who knows the worst thing I did, the truth that no one else can ever know, and now it seems she wants to punish me for it. Isn't that what I deserve?

–

It's not until the sound of the key in the door that I realise the kitchen has grown dark.

'Shit,' I say, slamming my laptop shut and running to the living room to get in there before my husband does. The girls are cuddled around each other, eyes glued so comically to *Peppa Pig* that they don't even acknowledge my rushed entrance. It's only when Mark appears in the doorway that their trance is broken.

'Now, this is exactly what I like to see,' he says, shrugging off his jacket and smiling at the sight of us. He's always telling me to slow down, that it's okay to spend the afternoon with the girls watching TV; that I don't always have to be 'doing' things, 'achieving' things.

After he's finished saying hello to the girls and set them back in front of the TV, I jump up from the sofa and pull him close, breathing in the smell of the outside that clings to his work shirt.

Eventually, Mark gently pulls away and I'm embarrassed to find my face is wet with tears.

'Em…' he says. 'If going back to work is too much…' He lowers his voice so the girls don't listen in.

'It's not,' I say, fiercely wiping at my wet face. 'I'm just being silly.' I look down and see Lara's worried face looking back up at me. 'Happy tears,' I cry. 'Mummy's just so happy to see Daddy.' But my voice sounds weak, high-pitched, altogether just not quite right.

'You take them up for a bath, I'll make a start on dinner,' Mark says. 'Spaghetti okay?'

I nod with a tight smile and take the girls upstairs.

-

'Em,' Mark says a little later over dinner, 'it's just us now, come on. What's up?'

I clear my throat and try to shake the thoughts from my head. 'Nothing, I'm just knackered.'

Mark smiles and clears our plates; I'm surprised to find I've scraped mine clean. Mindless eating.

'It'll get easier,' he says, planting a kiss on the top of my head. He takes the plates to the sink and starts running the hot water to wash up. I close my eyes and try to stop my thoughts from whirring.

'I bought us a treat,' Marks says, as I realise he's sitting back at the table next to me. He produces two chocolate eclairs – my favourite – and beams at me. 'Not totally useless, am I?'

The words make me flinch; I've called him that so many times to TwoIsTrouble. I never meant it; not really. But it just felt so hard sometimes, being the one left with the girls all day, especially after the accident. I never meant what I said. Mark is everything I could hope for in a husband. But that site, it brought out the worst in me.

Made me say things I wouldn't ever say aloud; think things that I'd never thought before.

'You're not useless at all,' I tell him.

'Hey, enough of that,' he says, following my eye-line to the closed laptop. 'No more thinking about work.' He pushes the laptop away and with it my notepad which is still open on the list I wrote about that bloody woman. He reads it aloud, 'Woman. Mother to identical twin boys. Lives in South West. Married. Stay-at-home mum.' He frowns. 'What's this?'

My cheeks redden. 'Oh, it's just for work. Customer profile for—'

He laughs. 'Really? You've been back one day and you've managed to find an account where the customer is basically you?'

I frown and look at the words. It *is* me; except for the twins being boys, every other detail is my exact life up until yesterday, when I dropped the stay-at-home mum part. I don't know why this surprises me. It's the reason I got on so well with TwoIsTrouble in the first place. On paper, she was just like me. Is that why she was so desperate to convince me not to go back to work? She didn't want to lose the one person she could rely on to be as miserable as her? Anger curls in my stomach. That's why she's doing this, isn't it? She doesn't want me to be happy. She *wants* me to be miserable. She wants me to be back on MumsOnline, sharing tales of despair with her.

'No. That type of woman is nothing like me,' I tell Mark as I dig my fork into the chocolate eclair. 'Nothing like me at all.'

Nine

Then

Who am I?

When I was pregnant with D1, I spent little to no time thinking about what kind of mother I'd be. I guess I was too young, too stupid to realise how it was going to change everything. What kind of mother was I to her? I think a good one, sometimes, in some ways. I wasn't a proper mum though – not like I'm supposed to be now. It's fine to be the kooky, irresponsible, fun mum when you're young and beautiful. It's fine to leave the baby with the grandparents (thank GOD for D1's grandparents) and keep going to work like you're still you. But how could I be that with the twins? I'm married now. To a proper man, an adult. Not like D1's dad. We were never proper parents, just kids who ended up with a kid of our own. She was a good kid then, too. Easy to please. Always smiling. She'd hold my hand everywhere we went, never let anyone pass us by without shouting and waving 'hello!' at the top of her little voice and always running to our shabby front door with utter joy. Everyone was always telling me just how happy she always seemed, despite the second-hand clothes and wild curly hair that would never stay in its plait. But everything is different now. I can't just let the girls choose whatever they like from the charity shop or let them outside with wild hair. Now we have a proper house, with a big kitchen that always needs to be cleaned and a garden that is always overgrown despite H telling me to sort a gardener. That's what a proper wife would do, isn't it? It's not fair that I can't be either a good wife or a good mum. The twins need me to be and so does H.

And the thing is, I think I could be, if it wasn't for D1. She's always there, a constant reminder of my shortcomings. I want to shake off the old me and become the kind of mother you see on TV; the ones who always have the fridge stocked, who have meals on the table for their handsome husbands when they arrive home from work, who breastfeed with ease. But I'm not like that and yes, I do blame her. If I had time to concentrate on the twins instead of always having to pander to her, everything would be fine. But she just won't leave me alone long enough to do anything. And I'm tired. All the bloody time. Where's that little smiling girl now? She's gone, and I'm left with an extra child who screams and whines and moans relentlessly, grabbing my body for warmth that I can't give her any more. I'm so tired. This isn't how it's meant to be, is it?

Ten

Now

The next day, I'm back in the office. The morning has been manic; I snoozed my alarm for five minutes too long and had to speed everything up to accommodate the lost time. But I've made it in, I'm here sitting at my desk like there's nothing to worry about except the crippling panic I feel every time I open the pitch document I should be working on.

It's just gone three p.m. and I've been checking my phone all day, expecting the worst from TwoIsTrouble, but so far there has been no further contact. My concentration is completely frazzled and I know I must look a wreck. I've not left my desk since I sat down this morning, reading and re-reading the brief for the pitch we have on Monday. It should be easy, a corporate PR strategy for a baby food company that came under fire last year when an employee sold a story to the *Daily Mail* about the head office's rather shady practices to their own pregnant employees. Not ideal for a company whose primary market is mothers. I finally managed to get that stupid media report to save after asking one of the interns to show me, and the new system really isn't as complicated as it felt on Monday. Yet every time I try to gather my thoughts in any sort of order, nothing comes. All I can think about is how if TwoIsTrouble ever spills my secrets, I'll be the negative PR story.

'How you feeling about it?' Alyssa appears by the side of my desk and asks. I minimise the PowerPoint screen, not wanting her to read my ill-thought-out words.

'All good,' I say, shrugging. 'Nothing I haven't done before.'

She nods and smiles tightly. 'Of course. Must be weird though, having all that time off and coming back to it.'

'You know what they say… like riding a bike.'

She laughs. 'I'm not sure anyone does say that any more, but I get your point. It'll be great to see how you approach this; we could do with getting some traditional methods back here. Everyone else is so young, we do tend to approach everything digitally only. Did I see you had some ideas for print?' She nods at my screen.

'It's not really ready for…'

'Don't worry about that,' she says and pulls up a chair next to my desk. I have to awkwardly shift my chair over to avoid our arms touching but Alyssa is oblivious to my discomfort and takes over my mouse, bringing my presentation back up.

Before I even have a chance to convey how utterly infantilising her taking over like this is, she bursts out laughing.

'Oh, that's great,' she says, nodding along with my shoddily sketched out idea for a print campaign involving hand-drawn cards sent to mothers across the country to thank them for their work.

Despite myself, I smile and feel something I haven't felt for a while.

'I wasn't sure… Thought it was a bit… obvious?'

She shakes her head. 'Not at all. I think it'll really speak to their customers. I love that you've gone back to the roots of the brand and used print – everyone now is so stuck on everything being digital. Sometimes the old methods really are the best. I'd be happy to never run an online campaign again.'

I bristle and glance around the open-plan office, hoping no one else just heard the dig. 'I'm hardly old, Alyssa.'

'What?' She crinkles her perfectly dainty nose. 'I didn't say you were.'

My cheeks flush and I rub my face. 'You didn't need to. I know what you mean, I know what you think of me. That I'm old and outdated and that my campaign ideas are tired. I know everything is online—'

'Woah! Seriously, Emily. You've totally misunderstood me, I promise.' She rests her hand on top of mine and looks at me with wide eyes. 'Trust me, if you ask anyone in this office they'll tell you how I feel about online campaigns…'

This time, it's her who's blushing and the bravado I thought I saw in her is gone.

'What do you mean?'

She laughs and waves her hand in front of her face. 'Oh, it's nothing really. The first campaign I ran went viral, which is great, except not in a good way. And I was the one that the trolls decided to go for over it.'

I'm glad no one is sitting near enough to us to hear the story Alyssa then tells me, though it becomes clear during the telling that everyone in this office is well aware of it already. Alyssa explains how, after a particularly ill-thought-through campaign involving an 'activist influencer' who turned out not to be all that they seemed backfired, she was targeted by online trolls for over a year.

'I nearly left the job altogether,' she tells me. 'But Daniel convinced me to stay. I'm glad I did. I do love PR, despite that pretty gross experience. I'm just more careful now about what I put online.'

I tell her that I understand, and that I'm so glad that when I started my career, we never had to put our names out there at all.

She shakes her head. 'That's the worst bit, though. Nothing about the campaign even used my real name; we knew it was going to be a divisive one so I used an alias online – made up a username so people wouldn't find me if it backfired.'

I frown. 'So how did they find you?'

She looks down, clearly embarrassed. 'It was the stupid username. I'd used it before; I hadn't remembered but I'd written this cringey travel blog in my gap year on Tumblr and posted everything with the same username. It was so stupid of me. I still can't believe I didn't think of it. All they had to do was put my username into Google and it found everything I'd ever written on the internet...'

I know I should say something of comfort to Alyssa, tell her it wasn't her fault and apologise for how I've treated her this week. I should explain that my frostiness towards her was due to my own insecurities and act like the mentor Daniel hoped I would be when he gave me this job. But I can't.

All I can think is that Alyssa might have just helped me to finally find TwoIsTrouble and put a stop to all of this.

–

She's easy to find. Alyssa was right; all you do is put someone's username into Google and just like that, everything they ever did online is there for everyone to see. My heart races as I scan through the results, my eyes greedily absorbing the words flying across the screen. There is so much here to discover. I click through to an Instagram profile which reads:

> Mama to two beautifully identical naughty boys! Sharing my daily #MamaStruggles and forever playing guess who!

It's her. It must be her. The small circular profile image is of a plain woman around my age. She has 327 followers but is following over 5,000 people. I scroll through her posts. She writes like those typically cringey 'Instamums' who get paid to promote baby food on their feeds. But she isn't an Instamum, she's just a mum. Her posts have three, four likes each. No comments. They're badly lit, badly shot, the captions below them badly written. The whole page reeks of desperation. Who is this woman? I zoom in on one photo of her with two identical twin boys, around the same age as the girls, I think, but it's hard to tell. She has blonde hair, pale skin and grey-blue eyes. Everything about her face is forgettable. I click on her profile picture which is coloured on the outside, signalling she's recently added a story.

'Hi mommas!' Her nasal voice rings out through my laptop speakers and I jump to silence it and grab my headphones. A few curious glances dart my way from my colleagues but I laugh and apologise as if it's nothing. With my headphones in, I replay the video.

'Hi mommas! I don't know about you but I'm so tired today. These two terrors kept me up all night!' The camera pans from her face to the twins beside her. One of them smiles gleefully at the camera while the other bats it away with a closed fist. 'If anyone has any tips about how to get through the day without any sleep, send it my way – I'll need it!' She signs off with a laugh and the next story is a filtered selfie with coffee cups over her eyes.

'Researching Instamums?' I hear Daniel's voice from behind me and yank the headphones from my ears while minimising the screen.

'What?' I say, turning around in my chair to face him.

He frowns and nods at my screen. 'That woman on your screen,' he says. 'Is it for the Browngate pitch? Only she's…'

'Oh, that, yes. I was just looking for someone—'

He shakes his head and stops me. 'Sorry, Emily, I don't mean to be rude but, really? This campaign it's got to be… Aspirational. If you're going down the influencer route, let's not get all "woke" about it, yeah? I know women say they want to "see themselves represented"' – he does air quotes around this – 'but you and I both know that's crap. And trust me, Browngate are not going to want some knackered-looking mum who hasn't quite lost the baby weight.'

I flinch at his harsh words, momentarily forgetting that the woman he's so harshly disparaging is no longer a friend.

'Don't look at me like that, Em,' he laughs. 'You know what I'm saying!'

I manage a laugh back despite wishing I could tell him what a pig he can be. 'Yeah, I know,' I say, batting away his comments. 'She's not someone I'm seriously looking at for this. It's just research. Don't worry.'

Daniel hovers around my desk for a while longer offering ideas for the pitch but I can barely hear a word he's saying. I nod in all the right places but I'm desperate for him to go away so I can get back to my 'research'.

In the end, it's Alyssa who saves me from Daniel's monologue.

'I'm heading off for the evening.'

'What? Part-timer!' Daniel jokes and I see the smallest eye roll from Alyssa as he laughs.

'It's five o'clock. Want to walk out with me, Emily?'

I don't need any encouragement and grab my things and shove them into my bag while calling goodbye to the office.

'I'm this way,' Alyssa says, pointing in the opposite direction to me.

'Okay, bye,' I say, knowing I should use this time in private to apologise for the way I've been with her so far but I don't know how to without sounding totally ridiculous. She'd never understand.

'Are you okay, Emily? You look a bit…'

'I'm fine,' I say, trying to smile. 'I don't want to be late to pick up the girls…'

'Of course,' she smiles, going gooey-eyed again and I wonder if despite her career-driven appearance she actually dreams of being a mum. We say our goodbyes and I walk the rest of the ten-minute journey from the office to the car park with my eyes glued to my phone, much to the annoyance of everyone I bump into.

By the time I reach my car, I'm sure that this woman is my TwoIsTrouble. I've gone back through her highlighted stories. Endless reels of her asking for parenting tips, sharing every single thought she has about her twins, even a few shots of her actually crying while filming. There's something else I've noticed too; she's never with anyone.

It's just her and the boys, all the time. No husband, no partner, no friends.

There is something not right about her posts, the way she talks to the camera on her stories like a celebrity and yet, going by the lack of comments on her posts, no one is watching. So who is she doing it for? As I yank the car into reverse and back out of the car park, a horrible thought occurs.

Did she make these videos in the hope that I would find them?

-

The drive to pick up the girls goes by in a haze and by the time I arrive, the evening is starting to draw in. Golden hour. I grimace at the phrase; something influencers use to describe the best light of the day for selfies. Why do I even know that? Before getting out of the car, I instinct-ively reach for my phone and check my email, Facebook, Instagram and Twitter. No messages. I hate that every time I'm away from my phone, even for a short drive, the fear creeps in that she's going to have done something. Said something. I remind myself that she hasn't got all the power any more, not now that I know who she is. I put my phone back in my handbag and get out of the car.

The girls' nursery is a small grey building covered in pink dots, called Polkadot Daycare. The name put me off at first – I asked Mark how we could trust anyone who would paint giant pink polka dots all over their building with our girls. But it's the best in the area, recommended by all the local yummy mummies and in the end, I realised my own misgivings about it were ridiculous.

A few other mums lurk around the gates, waiting for their children. The nursery has different pick-up times:

midday, three p.m. and six p.m. There is something almost shameful about being here for the six o'clock one. The 'mothers who can't give their children more time' slot. The 'mothers who work' slot. The 'not quite good enough' slot. I shake the thought, unwilling to give it any more room in my brain.

I don't know these women yet, the other anxious waiters, but they seem to know each other. I smile tightly at one of them. She returns my smile then trains her eyes back on the door. It's a funny feeling, waiting for someone to allow you access to your own children. Especially after they have been yours and yours alone for every moment of their lives up until now. I resisted putting them into nursery for the thirty hours we got free when they were old enough; I did try it for a few weeks at Mark's insistence but I hated being without them. Everyone told me I'd relish the free time, as if by relieving myself of my children I'd somehow become thinner, healthier, better all round. But it didn't work for me. They'd be dropped off in the morning and I'd return to the house in a state with no energy to clean it and instead find myself at the kitchen table, scrolling MumsOnline until TwoIsTrouble came online, then we'd waste hours sharing how tired we were, what a state our houses were, how our brains couldn't really function enough to be useful any more, and then it would be pick-up time and I'd feel more guilty than ever that I'd not magically morphed into a better version of myself in my six hours of freedom. But it's not like that now; today I've done a whole day of work and I feel tired in the way it's okay to feel tired, when you've earned it.

Finally, a young woman I recognise appears in the doorway. Katie, I think her name is.

'Hi ladies,' she calls, waving us over. The four of us rush towards her; the woman I smiled at giggles and makes a joke about us being as bad as the kids.

Inside, we're asked to wait outside the main room. I've been in there before, when Mark and I came to look around. Now, I can only see through the top glass of the door. I can't see the girls, but I see their pink coats hung up on the wall, side-by-side. My eyes search the room in desperation, looking for their blonde heads.

'Don't worry,' the woman I smiled at says. 'They'll be getting their end-of-day apples.'

I frown at this friendly stranger. 'What?'

She laughs, making the skin on her freckled nose wrinkle. 'They call it a treat… Funny, because when I offer cut up apple slices at home, Jake, my son, won't touch it. But from Katie? Well, it's like gold dust.'

I laugh tightly, my eyes nervously returning to the door.

'I'm Holly,' the woman says.

'Emily,' I reply. 'Sorry, I'm a bit on edge. This is only the second day they've been in. First day I've picked them up.'

She smiles and nods, like she's seen it all before. 'You do get used to it. Jake's been coming for just over a year. Probably too long, to be honest. But I was desperate to go back to work as soon as I could.'

'How old is he?'

'Just turned two.' Holly beams as she pulls out her phone and shows me a photo. I tell her the only thing that you need to say to adoring mothers; that he's lovely. 'What about yours?'

I smile, my hand already flicking through my favourite photos on my phone to show her. This is something I have learned to be prepared for. It's no good to have to scroll through your entire camera reel while strangers wait for pictures; you have to have the best ones saved in your favourites folder. I have a collection of over 300 – it's hard to choose just one. But they're in order, so it's easy to find the most recent, most beautiful photos.

'They've just turned four,' I tell her, holding up a photo of the girls that we took on their birthday a few months ago, their faces lit by warm candlelight, cheeks pink with the excitement of it all.

'Twins!' Holly squeals, her face lit up in delight. 'Oh, wow. They're so beautiful,' she sighs, her face glued to my phone.

A swell of pride fills me; this reaction never gets old.

'Thank you,' I say, moving my phone away from her to flick through more photos to show. 'They're certainly a handful,' I laugh, smiling at Holly. Perhaps she can be my new mum friend. The idea quickly takes hold and I smile wider as I imagine chatting each day as we wait for the kids, catching up about our work days.

'God, I bet.' Holly looks up from the phone and stares at me, her head tilted to the side, suddenly serious. 'Is it just the two of them?' I open my mouth to reply but find I can't. 'God, what am I saying? *Just* the two, as if two is easy! Sorry,' she says in a rush. 'I didn't mean that. I can't imagine having two at the same time. Sometimes I feel like I'm losing my mind with just the one. Did it send you totally bonkers at first?'

I bristle. 'No.' I put my phone away and Holly takes a step back. 'It didn't.'

'Oh, I didn't mean anything like... Well, I just meant—'

Holly blushes and looks down at her hands. I battle with myself to apologise; this poor woman is trying to be my friend. Why can't I just talk to other mums like a normal person? But her words cut. Yes, something did send me 'totally bonkers', I want to say. But it wasn't '*just*' the two of them. And maybe I'm still a little 'bonkers' right now. But to admit that would risk falling back into it. And whatever happens, I can't do that.

'I'm sorry, I—' I start to mutter an apology as the door swings open and our attention is pulled towards the noise of our children escaping.

'Emily?' Kate calls my name from beside the door. I turn briefly to Holly to say goodbye but she's already walking away. Another chance at friendship lost.

I move through the other women towards Katie.

'Hi,' I say.

'Hi, Emily,' she says. 'Lovely to see you again.'

'Is everything okay?'

'Oh yes, of course,' Katie smiles then tells me the girls have been doing their colouring and the assistant was having a hard time tearing them away. 'I just wanted to catch you for a quick chat while you're here.'

She smiles and leads me through into the main room. The miniature desks are strewn with crayons, paper and splodges of paint. I notice that none of the other mums are being led away like they've done something wrong and can't help but feel uneasy.

'Mummy!' I hear Ella's squeals before I see them both.

'Hello, darlings.' I bend down and they wrap themselves around me in a tight hug. 'Have you been good?'

'They've been very good,' Katie tells me as the girls nod earnestly.

I work my fingers through Ella's hair; she's somehow managed to turn the tight plaits I gave her last night into an almost seventies bouffant in the few hours since she's been gone.

'Girls, do you want to go and fetch your backpacks from next door while I talk to Mummy?'

They toddle off together and Katie smiles at me tightly and perches herself on the edge of the desk at the front of the room.

'I just wanted to check in, really. See how you were feeling now?'

'I'm fine. Why wouldn't I be fine?

Katie's cheeks colour and I can tell she's incredibly uncomfortable with this conversation.

'I was a little concerned after our phone call at lunchtime...' She says. 'I know the first few days of going back to work can be so hard on mums and I just wanted to make sure that—'

'Sorry, Katie. I really have no idea what you're talking about.'

'The conversation we had at lunch today, Emily. You said you thought you'd need to pull the girls from nursery altogether because you weren't... coping at work...'

I shake my head. 'I didn't!'

She opens her mouth and then closes it again, looking at me like I'm totally mad.

Before I can say any more, tell her she must have me confused with one of the other parents, the girls noisily run through, wrapped up in their matching coats with their bags strapped to their backs.

'Ready!' they cry in unison. This pulls Katie from her fish-gasping-for-water look and she smiles broadly and claps her hands.

'Don't you two look delightful!' The girls' faces light up at the praise and they giggle before holding hands and walking towards the door, ready for home.

'Emily, it's okay if you're finding things difficult. Honestly, there's no judgment here. Mark has told us about your history and what happened last year with—'

'Will you please not talk about this in front of my children?' I whisper sharply.

Katie takes a step back and turns bright red. 'Of course. I'm sorry. But we do need to discuss that phone call.'

'You must have me confused with one of the other mums,' I tell her, my tone now falsely bright as I see the girls watching us.

Katie nods but her smile is gone. 'Okay. Let's pick this up at a better time. It's obviously been a tricky day for you. I'll set up a time when you and Mark perhaps could come in without the girls.'

To that, I don't even reply. Because now I realise that Katie hasn't got me confused with another mum. She really thinks we spoke today. She must have spoken to someone. That someone wasn't me.

But I can make a pretty good guess who it was.

Eleven

Now

It's raining as we leave Polkadot, and fat cold drops spill onto my face as I shout at the girls to hurry up across the car park. I bundle them into the car and strap them tightly into their car seats, my head throbbing.

'Ow!' Ella cries.

'Sorry, sorry, darling.' I rush to release the tension from the seatbelt which I've yanked across her chest. 'Better?' She nods solemnly but won't look at me. It's enough to make me take a breath. I apologise again and kiss her head, then secure Lara into her car seat with more tenderness. Nothing hurts like the pain you feel when you've hurt your children. Accident or not.

At the wheel, I take another deep breath before turning on the engine. The rain has stopped, the angry shower over as soon as it started. Sun peeks through the clouds, lighting the puddles in the car park. Everything feels better for a second. I put on the girls' favourite audiobook for the fifteen-minute journey home and allow myself to consider what has just happened.

TwoIsTrouble rang the girls' nursery and pretended to be me. It must have been her. By the sounds of it, she put on a very convincing performance. For what purpose? I think back to how Katie looked at me; the worry that filled her face as she asked if everything was okay. She thinks I'm unstable. But it wasn't just the phone call that made her think that; she said Mark had told her about what happened before. How could he? We promised we'd make this a fresh start; what was the point if he was going to rake it all back up? My ears grow hot as shame and fury flow through me. I grip the steering wheel tighter.

'Mummy!'

I slam the brakes.

The car jolts to a stop just in time; the red lights in front of us glare angrily as two women step out to cross the road. My hands shake against the steering wheel as the lights turn back to green. Horns blare from behind, the sound echoing in my ears as I force myself to drive forward to silence the noise.

I snatch a look in the rear view mirror; the girls are silent, staring at me with their big blue eyes. My scalp itches.

'Silly Mummy,' I say, forcing a laugh. 'Aren't I?' They stare on, not convinced by my false jollity. 'I know you sometimes get a bit… scared when Mummy drives, but it's okay. I promise. Let's not tell Daddy about the red lights, okay girls?'

I train my eyes back on the road, not allowing myself to get distracted again as I crawl along, my speed no higher than twenty miles per hour. 'Promise me, girls?' I say. 'You don't want to make Daddy worried, do you?'

'No,' Lara says quietly. Always the first to come to my rescue. 'We promise, Mummy.'

It's not a good feeling; the one you get from forcing your children to lie for you, but I've found it's better than the alternative.

By the time we get home, Mark has already changed from his work clothes into his joggers and a sweat top and has set the table for dinner. He's got his music on loud in the kitchen and Sam Cooke croons away in his deep, longing voice, as Mark picks up the girls and spins them around. They giggle manically and any sign of the car journey's fall-out vanishes from their faces. Relief washes over me, followed swiftly by guilt. How am I back in this situation where my whole life feels so close to shattering? But this time, it isn't just in my head. This is her doing.

'Can you give them some tea while I get changed?' I ask Mark before even saying hello. 'I'm desperate for a shower.'

He tells me of course and I run upstairs into our bathroom, my phone in my hand. I turn on the shower, take a seat on the closed toilet, and begin to scroll through TwoIsTrouble's Instagram page again.

Sarah.

That's her name. Such a plain, normal name. I zoom in on her face again, looking for the signs of madness that I'm sure live behind her eyes. This is the woman who pretended to be me today. She called my children's nursery and faked my voice. Why? Why would any sane person do that?

Suddenly, a thought hits me and I can't believe I haven't considered it before.

Her pretending to be me, to make me look mad, isn't the most terrifying part.

What I should be afraid of is this: she knows where my girls go to nursery, which means she knows how to reach them.

There is only so long I can get away with hiding in the bathroom, so after half an hour of what can only be described as cyber-stalking Sarah, I jump under the hot water quickly and wash my hair so Mark doesn't wonder what I've been doing up here.

I've managed to find out a lot about this woman. Unlike she told me online, she lives in the South East, not the South West like me. Her house is somewhere in Wantage; I've worked that out from the various tagged locations in her desperate posts. There's a coffee shop she seems to spend a lot of time in, called Beans and Dreams. Her boys are two, not four like she told me, but that's hardly surprising; she also lied about not being a psychopath. She doesn't seem to work, but it's hard to tell that from photos, and I'm pretty sure she lives in a new build. I've thought about messaging her, but I'm sure she'd just block me. I'm not going to give her the option of getting out of this so easily.

'Emily?' Mark shouts up the stairs as I pull a brush through my wet hair. 'Dinner's almost ready.'

'Just give me a minute!' I shout back, annoyance sharpening my tongue despite myself.

I could call the police. Tell them what she's doing. But then I'd have to admit everything else; explain our relationship. They'd want to look through our messages, wouldn't they? And I can't let them do that. My scalp yelps in protest as I yank the brush through my hair. I've got to make her leave me alone. Before she does anything worse.

I roughly towel-dry my hair and pull on some leggings and an oversized top. My face is red and puffy from the hot shower so I rub on some foundation to cover it before going back downstairs.

73

The smell of sweet Chinese spices wafts from the kitchen and I feel my mouth water. Mark is such a good cook; he always has been, but he really stepped it up once the girls arrived. He told me he wanted to make sure he knew exactly what was going into our bodies, to make sure we were getting all the vitamins and nutrients we needed to be the healthiest we could be. It should have made me feel cared for, loved, but all I remember feeling at the time was a sense of jealousy. Why had he not cared about those things before? Why did it take the girls for him to look after us better?

By the time I became friends with TwoIsTrouble, the fog had lifted enough that I realised that feeling was unfair and totally unlike me, but I had other reasons to gripe by then. She'd moan that her husband never cooked, never even considered that he might need to stop at the shop on his way home from work, instead of assuming that she'd always have dinner under control. She always did, she told me, but why didn't it occur to him that he might also be responsible for feeding them? I couldn't match her complaints in the same way, so instead I offered stories of the chaos of our kitchen. How Mark insisted on making everything from scratch, even blending his own spices, every single night when all I wanted was to bung something in the oven and be done with it. Some days, the never-ending cycle of eating and cleaning felt so overwhelming I hated the very smell of food. I'd write to TwoIsTrouble that I'd be happy to never eat again.

I wasn't lying then, but I can't imagine feeling that way now. Yes, our kitchen is still in a semi-permanent state of disarray. But it's a state caused by love; by my husband going out of his way to make food that will bring a smile to my lips on days when nothing else can. It's one of the things Mark takes real pride in. Before he became a dad, he'd say he couldn't wait to have a special meal that only he could make for our family. *Be good tonight and Dad will make his special Bolognese*, he'd imitate me saying to our future children. We'd laugh as we imagined a life like that, where we were the grown-ups, the ones taking care of everything, keeping a family safe.

'I'll take them up,' Mark says now, meeting me in the hallway. 'Do bedtime. Can you just keep an eye on the rice? Everything's on timer.'

I nod and kiss the girls goodnight as he takes them upstairs. Bedtime is another part of our daily routine that Mark has always done his fair share of. I'd read TwoIs-Trouble's complaints in this area and watch as the other women shared her frustration, offering words of support and solidarity in a way that I never could.

There is something somewhat isolating about having a husband so good.

Women don't warm to you in the same way when you don't have horror stories to compare. I realised that early on; no one wants to hear your complaints, no matter how bad, if another element of your life is perfect. No, it needs to be all falling down before you're given any sympathy. Perhaps that's why I tried to demolish all the good things I had.

In the kitchen, I check the rice isn't boiling over and lay the table. The oven timer is set for fifteen minutes and I can see chilli-glazed salmon gently roasting inside, the skin becoming sticky and delicious under the heat. I sit at the table and get out my laptop. Google Maps tells me the drive from here to TwoIsTrouble's home town, Wantage, is just over an hour. Plenty of time to make it there and back tomorrow while Mark is at work. He never has to know about any of this. The more I think about it, the less insane the whole plan seems. I just need to confront her, face to face. Scare her into stopping this insanity. Internet bullies are known for hiding in the shadows; like all bullies, they live in fear of the tables turning on them. TwoIsTrouble, *Sarah*, is a woman desperate for attention. Acceptance. It's so obvious to me now that I can't believe I didn't see it before. I was her only friend. That's why she can't cope with me leaving the site. Though why she thinks ruining my life is going to somehow lure me back to the forums is beyond me; but she hardly seems like a rational person.

Tomorrow, I'll put a stop to all of this.

'Em, are you all right?' Mark says, breaking into my thoughts. I snap the laptop screen closed and force a smile, the weight of it pulling at my cheeks. 'The timer… Em,' he says as he runs to the oven. The sound comes into focus then. The repetitive *ding, ding, ding,* of the oven.

'It just started,' I lie. 'I was about to—'

'Shit,' he shouts, pulling the tray from the oven. The salmon is shrunken and black in the middle of it. 'Sorry, I must have put the timer on wrong. What a waste…'

'It doesn't matter. There's rice and veg… It's fine. I'm not even that hungry,' I say but the rumble of my stomach betrays me.

Mark puffs out his cheeks and shakes his head. He hates it when things like this happen. He told me once he feels like he's failed me when the food he cooks doesn't turn out right, that it's his job to look after us.

'Did the timer really only just go off?' he asks, looking at the rice which I can now see is also ruined. It's stuck to the bottom of the pan in burnt patches. How did I not notice all of this? Annoyance twinges on my lips as

I tell him again that yes, he must have timed it wrong. He frowns and I'm not sure he believes me, but Mark is too kind to call attention to my absent-mindedness.

Too kind, or too unwilling to consider that it could be happening again.

–

We have fish-finger sandwiches in the end. A children's dinner but exactly what I needed; simple, comforting. As I stand at the sink and dunk the dishes into hot soapy water, I feel Mark behind me.

'Everything is okay, isn't it?' he asks.

I watch his reflection in the window, the dark night outside a black mirror wall in front of us. He's looking down and fiddling with his sleeve like a little boy.

'It's fine, I promise. Work is fine. I'm just tired. It's hard getting used to the hours.'

'And you'll tell me, if anything starts to feel… off, again, won't you?'

I look away and scrub at the already-clean plate in my hand as I promise him yes, I'll never let things get bad like they were before. I swear, I'll never let it happen again.

Twelve

Then

My Daughter Is Turning Me Insane

I'm so fucking angry I can barely write this. H isn't home yet and I need to vent. Like he'd even listen if he was here. He never listens to me any more. If I tell him later what happened today, he'll probably just laugh. He finds everything so fucking funny lately. This isn't funny.

The girls had their twelve-week check-up today at the hospital. We had to take the bus into town because I'm still not confident enough to drive − I never used to have to, everything was on the doorstep − and now every time I get behind the wheel I think of how many accidents happen on these awful country lanes and I just can't stop picturing the car crushed into a metal ball; us all dead inside.

Anyway, H said he tried to book a taxi but he left it too late and no one could pick us up in the end. I was fuming. The obvious thing would have been for him to stay home from work and take us himself but, of course, that wasn't an option. It never is. So we had to deal with the bus. Have you ever tried getting on a bus with newborn twins and a five-year-old? H certainly hasn't, that's for sure. He told me to stop being so dramatic; it should be fine. Everything would be fine. I should have known there and then that the whole day would descend into absolute chaos.

By the time we got to the hospital, I was damp with sweat, the girls were both crying and D1 was insisting on holding my hand so tight with her clammy, sticky fingers that I felt like she was glued to me. Does everyone suddenly understand the reason behind spontaneous combustion since having children or is it just me?

I shouldn't have screamed at her, I know that, but she just wouldn't let go and I was trying to get the double pram through the too-small doorframe before our appointment time passed by and I just needed her to get her sticky hands off me for one bloody minute. The look on her face when the words flew out of my mouth made me feel like I was cracking in two. But the girls were howling by then, their tiny puffy faces red with the exhaustion of it all, and I just couldn't deal with D1 adding to it. So I snapped again. Told her to shut up. She isn't a baby any more.

She let go. Then ran. Yes, my own daughter sprinted through the hospital corridors away from me like I was attacking her. What could I do? No one was around to help me, the corridor was completely empty and I was left standing there with that stupid bloody pushchair that's too big to fit anywhere, screaming at D1 to come back. I watched as her little red coat disappeared around the corner.

Do you know the worst bit about it? For a moment, when she was gone, all I felt was relief.

Thirteen

Now

I slam my mobile on the table in frustration. Mark's mum won't take the girls today. She's got a hair appointment, apparently, and cancelling on the day would see her 'on the wrong side of Tina for months' so she won't. That means the girls are going to have to come with me. It's not ideal by any means; I hate the thought of that woman setting eyes on them. But if I don't go today, I know I'll lose my nerve. And I need this to be over for their sakes as much as mine. They deserve a good mother, and I can't be one with the threat of TwoIsTrouble spilling all my secrets hanging over my head.

Mark asked what we were going to do today before he left for work. I vaguely referenced a trip to the shops to get a present for one of the girls' friend's birthday parties. He looked so pleased that the girls were finally making new friends, as if this was proof that our fresh start was working. I felt bad lying to him, but it is for his own good. If he knew what was really going on, he'd be horrified and the very last thing Mark deserves is more stress caused by me. I can fix this on my own. No one ever needs to know.

'Right, girls, time to get dressed,' I call through to the living room where Ella and Lara are happily watching *Peppa Pig* in their pyjamas, a Fruit Shoot each in hand.

Upstairs, I pull out clothes from their shared wardrobe at random and tell the girls to hurry up. They pout but I do get them dressed eventually, though perhaps I should have taken more care over their outfits. They are far from matching today; Ella in a pale blue top with a pink skirt and Lara clashing horribly alongside her in green leggings and a black and red flowery top. Never mind. They won't be getting out of the car anyway. I'm going to confront Sarah on the doorstep; the whole thing will be over in a matter of minutes and we can come home and cuddle up on the sofa and watch Disney films for the rest of the day. A nagging voice in the back of my head tells me that it can't possibly be that simple; that I deserve to pay for what I've done and I can't walk away yet again from my mistakes Scot-free. But what else can I do? Let her rip my family apart and have the girls and Mark once again suffer the consequences of my actions? No. That can't happen again.

But as we walk out of the house and I pull the front door closed behind me, I hesitate. This really is madness. Why am I doing this? I don't need to drive to bloody Wantage and confront a stranger. What's she even really done, when I think about it? Yes, she could ruin me if she wanted to, but she hasn't. All she's done is send me a few unwanted messages which have stopped since I blocked her. Perhaps I'm making something of nothing here. The person in the park who watched us, the postcard through the letterbox, even the phone call to the nursery, there's no way of knowing any of those things are connected. It could all just be a horrible coincidence, a figment of my overly stressed, guilt-ridden mind. If that's true, we can go back inside right now and pull our still-warm pyjamas back on, get the duvet and snuggle up on the couch.

'Girls,' I say, my hand still on the doorknob, ready to call them back, but then my phone beeps.

My heart tugs with the now-familiar jolt of panic. I yank it from my coat pocket and stab the screen.

Mark.

Not her.

Just Mark.

> Everything okay? Wish I was at home with you x

I close my eyes and take a deep breath. That feeling, the sharp pang of panic every time my phone goes off, that's the reason I can't go back inside and watch Disney films. It's why I have to confront her, to at least find out if these things are in my head, or if she really is trying to ruin my life. Until I know for sure, I can't be a good wife, nor a good mother, not a good anything to anyone. And my family have had to put up with enough of that behaviour from me already; I can't put them through any more. They deserve so much better.

'Come on,' I say to the girls as I march towards the car. 'We're going on an adventure.'

–

Traffic getting out of Cheltenham is ridiculous. The girls moan the entire time; they're bored, they're hungry, they want to go home. I turn up the radio and ignore them as frantic pop music fills the car. I have no idea who is singing. A girl. Or a woman, I should probably say. There was a time when I could have named every song played on Radio One; when every singer felt like a woman to me rather than a school child. I look at the people on TV now and feel so old. They all look like children. Whoever they are. Mark laughs if I ever complain about it. '*It's called getting old, Em.*' Like there's no shame in it at all. He can sink into this new stage of life like a comfortable Sunday afternoon film while I silently rage against it.

By the time we pass through the worst of the traffic, we've already been in the car for thirty minutes. Google Maps tells me we'll arrive in just under an hour.

'Where are we going?' Ella asks for what feels like the hundredth time.

'I've told you, we're going to see someone Mummy knows.'

'Who?'

'You don't know her.'

'What's her name?'

I grit my teeth. I don't want to tell the girls anything about Sarah. Not even her horribly normal name. So I lie. I make up a story that's so much nicer than the truth. Maybe that makes me a bad mother, but isn't my job to protect them from the true ugliness of the world, until they're ready to learn it for themselves?

As we arrive in Wantage, sun starts to spill through the clouds and I choose to take that as a sign that I'm doing the right thing, for once.

–

I've parked outside the coffee shop I know she goes to. We've only been here for ten minutes but already I've realised this is a totally stupid idea. In my head, I had a vision of us arriving and her sauntering up the street, as if she knew I would be here. But no one has passed at all and the cafe is near empty. The girls' boredom is reaching breaking point and I can't sit here for much longer.

'Mummy is going to go and check where her friend is. You stay in the car and I'll be back in a minute,' I tell the girls. Ella huffs like a stroppy teenager and I see a flash of my future. Despite everything, it makes me smile.

I walk across the street, double-locking the car, and into the cafe.

I can see why Sarah comes here. The decor is Instagram-perfect. Despite the atmosphere being cold and unwelcoming, even I understand how easy it would be to create a beautiful photo of the dark, handcrafted wood tables with the single tulip in a thin glass in the middle. Everything about this place is dying to be shared.

'Hi,' I say to the young woman behind the counter.

She smiles and raises her eyebrows as if encouraging me to get on with my order.

'I was hoping you could help me? I was supposed to meet my friend here but she hasn't shown up and I'm a little worried about her...'

The women's eyes flicker with interest, if not concern.

'Her name's Sarah? She comes in here a lot.'

A twinge of recognition on the woman's face.

'What time were you meeting her?' she asks.

'Half an hour ago. I've been waiting outside.' I wave vaguely towards the car and watch as she registers the faces of the twins in the back. 'I met Sarah online; on her Instagram page, you know it?'

The woman shakes her head.

'We've both got twins, so you know, we made friends. I wouldn't usually worry or bother you with it... but Sarah has seemed a bit...' I drop my eyes then and fake a pause.

'I'm just a bit worried about some of the things she said. It's why I rushed over today. I'm not from around here and we've driven for over an hour to see her. It's not like her to not answer my calls.'

The woman shakes her head. 'I'm not sure what you want me to do about it?'

'I don't have her home address. I was hoping you might?'

After a moment of awkward silence during which the woman seems to be assessing me for signs of being a stalker, she eventually must decide I'm not one, just another mother of twins. The status so often renders me invisible, but it also has its benefits. Everyone wants to believe mothers are good, even in the face of evidence to prove otherwise.

'I don't know the number but she lives on the Oakgrave Estate, one of them on the first row.'

I thank her, swallowing my enthusiasm in order to not raise any suspicions, and leave the coffee shop. The girls are full of questions as I get back in the car; why did I leave them, why couldn't they come in to the cafe, why didn't I get them a Fruit Shoot? But I ignore them as I input the new location into Google Maps. It tells me we're so close we could just walk, but I don't want to be far away from the car. Just in case.

We drive the one-minute journey in silence and I pull onto the Oakgrave Estate. It's a typical new-build housing development. Identical houses crammed into each other. Cars lined up alongside the road, as if the developers didn't consider parking in their plans. I look down the street and feel my head pulse. The woman from the cafe said Sarah's house was on the first row but failed to mention so were about sixty other homes.

'Mummy! What are we doing?' Ella cries from the back seat, her frustration at the lack of 'adventure' in our supposed adventure becoming audible.

I turn to look at her and put on a smile. 'I told you, darling, I'm looking for someone. It won't take long, please be patient.'

'Phone her!' Ella shouts, as if I'm the most stupid person in the world.

'I haven't got her number. So I'm going to sit here just for a minute and work out which is her house, okay?'

Ella glares at me from under the curls of her fringe then turns her stroppy face to the window. Lara watches our exchange anxiously.

It doesn't take me long once I start looking through Sarah's Instagram account to discount a huge number of the houses in front of me. From her stories, I can tell her door is green, not cream or black like some of them on the road, and that she has a small front garden. There's also a lamppost outside her bedroom; I know because she posted complaining about how hard it was to get any sleep with twins even without a light glaring into your room twenty-four/seven. It's that final detail that brings me to her front door.

The girls stay in the car. They whine, of course, but I don't want this woman anywhere near them, for their safety as well as my sanity. I march up her path and strike three quick knocks on the door. The paint up close is peeling. No one else is out on the street and the whole place has a feeling of abandonment. The houses are okay looking – standard red-brick new-builds – but there's no sense of life on this estate. This is good; if we're to have a showdown on the doorstep, at least no one will see.

The door flings open.

There she is. I stare at this stranger and search for signs of familiarity in the woman I've bared every element of my soul to, shared unspeakable thoughts with. But nothing in her face shows any signs of recognition and for a moment I falter.

'Sarah?' I say. She nods, a small smile on her chapped lips. 'TwoIsTrouble?'

Her eyes light up and she nods manically. 'Oh my gosh, yes, that's me!' She lets out a nervous giggle, apparently thrilled at being recognised as an 'influencer'. I wait for her to understand who I am, what I'm here for, but her face is the picture of innocence. The silence spreads too far between us and her smile begins to slip. 'Do I know you from Instagram?'

I let out a snort. 'Are you kidding?'

Her eyes narrow and she moves to block the space in the open doorway. 'Sorry, I don't understand what's happening. Who are you?'

'You know who I am, Sarah. Cut the bullshit.'

Behind her, there's a loud crash and then the cry of a small child. She instinctively turns to the noise, then, as if remembering I'm here, moves to slam the door shut.

'Wait—' I shove my foot in the closing door.

'What are you doing?' she shouts. The screams of the child persist and she's torn between stopping me from entering and attending to her son.

'We need to talk,' I say, calmly. 'Go and see to your son, but I'm not going anywhere.'

She glares at me, her cheeks now an angry red and scoffs like this is total madness, but then does walk away, leaving the front door open. I glance across the road to check on the girls. Their faces peer out of the locked car windows. They're fine. It's all the reassurance I need as I step into Sarah's home and shut the door behind me.

I hear her consoling her crying son as I move through the hallway. It's a tip. The kind of chaos that only another mother of young twins can recognise and not judge. In the small square kitchen off the hallway there are piles of dirty dishes in the sink. Laundry sits unwashed in a pile in front of the washing machine and, inexplicably, there's a large toy bear on the counter with his fluffy insides spilling out. In the hallway, the double pushchair makes it almost impossible to pass through as I inspect the photos on the walls. Most are shots of Sarah's boys; staged photos, the sort of thing you see Groupon offers for where you end up in a dingy ill-lit studio with too much make-up on your face and a sense of bitter disappointment in your stomach.

She always led me to believe she lived in a house similar to mine. We bemoaned the constant cleaning of our bi-fold doors, covered with sticky finger marks from our children. Complained of the chaos of prams in the hallway, but never with the understanding that one of our hallways was quite literally no wider than a pram. Did she actually say anything about her house or did I just assume that her house was like mine? For a moment, I forget to be angry at her and just feel embarrassed at my own lack of self-awareness. How galling it must have been for her to listen to my complaints. How spoiled I must seem. Is that why she's tormenting me now?

Sarah spots me in her hallway and screams. 'Get out!'

I hold up my hands like a burglar caught in the act. 'I just want to talk to you.'

Her eyes rove over me manically. 'Who are you? What do you want?'

'Come on, Sarah. You know who I am.'

'You're fucking mental. Get out – now. I'll call the police—'

'Are you sure you want to? After everything you've done to me?'

She shakes her head and reaches for her phone. I rush forward and knock it from her hands. We both stare at it on the floor in shock.

'Stop pretending,' I shout. 'It's me. Emily!'

She continues to stare, no sign of recognition.

'MotherOfTwins?'

Again, nothing.

'Look… Emily? You're really scaring me. I've got two children in the room next door, and I really, really would like you to leave now.' Her voice shakes and I realise that she's scared.

She's scared of me.

I take a step back and collect myself. This is insane. I'm being insane.

'I need you to leave me alone,' I say quietly. 'Whatever reason you have for doing this, I just need it to stop.'

Sarah nods slowly and crinkles her brows. 'Okay,' she says and my heart clenches. Finally, I'm getting through to her. At that moment, there's a bash against the door behind her and Sarah's face breaks. 'That's my son,' she tells me. 'I'm going to open the door, okay? I just need to check on him.'

'Of course…'

She holds my stare for a second longer then opens the door. The child comes toddling through, his chubby little face filled with glee at the sight of his mum. I open my mouth to tell her how beautiful he is, but then remember why I'm here. This isn't a nice catch-up with a friend where we can coo about the gorgeousness of our children. This woman is my enemy.

Sarah reaches down to pick up her son and nuzzles her face in his head. As she does, his double appears in the doorway and tugs at her trouser leg to be picked up too. She looks between him and me and chews her bottom lip. She can't hold them both while standing up. I know it, and so does she. You think you'll be able to when they're babies. Balancing one twin on each hip is tricky, but you get used to it. Then suddenly, they stop being babies and you can't do it any more. You have to choose which one to cuddle. Which one to carry. It's awful. I remember it so well. The constant guilt of physically not being enough for your children.

'Let's go in there,' I say, nodding towards the living room behind her.

She sighs but nods, knowing that there's no way we can continue this conversation in the hall with her boys like this.

The living room is perhaps even more chaotic than the hallway. Chaotic yet somehow cosy. There's a two-seater sofa up against one wall and a cuddle chair on the other. It's worn, sunken in the middle where Sarah must have lain on countless evenings with her sons on her chest. I look around the room for a laptop, desperate to see evidence of her obsession with me, but find nothing.

Sarah sits uncomfortably upright on the cuddle chair with the boys, hugging them close to her like I'm the danger. I sit on the sofa, my hands poised in my lap, desperate to show I am the calm, rational one in this situation.

'Look,' I say, trying to keep my voice level. 'I don't know why you're doing this. But we were friends once, and I'm asking you, as a friend, to just stop now.'

She stares at me, her chest rising and falling too quickly as she pulls the boys tighter to her.

'Okay,' she says again. 'I'm sorry, Emily…'

I let out a breath. This is all going to be over soon. I knew I was right to come here; she just needed to see me as a person, to think about her actions beyond the screen. She's sorry; that means she'll stop.

'But I really think you might have me confused with someone else.'

I shake my head, angrily. 'No. No, I don't. You're Sarah. You've got twin boys. You go by the ridiculous name TwoIsTrouble.'

'Yes, all of that is true, but I don't know you.'

'Yes, you do!' I shout, slamming my hand against the side of the sofa. 'You do know me. You know everything about me. You know all the things I don't want anyone to know and you're using it to torture me!'

Despite myself, angry embarrassed tears spill from my eyes. Sarah looks horrified as her own boys start screaming at my outburst.

'I don't know what's going on, Emily, but I promise you, I've no idea what you're talking about.'

–

I clutch at the too-hot mug of tea in my hands as I count backwards from ten, over and over again.

We're still in the living room, but now Sarah is less terrified of me. She's set the boys loose and they play on the floor between us, ramming plastic toy cars into each other with a level of violence that feels inappropriate after my earlier scene.

I was wrong.

Sarah isn't TwoIsTrouble; simply another mum who happens to use that same stupid username online, desperate to meet other mothers of twins. To make a connection with somebody, anybody, to stop her feeling like she's the worst mother in the world. I've told her a bit about TwoIsTrouble, my TwoIsTrouble. That we met online and she's now stalking me in real life. Sarah's eyes widened as I told her the story, leaving out the worst parts, the parts that would make her recoil from me and I could see that she was thinking about her own Instagram, wondering if this sort of thing could ever happen to her with all her oversharing.

'It's my girls that I'm scared for...' I tell her now, then jump up. 'Oh my god!'

'What?' Sarah cries.

'The girls. My girls. They're in the car!'

I slam the tea down on the coffee table and jump up.

'It's okay, don't worry. Bring them in, it's fine,' she says but I'm already running out of the door and into the road.

I yank open the car door and feel my legs shake beneath me as the girls' faces stare back at me.

'Sorry, I'm so sorry. Mummy got stuck in the house and—'

'Hello!' Ella shouts, her eyes looking straight past me.

Sarah has followed me out, her face etched with concern.

'Hello,' she says, smiling at the girls. 'I'm Sarah. What are your names?'

'We should go,' I say, flushed with embarrassment at how nice she's being given what I've done.

'I need a wee!' Ella cries.

'Me too! Wee! Wee!' Lara follows her sister's lead.

Sarah tells me to bring them inside, her hand soft against my back. I unstrap them from their car seats and we walk back across the road together to Sarah's, my whole body burning with shame and embarrassment. I don't deserve her kindness.

It doesn't take the girls very long to make friends with Sarah's boys. After they've been to the bathroom, they sit happily on the floor playing together, Ella taking the lead as always while the boys stare up at her in awe.

'I'm so sorry,' I tell Sarah again. 'I'm not normally like this…'

She smiles. 'Well, you're not exactly in a normal situation.' She takes a sip from her mug as we both watch our children. 'I think you need to tell your husband,' she says. 'You can't go on like this.'

I nod, not taking my eyes off the girls to meet her gaze. I haven't told her everything. Sarah doesn't know the extent of the secrets I've shared with TwoIsTrouble. She doesn't know what I stand to lose if the truth comes out.

I tell her that I will, promise to keep in touch and apologise again for my insane behaviour. After a few minutes, I gather the girls and we leave.

Fourteen

Now

The journey home seems to take forever. I can't stop thinking about what I've done today; dragging the girls to a stranger's house to confront them. How did I ever think that was a good idea? My inability to think rationally scares me; I can feel myself slipping back into how I was before. As I pull into our driveway, I'm relieved to see the girls have fallen asleep in their car seats. I hope today isn't a memory that they'll carry with them; and if they do, I hope they just remember sitting in a stranger's living room, playing cars with twin boys and not the tear-soaked horror on their mother's face. They've enough of those memories to last a lifetime.

We sit for a few moments on the driveway, the girls gently snoozing in the back as I try to gather myself. I hate that I did this today. Whoever TwoIsTrouble really is, she has one goal: to make me look insane. And what am I doing? Acting it. Proving her right. She didn't force me into what I did today – I chose that. I think back to the words my therapist would repeat over and over as I sat in her office the weeks after the accident. *You choose how people make you feel. Never give anyone else that power.*

She'd be horrified if she could see me now. I've allowed a stranger to control every moment of my life in the last few days and only I can put a stop to that. But it won't be by driving around accosting strangers in their homes, or dragging the girls on insane 'adventures'. Or by lying to Mark.

But even as I think it, I know that there's no way I can be honest with Mark about this. He's stood by me through everything; after the accident he never blamed me for what I'd done, what I'd taken from him, from all of us. Not once. But if he knew the truth, how could he not? I'd lose him, the girls. I'd lose everyone. TwoIsTrouble holds all the cards right now and could ruin my life with a single email to my husband. She'll be the sort of person to have kept screenshots, won't she? I imagine her sending my confession about the accident to Mark, perhaps not even adding a note with it. Just the screenshot. That would be enough. But wouldn't she have done it by now if that's what she wanted? Perhaps this isn't even about the accident. I told her about it early in our friendship, over a year ago and she's only brought it up once since then – recently, when I told her I was going back to work. When she did, I brushed it off, like it was nothing – like she was overdramatizing what I'd confessed. Not long after that, I deleted my account hoping that would be the last of it.

If this was about the accident, if she knew the significance of what I'd told her, surely she would have pounced on it when I first admitted the truth? Not waited a year until I warned her I'd be spending less time on the site because I'd soon be back at work to bring it up again. Her reply was instant.

> TwoIsTrouble: Babe, are you sure you want to do that? Aren't you worried about all the stress that will come from going back?

I told her I wasn't, that I'd be fine and I was ready to get back to the real world.

> TwoIsTrouble: Really? Given what happened last
> time you were stressed, I would think you'd be more
> careful. You wouldn't want to cause another accident
> – imagine if it was one of the twins you didn't get to
> bring home this time…

I thought I was going to be sick at my laptop. I had originally told her not long after the accident happened, when I was still freshly bruised and broken, inside and out. In the days after, still barely functioning, I managed to convince myself that she would forget what I'd confessed to; that we could pretend it had never happened. A totally ridiculous hope but one I'd clung onto, but here she was a year on, remembering it all and using it against me.

Or was she? For the first time, I consider an alternative motive behind her words. I was her only friend, from what I could tell. We were as lonely as each other and I'd just told her I was leaving her for good, that I wanted to get back to 'the real world', as if the one she and I had created during the last year online meant nothing. Perhaps this isn't about what I did. Perhaps I'm letting my own guilt and paranoia create a situation that isn't even happening. Perhaps she just wanted my attention. *You shouldn't give in to their tantrums; they just want attention.* That's what she'd always say when I'd tell her about my latest ploys to soothe the girls. I let out a strangled laugh as I think it. Is that what I should do here? Simply ignore TwoIsTrouble and hope she tires herself out? I look at the girls in the back seat, sleeping soundly, and nod decisively. Yes. That's exactly what I'll do.

So, I won't be running around like a mad woman any more. I'm not going to try and find the real woman behind TwoIsTrouble, I'm going to let it go.

A tap on the window makes me jump but I'm relieved to see it's only Joanne, Mark's mum. She gives a funny little wave and steps back as I open the door.

'Everything okay?' she asks.

'Fine. Yes, just waiting a second for the girls to wake up,' I say, nodding to them in the back of the car. They haven't stirred and I'm dreading waking them up. They love their sleep, but they don't love it being interrupted. Mark says they take after me in that regard.

Joanne frowns. 'You'll be sat here all day. I'll wake them.' She opens the car door before I can stop her.

I roll my eyes behind her back. I love Mark's mum, I really do, but she always thinks she knows best. We had a whole separate forum for it on MumsOnline. 'SMMILS' – standing for 'Shit My Mother-in-Law Says'. This would be an excellent one to add. The pile-on would be immediate. *Why do they always have to undermine us? So insensitive! As if she knows your kids better than you.* Their replies would give me a momentary relief; confirmation that I wasn't the problem, everyone else was. But then the guilt would seep in at night, or when Joanne did something kind and I'd remember all the nasty things I'd written about her. She's never deserved my anger. Not once.

'Nanna!' Ella shouts, waking up Lara. She squirms in her car seat, delighted as always, to see Joanne.

'Hello, my darlings. Shall we get you out of these horrid car seats and go and have a cup of tea?'

-

Once the girls have settled down with some colouring in the living room, Joanne and I sit at the kitchen table with two cups of tea.

'What time does Mark usually get home?'

I glance at the clock on the wall. 'Around six. Sometimes later if he gets held up.'

She tuts. 'You're lucky, you know. When Mark was young, Alan and I would often not make it through the door until after dinner. Never did Mark any harm, mind. Though once we were home, we didn't have the distractions you do, I suppose. Work was left at work. I see you both on your phones at the weekends too, no doubt answering emails...'

I murmur agreement and blow on my tea.

'How are you finding it then, being back at work?'

I shrug my shoulders. 'Not so bad. It's nice to be out of the house.'

'Well, that's nice. I did wonder how it would be... You know, whether it would be too much.' Joanne looks across the table knowingly but I return her worried gaze with a tight smile, irritated at my irritation.

'It's fine. I wanted to go back. It's good for me, for the girls, for all of us. I can't sit at home forever—'

The ring of the house phone cuts through my reassurances and I get up to retrieve it from on top of the microwave where it's been left despite my relentless nagging at Mark to put it back in its holder. The batteries are probably almost drained now.

'Hello?' I say.

'Hi, it's me.' The sound of my sister's voice makes me inwardly groan. Alison is the last person I want to speak to right now.

'Hi, everything okay?' I leaf through the pile of unopened letters that have been left underneath the phone. Mark never opens his letters, says he never gets anything exciting so what's the point? I rip open a few while my sister talks.

'Yes, fine. I just wanted to check we were still okay for Saturday?'

'Saturday?'

She sighs loudly and I put the letters back as I move across the kitchen to check the calendar. There's nothing in for Saturday.

'Yes. We said we'd meet to talk about the house.' Her tone is hopeful in a way that breaks my heart.

'This Saturday?'

She's silent on the end of the phone and I regret my words immediately. 'Sorry,' I say, as if remembering. 'But yes... I'm sure Saturday is fine.'

'You forgot.'

'No. I didn't forget, I just got my weekends mixed up.' I keep staring at the empty calendar in front of me. Why didn't I write this down? I always write everything down.

'Okay,' she says. 'So, shall I come to you?'

'No,' I say, perhaps a little too forcefully. 'Let's go for lunch. I'll find somewhere and text you,' I add to try and cover my obvious resistance to her coming to the house.

The idea of us meeting for lunch, like proper sisters, placates her and we're off the phone within minutes of the arrangements being made. I hang up and feel Joanne's eyes on my back.

'Who was that?'

'Oh, just my sister.'

Joanne raises her eyebrows. 'That's nice. Sounds like you have some nice weekend plans to look forward to?'

I pick up our mugs from the table and take them to the sink, my back to Joanne. I pour my cold, almost untouched tea down the drain.

'Do you want me to have the girls? I can rearrange tennis!' She sounds so eager at this, and I know she's pleased that I've got some sociable-sounding plans. She worries I don't have enough of a social life; I've heard her say it to Mark on the phone when they think I can't hear them talking. I know she'd prefer me to be one of these women who's surrounded by other mothers, always going on coffee dates and group holidays and I wish I were too. But it never works out. I guess I'm not all that likeable in real life, not any more.

'No, they'll be fine here. Thank you, though.'

'But on Saturday—'

'Mark can have them.' I turn on the tap and let the water run hot, swirling washing up liquid through the mugs.

'He's got his fun run, hasn't he?' Joanne says and I grit my teeth. Another thing I forgot. I walk back to the calendar and shake my head.

'No, that's not this month...'

Joanne appears beside me and laughs. 'Oh, Em, you're a month behind!' She takes the calendar off the wall and flicks the page over from February to March. Sure enough, there it is, scrawled in Mark's handwriting: 'Fun Run 12 – 2' alongside 'Alison – lunch' written in my own. 'I think perhaps going back to work is getting to you more than you think!' She jabs me lightly in the ribs with her elbow, trying to make light of it all but I feel a wave of panic.

I'm making stupid mistakes again. Just like before. And seeing Alison is guaranteed to make all of it worse.

Mark gets home later than usual; it's nearly seven by the time he strolls through the door so the girls' bedtime routine is pushed back and everything seems to drag on forever. After we've eaten, tidied up from eating, and put them to bed, Mark's phone goes and he disappears upstairs. I sit on the sofa and flick through the channels mindlessly, eventually settling on a BBC period drama that I heard one of the women at work mention earlier in the week. The characters saunter around on screen in their heavy gowns and white powdered faces as if they've not a care in the world.

The sound of Mark clearing his throat in the doorway draws my attention away from the screen.

'You want to watch something?' I ask him.

He sighs and leans against the doorframe. 'Mum just phoned.'

I wait for him to continue but he doesn't, so I go back to staring at the TV screen. Eventually, he walks across the room, takes the control from my hand and sits next to me. He flicks the TV off.

'I was watching that.'

'Em, come on. Will you look at me?'

I huff like a sulky teenager and turn to face him. 'What? What do you want?'

His jaw is hard set and my stomach tightens at the sight of it.

'What? Mark, what's happened? Is it your dad?'

With that, his jaw releases and he shakes his head. 'No. No, they're fine.'

I let out a deep sigh.

'You didn't mention that Mum came over earlier.'

I shrug. 'This is literally the first chance we've had to have a conversation.'

'That's not exactly true, Em.'

He's using his patient voice with me; the one that has the opposite of its desired effect.

'What have you done today?' he asks.

I click my tongue against the back of my teeth and tell him we've been to see one of the women from the girls' nursery, my mind conjuring up a name.

'Mum said you didn't seem right, when she came over.'

'Right,' I snap. 'So, she's coming over to check on me then phoning you after to report in? Great, thanks for that.'

Mark rubs his forehead and breathes in. He hates fighting. He'll do anything to avoid a row. 'What's happened? Has something gone on today?'

'No, I told you what happened today. I saw Sarah—'

'I thought you said Sian?'

'What?'

'You said you'd been to see Sian.'

'Why are you questioning me? I said Sarah, my friend Sarah from nursery. Do you want to check my phone? See our WhatsApps?' I grab my phone from the side of the sofa and shove it into his chest.

He doesn't react for a moment, then calmly takes my phone and places it back where it was. 'No, Em. I don't want to do that. All I want to do is know that you're okay. And this?' He puts his hands out. 'This reaction, it shows me you're not.'

Fifteen

Then

First Day Back To School!!!

The day has finally come. I've been counting down the hours until this moment and it's finally here. I'm writing this from the kitchen table, a still-warm coffee in front of me, the girls asleep in their cot upstairs. It's eleven a.m., and for the first time in months, I have a moment to myself.

D1 didn't want to go today. Of course she didn't. All she wants to do lately is hang off me like a limpet. She's becoming clingier every day and always looks so sullen. H tells me it's nothing to worry about, that it's to be expected now that she isn't my only baby. She isn't a baby at all, I told him. He smiled and told me no, she isn't. That's the problem.

I know he thinks I spend too much time worrying about D1 but I can't help it. All I want is to be able to concentrate on the girls, to enjoy these precious months where they are reliant on me in every single way, to be able to give myself over to them like I did to her. But I can't. She won't let me. Is it always this way with second children? But it's worse with us, of course. Because the girls are both my second and third children bundled into one package. Two perfect, matching, beautiful babies. And D1 is jealous of that, I can see the jealousy oozing from her with every glance she gives the girls, but it's not their fault they're here.

I wish she could learn to love them like a big sister is supposed to.

Our neighbour came by yesterday afternoon with a Victoria sponge that she'd bought from the WI fayre in town. H was out on some sort of run with his work friends, even though it was a Sunday and one of the only days we get to spend time together as a family, so I invited her in. I'd not realised how bad the house had got until I saw it through her eyes. She didn't say anything, of course; she didn't have to. I watched her taking in the pile of washing that sat in front of the machine, spilling from the basket; the sticky kitchen sides littered with toast crumbs, splodges of jam from D1's breakfast, half a banana that I must have been eating at some point or other. She smiled tightly and raised her eyebrows before telling me she remembered what it was like.

D1 sauntered in then, a smile on her face that I hadn't seen since before I brought the girls home. The neighbour asked her if she was enjoying being a big sister and D1 nodded enthusiastically. I love it, she said. I snorted, I couldn't help myself. The neighbour looked up at me in shock and I laughed to hide my embarrassment. She's been rather a handful lately, I told the neighbour. D1's eyes filled with tears and she ran out of the room. I swallowed my anger. She always does this. Makes me look like I'm a bad mother. But no one knows what she's really like, when it's just us. No one sees that.

The neighbour didn't stay long after D1's outburst and H didn't come back for hours. It was just me, the girls, and DI. Again.

But still, that was yesterday. Today is a new day. Today, D1 is far away for six whole hours and I can relax. This is the time when I can start to get myself back. I cut a big slice of Victoria sponge and sip my coffee while my beautiful babies sleep. Later, I can push their pram through the park without worrying about

DI's sticky hands clinging onto me, veering the pushchair off the path. Today it's just going to be me and the girls.

Everything is going to be all right. I'm sure of it.

Sixteen

Now

The next day, I wake up late to find that Mark has given the girls their breakfast and made me a cup of coffee, left on the bedside table.

'I'm heading in now,' he tells me, as he appears at the bedroom door. 'They're in front of the TV but will probably only stay quiet for ten minutes or so when I'm gone.'

'I'm getting up,' I tell him, reaching for the coffee. 'I don't know why I slept so late, sorry.'

He waves away my apology. 'Your body obviously needed it.'

He says goodbye and I wait in bed until I hear the door slam. Last night, after a few tears, I finally agreed that I'd take the day off today. Mark said he would phone Daniel directly, the idea of which makes me hot with embarrassment.

Mark's treating me like I'm ill again. I should be grateful – how many women would love a husband who attends to their every need, lets them sleep in and sorts the children out for them? But part of me is furious at him. I wish I could tell him the truth, wish he didn't jump straight to the conclusion that I've become mad again. I get out of bed and quickly change into yoga leggings and an off-the-shoulder black top; my uniform for staying at home. It was one of the things my therapist advised me early on to do. 'Have a routine even on days when you aren't going anywhere. Get up, get dressed, it doesn't matter what you wear as long as it's not pyjamas.' I followed the advice to the letter, always a stickler for rules.

I go downstairs and make myself a slice of toast after saying good morning to the girls. They barely register me; they're having a twin-talk, their heads pressed together as they mumble words unrecognisable to the rest of us. I didn't sleep well last night, tossing and turning so much that Mark got up and slept in the spare bedroom. Both of us do that a lot; it used to be a source of anxiety for me; it felt like if we ever spent a night apart we were somehow admitting defeat in our marriage. But I don't think like that any more. Sometimes, we just sleep better alone. I wrote about it once on MumsOnline. I got a lot of angry comments from women who couldn't imagine the luxury of having a spare room alongside kids' bedrooms. I didn't tell them we also have an office.

I got a lot of messages about how worried I should be too, that we chose to spend the night apart. A lot of people showed me articles about 'sleep divorces' where couples permanently split after losing the intimacy of sharing a bed. It didn't help my worries. TwoIsTrouble did, though. She told me she and her husband had done it for years, even before she'd had the boys, and she said they were perfectly happy. It made me feel better, to have someone confirm that my life choices were okay.

She wasn't always bad, I realise now. Perhaps she had once wanted to pull me up, make my life better, like a true friend. As I spread butter across my hot white bread I wonder, what changed?

My mobile buzzes from the kitchen table and I'm nervous when I see an unknown number on the screen.

'Hello?'

'Hi, Emily. It's Alyssa.'

'Oh, hi.'

'Look, sorry, I know you're not well but I wanted to give you the heads-up about something.'

I walk through the living room while Alyssa talks. She tells me how she heard Daniel talking to one of the other PRs this morning about me calling in sick; ranting and raving that I was going to fuck up the Browngate pitch.

'Sorry,' she says, breathlessly, after retelling the whole story. 'Maybe I shouldn't have called. I just think he's being so unfair. It's your first week back and—'

'Don't worry,' I tell her, forcing myself to be calm. 'Thank you for telling me. I appreciate it. Daniel's always been rather melodramatic… But it's good to know when he's losing his sh—' I catch the word before it leaves my mouth, aware of the two little faces staring up at me. 'Well, you know what I mean. I'll sort it, thank you.'

I wish I'd been kinder to Alyssa on day one. It's hard to believe that I've become the sort of person who sees other women, younger women, as a threat. Would I have called a colleague at her age and done them this kindness? I like to think I would have, but I was so blindly loyal to Daniel back then I'm ashamed to admit that I may well have let someone else hang out to dry if it meant staying in his good books. Alyssa isn't like that. She's a better person than me.

After we hang up, I guiltily pull out the *Frozen* DVD and switch it on. The girls are instantly transfixed as the bright animation starts. I fire off an email to Daniel to let him know I'm still working on the pitch today and promise that it'll be perfect by Monday, ready to present.

His reply is instant. *Good stuff. Knew you wouldn't let us down!*

He always used to say that. I was the one on the team who he could rely on; who understood that he expected us all to go above and beyond and I got it. I used to bask in his praise but now as I look at his words all I feel is panic. I'm not that person any more. I'm not reliable. Organised. Effective. I'm not anything that I used to be.

I take a deep breath as my heart starts to race. I can do this. I can write a pitch presentation; I've done it a million times before. *Not since then*, the nasty little voice in my head says. I silence it and focus on my breathing.

I can do this. I can do it all.

—

A few hours later and I can finally shut down my laptop. Outside, the early spring afternoon is calling and I wrap the girls up for a walk to the park. They've dutifully sat through *Frozen* followed by endless episodes of *Peppa Pig* while I've worked. I don't know what I was so worried about before; I've got to stop letting myself get so worked up. I text Daniel saying the presentation is done and send him a link to the shared drive I've saved it on.

You're a star!

He replies after a few seconds and I smile. Before I put my phone back in my pocket, I see another text. My sister, reminding me about our meeting tomorrow. I'm not going to reply now; I don't want to think about

Alison. Nothing good happens when I do. I tap out a text to Alyssa saying thank you again for giving me the heads-up earlier. She replies instantly with a thumbs-up emoji and tells me that Daniel is looking at my presentation right now in the office and, most importantly, he's smiling.

I bask in the adrenaline buzzing through me; zesty little sparks flit across my chest as we walk down the road to the park. This is what it used to feel like, I realise. Finishing a presentation, a pitch, anything for work. I'd start with panic, then I'd smash it. Every time. I used to be a person who could do things and that's how I feel right now.

'What are you laughing at?' Ella says.

'Nothing,' I say. 'I'm just happy.' I didn't realise a giggle had escaped but why shouldn't I let it? I did something good today, something that didn't involve me being a mum, something that said to me and to everyone else: *Emily is a person who does things.* But more importantly, I didn't let TwoIsTrouble get in the way. I did what I had told myself I would; I stopped obsessing about her and let it go. And things got better.

We practically skip down the road together to the park and the world seems brighter. As the early spring sun catches my cheeks, I feel it filling me up from the inside. Things are going to be okay. This is a sign. I thought I couldn't do it. I thought I couldn't be the old me again, but look at me now! Perhaps I'll ask Alyssa for a drink after work next week. Maybe we could be friends, even with the age gap, and then everyone can stop worrying about me.

At the park, I lift the girls into the baby swings and stand behind them, pushing them as they soar through the air. I'm so practised at this that I can do it one-handed and I allow myself the luxury of flicking through my phone as I push. I never realised that looking at your phone in public was a luxury until I had the girls. The looks you get for doing it are shocking. We talked about it on MumsOnline, how enraging it was to be judged for the simple act of checking your phone in the presence of your children. Even when they're babies, people stare at you like you're a terrible mother if you take your eyes off them for a single second to check your phone.

Fuck it. Today I don't care. Let them look. Let them judge.

I giggle again, feeling like the rebellious teen I once was but realise my show of defiance is wasted as there's no one in the park to watch me, or care, anyway.

The girls chatter away to each other as I push, occasionally shouting, 'Higher, higher Mummy!' as I scroll. On Facebook, I'm drawn into an article showing before and after photos of Kim Kardashian's mansion. Ghastly. Then, I flick to Instagram where I devour a series of posts from old friends showing their children's birthdays, a close-up of a glass of wine after a long week, a bunch of roses from a charming husband. Why are other people's lives so intoxicating?

I click onto the stories reel and let them play out one by one. I watch celebrities and nobodies alike broadcasting the details of their days.

And then my stomach drops.

TwoIsTrouble appears on my screen. Or, as I now know her, Sarah. I turn up my speakers as I watch the close-up video of her face.

Hi, mammas! I've been wondering about whether to post this or not but I just felt like I had to. The weirdest thing happened to me yesterday. This total stranger,

The sound of a scream stops me and I drop my phone as I look up to see Lara face down on the ground.

'Oh my god, Lara!' I run to her, my heart pounding in my chest, and scoop her up. Her face is scratched and her eyes pool with tears. She looks at me for a second, not quite knowing what to do, and then she screams. Tears pour down her face as I try to calm her, my ears ringing with the sound of her sobs mixed in with the squeals of horror from Ella still stuck in her swing.

'Is she okay?' A man appears beside me and kneels down on the asphalt. 'I saw her fall from across the park.'

'Mummy! Get me oooooout!' Ella screams from behind us.

'Shall I?' The man asks me and despite him being a total stranger I nod, my hands too full of Lara to do anything else.

'Are you okay, darling? Where does it hurt?' I say to her.

'Everywhere,' she says in a tiny voice and my own body pulses with pain in response.

'You *pushed* her!' Ella yells at me as the man puts her down. Her face is red and she thumps me on the arm and yanks Lara from me.

'Ella,' I shout, as I loosen my grip on Lara, not wanting her to be tugged. 'Stop it.'

'Shall I call someone?' the man says.

Both girls are backing away from me now, their faces red with indignation. I stand up to bring myself level with the man before replying.

'We're fine,' I say.

He frowns and glances down at the girls. 'Is your husband at home?'

'What?' I snap.

'Or your mum? Anyone? A friend?'

I shake my head and tell the girls to come on as I grab their hands. They pull away from me and shout. 'Stop it,' I tell them. 'Stop being silly, we're going home.'

I start to walk off but the man steps in front of me. 'Look, I really think you need someone to be with you. I don't feel right just letting you walk off like this after what I just saw.'

'What are you talking about? She fell, that's all. She's basically still a toddler! They fall all the time. Excuse me,' I say, pushing past him.

'She fell because you pushed her.'

I stop in my tracks, the heat of his words licking at my back.

'You were on your phone. I was watching you. I should have stepped in before but I thought… God, you know what it's like now, being a man… You can't tell a woman anything without being called out as a sexist. But you weren't paying attention.'

I whip around to face him. 'Are you joking? She fell out of the swing. She's fine!'

'She's not fine. She's got a cut on her face, and neither of them want to go with you.'

I let out a high-pitched laugh. 'I can't believe this. My children are none of your business. This was an accident and you're blowing it out of proportion.'

His cheeks redden and he looks around the park. There are a few other families here now. I hadn't noticed before, but we've drawn a crowd. Embarrassment itches at my scalp as a sea of concerned faces stares back at me. We are this afternoon's spectacle and I realise the crowd aren't going to let me just walk away without making this worse.

'I want Daddy!' Ella shouts and I hate her then as she runs back towards the man. The stranger.

Lara, at least, has some loyalty in this show of public humiliation and she doesn't follow her sister immediately but one look from Ella makes her feet move and I'm left facing my children, alone.

'This is ridiculous,' I say again. 'Completely ridiculous.' But I get out my phone, and I call Mark.

Seventeen

Then

The School Meeting

Well, I certainly feel stupid. I read back my last entry and can't believe how naive I was. I really thought things would get better when D1 went back to school. I thought she'd learn that life couldn't revolve around her any more, that other people sometimes had to come first. But they've just got worse.

The school called me this morning. D1 had been gone for less than an hour. I was lying upstairs with the girls either side of me, listening to their sweet baby gurgles as the mid-morning sunlight fell over my face. It was bliss. Pure bliss. Then the phone rang. I'm starting to think that D1 does it on purpose; she has a way of ruining every perfect moment even when she's not physically there.

The school wouldn't tell me what it was they wanted to see me about; they just said it would be better if I came into the school. I've got twins, I told them. I can't come traipsing across town with newborns! But they insisted. So I did.

By the time I arrived, it was past lunch and I realised too late that I hadn't eaten anything that day. This happens to me a lot now. Is that normal? I don't know how I'm supposed to find the time to feed myself when I'm so busy feeding everyone else. Maybe that's why I've completely failed to breastfeed. Not enough nutrition in my body to feed my children. Another way I'm failing.

But this isn't about that. This is about D1.

I knew it was going to be something really bad as soon as I saw her teacher's face. She smiled in the way that women often do at me now. Is it like this for everyone with babies? That smile can kill me some days. It says, you look knackered. It says, I'm glad I'm not you. It says everything I don't want to hear. Least of all from D1's teacher.

She sat me down and asked if I'd like the school receptionist to watch the girls while we talked. I didn't mean to shout but I think I might have. I'm embarrassed to think about it, actually. The way I acted when she suggested taking the girls from me for a moment. But still, she isn't a mum. She wouldn't understand how it feels to have someone suggest you can't look after your own children.

So the girls stayed with me while the teacher talked. She told me she's worried about D1. Said that she hasn't been herself since she's been back at school. Asked if everything was all right at home. All right at home? I laughed. The girls started crying. If you haven't noticed, I snapped, I've got my hands full with these two right now. The teacher told me she understood, gave me another of those enraging pity-filled smiles, then had the nerve to say that it was totally normal for D1 to be feeling left out now that her sisters had come along, and suggested I make an effort to spend more alone time with her.

I've never been so angry in my life.

How dare she suggest that I'm not paying D1 enough attention? I tried to explain that D1 is horribly jealous of the girls, that she doesn't want to be involved in anything when they're around and, in case she hadn't noticed, the girls were rather dependent on me right now. The teacher looked at me like I was insane. I am SO sick of people looking at me like that. It used to be that *when I said something, people believed me. Now, everything I say is viewed through the lens of me as a mother. A tired, over-emotional, doesn't-know-what-she's-saying mother.*

D1 has obviously been playing the same game that she did with the neighbour. From what she tells me, she absolutely loves her little sisters, the teacher said. I shook my head, then decided against arguing. What's the point? I know D1 is only a child, and I shouldn't be reacting like this to her games, but some days I just want to scream.

She's not normal. There's something VERY wrong with my child. So why am I the only one who can see it?

Eighteen

Now

'I'm heading off now,' I say to Mark's back.

'Okay,' he says without turning. He's frying bacon, the fat spitting up from the pan in tiny angry specks. Usually, I'd tell him off for this; *use the grill*, I always say, *there's so much fat when you fry it*. But today, I daren't criticise him for anything. He's barely speaking to me as it is.

He's furious about the park incident. But so am I. When I called him to save me from the angry mob, I knew he'd be upset. Who wants to get a call from their wife in the middle of the working day to say that she's being held by a pack of strangers, accused of hurting their daughter? But I didn't think the upset would be directed towards me.

He came as fast as he could but his office is a fifteen-minute drive, so the mob and I awkwardly stood in the park in a face-off scenario while we waited. By the time Mark arrived, the girls had got over their dramatics and were playing in the sandpit.

I listened in silent horror as the man who started it all explained what had happened. How he'd been watching us from across the park, concerned that I was so engrossed in my phone. He saw Lara climbing out of the swing and watched as I continued to push anyway. He wasn't saying

I'd done it on purpose, of course; he couldn't see from his view whether I knew she was half out of the swing or not. But either way, if I'd been looking at her, instead of my phone, it would have never happened.

I waited for the end of the story, my cheeks burning with shame and rage at this stranger's characterisation of me. He said enough to flavour the story with a pinch of terror, just the right amount of doubt that perhaps I did do it on purpose. Perhaps. But probably not. Who was he to say?

I waited for Mark to tell him where to go. To jump to my defence. To tell this stranger that I would never, ever, do that to my daughter.

But he didn't.

He thanked the man. *Steve*, he told Mark his name was, as he shook his hand. Mark thanked him for his concern. Thanked him for calling. Thanked him for looking out for the girls.

And then Mark picked the girls up, one in each arm, and marched from the park, leaving me standing alone. Ashamed. Embarrassed.

I fled from the park and walked home on my own, my empty hands shaking by my sides where they should have been held by the girls, unable to believe what was happening. When I got into the house, he was upstairs with the girls and I waited in the living room, unable to force myself upstairs.

'Her face is scratched,' Mark said through his teeth when he finally came down. 'She's only just stopped crying.'

My cheeks burned under the glare of his unchecked anger. 'It was an accident, Mark.'

He shook his head and breathed in deeply. 'Was it?'

I jumped up from the sofa then, and the shouting began. I didn't conduct myself that well, I admit. I wanted so badly for him to tell me that it wasn't my fault, that of course it was an accident, that it could have easily happened to anyone, to him. But he didn't, he still hasn't. Instead, he told me he couldn't trust me at the moment. That he knew it was a mistake letting me go back to work.

Letting me. That made me rage. We've never been that sort of couple; Mark is not that sort of man. And yet, he said it.

He slept in the spare room and I woke up alone. It's not the first time we've fought so badly that we've slept apart, but he always ends up back in our bed sometime during the night, so that by the time we wake all is forgotten, our bodies curled around each other's where they belong. But today, his anger has carried him through the night and leaked into our Saturday. My own anger has fled and in place of it is a hot, needy desperation to make things right but I know he needs time to cool.

This morning, we've moved around each other in silence, our attention focused on the girls. He went for a run in the end, something he did often when we met but now only when he needs to clear his head. He said it would make up for having to cancel his fun run and guilt crawled over me then, as well as annoyance. He could have got Joanne to look after the girls this morning; there was no reason not to. But he said he didn't want to leave them when they were so upset from yesterday. I couldn't help but roll my eyes at that, as if I was happily going out without a care in the world for them while he was staying behind like the good one. Always the good one.

I leave the smoke-filled kitchen from Mark's frying bacon and walk into the living room where the girls are cuddled under a blanket watching television, again. I dread to think how many hours they've consumed this week.

'Mummy's going out now,' I tell them from the doorway.

Lara looks up at me with her eyes wide and gives me a small smile. My body aches as I catch sight of the scratch on her face. It's small, barely anything, but the red scratch doesn't belong on her porcelain skin. And it's my fault that it's there.

'Bye, Mummy,' she says, her voice small. I walk across the room and position myself between them on the sofa. Ella grumbles but Lara cuddles into me, the soft lumps of her warm body fitting perfectly into mine.

'You know Mummy didn't mean to hurt you yesterday, don't you?' I whisper to her.

She nods.

'I love you more than anything in the whole wide world, you and Ella. You know that, don't you?'

'Yes, Mummy,' she whispers.

I cuddle her closer; the beat of her heart echoing my own. I think about how she used to live inside me, where the world couldn't hurt her. Where I couldn't hurt her.

'You're going to be late,' Mark says, his voice from the doorway breaking us apart. I meet his eyes and feel a rush of relief as a small smile crosses his lips. I give both girls a kiss on the head and walk out the door.

–

By the time I arrive at the restaurant to meet my sister, I'm fifteen minutes late. Traffic was ridiculous getting through town and my jumper sticks to the sweat on my back. I see her as soon as I walk in, sitting by the window with a scowl on her face.

'Sorry,' I say, as I sit down. 'Traffic was—'

'It's fine. Don't worry,' Alison says, smiling too brightly. 'I ordered you a wine.'

'Oh, thank you,' I say. I don't usually drink in the day, especially if I'm going to drive, but she pushes the glass towards me and I take a sip. I don't want to start this conversation by upsetting her. I can't remember when we last sat down together – certainly not in the last few years, if at all, at a restaurant like this. We've never been close as adults. I have a hard time even believing Allie really is an adult. She's five years younger than me but it seems more, probably because she's never really left home or done anything with her life. Since Mum died last year, we've barely had any contact at all. She tried to get in touch after the accident, but I couldn't bear to see her; or anyone really, in those early days.

'So, how are you?'

'Fine,' I say, my smile tight. 'I went back to work this week, so a little... well,' I laugh, 'hectic, I suppose. You know what it's like.'

'No. Not really.' She takes a sip of her wine and looks across at me, a tinge of sadness clouding her eyes.

Shit. I always say the wrong thing to her. 'Just busy, I guess I meant. You know what it's like to be busy.' I fumble my words, coughing to cover it. 'How are you?'

She shrugs. 'Same old. Nothing much to report.'

I pick up the menu and suppress a sigh. I've always found it so hard to talk to Allie. Well, actually, that's not entirely true. As a child, I could never shut her up. With the age gap between us, she mostly just drove me crazy with her chattering but since we've been adults... well, really since it's just been the two of us, we barely manage to hold a conversation for more than a few minutes. I find it hard to be near her, if I'm honest. She reminds me too much of what happened and there's nothing between then and now to talk about to fill the gaps. Allie has a very dull job doing something to do with computers – exactly what I've never been sure of. She works from home and as far as I know, her love life is non-existent.

'Do you know what you're having?' I ask to break the silence.

'Chicken salad.'

I scan the description and frown. 'I think I'll go for the spaghetti.'

She laughs.

'What?'

She shakes her head and smiles as she sits back in her chair. 'Just funny, isn't it? I go for salad and look like this, yet you go for carbs and look like you.'

I scrunch up my face and put the menu down. She always does this; acts like she's so much worse off than me. The ridiculousness of it is that she's as thin as anything. If she wanted to be, my sister would be beautiful. But she hides it under unstyled hair, unplucked eyebrows and ill-fitting clothes. And of course, the permanent frown she wears that creases her brows and purses her lips. Sometimes I wonder if the comparisons she makes between us are for my benefit, as if she can somehow address the obvious favouritism my mum showed towards her that she never quite lived up to.

I start to tell her to stop being so silly, that she looks great, but I'm interrupted by a young man who comes to take our order. It's a relief; she takes compliments about as well as I give them.

'It's going to be a bit of a wait, I'm afraid,' the waiter tells us. 'Kitchen is rammed.'

'How long is a bit of a wait?' I ask.

He waves his hands and looks put out. 'Forty, forty-five minutes?' He goes up at the end of the sentence like he's asking me. 'We're going as quick as we can, I'm afraid. Can I get you both another drink while you wait?'

We tell him no and off he scuttles, leaving us with just each other again.

'Well, at least it gives us plenty of time to sort out everything…' I say.

She smiles tightly and reaches into her bag below the table, taking her cue to turn this from a friendly sisters' catch-up into what it really is.

She places a manilla file on the table and my eyes rest on her childlike handwriting on the front. It hasn't changed at all. She's written the words 'Mum's House Things' on the cover, like it's a school report. It's thick; paper spills from the sides, sheets with creased edges; well-thumbed. I imagine she knows everything this file contains, inside out.

It shouldn't really be like this. I am the older sister; I should be the one taking charge. But I was never the one closest to Mum. And Allie still lived at home when Mum died. Lived? Lives? I realise I have no idea.

'Are you still staying there?' I ask.

'What?'

'At Mum's.'

'Why wouldn't I be?'

'I was just wondering… I didn't know if you'd have moved out now that it's just you there.'

'And gone where?' she says tetchily.

I sit back in my chair and shrug. 'I was just wondering; I just thought perhaps you'd have…' I drift off, not wanting to address the fact that she really should have somewhere else to go by this point in her life. I wish she would shake off some of her sadness and grief and start her life. But it's none of my business. 'I thought maybe you'd have moved into a place of your own, maybe with some friends or something. That's all.'

She rolls her eyes and I glimpse the petulant little sister she used to be. 'Right. Well, that house is my home, and I like living alone so I plan to stay living there for as long as I can. Though of course, that's partly up to you.'

'Up to me? Why?'

She sighs and pulls her chair forward, making it squeal against the floorboards. 'Don't you read any of the emails I send you?' she asks. 'You own half the house. That's why we're here.'

I look down, embarrassed. I don't read her emails. Not all of them. They're very long and I've been so caught up with everything lately with the girls it's just not felt like a priority. I know I own half the house; of course I know that. Mum has been dead for a little over a year and she left a will laying everything out for us; a fifty-fifty split between Alison and I. I was so shocked to see myself equally included alongside my sister that I never thought beyond the fact; never considered what it meant to own half the house, what I might decide to do with it. So, Alison and I have barely discussed it until now.

'I'm sorry…' I say, taking a deep breath. 'To be totally truthful, no. I haven't read all of your emails. It's been total chaos at home and I'm struggling to keep up with everything.'

With this admission, my sister does something I do not expect. She smiles at me, her lips parting to reveal perfectly white, straight teeth.

'Don't worry,' she says, leaning across the table, almost taking my hands in hers. 'You're here now. We can sort it all out, together.'

—

Over the course of lunch, we somehow manage to hold the first proper conversation we've had in over a year. She listens as I tell her about the stress of going back to work, leaving out any details of the chaos of MumsOnline, and even offers to look after the girls if ever I need it. We've not been close for such a long that the offer comes out of the blue and I'm vaguely lost for words when she makes it. But we manage to move on from my obvious shock and I graciously accept the offer, though I can't imagine a time where I would really leave the twins with her. We just don't know each other well enough any more and Mark would never allow it; he's had a handful of conversations with Allie over the years at family occasions, but they've got no real relationship. He'd never trust her with the girls. The thought makes me briefly sad, as I imagine how things could have been if we were a different kind of sister – the type that regularly goes for lunch on a Saturday, that is in and out of each other's houses like their own. But we were never going to be sisters like that, so the disappointment is brief, a fleeting moment of grief for a long-dead idea.

'It's really nice to talk,' Allie says. 'I've been so… well, lonely, since Mum died.' She looks away but not before I see tears pooling in her eyes.

'I'm sorry, Allie,' I say, colour rising in my cheeks at her obvious emotion. 'I should have been there for you. Things have just been… hard.'

'I know they have. But not now, right? Your life seems pretty perfect…' She wipes a tear from her cheek and looks up at me. '…with Mark and the girls and your job. It's almost like it never happened.'

'It's not like that,' I blurt out, wanting her to stop talking. My thoughts race with panic at the idea that she's going to make us have this conversation right here at the restaurant, surrounded by strangers, and I rush to instead fill the gap with the first thing that comes into my head. 'Things aren't perfect at all. I'm so stressed about going back to work and everyone wants me to just be fine, to get on with everything but I can't, because all I can think about is this bloody woman who won't leave me alone…' I stop the words from spilling out any further, my cheeks hot with embarrassment at my outpouring, but it's too late.

Allie leans forward. 'What? What do you mean?'

I shake my head. Now that I've started this conversation I'm unsure if I should have said anything. But perhaps talking to someone else, someone who isn't Mark, will help. 'Someone rang the girls' nursery and… they pretended to be me.'

'What?' Allie says, her head cocked to one side, confused. 'And said what?'

I scratch behind my ear, wishing I'd not started this. 'Nothing, really. They said I wanted to pull the girls out of nursery or something; that I wished I hadn't gone back to work.'

Allie's nose crinkles as she sips what's left of her wine. 'That's so weird. Maybe someone wanted their place?'

She nods to herself, warming to the idea. 'Some local yummy mummy desperate to get her kid into the nursery, perhaps?'

I consider this and for a second, wonder if she's right. What if it wasn't TwoIsTrouble at all but some insane mother trying to get her kids into Polkadot? It is a very competitive nursery; we put the girls down on the list as soon we moved house, knowing it could take up to a year before a place came up. When they called to say two spots were finally free, it was one of the many things I took as a sign that I was meant to go back to work.

'What did Mark say?' Allie asks.

'Oh, I didn't tell him.'

'What? Why?' She looks shocked and unsatisfied with my explanation that I didn't want to worry him with it. 'I always thought you and Mark were one of those couples who told each other everything.'

I sigh. 'We used to be, I think children change things.'

Allie nods thoughtfully as the waiter brings over our main courses.

'I'm sure it's nothing,' Allie tells me. 'I wouldn't worry too much about it. It's hardly like someone is out there wanting to get you, is it?' She rolls her eyes as if this is the most unlikely scenario in the world and I agree, wanting to change the subject. Hoping she's right.

As we eat, we manage to get through most of the complicated legal things to do with Mum's house and I'm glad of something logical to discuss. When the waiter clears our plates away, Allie tells me that I need to review the documents she's sent over on email and I tell her I will.

'Could you do it now?' she asks, her voice small and childlike. 'I'm sorry to push you but…'

'No, you're right to,' I say. 'I'm sorry I've not done this before.' I reach into my bag to find my phone and notice my work laptop is still in here, so grab that instead.

After a few minutes, I finish reading the final document – an agreement she's had drawn up by a lawyer – and lower my screen.

'I should have made more of an effort to help you with all of this after Mum died,' I tell her.

'It's fine, honestly. You had a lot going on. Still do, by the sounds of it.'

'Mmm,' I murmur my agreement. 'But it's not an excuse. I should have helped, and I will do more, I promise.'

She smiles and sits back in her chair. The afternoon sunlight flits across her face and I think how pretty she is when she looks happy, which is followed by a tinge of guilt at how little I've seen her look this way in my presence before. I move my eyes back to the screen and make a decision there and then.

'I'm fine with this,' I say, waving at the screen. 'All of it. I'm happy to sign it now.'

A huge smile covers her face. 'Really? Are you sure?'

I nod.

'You don't need to speak to Mark?'

I should, really. The agreement she's had drawn up says that I'm happy for her to carry on living at Mum's house indefinitely, as long as she splits any profit from the house sale as and when she decides to move. It's an agreement that is totally in her favour and means I won't see any money from the house now, or maybe ever. But it feels like the right thing to do. Profiting from that house at the expense of Alison is something I could never do.

'We've briefly talked about it before,' I tell her, which isn't totally untrue. I told Mark after Mum's death that the house was half mine, but that I didn't want to be involved with it. He didn't object at the time, though pointed out my share would be a fair chunk of money so to try and think about it rationally, but we've not discussed it since. 'It's your home. I have a house; we aren't desperate for the money from the sale right now.'

Her smile slips for a moment. 'No, I suspect not.'

'I mean, we're not exactly rolling in it,' I laugh, to cover the awkwardness. 'But like I said, I'm working now, and Mark's job is good, so…' I trail off, aware of how different our circumstances are. 'Look, if you feel funny about me signing it now, let me talk to Mark about it and I'll email it over as soon as I do.'

She smiles again and the awkwardness disappears. I'd forgotten how she could do this; create an atmosphere, good or bad, purely with the movement of her face.

'Yes, okay. Let's do that. That seems more sensible, doesn't it? Just make sure to do it soon or I'll have to get another agreement drawn up, and that one cost a bomb already!' She laughs. I frown, not understanding and she explains it was supposed to be signed when she first sent it over, two months ago. If it isn't signed by the end of this month, the deadline for the mortgage rate will have expired again and her solicitor will have to write up a new version.

'I'll do it this week, I promise,' I tell her. The waiter arrives with the bill and I tell her I'll get it, like a big sister should. I put my laptop back in my bag. 'I just need to go to the loo before the drive home. I won't be a sec.'

'Your pelvic floor's never the same, is it?' She laughs as I get up and I laugh back, wondering how on earth she even knows that.

In the bathroom, a mother and teenage daughter are waiting in line for the one cubicle currently occupied. I listen as they discuss their afternoon plans; the daughter is absolutely set on getting a dress from New Look that the mother doesn't approve of. Eventually, the daughter goes into the cubicle and I'm left along with the mother who smiles to herself once the daughter can't watch her, as if the argument is only for show. She knows she's getting that dress, and her daughter will love her for it.

Back in the restaurant, Allie is sitting at the table with her coat on.

'Ready?' I ask, picking up my bag. She nods, and we walk out together.

'Where are you parked?' she asks when we're on the street.

'St George's,' I tell her before remembering she hardly ever comes into Cheltenham, though it's not much more than an hour from the house. 'That way,' I point, instead.

'I'm the opposite, so I'll say bye now. It really was lovely seeing you. We never do this, do we?'

I shake my head and she holds my gaze intently, the green flecks in her hazel eyes shining in the afternoon sun.

'We should,' she says, decisively. 'Since Mum has been gone, I get so... Well, you know. I miss her. I don't like being alone.'

My heart aches at her words and I pull her in for a hug. As we wrap our arms around each other, the strangeness of feeling her so close to me only intensifies my guilt. This is perhaps the first time we have ever hugged. Ever?

It can't be ever. But as we step away from each other, our cheeks flushed with mutual shock at the sudden turn in our relationship, I realise it is.

As I drive home, the smell of her dusky perfume clinging to my scarf, I decide I'm going to sign the agreement as soon as I get in. It's my house; my decision. I don't need to complicate matters and slow things down by waiting to convince Mark. I owe it to her to be a good sister after a whole life of being a bad one.

Nineteen

Now

'I'll take them in, Em,' Mark tells me as he scoops up a crying Lara in one hand and his coffee in the other.

'But it's my day,' I say.

He shakes his head. 'Doesn't matter. You've got your pitch, let me worry about them.'

I bite my lip and count backwards from ten as I look around the utter chaos of the kitchen. The girls' matching porridge bowls have been chucked in the sink with soapy water half-heartedly poured on them, coffee granules dot the surfaces and the milk's still out with its lid off.

'I'll sort it, don't worry,' Mark says, reading my thoughts.

The idea of walking out of the door and leaving all of the mess, the chaos, behind is alluring. I tell myself that Mark has had the luxury of doing this a thousand times before, why shouldn't I do it now? We made up on Saturday when I got back from lunch and have both been on our best behaviour since, desperate to gloss over the crack that the park incident formed between us.

'Okay. Thank you,' I say, picking up my backpack. 'Be good for Daddy,' I tell the girls before giving them both a big hug.

'Good luck today,' Mark says. 'Tell Mummy good luck, girls.'

They both shout good luck at me far more times than is necessary but I laugh and thank them, before walking out of the door.

It's a beautiful day outside; not too hot that I risk forming sweat patches on my new linen polka dot shirt, but sunny enough that the day feels full of hope. By the time I pull into the car park outside my office, I've rehearsed my pitch in my head from start to finish and I'm feeling as confident as I can.

–

'Morning!' Alyssa calls from behind her desk as I walk into the office. 'You're early!'

I smile and tell her that Mark's taken the girls in so I had some extra time this morning.

'What a sweetheart,' she says. 'Coffee?'

'That would be amazing, thank you.'

I go to my desk and unpack my bag; aside from us, no one else is in yet and I let myself spend five minutes flicking through social media on my laptop before I start, relieved as ever that there are no surprise notifications from TwoIsTrouble. A jolt of glee fills me. Perhaps she's gone. Perhaps Allie was right about the call to the nursery, and I could have been wrong about the card that came through the letterbox; there was no proof it was from her. Once those things are taken away, what's she really done to bother me, other than inappropriately message me on social media? Nothing. She's done nothing.

'Here you go,' Alyssa says, placing a coffee on my desk. 'So, how are you feeling about today?'

I take a sip of the coffee before answering. 'Good. Mostly. No, good.' I smile. 'Between you and me, I'm as convinced that I'll be brilliant as I am that I'll fall flat on my arse.'

She waves my concerns away. 'No chance, Em. I've heard Daniel bang on enough about how much of an absolute queen you are in a pitch, there's no way you can have lost that over a few years. You'll be great.' She gives my shoulder a squeeze before going back to her own desk.

I let her words land as I imagine Daniel using the phrase 'an absolute queen' and it's enough to make me laugh and reduce some of the tension I've been holding over the pitch. Perhaps I'll ask her for that drink tonight after work, if everything goes well.

Eventually, the office starts to fill. At around eight thirty, Daniel stops by my desk and asks me to come and see him just after nine. I follow him into his office, my heeled boots clipping across the floor.

'Glad to see you in nice and early,' Daniel says, taking a seat behind his desk. He motions for me to sit.

'Mark took the girls in,' I tell him.

'Big day today!'

I nod. 'Yep. I've got everything ready. Did you have a chance to look through my pitch this weekend?'

He nods. 'Looked great, Emily. Really great. The bit at the end, summing up what mothers really want?' He raises his hands in a clap and I fill with pride. 'You're going to kill it.'

We go over the specifics of the meeting: what time the client is arriving; how long we have to present; the other agencies we're up against. Both of us are fizzling with adrenaline. This was always the part of the job I was best at.

We finish prepping thirty minutes early and everyone scuttles back to their desks, or the kitchen for a brief moment of freedom. Everyone is sure I'm going to *smash it*, they told me all through the prep. While the expression makes me feel every bit of my thirty-four years in the face of the enthusiastic twenty-year-olds, it's also pumped me enough that I really believe I can do this. Back at my desk, I open my laptop and sign into my Gmail. My sister has emailed the contract over again.

> Morning Emily,
>
> Really was lovely to see you on Saturday. I'm sorry everything has been so hectic and stressful for you lately. I really did mean it about looking after the girls if you ever need it. Anyway, I've attached the contract again, it's a DocuSign so a digital signature is fine once you've talked to Mark.
>
> All my love
>
> A x

I check the time. Twenty minutes until the client arrives. I open the contract and briefly glance over it; it's the same one we looked at on Saturday. Signing this will make her happy; I don't need the money from the house. I'm going to do it. I'll tell Mark after, he won't mind. We don't desperately need the money right now. I click through the various pages and smile as the whoosh of my email flies into her inbox.

> All done! Was lovely to see you. Just running into a meeting but would love to catch up again soon.
>
> E x

At eleven, they arrive. I immediately click with Miri, the main person I have to impress today. Despite being annoyed at Daniel's assumption last week that we'll get on just because we're both mothers, he was right. We spend the first five minutes of the meeting exchanging toddler terror stories while one of the interns fetches coffees.

Then, it's time for the pitch. I feel the adrenaline rushing through my body as I stand to walk to the front of the meeting room. The intern – whose name I can't remember for the life of me – has set my laptop up to project onto the wall, my presentation ready and loaded from Google Drive. All I have to do is click the space bar to bring it to life. My hands shake as I press it, but then relief washes over me as my opening slide appears on the wall. I take a deep breath and begin.

I fly through the slides, watching Miri smile and nod at many of my points. The fear I felt earlier is gone, replaced by excitement. I'm doing this. I'm being the old Emily again. I can feel Daniel's relief when we near the end of the presentation and nothing has gone wrong. The room tingles with anticipation.

'So, to sum up. What do mothers really want? And how do we give it to them?' I say through my smile as I click the slider again, knowing this final point is one of Daniel's favourites. 'Security. Value. Honesty.' These are the words that come out of my mouth, but the faces in front of me are filled with horror, like I've said something totally obscene. I turn my head to check what they're seeing on the wall, maybe I'm on the wrong slide?

Then I see it.

In place of my carefully crafted words, is another slide entirely.

What do mothers really want?

To be free from the relentless fucking grind
of motherhood.

To go back to the day before the twins.

To remember who the fuck I am without
them.

To make them disappear.

'Is this some kind of joke?' Miri says.

Daniel looks at me in horror, but I can't speak.

He jumps in with a laugh. 'I think perhaps this slide has got mixed up with another one. Right, Emily?'

The client cuts straight back. 'And at what point in the pitch was it meant for? At which point was it appropriate to tell us you find motherhood a "relentless fucking grind"?'

Every part of my body burns with humiliation. I don't move. I can't speak. I just stand at the front of the room with everyone's eyes on me, saying nothing, doing nothing.

Daniel clears his throat as Miri and her colleagues stand up to leave.

'I'm sorry, Miri. Emily has been through a lot lately. Clearly, she isn't thinking straight.' He shoots a furious look at me. 'I'll walk you out.'

To make them disappear. The words repeat in my head like a chant. *Make them disappear.*

I don't move as they file out; only Daniel is able to look at me as they go. I hear him apologising to Miri repeatedly as they walk down the corridor, telling her that the slide was not part of the presentation he saw; that he should have never let me present; that I've been fragile since having the girls. I want to slip between the floorboards; to be sucked in between the spaces and cease to exist. To run. To *disappear*. I need to get out of this room. But I can't. I'm trapped.

I didn't write those words.

I wouldn't. Not like that…

'Daniel, I—'

He storms back in the room and stares at me.

'What the *fuck* was that?'

I shake my head as my body trembles. 'That wasn't… I didn't write that…'

'No?' He barks an angry laugh. 'Jesus Christ.'

'I'm serious, Daniel. I'm sorry, I know it looks bad, but I didn't write that. I swear. You saw my presentation, I sent it to you.'

Tears fall down my face as I beg him to believe me. He slumps down against the desk and shakes his head, the anger falling away.

'Mark was right; it's too soon. I shouldn't have let you come back.'

'What? No, Daniel, listen, this isn't me—'

'He warned me that something like this might happen. I should have listened.'

My stomach churns. I think of Mark phoning Daniel, telling him I'm basically a basket case. How could he do that to me?

'I don't know what Mark told you, but he's wrong. What happened today—'

'What happened today is that I put you in front of one of our biggest business opportunities for years and you deliberately sabotaged it. I'm sorry, Emily, but there's no coming back from that. I can't have someone so unpredictable on the team.'

I try to laugh but it comes out in a whimper. 'Unpredictable? You know I'm not like that! How long did I work here for? How many times have you seen me stand up there and deliver everything perfectly?'

He sighs. 'Maybe that's what you were like before, but clearly not any more. I'm sorry, Emily. I really am. But I think it's best if we call it a day.'

I close my eyes and feel humiliation pouring over my body.

'Maybe later down the line we can talk again, but this is clearly not the time for you to be working. Go and be with your girls.'

He sighs and rests his arm on mine as he walks past. 'I'm sorry, Em. I really am.'

Then he walks out and I'm left alone in the conference room, feeling everything collapsing around me.

Twenty

Then

Everything is getting worse

I'm trying to not be too dramatic about this, but H promised he'd be home for the girls' first birthday and he missed it. How could he miss it? I'd planned everything so perfectly: the two identical cakes with their initials on; the pink balloons lining the hallway; the bloody magician that he insisted would be perfect. Who gets a magician at a first birthday? The girls barely noticed him, of course. They're one. They have no interest in magic.

D1 was thrilled, though. Perhaps that's why H suggested it, actually. Perhaps it wasn't for the girls at all, but for her. He warned me that she might be difficult today, said it was important that we pay her some extra attention so that she didn't feel left out, as if I wouldn't naturally do this. I gritted my teeth and promised I'd try.

I love D1. Of course I do. But she's becoming more difficult every day. I know it's wrong and I shouldn't say it, shouldn't feel it, definitely shouldn't write it down, but sometimes I can't help but imagine what things would be like if it was just the four of us. Me, H, and the girls. The perfect family unit. Sometimes I think she knows this is how I feel, and maybe that's why she acts like she does. Does every mother live with this constant guilt that they're messing up their kids?

She was good at the party — as good as she can be, anyway. All the other mums think she's hilarious, always playing up to the camera, smiling sweetly and telling everyone how much she loves her little sisters. But I know it's an act. As soon as they're gone, and it's just us again, she ignores the girls completely. Sometimes her transformation is so severe I wonder if I'm going completely mad. Why can no one else see through her?

But today isn't about D1. I've got to stop focusing everything on her, on her bad behaviour. It's not fair on the girls.

They looked so perfect today. Their hair is starting to grow now; their blonde curls almost reach the tops of their ears. They're going to be so beautiful when they grow up. D1 once asked me why her hair didn't look like theirs. I told her she had her dad's hair. Whose hair do they have, then? she asked, frowning and looking at my own blonde curls. I told her they have their dad's. And mine. She pouted her lips and sighed, as if I'd somehow offended her with the reminder that their dad would never be hers. I wanted to tell her I know how she feels, but I didn't. Of course I didn't. She's just a child.

D1's dad wasn't there for her first birthday either, so she at least has that in common with her sisters. I keep telling myself that the girls won't remember it; first birthdays are for the parents, not the babies. But I'll remember. That's the problem. This time around, everything was supposed to be perfect. I thought H understood that.

He said that something came up at work. Something? What does that even mean? How do we let men get away with this shit time and time again?

I sat alone for most of the party without him. The other mothers just don't get it. They coo over D1 like she's the most amazing little girl they've ever seen, but they don't know what she can be like. I can't bear looking at her face when she does it. That's horrific, isn't it? To feel that way about my daughter.

But she knows what she's doing. She knows that she's playing them against me. Do you know what she said to the magician, in front of everyone?

Mummy said that if I'm not good today, you'll make me disappear.

I could have killed her. I really could. Sometimes, she has no idea how much I wish I really could make her disappear. Her and everyone else.

Everything seems to be getting worse lately, and I just don't know what to do.

Twenty-One

Now

In the car park, red-faced and tearful, I open my laptop. Gathering my stuff to leave the office was horrific; I could feel the eyes of everyone crawling all over me as I did it. Alyssa tried to talk to me but I shut her down and she retreated back to her own desk like a wounded animal. I shoved everything into my bag as quickly as I could and ran out to my car. Now that I'm alone, I can finally check the presentation file and try and work out what the hell has happened.

Last edited 2:14 a.m.

'What the fuck?'

How can that possibly be? I didn't wake up in the middle of the night and type this garbage.

Someone must have hacked into my account. Daniel?

I shake my head. That's ridiculous; it wouldn't serve Daniel in any way to do this. Someone else must have got into my account and changed the document.

No. Not 'someone'.

Her.

—

By the time I reach my front door, I've been through every emotion possible. As I twist the key in the lock, I feel the angry ball of rage that's been burning in my stomach start to soften. I'm home now; safe. Just take it one step at a time.

I walk through the front door and shove my bag down at the bottom of the stairs, letting out an enormous sigh. I have a few hours before I have to collect the girls, a few hours before Mark is home and I have to explain to him that I've lost my job. In the kitchen, I run the tap for a glass of water but stop as I hear a bang from upstairs.

Someone is in the house.

I stand perfectly still and try to drown out the sound of my own heartbeat thudding in my ears so that I can listen again.

Footsteps.

Is it her? Is it TwoIsTrouble? My hands shake as I gently turn the tap off and creep through the house. Suddenly, the footsteps get louder and I hear a drawer bang shut. I think of this stranger rifling through my things, her grubby hands caressing the girls' clothes and I want to be furious but for the first time since this began, I'm scared. What sort of woman would do this? I close my eyes and lean my head against the bannister, trying to prime myself to face her. There's another loud bang from upstairs then a voice.

'Emily?'

My body sags with relief. Mark. It's just Mark.

He pounds down the stairs and I frown as I see he's in a T-shirt and jogging bottoms.

'Jesus, Mark. You scared the life out of me. Why aren't you at work?'

He stands level with me in the hallway and shakes his head as he looks at me. 'Are you serious? How about you tell me why *you* aren't at work?'

I gulp and frown. 'I had to come back to get—'

He sighs and puts his hand on my arm. 'You were fired, Em. Daniel called.'

I turn and march away from him, feeling the embarrassment of his words all over my body. Mark follows and grabs my arm to twist me around.

'Emily, stop. Come on, you're being ridiculous. We need to talk about this.'

Concern is written in every inch of his face. He's looking at me like he used to, when I wasn't well. It shouldn't provoke this reaction in me, but it makes me furious. Those kind, concerned eyes always assuming the worst about me. So ready to save me.

'For god's sake, let go of me.' I shrug off his touch and flounce into the kitchen. 'I wasn't fired; you don't have to say it like that.'

I march into the kitchen and fling open the fridge where I empty what's left of a bottle of wine into a glass.

'It's barely two o'clock, Em—' Mark says but one look from me cuts off his words. I put the glass down on the side and leave it there. We both look at it like it's poison.

I sigh and let out some of the angry tension that's been weighing down my shoulders. I look up at Mark and he gives me a small, sad smile. More than anything I wish I could fall against him and tell him the truth, but every time I imagine trying to explain it to him, I picture his face crumbling at my words. And everything else they'd lead me to admitting…

'Tell me what happened,' he says, his voice soft. 'I just want to understand what we're up against.'

Anger flickers through me again. *What we're up against.* It's a phrase he always used to use before, when he'd come home from work and find me sitting in the middle of the living room, the girls screaming beside me, clothes strewn around the house, washing up spilling from the sink. And me, doing nothing. I asked him once if it was something he'd read in one of his self-help blogs, sneered at him for repeating internet pyscho-babble, when I was the one hiding upstairs with my MumsOnline friends like a dirty secret. *Is pretending we're in this together supposed to help me?* I remember snarkily posting about him. He could never understand that no matter what he did, my struggle was mine alone. It separated us in a way he could never understand.

Still, he tried. Like he's trying now. I can see him searching my face for answers, to try and understand how everything has gone so wrong in such a short space of time. When everything was supposed to be okay now. *Everything is going to be better*, that's what I promised him just a few weeks ago. Back to work. Back to me. Back to us.

Now, he's looking at me like I'm the same unwell woman who he used to have to force to get dressed when he came home from work and found me still in my unwashed pyjamas. I don't want to be that woman; I've worked so hard to not be her, to never be her again.

'I think you need to go back to Dr Aldred,' Mark says. He at least has the grace to look away from me now, his cheeks turning pink.

I shake my head. 'I've told you, I'm fine. This isn't…'

'This isn't what?'

'I'm not ill, Mark.'

He shakes his head and pinches his nose between his fingers. He takes a deep breath before calmly looking up and speaking to me, each word coming out slow and steady, like I am a child that he must not risk upsetting.

'I love you, Em. But this… your behaviour recently, this is how you were before. And I don't think either of us wants to let it get to a stage where—'

'A stage where what?' I snap.

He clenches his jaw and says nothing for a moment. I look away, feeling shame creep up the back of my neck.

'A stage where something could happen to the girls. Not again. I can't let that happen again.'

Tears flood my eyes and I dig my nails into the hard wood of the table. A sob escapes me as the memories his words conjure up threaten to overtake me.

Memories of the day that everything changed. The day that my behaviour stopped being a slightly awkward secret that Mark and I shared and become something big, ugly, terrifying. After that day, words like 'dangerous' became used with alarming frequency around me. I was a 'danger' to myself. A 'danger' to my daughters.

I don't want to go back to that place – not mentally, not physically. I can't. The mere idea that Mark thinks I'm even close to tipping into that place makes me want to scream at him. How can he not see that this is nothing like that?

'I'm not ill,' I say again. 'This isn't like before. I'm not ill—'

'The problem is, Em, that's exactly what you used to say back then, too.'

I choke down another sob as I realise nothing I say is going to convince him.

'I'm going to call Dr Aldred. She'll be able to see you for an emergency appointment. You might just need to go back on some medication. Don't cry, darling, come here.' He pulls me into his arms and I sob against him. He strokes my hair and tells me all the things I got so used to hearing back then. It's okay, it's not my fault, he's going to fix this.

The words wash over me like they always have. Mark can't fix things this time. I can't even tell him why.

Eventually, he moves me into the living room and pulls a blanket over me, like I'm a poorly child. I let him take charge; he's good at this. He's always been good at looking after me. His patience is relentless.

After he leaves the room, I hear him on the phone making me an appointment. I think about getting out my own phone and logging into MumsOnline to see if TwoIsTrouble has posted anything, but my body feels so tired, every part of me feels so tired and eventually I give in, close my eyes and wait for exhaustion to pull me under. But the relief doesn't arrive. Instead, my head is a jumble of thoughts and fears, words flying around that I can't stop.

Did I really say those awful words? Did I write to TwoIsTrouble and tell her I wanted the twins to disappear? Tears bubble up in my chest as I see myself hunched over the laptop in the middle of the night, Mark and the girls fast asleep upstairs with no idea of what was happening in the hours between two and four a.m.; the worst hours. The hours most people never see, unless they're out having fun. But those are the hours that always haunted me. They were the hours when panic would fill every fibre of my body, wrenching me from the safety of the duvet and into the cold, hard kitchen where I'd pull my laptop from the side and sit in the glow of the cold light, and type. She was always online when I needed her. Was it in these hours that I poured out my most disgusting thoughts? Wrote them down for the world to see? And now they're back and haunting me.

But even if I did once say them, I'd never write them now, especially on a work presentation. I'm not that far gone. Am I?

Twenty-Two

Now

Dr Aldred's office is the kind of place that makes you want to take off your shoes and get comfy. The walls are a muted grey, covered with huge, colourful prints of abstract art. You enter through the side door of her large Victorian townhouse, going straight up the stairs to the side of the house so that you never interact with her home. I often wonder if she worries about this constant connection between her home and work life, but then I see her and remember she is not the kind of woman who worries at all. She is a woman who has it all perfectly together. That's why women like me go to her, isn't it?

Today, I sit with my shoes firmly on, my hands clutched in my lap as I clench my jaw to keep my smile in place.

'Emily,' she says, smiling warmly. 'It's good to see you.'

I clear my throat and try to laugh. 'I wish I could say the same.'

She doesn't rise to my comment and instead sits back in her hardback chair and looks at me in silence. We sit like that for a few moments until I feel the familiar urge to talk.

'This isn't what it looks like,' I say.

She nods slowly before asking, 'What do you think it looks like?'

I roll my eyes. 'That I'm having a breakdown. Again.'

'No one is saying you're having a breakdown—'

'Mark is. That's why he called you, isn't it? To intervene before things get too bad.'

Dr Aldred says nothing and I'm left feeling like an insolent child. I've let the anger slip into my words and I know what I sound like, so much like the old Emily she's dealt with over the years. As soon as Mark began to notice there were problems with me, he dragged me straight here. I'm vaguely aware that this makes me luckier than most; that my husband is aware enough of the struggles mothers face that he could recognise the signs of destruction in me, and wasn't too proud to ask for help. But it's easy to be the hero. Much harder the damsel in distress, and I couldn't bear the idea of sitting in a stranger's office every week and baring my soul. In the end, it didn't even help, did it? I still became the villain.

I push the thoughts away and remind myself that Dr Aldred is no longer a stranger. Nor is she the enemy here.

'Why don't you tell me a bit about what's been going on?' she says in a soothing, honeyed voice.

'I'm sure Mark's already told you,' I say, unlacing my hands and staring at the patterned rug on the floor.

'We've spoken, yes, but I'd like to hear about you, Emily. What's been going on for you?'

'You won't believe me.'

She tilts her head to the side and smiles. 'Try me.'

I sigh and sit back in my chair like a stroppy teenager. 'I didn't write those things on the presentation. I really didn't.' Despite my exhaustion-induced panic last night, I'm sure that I didn't do it; there is no way I would deliberately sabotage my presentation. As sure as I can be. Whether I wrote those words to TwoIsTrouble at some point before, of course, is another matter and one that I'm not ready to go into.

'Okay. Have you said this to Mark?'

I nod.

'Do you understand why he might be concerned about this?'

'Of course I do, I'm not an idiot. I know what it looks like.'

'You've said that already, and I think what we need to do here, Emily, is talk about what's happened, and work out what we can do to support you. It's just you and me now, you don't need to worry about what I think, or what anyone else thinks. This is your space to talk openly.'

She holds my gaze with steely blue-grey eyes. She's heard so many of my confessions already. Could I trust her with this?

'I followed your advice,' I say. 'I came off MumsOnline.'

'That's good. That's a real step forward, Emily.'

I feel a twitch of pride at her approval. It's something she had been talking to me about for months, my unhealthy attachment to the forum that Mark knew nothing about. We talked about it in this office like I was an addict trying to kick a bad habit. This must be how it feels when those people stand up in meetings and say the line, 'It's been eighty-eight days since my last drink'.

'I felt really good about it,' I go on, 'like I was finally moving forward, like we talked about. I had my job, the girls were happy, Mark and I were happy, and I thought "I don't need this site any more". But then, that *woman*,' I spit, 'the one I thought was my friend—'

'TwoIsTrouble?' Dr Aldred interrupts and I'm thrown for a moment that she remembers the details of my life so well.

'Yes. Her. She found me.'

Dr Aldred turns her head to one side as if trying to decipher my words. 'Found you?'

'She found out who I really was.'

She nods. 'That must have been very upsetting.'

I can't reply. My throat is clogged with all of the words that I want to spill but I know that it's not the right time, this is not the right place. I focus on my hands in my lap. A piece of wool has come loose from the cushion I didn't realise I was cuddling and I pull it and wrap it around my fingers. We sit like that for what feels like hours but could be minutes; time has a way of warping in this room.

'I haven't told Mark,' I say.

Dr Aldred nods.

'He thinks it's just the stress of going back to work.'

'How has returning to work been?' she asks.

I puff out my cheeks. 'Does it matter? I won't be going back again.'

'I think it matters, yes.'

I let out a short, unhappy laugh. 'It was good. I mean, I was there for three days before I got' – I clear my throat and spit the word – 'fired, but before that. It was good. I felt like me again.'

'What did that feel like?'

I stop and look around the room, as if the right words might materialise in front of me. I wave my hands. 'In control. Useful. I don't know… like a person.'

'You don't feel like a person at home?'

I frown and snap, 'Of course I do. But you know what I mean. When I was doing the pitch… I felt like, I can do this. I remembered it all, I wasn't sure I would. I thought I'd forgotten how to think like that, but I hadn't.'

'It must have been very upsetting when they let you go.'

I grunt.

'Do you want to talk about that?' Dr Aldred asks, her head cocked to the side.

'No.'

We sit in silence until I hear the sound of children screaming from downstairs. Dr Aldred's eyes flicker to the door and I see her fighting to maintain her doctor mask when all she wants to do is go and check on her children.

'You can go, I don't mind,' I tell her. Her mouth twitches and she starts to shake her head but then another bang comes and she jumps up and runs out of the room.

She leaves the door open a crack and I hear the sounds of family life drifting up the usually sealed staircase. In place of her cool, thoughtful words, I hear Dr Aldred snapping at her husband that she's trying to work and can he for once just *take control of the children*. It's oddly comforting, to hear the cracks like this.

A few moments later, she comes back up the stairs and shuts the door behind her. She smooths down her hair and sits back opposite me.

'Sorry about that,' she says, her doctor voice back in place but the pink spots at the top of her cheeks remain; a stain on her perfect demeanour.

I shrug. 'It's okay. It must be hard trying to work up here with your family just below.'

Dr Aldred clears her throat and shifts in her seat. 'You were telling me about your job.'

I nod. I open my mouth to say that it's fine, but we catch each other's eye and I see something in hers that I hadn't before. A mutual understanding. This is a woman who understands chaos, who knows how to shut away the messy parts of life and carry on as if nothing is happening.

'It was her,' I say. 'The reason I lost my job, it was because of her.'

Dr Aldred frowns and taps her pen against her notepad. 'I'm sorry, Emily, I'm not sure I follow?'

'TwoIsTrouble,' I say. 'She's behind all of this.'

Her mouth twitches and for a moment I think I've lost her, that she's looking at me like the typical crazy mother opposite her, but then something else comes over her face and she tells me to go on.

'As soon as I deleted my MumsOnline account, she found me on social media and tried to get to me there instead but I blocked her,' I say, as Dr Aldred nods. 'Now she won't leave me alone. She rang the girls' nursery, pretending to be me. She sent a note through my door. I'm sure she was watching us at the park one day, too. Then, she got into my work presentation and changed the slides. I know it was her.'

Dr Aldred holds my gaze thoughtfully and I feel the heat of anticipation covering my body; this can only go one of two ways now.

'Okay. I understand. Can I ask why you think she's doing these things to you?'

I frown. 'What?'

'This woman, you say she's messing with your life. Why do you think that is?'

I shake my head and sigh impatiently. 'She wants to ruin my life.'

Dr Aldred nods, leaving a beat in between her question. 'Yes, but why?'

'I don't know,' I say, looking down at my hands in my lap. I've wound the cushion thread around my fingers so tightly that it's snapped, and my finger is left with a red, angry ring around it.

'She was your friend.'

'Yes.'

'Was she upset when you told her you were going to leave the site?'

'I didn't tell her.'

Dr Aldred nods. 'That must have been upsetting for her.'

'What?'

'If she felt you had abandoned her, it could have been upsetting.'

I laugh. 'Are you taking her side?'

'No, Emily. There are no sides.'

I twist my wedding ring around my finger and breathe in and out, counting from ten down, again and again. Calming myself.

'Sometimes it can be very hard when you make a big life transition like this.' Dr Aldred's cool voice cuts through my thoughts. 'Your mind can want things to stay the same, even with a positive change, and fight against it.'

'I'm not fighting anything. She is.'

Dr Aldred looks at me thoughtfully and writes something on her pad.

'She kept my messages. From before, from when I was really... not myself. Things I said about Mark, about the girls.' I feel my cheeks colour. 'The sort of thoughts I had when... you know.' Tears spring to my eyes at my own stupidity once again.

'You're worried Mark will find out about the things you said.'

I nod. 'That's what she put in the presentation,' I finally admit. 'I didn't write the words on the slides, I promise you I didn't. But I think they might be my words.'

I look down, unable to face her as I admit it.

'But I didn't mean them when I said them. You know I didn't. I know I didn't. But seeing them up on that fucking presentation in front of everyone... God, I've never hated myself more. Because I did think them, I did once wish everything would disappear. I did say that. Only to her. Now she's using that, using my words, sticking them together to make me sound totally insane.'

'Is that what you think, that the things you said before are totally insane?'

I sigh. 'That's not the point. I know the things I did before, the things I wrote, weren't me. But she's making them look like they are.'

'What do you mean?'

'She's using my words against me.'

'You're embarrassed by the things you said, the things you shared with this woman on MumsOnline?'

I laugh and frown. 'Of course I am. You know I am. It wasn't me talking. It was the illness. But she won't let me leave it behind.'

'Why do you think that is?'

I wave my hands, exasperated by this conversation. 'Because she wants to punish me!'

'Why?'

'Because I deserve it,' I shout. 'She knows about the accident. She knows!'

The silence after my outburst hangs in the air like a cloak, drowning out all other thoughts.

'You still feel guilty over what happened. There's no shame in that. But I do think you're underestimating

Mark. Remember, Emily, this isn't news to him. He knows about the accident, he knows how you were feeling before and after, and he stuck by you. Remember, this loss is not yours alone. Mark is right there with you.'

I shake my head. Because she doesn't understand. How could she? Mark knows about the accident, of course he does. But he didn't experience it; and the loss was not shared equally. He would never admit it, but he never felt grief in the way I did. How could he? Grief mixed with shame is a deadly combination; one only I had to bear. I keep the secret of my guilt from Mark not just to protect me, but him too. It's the darkest, very worst part of me and something few people know exists. Not even Dr Aldred.

But TwoIsTrouble does.

And no matter what Mark has put up with from me until now, if he knew this, if anyone knew this, I'd lose everything.

The shrill ring of a timer buzzes on the desk between us.

'That's all we've got time for today, Emily.'

My cheeks burn with embarrassment. The room becomes very still as I try to regain my composure but my heart is thumping in my chest at the thought of the admission. I stare at the patterned rug as I try to catch my breath. The clock ticks away in the background.

'Will you tell Mark that I'm okay?' I ask as I feel Dr Aldred stand up to open the door. 'Please, I'm not ill again. I'm really not.'

She turns around to face me, her expression impassive. 'What we've talked about today is just between you and me, you know that. But I will be recommending that we look at your medication, Emily.'

It's like a punch to the stomach. She doesn't believe anything I've told her.

'You think I'm making it up,' I say.

She shakes her head. 'I believe you think someone is out to get you.'

'They are,' I say.

Dr Aldred just nods and tells me her next patient is waiting.

'Try to remember all the good work you've already done, Emily. This is a small setback, nothing to be ashamed of. Sometimes medication just needs altering, that's all this is.' She gives me a small smile as she ushers me out of the room.

I walk down the stairs and out into the cool, fresh air, my body heavy with hopelessness. Dr Aldred does not believe me. If she doesn't, what hope do I have that Mark ever will? All they see when they look at me is a woman on the edge. A mother incapable of performing her role. How am I supposed to prove them wrong when my biggest fear is that they're right?

Twenty-Three

Now

'How was it?' Mark is leaning against the side of the car waiting for me as I leave Dr Aldred's office. The sky has turned from murky grey to blue speckled with sunshine in the time I've been inside and I squint at the sudden onslaught of light.

'Fine,' I say, then open the car door and get in, lightly shutting it to show that I'm fine. Not tense. Not slamming the door. This is not like it was before.

Mark always brought me to and from my appointments. It felt faintly ridiculous, to be honest, to drag him from work to ferry me around like the queen. *I can drive, you know*, I would snap at him on my worst days. But I'm not being that Emily today. Today I am calm. I am kind. That's what Mark needs to see.

He gets in beside me and we drive back towards home. I turn the radio on and let the bolshie Northern voice of the midday radio presenter fill the car. We listen for a few moments until Mark reaches to turn it down.

'You don't have to tell me what you talked about,' he says. 'But has it helped?'

I inhale a sigh and look out of the window at the busy high street as we drive through. I watch a too-thin woman drag a French bulldog through the lunchtime crowds, her face scrunched in annoyance.

'Yes,' I say. 'She's always helpful.'

'Good. Did she recommend…' He tails off, waiting for me to fill the silence.

'Medication, yep. So, I guess I'll be seeing her regularly again.'

'That's okay,' he says. 'That's good. It's not a step back, Em. It's a step forward.'

I murmur in agreement though I want to scream.

'And I don't want you to worry about your job. We'll be fine, I promise.'

I don't say anything.

'Do you think it'll be weekly again… that you'll need to see her?' he asks, his voice tentative.

A knot twists inside me as I realise why he's asking.

'Oh my god, Mark. It's too much. Isn't it? The cost of seeing her – we can't do it again!' I bury my face in my hands as a hot wave of failure flows through me.

Dr Aldred is not cheap. Mark has never told me how much, but I've Googled it, of course I have. Hundreds for every single session. When things started getting bad, Mark tried to get me seen by the NHS but the waiting list was long; too long. So we did what so many people can never do and we paid to skip it by going private. It's one of the reasons I wanted to go back to work, to finally start contributing financially to our family when I know my care, the move, everything I've done has caused us so much financial burden.

And now, not only am I bringing that cost back into our lives but I've lost my only way of paying for it.

'We're fine,' Mark assures me as I feel the car pull to a stop.

I open my eyes and see we're home. Mark rubs my leg and then lifts my chin to face him.

'I don't want you to worry about anything. But you're right, she isn't cheap. And realistically yes, it might be a little difficult without your income' – he holds his hands up to stop me as I cry – 'and I know you might not want to do this, but I do think it's worth us talking again about what's happening with your mum's house.'

I lurch back, then try to cover it by reaching for the door.

'I know you saw your sister the other day, and perhaps now is a good time to think about what we're going to do about it.'

'She lives there, I can't ask her to sell it!'

He shakes his head. 'No, of course not. But the house is half yours, and perhaps we can just talk to her about what that means. Arrange some sort of rent agreement? I don't know.'

My cheeks burn as I think of the document I signed yesterday morning while I was feeling so fucking fantastic about everything. It's too late to get money from the house. But how can I ever tell him that now?

'Yeah, you're right. I'll talk to her,' I manage to say. I can't tell him the truth; that I've let him down in yet another way.

'No, I can—'

I shake my head and smile, my jaw clenching tightly beneath it. 'Please, let me do this. I'm not totally useless, I promise. Let me do something to help. I don't want to go back to you being my carer.'

It's a cruel jibe but one that I know will work.

He sighs and then slowly nods. 'Okay. You talk to your sister, but leave everything else with me. I don't want you worrying about anything.'

He leans across the seat and pulls me closer to him before planting a kiss on my forehead. I smell the morning's coffee on his breath and breathe him in, wishing we could go back to how we used to be.

–

Mark works the rest of the afternoon from home and I curl up with the girls on the sofa, watching *Frozen* on repeat. I hear him on the phone to clients, the strong bellowing laugh he lets out every now and again reminding me that he is capable in ways that I am not. I've left my phone upstairs to stop me from seeking out any more interaction with TwoIsTrouble but I'm desperate to be left alone so that I can.

At five p.m., Mark comes into the living room and offers to take the girls to the park.

'I'll run you a bath,' he says and I smile and thank him, the heavy weight of guilt almost flattening me as he tells me he loves me, again.

As soon as he's gone, I jump out of the too-hot water and find my phone in the bedroom. Before I do anything, I need to talk to my sister. Perhaps there's a way I can still get out of this house chaos and Mark never has to find out what I've done. I wrap myself in a towel and take the phone downstairs; a conversation this serious has to be done in the kitchen with the solid, hard table beneath me.

Allie picks up after two rings.

'Hi, Emily.'

'Hi,' I say, my stomach already crunching beneath me. 'Are you okay to talk?'

'Yes, I'm at home,' she says and I wonder where else she would be; her job in some IT firm that I can never remember the name of is remote, and she never seems to go out with friends. 'Is everything okay?'

'I'm really sorry to do this, but... the contract, for the house. Is it too late to change my mind?'

'What do you mean?'

'I'm sorry, I know this is going to sound terrible but I can't sign it.'

'But you already have!'

'I know, but I shouldn't have.'

'Okay...' she says and sighs loudly down the line. 'What's going on, Emily?'

I close my eyes and rub my forehead. 'I didn't tell Mark.'

'Ah.'

'I know. I know. But he can't find out, he just can't. I shouldn't have signed it; it wasn't my place to do it. I didn't think it through and now Mark says we need the money and... I just don't know what to do. Is it too late to take it back?'

There are a few seconds of silence in which I prepare myself for an onslaught of anger, but then her voice comes back down the line and it's calm. Kind.

'Oh, Emily, why do you do things like this? Honestly! But no, it's not too late. I'll speak to my solicitor.'

'You've sent it to your solicitor?'

'Yes, I sent it across as soon you emailed me. But don't worry, I'll sort it.'

I feel the embarrassing, salty tears spilling down my face. My little sister, coming to my rescue. Why does everyone always have to come to my rescue?

'But what about you?' I ask a beat too late.

Allie sighs down the line and with it I hear years of frustration and disappointment. 'I'll manage—'

'But the house, it's your—'

'Emily.'

I drop the phone on the table and turn around.

Mark.

'Who are you talking to?'

The girls run into the kitchen shouting, 'Phone! Phone!' but stop when they see me.

I wipe my face with the back of my hand and try to smile.

'What are you doing back already?'

'Daddy forgot his phone,' Ella tells me.

'Girls, go in the living room, please,' Mark says, his eyes not leaving mine.

'But the park!' Lara squeals.

'Now,' he barks, which he never does, and their eyes grow wide. Lara grips Ella's hand and they trail out together. Mark walks behind them and shuts the living room door before returning.

'Who were you talking to?'

'Oh, just—'

'No. Don't lie. That was your sister, wasn't it?' His jaw is clenched and his nostrils flare; this is Mark at his most furious. It's something I rarely see and the sight of it is enough to make the tears start. 'What have you signed?'

I can't hold it in any more and the sobs overtake me.

'I'm sorry,' I cry. 'I'm sorry.'

The anger vanishes from his face and he rushes across the tiled floor to save me.

—

With the girls carefully hidden away upstairs with their colouring books, Mark and I sit down in the living room to talk things through. I've calmed myself down and so has he, whether through genuine compassion or for fear of the girls seeing him shout I don't know, but either way, the air feels less electric and we can finally talk.

'Why didn't you tell me?' he asks, his voice in the soft tone he usually uses on the girls when he wants them to tell the truth.

I resist the urge to lie. 'I wanted to help my sister and I thought you'd stop me.'

His nostrils flare and I see him visibly forcing his anger down. 'This isn't right, Em. You can see that, can't you? This was a huge decision and you've just gone off and done it. That's not like you.'

I scratch my arm and shrug. 'I didn't know I was going to lose my job.'

'That's not what we're talking about—'

'But it is! If I hadn't lost my job, and you hadn't made me go back to Dr Aldred, we wouldn't need the money so we wouldn't—'

'Jesus, Em. This isn't about the money!' He stands up and paces the room, the electric sparks back in the air, fizzling and snapping between us. 'How can you not see that this is about more than that? I'm worried about you. I'm worried you'd do something like this.'

'It's my house! It's not like I've done something insane—'

'You don't think this is insane?'

I grit my teeth and look away from him.

'You've signed away your legal rights to a house that's probably worth about a million fucking pounds. Even if we were rolling in it, you'd think that might be something you'd want to discuss with me. The sort of decision we might want to take more than five minutes to consider *together* as a bloody couple.

'I took more than five minutes considering it!'

'When? Between seeing your sister on Saturday and signing over the house on Monday, when was this long period of consideration done?'

The room falls silent and Mark stops pacing. He moves to sit on his knees in front of me. He grabs my hands and turns my head to his.

'This isn't normal behaviour, not for you. You can see that, can't you? It's not the money. It's the impulsiveness that scares me.'

I meet his eyes and try to stop my cheeks from burning.

He's right.

It was impulsive.

That feeling I had yesterday morning sitting at my desk like nothing could stop me… it was a feeling I wanted to keep. It's why I signed away my rights to the house without a second thought. It's the sort of thing I would have done before. Anything to keep that feeling.

I can't blame TwoIsTrouble for that. This one is all on me.

Twenty-Four

Then

My husband thinks I'm insane

H says I'm insane. It's taken eighteen months, but he's finally shown me what he really thinks of me as a mother. He screamed it at me tonight after dinner, after I told him what D1 had done. I shouldn't have told him; I should have learned by now that he'll take anyone's side over mine, even hers. Why can't he see what she's really like? He's never here, that's why. It's easy for him to saunter in a few nights a week when he's not working away and see the good bits. He can come in, read D1 a story as she falls asleep on his chest, then watch me give the girls their night feed while they gurgle happily, and imagine every night is like this. The picture of a perfect family. He's never here when D1 refuses to go to bed at all, or when the girls won't stop crying and D1 laughs. Yes, she actually laughs when the girls are screaming and I'm nearing tears myself. I hear her giggles from her bedroom. H sees and hears none of it. He's only here for the good bits.

He doesn't believe me when I tell him D1 has done things deliberately to upset me. But why else would she do them? Her jealousy is getting out of control.

I picked her up from school slightly late today. Five, ten minutes at the most. The way her teachers looked at me you'd think I was some sort of abusive parent. I tried to tell them that the girls are on a very strict sleep routine and I can't wake them before they're ready, even if it means I'm a few minutes late at the gate. It's a few minutes, what does it matter to them? They have after-school club running anyway for the children of the parents who really can't be bothered to spend time with them. I'm not one of those parents. I'm here. Every day. I'm here.

But anyway, D1 was obviously furious, because my sole purpose is apparently to be at her beck and call every second of the day. I took her to the sweet shop in the village to apologise, even though I really shouldn't have to resort to bribery to get her to behave, but today I didn't have the energy to be a good parent. She chose a milk chocolate bar in the shape of a puppy. Then refused to eat it. But I let it go; if she doesn't want to eat her treat that's down to her. By the time we got back to the house, I thought things were fine, that she'd forgiven me for being late. I left the girls in their playpen for a few minutes while I went into the laundry room for what felt like the millionth time that day. Do all toddlers produce this much laundry? The girls seem to smear unconfirmed substances on everything they own lately. I was coming back through the kitchen when I heard it.

BITCH.

Only it didn't sound like that. Because at eighteen months old, it's hard to form the 'tch' sound.

I stormed into the living room and heard the word again, repeated through giggles from both the girls. D1 was sitting in front of them clapping them on like it was the best game ever. I grabbed her by the arm and dragged her from the room. Yes, perhaps I shouldn't have been so angry, perhaps I should have calmly asked her to explain what she was doing, but at that moment I saw red. I saw her doing what she always does: trying to ruin my perfect girls by making them just like her.

The girls started crying, their pained cries scratching my ears through the walls as D1 screamed at me that she was just teaching them new words, why did I always have to be so horrible? They're bad words, I told her, you're deliberately teaching them bad words. She shook me off and reached into her pocket, pulling out the now melted chocolate puppy. She turned her scrunched up face towards me, eyes angry in a way I hope to never see again and said quietly 'Bitch is a girl dog. That's the word I learned today at school.'

Then the tears came and she told me she hated me. And I am ashamed to admit that I told her the feeling was mutual.

I don't know how long things can go on like this. I really don't.

Twenty-Five

Now

I know the house is empty as soon as I wake up. The air has a stillness to it that isn't physically possible when the girls are around. I lie back and close my eyes; my head pounds with a steady beat that starts at the base of my neck and creeps across my brain, holding it in a grip so tight it hurts to move. My phone beeps from the bedside table and I force myself to sit up.

> I've had to go into the office this morning.
> Girls with Mum, I will pick them up at 1.
> Take it easy today. Have left orange juice
> by the bed. Love you. M x

I reach for the glass of orange juice he's left me and swig it down in three guttural glugs. The last of it dribbles down my chin and I wipe it away, disgusted with myself. How has everything fallen apart so quickly? Just over a week ago, I was going back to work, leaving MumsOnline; everything was going to be good again. And now look at me. Not even trusted to look after my own daughters.

I trudge downstairs in my pyjamas and sit at the kitchen island with my laptop open, my fingers twitching at the

'No, Emily. I don't just mean that. I've been worried about you for a while. When I saw you on Saturday, you didn't seem yourself.'

I busy myself stirring milk into our coffees then walk to the island to place the mugs down. I take a seat opposite her and consider my response. My sister doesn't really know me. It's a sad but very true fact; so how can she possibly know what 'seeming like myself' is?

'Things have been a bit… all over the place lately.'

She laughs, not unkindly, but still it makes me frown. 'Sorry,' she says, noticing my expression. 'But that's a bit of an understatement, isn't it? You've not changed, you know. I remember when you had all that trouble with those bullies in your final year of high school and you just wanted to shrug it off, like it was a "blip". Seems like you're still trying to pretend.'

My cheeks burn, a buried memory coming to the surface. She doesn't know what she's saying; she would have only been eleven and cushioned from so much of what was really happening back then, but the reference to the past is still unwelcome.

'You should be worrying about yourself,' I tell her. 'Have you spoken to the solicitor about the house?'

Her face clouds at the unwelcome reminder that my husband is happy to make her homeless, but it passes quickly as she shakes her head. 'Don't worry about all that, we're sorting it. And don't change the subject, stop pretending everything your end is fine.'

'I'm not pretending. Things aren't okay, I know that.'

'We should talk about it.'

I shake my head. 'Honestly, I know you're trying to help but it's not going to help right now.'

'Em, you never want to talk about things.'

I swallow down the annoyance that's creeping through my throat and plaster on a tight smile. 'To be fair, you wouldn't really know about that.'

'You never want to talk about Beth.'

She looks at me dead in the eyes as the word falls between us. Beth.

The name we never say. Not in this house.

'I don't... I c-can't—' I stutter the words as I stand up from the island and back away. Every inch of my body pounds with the beat of her name.

Beth. Beth. Beth.

I close my eyes and shake it away.

When I open them, I focus on the details of the kitchen. Crumbs from this morning's breakfast not yet wiped away on the counter. The black dots that show Mark timed it wrong again. The smell fills my nostrils and I picture him lifting the burnt toast to his lips and crunching. The girls laughing in the background. Mark saying *silly Daddy* as they screw their nose up at the charred smell.

My breathing steadies as the pulsing behind my eyes begins to soften.

'I need to go into town to pick something up,' I say.

My sister frowns. 'Emily, come on. We need to talk about this—'

'Finish your coffee, no rush,' I say, moving across the kitchen to grab my car keys. 'Just pull the front door tight when you leave, make sure it locks.'

I give her a tight smile and tell her I'll give her a call soon about the house, then pick up my bag from the hallway and leave, shutting the door behind me.

Twenty-Six

Then

Two is the perfect number.

Three children is just too many.

I know, I know, I know. That's not what you're supposed to think, let alone say. But what if it's true? The world is made for families of four. Husband, wife, two children. Everything gets more complicated when you add an extra child. Too many for the car to be comfortable. Too many to book a holiday home. Too many for a babysitter to take. Too dramatic? It's true. You call around and everyone's all too happy to manage twins for the night, but add in the third daughter and the excuses start to come. I don't blame them. I know how they feel.

Three really is too many.

Twenty-Seven

Now

My medication is ready to pick up. Dr Aldred is always quick to write a prescription and Mark texted me earlier to make sure I didn't forget to collect it. I may or may not take the pills, I haven't decided yet. But at least if I fetch it like I'm supposed to I'm showing a willingness to get better. In the chemist, I line up behind an elderly man who leans against his walking stick as we wait. I hope my sister has left my house. I don't like the thought of her being there alone but I don't think she'd nose through my stuff. We're not kids any more.

'Emily Jones?' The woman behind the counter calls.

I move forward, ahead of the elderly man, and take the white paper bag containing my pills from her. She doesn't recognise me. This isn't the chemist where we used to go; this is closer to our new house. There's something nice about that; that this isn't the same woman who handed me these pills that ended up causing everything to go wrong. This is a new woman. And I won't give her the chance to recognise me, because I will not be here regularly. I will not be that woman again.

As I get back to the car, I realise I can't bear going home to an empty house, or worse, face getting back before Allie has left. I'll go and get the girls from nursery now; we can spend the afternoon together at the park and it'll be like this morning never happened.

–

As I walk up to the gates I focus on putting one foot in front of the other; I am fine. My girls will be with me soon, nothing bad is happening. I repeat it like a mantra as I walk, the pounding beat of my heart mocking me.

'Mrs Jones?' Katie appears at the door with a look of concern on her face.

'Hi,' I say, sheepishly. 'Sorry, I know I'm early. But I just—'

'They aren't here,' Katie says, her brow furrowed.

'What? What do you mean?' I grab the doorframe to steady myself as my world begins to crumble.

Katie's eyes widen and she opens her mouth, then shuts it again, apparently taking a moment to find the words.

'They were booked in but your husband phoned this morning and said his mum was having them…'

I glance through the door behind her, as if she might be lying but then a fuzzy recognition takes hold. I battle with myself over what is more likely to be true: I have forgotten the most basic facts of my daughters' care today, or Katie, the sweet day-care worker, is hiding them from me. Katie stares at me in alarm and I recognise the look so well. It's how Mark used to look at me every day.

'Sorry, Katie,' I say, feeling my cheeks redden. 'I must have forgotten, sorry,' I tell her, trying to keep my words calm. Measured. Not erratic. Normal.

'Is everything okay?'

BETH. Her name blares through my thoughts like a fog horn.

'Yes, fine,' I snap, desperate to drown it out. 'I just got confused.'

She eyes me carefully and I want to scream.

'Do you want to come in? The kids are outside with Melissa; we could have a quick coffee?' she offers. There's pity in her eyes and I feel my walls coming down.

'No, I'm okay. Really, I am.' I smile through gritted teeth. We say our goodbyes and I walk back to the car feeling my sanity slipping through my fingers. Beth's face fills my mind; her laugh shrill in my ears. 'Stop it!' I shout, then slam my hands over my mouth to cover the crazy thoughts from spilling out. My eyes dart around the street but no one is here to witness my shame.

This is what it used to be like. Forgetting. Confusion. Anger. Perhaps Mark is right; perhaps I am becoming ill again. It's Alison's fault. She should know not to ever mention Beth.

I get into my car and grip the steering wheel tightly before switching on the engine. I take my phone from my bag and open Mark's message from this morning. There it is, clear as day. He told me the girls were at his mum's. I take a moment to breathe in and out, slowly, carefully, before I drive. The journey passes quickly and before I know it I'm back on our street. Mark's car is on the drive.

'Mummy!'

I walk through the door and Ella runs down the hallway towards me, her face a picture of pure glee. I scoop her up and hug her tightly until she squeals. My body fizzles with love, then an ache so strong that I wince.

'What's wrong, Mummy?'

I realise too late that I'm crying. Ella's blue daisy-print top is spotted with my tears.

'Nothing, darling,' I say, but the tears won't stop.

Mark appears in the hallway, his face achingly sad. We meet each other's eyes and I feel my legs start to give way beneath me. He reaches me just in time and clutches Ella from my arms.

'Come on, you're okay,' he tells me as I sob. 'Els, go in the living room, please.'

I hear her feet patter away from us and guilt rises through my every limb. She shouldn't have to see me like this. I think of all the times I saw my mum flailing under the weight of her worries, and I want to scream at myself to stop. I never wanted to be like her, and yet here we are. I'm meant to protect my girls.

'Katie called me,' I hear Mark say and my head snaps up.

'What?'

'From Polkadot. She was worried about you.'

I clench my teeth and push Mark away as I wipe the tears from my face. He looks at me like I might break and it makes me want to scream. This isn't what I want; this isn't who I want to be. I think back to how, less than a week ago, we sat on the sofa sharing a bottle of wine and talking about how life was going to be from now on. How much better everything would be. I don't want Mark to slip back into the role of my carer. I'm stronger than that now.

'Did you forget?' he asks, his voice soft.

I shake my head. 'No, I just… I don't know why she had to call you.'

'I told you, she was worried.'

I rub my face and walk into the kitchen. 'Don't make this into something it isn't. I just misread your text—'

'Em, you were just stood in the hallway sobbing. We need to talk about this.'

I sigh and open the fridge; I take out a carton of orange juice and pour myself a glass with shaking hands.

Mark stands in the doorway and watches me. He's scrunching up the bottom of his T-shirt in his hands and his jaw's tight.

'What?' I snap.

He shakes his head and looks down.

'For god's sake, Mark. If you want to say something, then say it.'

He looks up and his eyes are full of tears. My heart constricts in my chest. I want more than anything to walk across the room and fix this, but I don't know how.

'I'm going to take the girls to Mum's for a few days,' he says.

'No!'

'It's for the best,' he tells me.

'You don't trust me around them.'

The statement flies across the kitchen and forms a barrier between us. Mark tilts his head and bites his lip. The look says it all.

'Em, you know I love you. And I'll do whatever you need me to…'

'Then stay.'

He shakes his head. 'I spoke to Dr Aldred and she agreed that it's better for us to have some space.'

Panic twists my stomach and I look down at the table.

'This isn't going to help,' I tell him through tears.

'What's been going on this week,' he says, 'it's not right. You've been so on edge, and the girls have noticed it. You know this isn't right. This isn't you.'

I sniff and bite my lip. How can I ever explain to him what's really going on?

'But I don't think the girls should be around you right now. I'm sorry – fucking hell, Em, you know how much it kills me to admit that. But they come first. We always promised each other that, didn't we?'

He lifts my chin up so that I face him.

'You made me promise last time that if anything ever happened again, I wouldn't let them witness it.'

I laugh, a hoarse, horrible sound that bounces off the walls.

'But this isn't like that,' I tell him, my voice high and erratic. 'I didn't mean…'

'It's just a few days,' he replies, walking across the kitchen and kneeling beside me. 'Just while we work out what to do to get you back on track. I promise, Em. All any of us want is for you to feel better.'

He stands up and kisses my head, then walks out, shutting the kitchen door behind him.

I hear him dragging the cases down the stairs and telling the girls to come and say goodbye.

I straighten up in my chair and rush to the sink to splash cold water on my face before they come in. I don't want them to see me like this. Mark opens the door and walks them through, glancing at me with tears in his eyes. I want to hate him, to be furious that he's doing this to me, but despite everything, I know he's only acting out of love. He's holding onto the promise I once forced him to make. The promise to never let the girls see me fall apart again. To never put them in a position where anything bad can ever happen again. He thinks he's doing the right thing; he's trying to protect them, to protect me.

Ella and Lara stare up at me uncertainly. The sight of their worried faces breaks my heart and it takes everything in me to summon up a smile.

'You're going to stay with Nanny, won't that be nice?' I hear myself say.

They look at each other, then back at me.

'Daddy's going to take you and I'm going to stay here and then I'll see you in a few days,' I tell them in the most balanced way I can manage.

They ask me why I'm not coming and I just shake my head and smile so tightly that I think my jaw might break, until Mark scoops them up and carries them out. I sit at the table with my head in my hands as he leans down to kiss my head and tells me he loves me, that he'll call me later. I sit like that for a long time after he's gone, wondering how everything could fall apart so quickly.

–

The sound of my phone ringing snaps me out of my state and I jump up from the table looking for it. Eventually, I find it but it's too late, I've missed the call. It's from an unknown number. I stare at the phone in my hand, willing it to ring again. Perhaps it was Mark, calling to say he's made a mistake; that he should have never left. But even as I think it, I know that's wishful thinking. There's no reason he'd call me from a blocked number and there's no reason he'd want to come back. Anger burns in the pit of my stomach at TwoIsTrouble for putting me in this situation. At myself for letting her. If I'd been a better mum, a better wife, it would never have been so easy for her to rip my life apart.

I grab my laptop from the kitchen table and open MumsOnline, suddenly desperate to make contact with her; to show her what she's done to me. I open the site and scour the threads for her username. I can't see any activity from her since we last spoke but when I open my private messages, the little green roundall is lit up by her name, showing she's online.

Are you there? I type.

Moments pass with nothing, then, she types.

> TwoIsTrouble: Yes.
>
> MotherOfTwins: Why are you doing this?
>
> TwoIsTrouble: You know why.
>
> MotherOfTwins: I don't.
>
> TwoIsTrouble: You can't be trusted with those little girls.
>
> MotherOfTwins: You don't know anything about my girls.
>
> TwoIsTrouble: I know everything about your girls. You told me.

My hands freeze over the keyboard.

Which one is your favourite today? She writes, goading me.

> MotherOfTwins: You're fucking insane.
>
> TwoIsTrouble: I think Lara. It's usually Lara, isn't it?

Seeing my daughter's name typed by her feels like a threat and I suppress a cry.

> MotherOfTwins: Leave me alone. This has gone far enough. I'm going to tell the police.
>
> TwoIsTrouble: Tell them what?
>
> MotherOfTwins: That you're harassing me.

She doesn't reply and I stare at the screen, begging for some sort of reaction.

> TwoIsTrouble: You're not going to tell anyone. You can't even tell Mark.

I don't know what to reply; all too aware that she's right.

> TwoIsTrouble: I'm doing this for them, Emily. They aren't safe with you. Mark knows it, so do you.

I shake my head and tell myself she's wrong. The girls are meant to be with me.

> MotherOfTwins: Mark doesn't know anything, he's only taken them because he thinks it's what I want.
>
> TwoIsTrouble: Taken them? What do you mean? Taken them where?

I curse myself for once again letting this stranger know the details of my life. She's always been able to trick me into telling her things I don't mean to.

> TwoIsTrouble: See, Emily. I was right. Mark knows you can't be trusted. He knows you're going to hurt those girls. Just like you hurt Beth.

I slam the laptop shut and scream into the empty kitchen.

Twenty-Eight

Then

Help me

It's easy to write it down and shout into the void. I feel like screaming it every second of every day. To the girls. To my husband. To strangers on the street as they pass me.

HELP ME.

Can't anyone see I'm drowning? Everyone says the first step to getting help is asking for help but what if you're asking and you're asking and you're asking but no one hears you?

I don't know how much longer I can take this.

Twenty-Nine

Now

I wake up with a start, unsure of what's pulled me from my sleep. I wipe saliva from the side of my face, too tired to even be ashamed of myself. I root around the sofa for my phone. It's light outside but I have no idea what time it is. After that message from TwoIsTrouble, I poured myself a large glass of wine and must have passed out on the sofa. The realisation that I've done what I saw my own mum do countless times before hits me with such force that I think I'm imagining the banging at the door at first. But then I hear the sound of Mark's mum's voice drifting through the letter box.

'Emily?' she calls. 'Emily, are you there?'

I sit upright and rub my eyes. Finally, my hands find my phone and I light up the screen. Eight a.m. What is she doing here?

'I'm coming,' I call through, though I've no idea if she'll hear me.

I grab the half-drunk bottle of wine from the coffee table and dart through to the kitchen where I hide it back in the fridge. Smoothing down my rumpled clothes, I walk through the hall and open the door.

'Oh, thank goodness,' Joanne says when she sees me.

'Joanne, what are you doing here?' I look down the street behind her as if Mark and the girls might be waiting to come back home. No one is there. A flicker of pain resonates in the pit of my stomach but I squash it down.

'Can I come in?' she asks. I nod and open the door wider for her to follow me through to the kitchen. I stand awkwardly beside the island as she takes a seat and looks up at me with a weary smile. 'Are you okay?'

I smile tightly and tell her I'm fine before asking again what she's doing here.

She frowns, as if her appearance should be obvious to me. 'Emily, what on earth is going on?'

I clear my throat and offer her a cup of tea.

'Mark should be here with you; they shouldn't be hiding out at my house! This is all ridiculous.' Two bright pink spots appear on her cheeks and I think this is the first time I've ever seen Joanne truly angry.

I sigh. 'It's better for them,' I tell her.

She tuts. 'Utter nonsense. I said the same to Mark. You're both acting like you're some sort of danger to those girls!'

I flinch.

'Emily.' Joanne stands and reaches for me. 'Come on, darling. You don't honestly believe that you're anything but a wonderful mother, surely?'

My eyes cloud with tears as I shake my head. 'I'm not. You don't know everything.'

'I know enough. I couldn't believe it when Mark turned up yesterday, like he was fleeing some sort of warzone! Ridiculous, totally ridiculous. He told me you'd made him promise that he'd take the girls away if there was any sign of you becoming ill. Is that true?'

I nod and look down at the floor beneath me, focusing on a spill that should have been wiped up yesterday. Perhaps I could get a mop and do it now, or would that only make me look more insane to Mark's mum?

'Honestly, I could kill that blooming son of mine. He shouldn't be entertaining this. You are not ill, Emily. You are not a bad mother. Do you hear me?'

I shake my head. I do not deserve her kindness. Would she still be here if she ever saw all the stories I've told about her online? How I've mocked her fussing over the girls, complained how her love suffocates me? Of course she wouldn't. No one would stay if they knew. There's only ever been one person who saw the true ugliness inside me, and they're gone.

'Come on, let's go and sit down and talk about this properly. It's time to face this head-on.'

I follow her lead as she marches into the living room. I wish for a moment that I could ever be as sure of myself as she is; that I could possess the type of certainty a mother needs.

'Mark told me you'd been to see the doctor again,' Joanne says when we finally settle into our places on separate couches.

I nod.

'And that she put you on some new medication.'

'Not new; she's put me back on what I was taking before.'

'Well, that's okay, isn't it? She's got you on the right track. There's no need for Mark and the girls to leave you here all alone.'

'There is,' I tell her. 'It's better if I sort this on my own.'

She tuts and tells me to stop being so ridiculous. 'Emily, you're struggling a little bit, that's all. There's no reason to exile yourself from your family like this. The girls need you, they need their mum.'

I start to cry as I hug the pillow in front of me. 'They need a proper mum, a normal, healthy one. Not me.'

'You're perfectly normal, perfectly healthy. The idea that you're not is utterly ridiculous. I told Mark so, too.'

We sit for a moment saying nothing, the noise of the passing traffic outside a vague reminder that life goes on as normal, despite us.

'He doesn't blame you, you know.' Joanne says this quietly, her eyes flitting between the window and me, not quite holding my stare long enough to make the words meaningful.

'He does. He should.'

She sighs and gets up from her sofa and comes across to mine. She sits so close I can smell the fresh scent of lavender laundry detergent and see the smudge of lipstick that has escaped into the wrinkles of her upper lip.

'Emily, honestly. What will we do with you?' She takes my hands and tuts. 'What happened… The accident. It was not your fault.'

I bite my lip and force my eyes to hold hers. We never talk about this. 'What happened' is only ever referred to like that. The 'incident'. The 'accident'. The thing we all want to forget.

'You weren't well, Emily. We all know that now. Mark knew it then. What happened could have happened to any of us. And the girls are fine. Really, aren't they? Everyone survived.' Joanna takes a sharp intake of breath, as if realising her mistake too late.

I think of the girls; their beautiful smooth skin, their blonde curly hair, their fresh indescribable deliciously perfect smell. And then I think of how they looked after the accident.

Their faces cut. Glass speckled in their perfect cheeks. Their hair flecked with fresh red blood. The smell of petrol and pain and fear embedded into their very essence. They weren't *fine*.

And not of all of us survived.

We went out as four that day and came back as three.

Mark and I had argued the night before. He'd reached the point where he was almost sick of me, I think now, looking back. He walked around as if the weight of carrying my unhappiness was just too much for him. I was trying; I was seeing Dr Aldred and taking my pills but every day I was logging onto MumsOnline and spending hours and hours talking to TwoIsTrouble and the other women about my life; their lives. Sharing and supposedly halving our troubles by doing so. But it just made me so angry. Angry at him, at the world, at everything. It didn't make sense to me that mothers were all so fucking unhappy and that no one seemed to care.

When my pregnancy test had come back positive a few weeks before, Mark was ecstatic. *Of course he would be*, I remember writing online later that night, *he's not the one who's got to deal with all of this again*. I tried not to show him that I was unsure about having another baby; tried my best to hide the terror of it all behind tight smiles and tighter assurances. But he knew. Of course he knew. That night, he finally confronted me.

'Do you even want this baby?' he snapped as I dragged my eyes from my phone for the first time all evening. I started to reply, to trot out the lie, but he saw the look on my face as I saw the heartbreak in his and, just like that, he knew the truth.

The morning after, I woke up feeling groggy; a hangover from tears late at night that nothing seemed to fix. The girls were needy – tetchy from seeing my bloated, tear-stained face no doubt – and Mark had left for work early without saying goodbye. When I went to take my three usual pills from Dr Aldred, something in my head told me if I doubled up just for that day, took six instead, that I'd feel better. That it would perk me up enough to get through things.

I don't know if the extra pills were what made the bleeding start. The internet has not been able to tell me and I've never been brave enough to ask the doctors, or anyone else. *Unfortunately, it's just one of those things*, they would tell me after. But I think I know deep down that it was; that I caused it. The worst thing was, the moment I saw the thick red clots on the tissue, that's the moment I knew I had been wrong. I *did* want my baby. I wanted them more than anything.

When I couldn't get hold of Mark, I bundled the girls into the car without a second thought, then floored it towards the hospital. I thought I'd strapped them properly into their car seats. I should have checked; I should have stopped. When I realised the double dose of pills was making me dizzy instead of perky, making my reactions too slow, I could have pulled over. But I didn't because I knew my baby was leaving me, having realised I was unfit to be their mother, and I desperately wanted the doctors to make it stop. To make them stay. But I should have never been driving in the first place. It was my fault that I lost our baby; my fault that I hurt our girls. No one knows that. Mark thinks, everyone thinks, I was so tormented by the miscarriage that I wasn't concentrating as I drove and that's why we crashed. How could I tell him the truth?

Risk them knowing that I not only caused my baby to die inside me but that I willingly put the girls in danger too? So I told no one. Except TwoIsTrouble, of course. She knows everything.

'Do you know what Mark told me after the accident?' Joanne says, cutting through my memories.

I shake my head.

'That he blamed himself.' Her cheeks colour and she gives me a sad smile.

'What? Why would he?'

'Because he thought he should have done a better job of looking after you. He knew you were suffering, and he said he still got angry at you about not being excited about the pregnancy.'

I look away and sigh. 'It wasn't his fault.'

'It wasn't your fault either. But both of you need to talk, Emily. You sitting here all alone still feeling guilty about what happened while he hides out at my house feeling just as bad?' She tuts loudly. 'It's ridiculous.'

The idea that Mark also blames himself for the accident makes me sag into the sofa. After it happened, once we knew the girls were okay – physically, at least – all I could think about was how much he was going to hate me. I never considered for a moment that he'd also hate himself. When he suggested moving house, not far, but far enough that I wouldn't have to face the concerned looks of the neighbours every morning or the empty room which he'd ear-marked for a nursery, I thought it was because he wanted to get away from my bad reputation. But maybe he also felt he had to run from his own.

We are not bad parents.

The thought hits me with such intensity that I actually laugh.

'Oh god,' I slap my hand over my mouth and apologise to Joanne. 'I'm sorry. I just… Hearing that Mark blames himself, it's just made me realise how awful this whole thing is. The accident, the car crash, the miscarriage,' I finally name it for what it is. 'It's been eating away at both of us, terrified that we're to blame, and you're right. We still have each other; we still have the girls. I hate that they were ever in that situation to begin with, that I put them in that situation. But it could have been so much worse.'

Joanne smiles and nods. 'Exactly. That's exactly what I told Mark. The miscarriage was awful, of course, but the doctors said it was probably already over by the time you crashed. You didn't cause it, Emily. And you'd never, ever put those girls in danger, I know you wouldn't. He knows you wouldn't. The only person left still doubting it, is you.'

I try to let her words sink in. Perhaps she's right.

'After all,' she adds. 'It could have been worse. It was early days, wasn't it? So much worse to lose a child later on.'

This breaks me. And I sob.

'Gosh, Emily. I'm sorry, that's… oh dear. I didn't mean that your baby wasn't important. I just meant, well it could have been worse, couldn't it?'

I want to tell her. I want to tell her so badly.

Yes, it could have been worse. At least this time the loss was only inside me.

This time.

I can't just forget that I've lied to Mark, not just about this, but about everything. He might forgive me for the pills, perhaps. He might forgive me for lying about it for a year. But if he knew the truth about what happened to Bethany, how could he see anything but what I see? A pattern of behaviour; a pattern of destruction. Blame and guilt anchor my body to the sofa as I allow myself to think of her. Why did I have to say her name to TwoIsTrouble? If I'd just confessed the truth about the pills and the accident and not brought the past into it, I might be able to get through this. But I'm trapped; I've trapped myself. She must have put it all together, what happened one year ago and what happened to Bethany. It's all connected. Mark won't forgive me. How can he, when I can never forgive myself?

A sob chokes me.

'Emily, please, come on.' I hear Joanne's words through my cries and feel her hand rubbing my back. 'It's okay. Everything is okay. Honestly, don't get yourself so worked up about it. Everyone's fine. Mark will see sense and come back with your girls, I'll make sure of it.'

I concentrate on levelling my breathing, stopping the sobs.

'You really don't think he believes that it was my fault?'

Her eyes widen and she shakes her head. 'Trust me Emily, no one thinks any of it is your fault. We all know how much you love your girls and what a good mother you are.' She pauses and takes in a little breath. 'I think it's much harder on your generation, you know. The expectations of motherhood are so high now. When I had Mark, I was warned about the "baby blues", as we used to call them. No one expected maternity leave to be fun, but your generation is supposed to not only rear perfect children but keep up a perfect life at the same time.' She shakes her head. 'There's no one way to be a good mother, Emily. But you don't have to be perfect, to never make any mistakes in your life, to be one. If the world judged women less harshly, perhaps you'd be able to see that on your own.' Tears spring to my eyes and Joanne takes hold of my hand. 'Honestly, anyone who thinks you could be capable of hurting your girls – or anyone else, for that matter – must be totally and utterly insane.'

She smiles and I return it weakly, but her words whir in my head.

Because I know for certain that two people believe me capable of hurting a child. One of them is already dead.

Now it's time to find the other.

Thirty

Two Is Trouble

Everyone thinks they know Emily Jones.

A mother of beautiful twins. A wife to a perfect husband.

None of them know the real you, do they, Emily?

None of them know what you've done.

What you'll do again if I don't stop you.

When I first found out the truth about what you did to Beth, I didn't want to believe it. Why would I? No one wants to believe they know someone capable of something so disgusting. So inhumane.

Murder.

What does it feel like when you hear that word, Emily? There was a time to me when all it conjured up was cartoon villains, boogie men in the dark.

Murder. It's not a word I used often because it sounds so very dramatic, doesn't it? Murders don't happen to normal people, in normal kitchens of normal families. And if they do, you know about it. Right? Everyone knows when a nice, normal family has their life ripped apart like that.

Not here.

No one seemed to notice that Emily Jones was a murderer. Or perhaps no one cared.

No one except me.

But I'm not going to let you get away with it for a moment longer. Everything is coming together now. I've waited so long to make you pay, and I can wait a little longer.

It isn't for me; I need you to understand that. This isn't some sort of revenge.

What I'm doing is for those girls. How can I live with myself, knowing I didn't do everything in my power to protect them? Now that I know the truth about what you did to Beth, I have to act. I have to save the girls. I won't let anyone else lose their life because of you.

Thirty-One

Now

Joanne leaves soon after that, once I've promised her I'll get in touch with Mark. It's still only midday, so there's no point in phoning him now, he'll be at work and we won't be able to have a proper conversation. Joanne offered to take me back to hers so I could spend the afternoon with the girls but I told her I needed time to sort my head out before seeing them. I think she was disappointed. In her mind she's solved the problem; she's talked some sense into me and so now Mark can come home and we can go on and be happy. But the problem remains: TwoIsTrouble. I think of all the things I've said to her about Joanne, the unkind picture I've painted of my mother-in-law who has done nothing but love me and I hate myself for it. Even now, Joanne is on my side.

But she doesn't understand the whole situation. While Joanne might claim that Mark doesn't blame me for the car crash, if he finds out about what really happened that day plus the truth about Beth then I'm sure that he will. How could he not? One "accident" is careless. Two is something else. But I can control this. It's all about the messaging, just like PR. The facts can remain the same but if I wrap it up in a more acceptable message, the outcome will be different.

TwoIsTrouble will have her version of the truth; the version I let slip one night after too many glasses of wine when I was feeling so sorry for myself, so much hatred for myself, that I could barely see. We never talked about my admission again, and I hoped that in some way she'd forgotten but clearly she hadn't. She knows Beth's name. But is that all she knows? What if my confession led to more… what if she went digging? She might have let one accident go, even knowing what she knew. But what would she have thought if she found out about the other one? Heat prickles the back of my neck. She'd have thought I was a monster. The truth about myself that I've always feared.

In our bedroom, I open my laptop and log back into MumsOnline to pull up our DMs. I haven't even looked back at exactly what I told her that night, but now I need to. To be sure that I didn't say more than I remember.

It takes me over ten minutes to scroll all the way back to the admission and my skin feels hot with shame as my eyes take in the words that led us there.

> TwoIsTrouble: How ru feeling today?
>
> MotherOfTwins: Crap.
>
> TwoIsTrouble: has something happened?
>
> MotherOfTwins: no. Nothing new. How are you?
>
> TwoIsTrouble: oh, you know me. Same old! What's going on?
>
> MotherOfTwins: I'm just so tired. Do you ever feel so tired you just want to stop the whole world so you can crawl away and hide?
>
> TwoIsTrouble: LOL yes, every day. Think it's called being a mum!

MotherOfTwins: Maybe

TwoIsTrouble: give yourself a break. You've been through a lot

MotherOfTwins: mostly my own doing

TwoIsTrouble: not really??

TwoIsTrouble: your mum dying wasn't your fault

TwoIsTrouble: the crash wasn't your fault. the miscarriage wasn't your fault

MotherOfTwins: I'm not sure that's true

TwoIsTrouble: come on, it's not like you made the crash happen!

MotherOfTwins: no. I know but still…

TwoIsTrouble: do you still think your DH blames you?

MotherOfTwins: he must. I blame me.

TwoIsTrouble: babe, if he blames you than he's a dik. Honestly you need someone who supports you more. He shouldn't let you feel like this!

MotherOfTwins: but what if he's right?

TwoIsTrouble: right about what?!

MotherOfTwins: that I'm a bad mum. A bad person

TwoIsTrouble: is that what he says?

MotherOfTwins: no. But I know he thinks it. Because I think it too

TwoIsTrouble: ur not a bad person

TwoIsTrouble: ur a great person who bad things have happened to

MotherOfTwins: what if it was my fault?

TwoIsTrouble: what do you mean

MotherOfTwins: if the miscarriage was my fault, if I had done it on purpose. Would you still say that about me then?

TwoIsTrouble: Babe, what are you saying?

TwoIsTrouble: are you there

TwoIsTrouble: you can tell me anything you know

TwoIsTrouble: no matter what you've done, I'll always be here

MotherOfTwins: I took too many pills

TwoIsTrouble: What?? Are you okay? Call an ambulance NOW

MotherOfTwins: no, not now. Before I drove

MotherOfTwins: That's why the bleeding started. I know it is. It's why I was driving like that – I was desperate to get to the hospital but I couldn't see properly. I shouldn't have been driving

TwoIsTrouble: Oh, babe. Why didn't you tell me before?

MotherOfTwins: No one knows. No one can ever know. Mark would never forgive me. It's all my fault

TwoIsTrouble: It's not. You were ill you didn't know that the pills would do that did you? It's not like you took them on purpose to get rid of the baby???

TwoIsTrouble: babe this isn't ur fault. you'd never hurt your baby like that – or the girls – would you?

MotherOfTwins: it wasn't the first time someone got hurt because of me. Someone I loved

TwoIsTrouble: okay…

MotherOfTwins: what if it's not just a coincidence that bad things happen when I'm around?

TwoIsTrouble: what do you mean? What else happened?

MotherOfTwins: it was my fault

TwoIsTrouble: what was?

MotherOfTwins: how do you know if something is an accident or if you've done it on purpose

TwoIsTrouble: ???

TwoIsTrouble: babe, talk to me

MotherOfTwins: what happened to Bethany was my fault. She always said it was and now I think she's right. This is history repeating itself

MotherOfTwins: If they knew what really happened to her, they'd never let me be a mother.

TwoIsTrouble: what do you mean? Who's Bethany? Is that what you were going to call the baby?

TwoIsTrouble: are you there? What's going on?

MotherOfTwins is offline.

–

I slam the laptop lid shut after I read it, my face burning with shame and disgust. The morning after my online confession, I remember waking up and feeling so sick Mark thought I was actually unwell. But it wasn't a bug that had turned my stomach, it was fear. I'd told a total stranger the worst thing about me, and there was nothing I could do to take it back. Instead, I told her that I'd had too much to drink the night before and to ignore any of my ramblings. We never spoke of it again and I blocked it from my mind. But I never forgot it; I'd wake sometimes in the middle of the night in a cold sweat thinking of what I'd done. It's why I became determined to wean myself off MumsOnline; off TwoIsTrouble. I never imagined for a minute that she'd discover who I was and use my admission against me. I hoped, stupidly fooled myself into believing, that she might have forgotten about it. Until she brought it up again and I knew I had to leave the site for good. All this time, I've been so terrified that she'll tell Mark what I said. But perhaps his mum is right – no sane person would ever believe I was capable of harming someone I loved. So, if I can just show TwoIsTrouble for what she really is – a mad stalker with a dangerous obsession with me – it won't matter what she knows. Or says she knows. No one will believe her anyway.

This whole time she's been playing a game, wearing me down to make me look so insane that when she finally does the big reveal – tying together my role in the accident and what happened to Beth – no one will doubt it. And I've helped her, every step of the way. I've lied to Mark, to my sister, to Mark's mum, everyone. It's too late now to tell them the truth about the note she sent, the messages, the presentation. I need new proof. I need to get her to do something else, but this time I'm going to be ready for it and Mark will be there to see just who the insane one really is.

I open my laptop again and brace myself to go back to MumsOnline. I need to draw her out, to get her to do something that shows everyone what she's doing to me. I look for our most recent messages, but they're gone. What the hell? In place of our conversation is the words '*Message history is temporarily unavailable'*. Our whole history is gone. I reload the page a few times, as if it might just reappear. But nothing. The chirpy, *start your conversation* generic messaging hovers by her name, urging me to write to her. Has she somehow managed to delete our entire message history? And if she has, why? Surely that's the one thing she has over me. Hundreds of words of incriminating evidence against me. Proof that I am a bad mother. A danger to the girls. Sweat pools on my upper lip as I continue to stare at the blank screen. I type.

> Why have you deleted everything? What do you want from me?

> ERROR: Message to user TwoIsTrouble cannot be sent. They may have changed their security settings or deleted their account!

This cannot be happening. I click around the site in desperation, as if her profile might magically reinstate the more I bash at the tracker pad.

There has to be another way to get to her. Suddenly, it hits me.

When she said she knew what I'd done to Beth, she didn't call her 'Bethany', the name she'd have found if she'd searched the newspapers, or public records to find out what happened. She called her by the nickname used only by those that knew her.

Beth.

A twinge of fear surges through me. Is it a coincidence? Did she simply shorten her name automatically? Or is TwoIsTrouble more connected to my family than I've ever considered?

I'm still considering this further clue an hour later when my phone rings.

'Hi Allie,' I say, seeing my sister's name on the screen.

'Hi. Everything okay?'

'Yes, sorry I was short with you yesterday.'

'That's okay. Is everything all right?'

'Yes… I'm glad you called actually. I've been thinking about what you said the other day. About Beth—'

I hear her sharp intake of breath.

'Could you come over?' I ask. 'I'd like to talk in person.'

'Now? I'm working. Aren't you?'

'Oh,' I say, looking at the time. 'Yes, of course. I didn't think. What about after work?'

'I would but my car's got a flat tyre. It's getting replaced tomorrow. Why don't you come here?'

'No. I can't…'

'Come on, Emily. You never come here. It'll be nice, I'll cook us dinner. Please?'

I sigh. There's no reason I can give to say no and she's right; I avoid my childhood home as much as I possibly can. It's where all my bad memories live. But perhaps that's exactly why I should go; the conversation I need to have with Allie is going to be uncomfortable anyway, why not get everything out of the way in one go?

'Okay,' I tell her and she lets out a little squeal of excitement that makes me smile, despite everything.

We arrange to meet at the house at five thirty, which gives me a few hours to kill. I text Mark to tell him I'll call him later and that I really want us to talk. He replies back instantly.

Yes, let's talk. I love you too. Always xxx

I clutch the phone to my chest and remind myself that no matter what happens, I can trust Mark to never let me down.

Thirty-Two

Two Is Trouble

I saw Mark today. He really is something special, don't you think? There's a quiet, rugged handsomeness that oozes from him that I'd never noticed before. He's always seemed so very put together. Boring, if I'm honest. You called him that once to me before, do you remember? It's not the worst thing you called him, of course. Useless. Stupid. Selfish. *A total fucking idiot* once, after he'd failed to load the dishwasher properly. I really had to bite my tongue over that one. You really are such a spoiled bitch.

You were wrong about him, anyway. Those women on MumsOnline would kill for a man like Mark. Your petty complaints about him were always grating when I'd compare them to the other threads and read about women being cheated on, hit, ignored, degraded by their husbands on a daily basis, and yet here you were with everything anyone could ever want and you still weren't happy.

We both know why.

It's hard to be happy when you're living with a secret like yours, isn't it? I thought you might come to that conclusion yourself eventually; that you'd see the root of your unhappiness wasn't the girls, or Mark, the unwanted pregnancy, or even me, but yourself. You were making yourself ill, Emily, by not telling the truth. You've been making yourself ill for years.

Mark agrees.

We've talked about it a few times now, usually over the phone but today was special because this time I saw something in his reaction to me that I hadn't ever seen before. Longing.

Yes, Emily. I hate to tell you but your loyal, lovely Mark looked at me with fuck-me eyes.

Who'd have thought it?

Men really are quite simple creatures when it comes down to it. All I had to do was dress myself up a little, wear a top that hugged my tits just a tiny bit, and that was it. Nothing happened. Not today. I didn't need it to.

We talked about you. About how worried he was. About what he might do now.

Emily.

I have to tell you something.

I'm going to take him from you. I only ever wanted the girls. But this seems too good to resist.

I wanted to keep them safe, but now I want him too.

Mostly, I want you to end up like I have: sad, alone, and destroyed.

Nothing more than you deserve.

Thirty-Three

Now

I slow the car to a crawl; the village hasn't changed at all over the years. The pub that looks like something straight from an English postcard still draws a small crowd to the front; they sit at the dark wooden tables with pints of beer enjoying the afternoon sunshine. I quickly scan the faces as I drive past, but don't recognise anyone. I keep driving, past the village shop which has had a makeover but still proudly displays Mrs Cranch's name over the door. It can't be the same Mrs Cranch though, surely? She must have been in her seventies when I was a child; we'd walk from the house into the village in summer just to get sweets from her shop, the only place that still did them in a white paper bag for a penny a sweet.

My stomach churns as I picture Beth coming out of the shop hand-in-hand with Allie, her face aching with a broad smile, so happy with her sweet selection.

I keep driving, my eyes glued to the road. I don't want to be flooded with memories like this. I'm not here for that; I'm here to talk to Allie and find out what, if anything, she knows about TwoIsTrouble.

The house, our house, comes into view a few minutes later. I pull up on the side of the lane and take a moment to catch my breath. I've not been here for a few years, but seeing it again, it feels like only days since I left. The huge dark green ferns still surround the house, blocking our lives from the view of any passing walkers. It makes it look so dark, so hidden. Which, I suppose, was the point. But how does Allie still live like this? She should be in a city somewhere, surrounded by people her own age, not hidden away in our dead mum's house like a recluse. She used to be so outgoing, chatting to everyone whether they wanted to listen or not, but after Beth died, everything about her changed. I guess I never let myself think about her part in this very much, but now that I do, I realise that it wasn't just my life that stopped that day: Allie's did, too.

I sit in the car for a moment and allow myself to look across the lane to Mrs Green's house. It's not her house any more, she died over five years ago, but seeing it still makes my stomach twist. The family who've moved in since have chopped back her prized rose bushes and installed a trampoline in the front garden. She'd be appalled. I smile as I think of her pursing her wrinkled lips and shaking her head. *A trampoline? In the garden? Whatever next*, she'd say.

Eventually, I drag myself from the car and walk up the path towards my old front door. The plants are untamed as ever; dandelions sprawl throughout the unmowed grass which shoots up like a jungle. When my stepdad Lewis lived with us, he hired a gardener to manage things but after he left, I guess he stopped paying them so they stopped coming, along with the cleaner. I don't blame him for leaving, with my mum the way she was it was hardly a surprise, but I do wonder how things may have turned out if he'd stayed and got Mum some help that wasn't solely focused on making things aesthetically pleasing. But he wasn't that sort of man – still isn't, by the sounds of the brief details I glean occasionally from Allie. He didn't even move that far away after he left, a few miles down the road, with his new girlfriend, now wife. But he may as well have left the country for all we saw of him after that. He wasn't my dad, and I can't say we ever had the sort of relationship where anyone would mistake him for it and I don't think he's a particularly relevant figure in Allie's life either, even now.

'Emily!' I jump as Allie calls my name from the front door. 'You're here.' She smiles widely and I'm reminded of just how pretty she can be as her blonde hair blows in the wind. I tuck my own dark strands behind my ear, feeling uncharacteristically aware of my appearance. 'Come in.' She opens the door wide and ushers me through to the dark hallway.

I'm hit at once by the smell of home; an indistinguishable mix of damp, woodsmoke and newspaper. Mum would always have newspapers all around the house; I don't know why because I don't remember ever seeing her actually reading them, but her fingertips were often darkened by the smudge of ink from the pages so she must have. Her absence in the hallway hits me with force and I'm surprised at the wave of grief.

'It's weird without her, isn't it?' Allie says. I nod. 'Sometimes I pretend she's still here.'

I must look worried because she laughs. 'Not like that, I know she's gone. But it gets so lonely in the house that sometimes I chat to her. Not properly, I know she can't reply. I haven't lost it, don't worry,' she tells me with a smile. 'Coffee?'

We move into the kitchen and I drag one of the old oak dining chairs from beneath the table across the brown tiled floor to sit. 'Tea, please,' I say and Allie nods and turns her back on me to boil the kettle.

The kitchen has barely changed at all. It's quite eerie and I remind myself that I'm an adult now; this house holds no power over me.

'How was work?' I ask once Allie places a mug of tea down and sits across from me.

'Oh, fine. Same old.'

I smile and nod, unsure of what to say next. The fact that I know nothing about Allie's job, so little that I can't even think of a suitable follow-up question, only highlights the bizarreness of me being here at all.

'It's weird, isn't it?' she says before taking a sip of her tea.

'What is?'

'This. Us. You being here. It's just… weird.'

I avoid her gaze and sigh. 'Yeah, it really is. I just find it so hard being back in the house… You know?'

We fall into an awkward silence as we sip our tea; mine is so hot that it burns my tongue but I swallow anyway, desperate for something to do. Where has the easy manner we found at the restaurant last weekend disappeared to? It's like the house has stripped us of the ability to pretend we're anything other than strangers to each other. But we're not, not really; we're family. Allie knew Beth, loved her; she's one of the only people who can really understand.

'Look, this is going to seem a bit out of the blue. But the reason I wanted to see you today was to talk—'

'About Beth?'

I nod.

She smiles sadly. 'I thought so. Ever since I brought her up yesterday I've been waiting for you to call.'

'Why?'

She shrugs. 'You never talk about her, but then nor do I. Not to you. Mum and I talked about her all the time.' She smiles at the memory but then her face clouds. 'But with you… I don't know, it's always just felt like you wanted to forget she ever existed.'

Her words sting and I shake my head. 'That's not how I feel at all. Jesus, Allie, do you really believe I don't think about her? I think about her all the time. I always have.'

'Then why don't you ever talk about her? Do you and Mark ever—'

'Of course we do!' I lie. 'It's not like I want to pretend she never existed. I loved her! She was my…' I trail off, a lump in my throat stopping the words.

Allie nods and looks down. 'I know. I didn't mean… I just, I guess I never felt you missed her like I did.'

A familiar rage burns inside me; Allie always felt more entitled to her grief than anyone and it just made me hate her for it. I was the one who deserved to feel Beth's loss like a puncture. I lost everything the day she died.

'I couldn't just fall apart when she… I had to look after—'

Her head shoots up. 'But you didn't fall apart at all. It wasn't normal to just go on as if nothing happened.'

I wave my hand like it doesn't matter, but my cheeks burn. 'Sometimes it's easier to pretend. It's the only way to get through it.'

'Not all of us can do that.'

I bite my lip. 'I know.'

'Mum fell apart. You barely seemed to care about her in all of this.'

'How could I care about her? I was trying to make sure the rest of us survived it!' I shout, the words bubbling up before I can swallow them. 'Mum never cared how I felt.

She should have been there for me. I was broken after Beth died, she knew I was, but all she cared about was herself.'

Allie clenches her jaw and drums her fingers against the table. 'She just couldn't cope.'

'She could cope, Allie. She just didn't want to cope with *me*.'

The truth sits between us like something ugly and unspoken. After Beth died, our mum could barely tolerate being near me. There was no space for my grief in this house. Allie will never truly understand why. That was a secret only my mother and I shared.

Silence fills the kitchen as neither of us know what to say. We never talk like this; the past is consigned to the past, where it belongs. My eyes fall to the kitchen window, into the garden where dusk is setting in. You can see the tall reeds that line the pond from here and I shudder at the thought of the dark waters they hide.

We moved to this house not long before Mum and Lewis got married. We'd been perfectly happy in our little flat above the precinct – at least, I had – but of course it wasn't big enough for the three of us, and nothing like the sort of place a man like Lewis would live even if it were. I can still remember my mum telling me we were going to move. Lewis came over one night with a pizza in a takeaway box. The smell of pepperoni still reminds me of him though I'm pretty sure that was the only occasion he ever brought me pizza. It wasn't really his style.

When he told us about the house we were going to move to, I had no idea it was going to be so grand. He talked about the massive garden I'd be able to play in, so different from being stuck in the flat with no outside space. He'd mention *the pond*, and the name's always stuck, though what this house really has is a lake. It's big enough to swim in, though I'm sure no one ever does any more. I remember when we first moved in on a sticky weekend in July; even though I was trying so hard to be angry at Mum for making us move, I couldn't help myself from squealing with excitement when I saw the pond. It was like something from a book; the little paddleboat moored up on the jetty just begging to be taken out. Mum wasn't as happy.

'Lewis, is that safe?' she asked, twisting her cotton dress in her hands.

He frowned and pulled her hands away before tutting at the creases she'd made in the fabric. 'Of course it's safe. Why wouldn't it be?'

'What if she falls in?' my mum said, eyes glancing over the pond as if the water might rear up and take me under any second.

'Don't be ridiculous. I grew up here. It's perfectly safe. Just tell her not to be stupid, and there won't be any problem.' The last line was delivered to me, Lewis's thick brown eyebrows raised as if daring me to disagree.

I was always surprised that he gave the house to Mum in the divorce; it had been in his family for decades. But I suppose he just wanted a clean slate after what happened. To move on without the ties to the past. Sometimes I wish he'd taken it from her; perhaps then she would have been forced to move on, literally and emotionally, and taken Allie with her.

I study my sister from across the table. She smiles back as if she knows what I'm thinking and wants to prove me wrong. It's a smile that says, 'I'm fine. Don't worry. I'm coping.' But I recognise that smile; it's the one I see every day in the mirror, the one I plaster on before I leave the house each day.

'You should talk to someone about what happened, Emily.'

I shake my head involuntarily and she tuts.

'You should,' she says again. 'It… it helps.'

'You talk to people about it?' I snap.

Her cheeks blush and she instantly drops her gaze. She shrugs and slides her coffee cup closer to her. 'Not really… Well, sometimes.'

'Who? Who do you talk to?'

'Mum told you, didn't she?' Her eyes shoot up but this time they're defiant. 'I asked her not to.'

I frown. 'No. Told me what?'

Allie cocks her head and purses her lips as if deciding if I'm lying. 'I go to a grief group. Okay?'

I grit my teeth. Of course she does.

'Why wouldn't you want me to know that?'

She throws her hands up. 'I don't know. I don't know what will set you off.'

'What do you mean?'

'You're so strange about it, Emily. You always have been; you've never wanted to talk about Beth and if any of us do it's like we're weak or something. But I can't be like you, I can't just shut my feelings away.'

'That's what you think I do?'

She sighs. 'Isn't it?'

I sit back in my chair and bite my lip. Outside, rain starts to patter against the windows and I close my eyes and listen to the sound as I feel my walls coming down. When I open them again, Allie has her arms crossed against her chest and her bottom lip pushed out; something about the sight of her looking so much like her younger self makes me smile, melting my rage to an embarrassing pool.

'What? Why are you smiling?'

'You just look so much like you used to,' I say. 'So stroppy.'

She laughs and the tension is broken.

'I think it's great you're going to a grief group.'

She raises her eyebrows.

'No, honestly. I really do.'

'It helps. You should try it.'

I nod, though I know there's nothing anyone could do to get me to go to something like that. The idea of ripping open my chest and baring all makes me shudder.

'Where is it?' I eventually ask to fill the silence.

She tells me the name of a town a few miles away. 'Charlbury town hall. I wanted it to be out of the village, I didn't want to see people we knew.'

'What do you talk about?'

She waves her hand and looks out to the garden. 'I don't know. Just... Everything, I guess. It's good to have strangers to confide in. Do you know what I mean?'

Something about the way she says it makes the hairs on the back of my neck stand up, because I know exactly what she means.

'Do you talk about me?'

She bites her lip like she used to when we were kids and I'd found her doing something she wasn't supposed to. 'I talk about a lot of things.'

'Me?'

She nods and looks away.

'Allie, you know I don't like people knowing my business.'

'It's fine, honestly. The whole group operates on a mutual understanding – what's said in group goes no further. That's why we can all be so open. Everyone knows each other's secrets.'

Just like MumsOnline.

'You should be careful. Sometimes strangers can be the worst people to confide in.'

She rolls her eyes. 'Oh, I know that. There was this one woman who came for a bit and…'

'What? What happened?'

'It doesn't matter; she stopped coming. Things got a bit weird.'

My ears prick up. 'When?'

She shrugs. 'A few weeks ago. I don't know what happened really.' Allie shifts uncomfortably in her seat. 'We got really close, I thought she was going to become a proper friend but then… I don't know. Sometimes I think the way Beth died makes it hard for people to sympathise with us. Do you know what I mean?' Allie looks down and my heart aches for her. I wish I could tell her how much I know that feeling.

'Did you tell her a lot about Beth? About us?'

She nods. 'Yes,' she says. 'I told her everything.'

'Everything? What do you mean, everything?'

Allie shakes her head and sighs, still keeping her eyes glued to the floor. 'You know, just what happened and what it was like after.'

'What do you mean by "things got a bit weird" with this woman? What was her name?'

Allie looks up and narrows her eyes. 'We're not really supposed to talk about the other people who go there.'

'What, so you can't even tell me her name?'

'Vicky. Her name's Vicky. She just got a bit clingy, I don't know how to explain it. We would WhatsApp between the meetings, we started sending voice notes 'cause it took so long to type but she would leave me these ten-minute ones, really intense and I wouldn't always respond...'

'When was this?'

She puffs her lips as if trying to remember the exact date. 'I don't know. I met her about a year ago, I guess? The messages were more recent, maybe six months or so?'

'Why didn't you respond to her?'

Allie shrugs. 'It got a bit weird. She'd lost a daughter.' Allie's eyes flick up and she bites her lip, either worried at the reaction this will get from me or guilty at spilling this woman's secrets. 'She used to leave these long rants about how so many women didn't deserve to be mothers and she wished she could do something about it.' Allie pauses and frowns. 'I know it was the grief talking, 'cause you do feel this sense of injustice at the world once you've lost someone you love. Don't you?

'I guess she thought I'd understand how she felt, like I'd be angry too and want to rant with her. But I didn't, I'm not angry, not any more. Too much time has passed.'

My throat has grown so dry while listening to Allie that I have to get a glass of water before I can reply. 'Do you have the voice notes? Can I hear them?'

Allie shakes her head. 'She deleted them all. That's one of the things I thought was so weird. She stopped turning up and then I went to WhatsApp her 'cause I felt guilty that perhaps I'd not been there for her, but all our chat history had been wiped and my message wouldn't send. I think she blocked me.'

I grip the side of the table and close my eyes. Is this the woman who's been tormenting me? Grief-stricken and furious at the world, did she target me as one of those parents who didn't deserve a second chance? And if so, what will she do to make sure I don't get one?

Thirty-Four

Now

Vicky. Vicky. Vicky.

Her name has played on repeat since I left Allie's last night. It nearly all adds up; they could have met just before TwoIsTrouble found me online. But why would she? And how? That's the part I can't make sense of. Did she hear Allie's stories about me and somehow track me down to find out more?

I couldn't bear to ask Allie much more about it. After she told me they hadn't spoken in weeks, she began to cry when she realised how angry I was that she'd told a stranger any of our secrets and I didn't want to push her further. It didn't feel fair. I love my sister, but she's always been incredibly naive; trusting to the point of idiocy. That's not fair, either. Allie's just normal; she didn't have to adapt the way I've had to; to learn that the people you love the most can cause the most fatal wounds.

It's Friday afternoon and I've wasted most of the morning debating whether to try and find this mysterious Vicky. Allie never got her last name and doesn't know where she lives other than it's near Charlbury. They never spoke about anything except their losses which left Allie with a slim picture of this woman's life. The similarities between their friendship and mine with TwoIsTrouble are too close to ignore.

All Allie can have admitted in the grief group sessions is the truth as she knows it. She never found out what really happened to Beth; I made sure of it. So, even if she poured her heart out to the group, laid bare her darkest fears over what might have really happened, she could have never said enough to cause anyone to suspect me. But if Vicky put together Allie's stories with my confession online… well, that would be the end of everything, wouldn't it?

My phone rings and I jump to answer it when I see Mark's name on the screen.

'Hello?'

'Hi, it's me.'

In the background, I hear the sound of a busy street. I look outside into our garden and the sun is shining. I picture Mark walking through the high street on his lunch break, his sunglasses on, the phone cupped to his ear trying to drown out the sound of the passers-by.

'Are you okay?' he asks.

I walk towards the fridge, opening and shutting the door as I realise there's nothing in there I want. 'Yes,' I lie. 'I'm okay. How are you? Is everything okay with the girls?'

'Yes, everything's fine. Hold on a sec.' The phone is muffled as I imagine him putting his hand over the receiver. I can still hear him as he orders his lunch; tuna salad on brown bread to go with a flat white. The mundane details of his day make me smile yet tear something deep inside me.

'You still there?'

'Yes,' I tell him.

'Sorry, just grabbing some lunch—'

'O'Hara's?' I ask, Mark's go-to lunch stop when he has nothing with him.

'Yeah,' he says. His voice is agitated and I want to ask him if he's having a stressful day; why he didn't have time to make lunch to take with him as I know he prefers to do. *They can never get the tuna to mayo ratio right!* he's told me before as I've sat watching him diligently making his sandwiches for the next day on a Sunday night, laughing that he won't just buy something during the day like a normal person.

I remember him telling me once that a colleague had made some joke about his sandwiches. Something about 'having a word with the wife' about the state of them and he was baffled; he couldn't understand why anyone would think that I made his lunch for him. I should have found it reassuring, knowing that my husband was not an old fashioned moron who believed women belonged in the kitchen, but this was back in the days when everything made me feel like I was failing, and all I could think was that his colleague had it right. That a good wife would make his lunches. So I did, for a while.

'Hope they haven't put balsamic vinegar in it,' I say to Mark now and he laughs, loudly and all at once, like he never expected to again.

'Honestly, Em, I don't think anyone in the world would put balsamic vinegar in tuna mayo except for you.'

I got a bit obsessed with his lunches after that comment. I'd try and make them more elaborate every day, which was totally ridiculous as all Mark ever wanted was a plain tuna mayo sandwich with a little butter. I'd ask on MumsOnline what everyone else made for their husbands; I even briefly joined the cooking forums to hunt down the perfect tuna sandwich recipes. Yes, people really do share 'recipes' for tuna sandwiches. One woman said the secret to it was to add a 'ghastly amount' of black pepper and a 'heroic dash' of balsamic vinegar to the tuna. Mark found it absolutely hilarious when he bit into his sandwich; he called me from the office to ask me what on earth I'd put into it. I did laugh, that time. Even I could see that my attempts at being an old-fashioned house-wife were comical and so Mark went back to making his lunches and I promptly left the cooking forum, never to return again.

'Listen, I just wanted to check in...' His voice is low against the sound of the street and the kindness in his tone makes me close my eyes to block out the sight of our empty kitchen; the empty chairs opposite me where the girls should be.

'I miss you,' I say.

The sound around him seems to disappear and I fear for a moment that he's hung up but then he says, 'I miss you, Em. This is awful.'

I open my eyes and hold the phone tight to my ear. 'Where are you? I could come—'

'No. No, don't do that.'

'Please, Mark. We need to see each other.'

'I know, I know. But I've literally had twenty minutes to go and grab some food before my next meeting; I'm stood outside the office now. I need to go in.'

'Oh... okay.' I stand up, then sit down again. I have nothing to do. Mark is the one with the job; the purpose.

'Why don't you come over after work?' he says and my heart leaps. 'Come see the girls at Mum's. Stay for dinner? We can talk...'

I tell him I will and we get off the phone.

After we've hung up, I sit alone in the kitchen for a long time, listening to the sound of the silent, empty house. Whatever happens, I need to get Mark to come home. He and the girls belong here with me. Without them, I'm nothing.

-

After four hours wasted Googling combinations of 'Vicky / Charlbury / daughter / death' to return nothing of any use, at four p.m. I head upstairs and get ready to see Mark and the girls. I take my time choosing my outfit, finally deciding on one of my nicest flowing dresses, then clip my hair half up and put on some make-up. I stand in front of the mirror and inspect myself. I can't do anything about the dark bags under my eyes but I think Mark will be suitably impressed with my appearance. I frown at myself in the mirror; Mark doesn't care about things like that. He never has. When I was first pregnant, I spent an incredible amount of time measuring every inch of my body, checking it against stats on the internet to see if I was getting bigger than I should be. Mark would take the tape measure out of my hands and kiss my bump, telling me I was perfect, my body was perfect. All of my insecurities, my anxieties, are my own. He's never given me any reason to believe I wasn't good enough exactly as I am. But my stomach dips as I think of him taking the girls and leaving me here. Is that really him supporting me? Loving me no matter what?

I shake my head. *It's for their protection*. The words taunt me, like a cruel joke.

But it's not me that they need protecting from. It's her, whoever she is.

The drive over goes quickly and I'm soon parked out in front of Mark's childhood home in the centre of Cheltenham. His parents have never moved and the house is much the same as when Mark grew up there as a boy. It's a quiet street despite being so central, tucked out of view. Most of the residents are retired so their gardens are styled to perfection. Whenever Mark's dad comes to ours, he makes grumbling remarks about our lack of garden, pulling weeds out from between the patio stones as he tells us that we need to get on top of things. There are no weeds in their front garden, not a chance. Lining the path to the front door are huge orange tulips that dip and sway softly in the wind. I feel myself relax; their home is so different to the one I grew up in. I think of the chaotic rose bush that splayed out from our front garden, the thorns that would grab hold of your ankles as you walked down the path on the way to school that appeared after Lewis left and the gardener stopped coming. I don't remember his name but he'd come a few days a week and I'd wave to him from the window as he chopped, pruned and styled our garden to perfection. So much of our lives fell into disarray without Lewis' tight grip.

'Emily?' I'm so lost in thought that I don't realise I'm standing at the open front door.

'Hi,' I say to Mark.

He tilts his head to the side and smiles. 'Hi.'

I feel a flush of happiness at his smile and ask if I can come inside. He moves back and ushers me in. The hallway is dark compared to the bright sunlight of the day.

'Where are the girls?'

'Mum and Dad have taken them to the park… to give us some time to talk.'

'Sorry, I'm early, aren't I?' I say, looking at his open laptop on the kitchen table.

He shuts it and smiles. 'No, you're perfect.'

I sit down at the kitchen table and try to form the words to start this conversation.

'Do you remember the first time I brought you here?' Mark asks. I look up; he's smiling at me. I nod.

'I was terrified,' I say, remembering the feeling.

Mark brought me to meet his mum only a few weeks after our first date. I say his mum, but his dad was here too. His mum is just the sort of woman that only really ever gets talked about on her own. Mark's dad is lovely, but he's just in the background, almost. His mum commands the room, whatever room she's in. His dad is perfectly happy standing back and admiring her from afar. It's one of the things that drew me to Mark; seeing that he'd grown up with a family like this. So normal. So kind. He's an only child, which probably helps. Things are always so much simpler when there's just one of you. Mark's mum treated me like part of the family from day one. She acted like there was no doubt that Mark and I would get married, have kids, and be happy from then on. I liked it. That certainty that I was here to stay.

'Your mum came to see me,' I tell Mark now.

He frowns. 'What? When?'

'Yesterday.'

He sighs and shakes his head, muttering, 'For god's sake,' under his breath.

'No, it was helpful. I was really glad she came; it was good to talk.'

Mark stands up and goes to the coffee machine. He takes out two stoneware mugs and starts making us drinks.

When the grinding sounds of the machine stop, he sits back down and places the mug in front of me.

I look down at the mug and laugh. 'Rabbit?' I ask.

He grins. 'It was meant to be a heart.'

I tilt my head and try to see the shape in the coffee foam in the way he intended.

'I'm sorry,' he says.

'I'll forgive your lack of Starbucks skills—'

'No. Not for that. For leaving… it was…'

Our eyes meet and my chest tightens at the look on his face. 'It's not your fault, Mark.'

He sighs and looks away. 'It wasn't the right thing to do. No—' He holds his hand up to stop me interrupting. 'I know what you're going to say, but don't. I shouldn't have left you. No matter what's going on, I'm supposed to stick by you… be a good husband, a good dad.'

'You are,' I tell him.

He shakes his head and keeps his eyes glued to the table away from me. I get up and crouch in front of him so he can't avoid me.

'You're the best husband. It's me… I'm a bloody nightmare.' I try to laugh but tears prickle the back of my eyes because Mark still won't look at me and I hate that I've done this to him; to us. Perhaps Vicky is right; perhaps some women don't deserve to be mothers. But Mark was made to be a father and I *am* a mother, whether I deserve it or not. I'm not going to let her, or anyone else, take that from me.

Thirty-Five

Now

I hear them before I see them; the melodies of their sing-song voices float down the hallway making my heart burst. Ella is chattering away as usual and Joanne is doing her best to keep up but her replies sag at the end of each sentence. *Yes, darling, I'm sure the ducks do have enough food. No, I don't think they get cold overnight.* A smile pulls at my lips as I listen to the whirlwind way my daughter's brain works; questioning everything, thinking about everyone. I slide the cup of coffee away and brace myself to see them, wishing away any leftover worry staining my face. Mark was right that I never wanted the girls to see me going through a breakdown again, it's too painful and scary for them, but I'm not breaking down. I can do this.

'Mummy!' Lara bowls in first, her cheeks pink and hair sticking on end from the wind outside.

'Hello, darling.'

She flings herself into my arms as Ella runs through and does the same. Their bodies curl into mine and for the first time in days, I feel whole again. This is where they belong; this is how things should be. I breathe them in and try not to flinch at the unfamiliar smells. Hints of Chanel No.7 cling to their skin; Joanne's favourite. I close my eyes and imagine taking them home right now and scrubbing them clean. They should smell like me. Like us.

'Where have you been?' Lara pulls back and asks with the tone of a tiny school teacher. Her bottom lip pouts and I laugh.

'Where have *you* been?' I retort.

She narrows her eyes and looks at Ella like this is a trick. 'Here, Mummy. We've been here.'

I pull her back in for a cuddle, all too aware that the room is watching us. I'm not ready to explain to my daughter why Daddy took them away.

'Right, best start on dinner then, hadn't we?' Mark's dad, Alan, says. He's wearing the Weird Fish pullover that I bought him for Christmas and something about that makes me feel safe. It's a visual reminder that I'm part of this family, even when I'm not physically here.

'Why don't you take the girls upstairs, Emily? We can manage all of this,' Joanne says.

I should say no, offer to help make dinner like I always do but the opportunity to spend time alone with the girls is too alluring and we run out of the kitchen hand-in-hand, like school children finally allowed to play.

—

'Mummy, if we stay here forever can we get another bed because I don't like this one.'

'What? No, Ella, you're not staying here—'

'Are we going home now?' Lara cuts in.

'No 'cause we're having sausages,' Ella replies, before pulling off her jumper. 'Too hot.'

'Me too.' Lara does the same.

We're in the guest bedroom, or as Joanne calls it, 'the girls' room'. In fairness, she's right – this isn't a room for any sort of visitors; it has the girls stamped all over it. As soon as Mark told her we were having twin girls, Joanne turned this room into a little girls' dream bedroom. The walls are painted a light pink with a hand-drawn rainbow covering one wall. Joanne added the rainbow herself once the girls were old enough to appreciate such things. I was supposed to help her but it was during the days when I didn't really do anything much, let alone follow YouTube tutorials on how to paint the perfect rainbow arch with my mother-in-law. It took her weeks; I remember Mark beaming with pride when she'd WhatsApp him progress pictures and feel a stab of guilt at the memory of my lacklustre responses. Now, I run my fingers along the paint and notice it hasn't faded at all over the last two years. She must touch it up. I think of their bedroom at home and try to remember the last time I did anything to make it nicer, but I can't.

'Shall we paint your bedroom at home?' I ask.

Ella frowns. 'Why?'

'To make it nice. I could do you a rainbow.'

'We've got a rainbow here.'

'But don't you want one at home? In your proper bedroom?'

Ella shrugs.

'Can we do clouds?' Lara asks, her face lighting up. 'On the ceiling?'

'Yes, we can. I'll paint you big fluffy clouds to sleep under.'

'Got stars here,' Ella says and I bite back annoyance.

'Yes but when you're back in your bedroom—'

'Can we go now?' Lara asks again.

The urge to scream 'yes!' is on the tip of my tongue, but I swallow it. Mark and I didn't talk about when they'd

233

be coming home and I don't want to make my daughter a promise I can't keep. She'd never forget it.

'Not right now, darling. Nanna is making us a yummy dinner.'

'Okay,' she says, shrugging.

I sit down on Lara's bed as the girls huddle in the toy corner, debating between themselves which of the toys from their excessive pile they should play with first, bored of our conversation. I try to talk to them some more but they're deep in twin-talk now, totally caught up with each other. I try not to think of the stupid TikTok videos I've seen where parents are reunited with their children; the little girls always squeal and cry, so happy to be back in their parents' arms. Why don't the girls feel that way about me? But then, why would they? The videos I watched are of parents separated by war; by work; by things out of their control. Our separation is wholly my fault. No one has been keeping us apart; that's all on me. A deep sense of dread builds in my stomach; this isn't the way it's supposed to be. I'm supposed to feel happy; I'm supposed to feel totally overjoyed at being near my daughters again. Nothing should be bothering me. I watch the girls, totally fine without me, and think that perhaps Mark did the right thing taking them away from me. Perhaps they are better off without me, in a room that is safe and clean and tidy, where no malicious stranger is watching them.

'Read us this one?' Ella suddenly says, turning around to face me, and just like that, under the adoring gaze of my beautiful daughter, I know their place is with me.

She climbs onto the bed with me and presses a book into my hands. Lara follows suit and curls up on the other side of me, resting her head on my stomach. The weight of them brings me back to earth.

'I've missed you so much,' I whisper to them.

'We missed you, Mummy,' Lara says and buries her head into the crook of my arm, her warm breath tickling me as my heart beat slows to match theirs. I close my eyes and bask in their affection.

'Read, Mummy,' Ella commands and I laugh.

'Okay, okay… Right. What are we reading?' I look at the book Ella has given me and frown. It's an old copy of *The Twits* by Roald Dhal, and I'm surprised to see it here. Joanne prefers new, pristine books and this looks like a charity shop copy. 'Has Nanna been reading this to you?'

'No.'

'It looks a bit old and dirty,' I say, flipping the book over to read the back cover. 'I think I read this when I was little.' I have a vague memory of the story and then I remember seeing a quote from the book going around Twitter; something about ugly thoughts making you ugly on the outside. 'Let's pick another one.'

'No!' Ella cries, grabbing the book from me. 'This one!'

I sigh. 'Okay. I just… It's not a very nice story, darling. And the book is old and grubby. Did Nanna give you this one or did you take it from one of the bookshelves in the living room?'

'Daddy gave it to us,' Ella says, sitting up to face me in defiance.

'Not Daddy,' Lara says, shuffling herself up too and shaking her head. 'It was a—'

'No!' Ella shouts and leans across me to whack Lara on the arm.

'Ella! Stop it. We do not hit. Say sorry. Now.'

She pouts out her bottom lip as Lara's eyes fill with tears.

'It's secret,' Ella says to her.

'What's secret?' I ask. 'Who gave you the book?'

'Daddy's friend,' Ella whispers with a smile on her lips. Lara looks between me and Ella in horror, her mouth forming a perfect O.

'What are you talking about, Els? Who's Daddy's friend?'

'Secret!' she shouts again, this time followed by manic giggles. 'Not telling!'

The lurking dread starts to crawl through me again as I look between my daughters. Lara is looking up at me with something that looks a lot like pity but I shake that thought from my head. Lara is too young to know that emotion.

'I don't want to read this one,' she says instead, taking the book from my hand and burying it under the covers. She gets up and trots across the room to get another book and brings it back to the bed. 'This one,' she says, pressing it into my stomach.

'Darling, tell Mummy the truth.' I take the other book out from beneath the covers. 'Where did you get this book?'

Ella giggles again, like this is all one big game while Lara shoots worried glances between us. She pulls me close to whisper in my ear.

'Daddy has a friend but he says we're not to tell you.'

Her words are almost drowned out by Ella crawling over me to yank Lara away but I heard them.

'Secret! It's secret!' Ella shouts, pressing her hands over Lara's mouth.

'Stop it, Ella. Enough.' I pull them apart and try to stay calm despite the ringing in my ears. 'Stop being silly, please. This is really important, okay. I won't tell Daddy you've told me. But is this new friend a lady?'

Lara and Ella look at each and seem to agree something in silence because they both turn back to me and nod, their big round eyes hollow.

–

We're in the dining room, which in itself shows something is not quite right. The dining room is only used for proper occasions; birthday dinners, Easter Sunday, Christmas. A Friday night dinner with the girls would not usually merit getting out the fancy knives and forks and laying the thick black placemats out on the eight-person table. We should be in the kitchen, around the chunky pine table with the crayon marks all over it from where the girls couldn't stick to just drawing on their paper and strayed out onto the wood. That's where normal family meals are held.

I watch my husband from across the table and try to search his face for the person I know. Everything about him is exactly the same; I know his face so well that sometimes I'm not even sure I look at him any more, just the memory of him instead. The dark, erratic eyebrows that always have at least one stray hair poking bolt upright instead of in line with the others; the dimple on his left cheek when he properly smiles. Just the one. His big, broad mouth that opens so wide when he laughs that you can see right through to his tonsils.

He catches me studying him and smiles. The dimple doesn't appear.

'You okay, Em?'

'Yeah, course. Could you pass me…'

I don't have to finish my sentence, he picks up the salt, knowing what I want.

'Thanks.' I look away from him as I grind the salt onto my plate.

'Mummy!' Lara squeals, giggling. 'Naughty! Too much!'

'Whoops,' I say, breaking out of my trance. I look up; Mark is frowning at me. I smile and cut up my food like everything is fine. 'How's Linda doing, Joanne?' I ask to break the silence.

Predictably, Joanne launches into a detailed account of how her friend is handling the latest round of rejections from her recent foray into online dating. Her husband left her last year.

I cut into a potato on my plate and hold in a grimace as the tang of an unbearable amount of salt coats my tongue. I focus on chewing as Joanne talks at me.

'So, yes. Not very nice, really. You'd think men would get better as they get older but—'

'Why did she leave her husband again?' I ask.

Joanne's cheeks go pink as she looks at the girls. 'Oh… you know. Just one of those things that happens some-times…'

'An affair, wasn't it?' I say, looking at Mark. 'Didn't she find out he had another woman?'

'Oh, well. Maybe that's something that little ears don't need to hear,' Joanne says but I don't take my eyes off Mark. He frowns back at me as I search for the twitch of his eyebrow that will let me know he's lying.

'What's little ears?' Lara says and Mark drops my gaze to reply to her.

'Ears that are too little to hear big things. Now, eat your sausages.' His eyes fall back to his plate where he chops up his food into neat, mouth-sized bites.

Joanne and I stand side-by-side at the sink. She washes; I dry. Like always. The girls sit at the kitchen table behind us, colouring in with thick felt tip pens.

'I'm glad you came tonight,' Joanne says, her voice low to avoid little ears listening in.

'Mmm.'

'I know it's hard, love. But you two will get there.'

I keep my eyes focused on the window in front of us as I wrap a plate in a tea towel to dry. The evening is starting to darken.

'I can put the girls to bed,' she says. 'If you and Mark want to go and have a proper chat.'

'No,' I say, shaking my head. 'Not tonight.'

She hands me a wine glass and I take it by the delicate stem.

'I think you should, love. Honestly, it's no bother for us.'

'No,' I snap, rubbing the glass dry. 'I don't want to—'

'Careful!' she says, just as the glass breaks in my hand. 'Oh gosh, don't worry – here we go…' She takes the stem from my hands, leaving me holding the top half of the glass.

I marvel at the clean break.

'Are you cut?' she asks.

I shake my head. 'I don't think so. Sorry, I don't know—'

'Don't worry about the glass, you silly thing. Let me see.' She removes what remains of the glass from my hands before inspecting them. 'No harm done. They're ever so fragile, those stems. I said to Alan the other day, I know it's very trendy nowadays to have these big huge glasses with these thin stems but it's hardly very practical, is it?' She tuts before rustling in the under-sink cupboard for newspaper to wrap up the broken glass.

'Why don't you go into the sitting room? I'll finish this up.'

I nod obediently and the girls follow me out.

–

In the living room, I sit on the opposite sofa to Mark, watching him as he watches the television; a wildlife documentary that in any other situation would be calming but tonight just feels out of place. Mark's dad sits beside him, transfixed by the swirling images of brightly coloured fish that swim across the screen.

'How's work?' I ask Mark. His eyes flit from the screen to meet mine.

He shrugs. 'Fine. Same, really.'

I nod. An awkwardness hangs between us as we struggle to find anything to discuss. The tension must be bad because Alan, not usually the most perceptive person, says he'll take the girls upstairs for their bath and quickly leaves the room, calling for Joanne to come and help him.

Mark laughs once he's gone. 'Feels like we're teenagers on a first date.'

I smile but my heart pangs. All I can think about is Lara's admission: *Daddy has a new friend but it's a secret.* I've always thought that if I had any sign that Mark was having an affair, I'd confront him. We talked about it on MumsOnline often. One of us was always being coun- selled by the others on how to deal with their cheating husband. So many women refused to do anything about it, other than log in and share their pain online every night.

I found a text on his phone.

My friend spotted my boyfriend on Tinder.

I heard one of his mates joking about my husband shagging around in the pub.

I'd always say the same thing: confront him! Leave! Take the kids. Do whatever you have to do but don't put up with it. But I get it now; that compulsion to bury your head in the sand at the first sign of a problem. Because if you ask them, you might hear something you don't want to know. Could Mark really be capable of cheating? Everything in my body tells me no. Not my Mark. The man who makes chicken soup from scratch the second I so much as cough. Who leaves me a mug and coffee pod on the kitchen counter each morning ready for my first cup. The girls must be confused; he'd never lie to me. My mouth twitches, ready to joke about the silly thing Ella said but then Mark speaks and I'm floored.

'Look, I know this is hard but I think maybe the girls and I will stay here for just a bit longer.'

'What? I thought you were going to come back... I thought that's why I was here.'

He shakes his head. 'I know. I thought that too. I did, Em. Honestly, there's nothing I want more than to come home but seeing you tonight like this...' He looks away and colour rises in my cheeks.

'Like what?' I screech, trying and failing to keep the hurt from my voice.

He scratches the back of his head the way he always does when he's stressed. 'You're not yourself, darling. I just don't know if the girls—'

'If the girls should be around me?'

He bites his lip and nods slowly.

'That's bullshit,' I hiss. 'At least have the fucking guts to be honest, Mark.'

'Em,' he whispers too loudly. 'They'll hear you, stop it.'

My body pumps with a mix of fury at his words and embarrassment at the thought of my own being heard by his parents and my daughters upstairs. I take a deep breath and try to calm down.

'I know what you've been doing.'

'What?'

'Why have you really left?'

He frowns and shakes his head. 'You know why. We promised each other that if you started acting like this again that I'd make sure the girls didn't—'

'It's convenient, though, isn't it?'

'What are you talking about?'

'Well, having a get-out-free clause.'

He opens his mouth and shuts it before ticking his tongue against his teeth. Anger reddens his cheeks as he shakes his head slowly. 'I can't believe you'd say that to me. You really think this is what I want? To be hiding out at my parents' while you're all alone?' His hands ball into fists on the cushion. 'I hate this. I hate all of it. Don't you think I wish you could just—'

'What? Disappear?'

He lets out a sound that's a mix between a laugh and a cry. 'No. I just wish you could be normal.'

Silence falls between us and he stands up. He won't look at me but I feel his words crawling over my skin, eating into my brain. As he turns to walk out, I say, 'Who is she?'

'What?' He turns around, his face red.

'Your new friend.'

'What are you talking about?'

I roll my eyes as a lump sticks in my throat. 'The girls told me. You shouldn't trust four-year-olds with secrets.'

He sighs and shakes his head.

'Who is she, Mark?'

He doesn't say anything and I feel my life slipping away from me like it never existed at all.

'Is she "normal"?'

He snaps his head up and looks me dead in the eye. 'The fact you could even think that I'd do that to you tells me everything I needed to know about the state of our marriage.'

–

After Mark storms out, Joanne appears in the living room and tells me it might be better if I leave the girls for the evening; they are apparently very upset at hearing me shout. I can't bring myself to be mad at Joanne for this, or suggest that she confront her son about what is really going on, because she pulls me in for a hug and tells me everything will be all right, and I just need to believe her. But I can't leave without saying goodbye to the girls, and so I sneak back into their room under the guise of going upstairs to the bathroom. I hold them close and tell them how much I love them, then lift that stupid book from the room and hide it in my handbag. Whoever Mark's other woman is, I'm not having anything she's touched anywhere near my girls.

Thirty-Six

Two Is Trouble

He called me as soon as you left, you know. *I shouldn't have asked the girls to lie.* He's sweet, your husband. A little bit clueless, but perhaps that's why you chose him. You needed someone who wouldn't dig too much into your life, didn't you? But he's not a bad man. Not at all. You really don't deserve him.

When you used to tell me about him on MumsOnline, I pictured a totally different man. The sort of husband you see on those shitty soaps; always working, never around, not interested. But you weren't really telling me about Mark, were you? You were concocting some sort of backwards fairy-tale for us all; desperate to garner some sympathy. Mark's always been there for you, no matter what you do.

He's very worried about you. Everyone is, apparently.

I'm glad you found the book. Did it make you think of her? You told me once that you were a lazy reader when you first became a mum, that you just read the same words over and over like a chant because you could never be bothered to read more than the first page. I bet you don't do that any more.

I wonder if you remember doing it at all.

You've scrubbed Beth so clearly from your life that I bet nearly all your memories are gone. Wiped clean.

But you can't just forget her. You can't pretend it never happened.

I won't let you.

Thirty-Seven

Now

The house feels cold and unloved as I walk in and I'm hit by the thought that if Mark leaves me, this is how it will always be. An empty house. No endless questions from the girls; no one standing in the kitchen with a glass of wine anticipating my return; no relentless melodies from *The Greatest Showman* blasting from the living room as the girls put it on for the hundredth time.

I'll be totally alone. I grip onto the bookcase in the hall to hold myself up. He couldn't take them from me, could he? The idea of Mark and his faceless yet impossibly beautiful 'new friend' becoming the perfect mum and dad to my perfect twins is so unbearable that a moan escapes me. How is this happening?

The sound of my phone ringing from inside my bag pulls me out of my despair as I imagine Mark desperately calling to tell me that I'm wrong, begging me to come back, but it's Allie's name I see on the screen. I cancel the call, but she tries again and I don't have the energy to ignore her.

'Hi, Allie,' I say as I move into the kitchen and slump down at the table without bothering to turn on the lights.

'Are you okay?'

'I'm fine.'

'You don't sound it?'

'No. Well, I'm not… really.'

'What's happened? Are the girls okay?' The concern in her voice pulls at my heart and I rub at the spot between my eyes that's thumping.

'They're fine. They're with Mark.'

'Where's Mark?'

'Gone.'

'What? Emily, what's happened?'

'Nothing, it doesn't matter. What were you calling for?' I trace my fingers along the ridges in the table where the girls have pushed pens too hard through paper and left dents in the wood. Are they asleep right now? They were quiet when I left. Ella turned her face away from me as I tucked her in, but Lara hugged me so tightly I thought my heart might pop. Perhaps I should have demanded I take them back with me. It's not normal, is it, for the father to be the one who gets the kids?

Too late I realise Allie has been talking down the phone.

'Sorry, I was just… What did you say?'

'Which bit did you miss?'

'Um… All of it… Sorry.'

She laughs. 'Don't worry, it doesn't matter. I don't really know why I called you about it.'

'About what?'

'Oh, nothing honestly. I was just babbling on about the woman… the one I told you about yesterday. Vicky? From grief group?'

'What about her?'

'She got in touch. Tonight, she texted me. It was just weird, after we spoke about her yesterday, you know. Like she knew or something.' Allie laughs. 'I just wanted to tell you.'

'What did she say?'

'Not much. She wanted to apologise for how she acted before… She said she's moved away up North to be near her parents. She said she's getting proper therapy now and that the grief group was actually just making her worse.' Allie sighs loudly down the line. 'Sad, really.'

My head throbs as I try to untangle this. Is this yet another lie? A way to throw me off the scent?

'Emily, are you all right? What did you mean when you said Mark's gone?'

I sigh and get up to switch on the lights; the glare burns my eyes and intensifies my headache as I blink to try and shut out the brightness. 'Just that. He's gone. He's taken the girls.'

'What? Why?'

'Well… depends who you ask.'

'So the girls aren't with you now?'

'No. He has them.'

'Oh, god, Emily. I had no idea. I'm so sorry.'

'Mmm, me too.' I look around my spotless empty kitchen and yearn for the mess and the noise of our usual Friday nights. Plates should be piled up by the sink with the remnants of a leftover Thai takeaway yet to be cleaned up, Mark should be hovering by the sink encouraging me to have just one more glass of wine. How many Friday nights have we spent like that? Too many to count. Too many to appreciate; just another night in. Same old Friday. What I wouldn't give to rewind the clock and be back there.

'Shall I come over?'

'No,' I say, shaking my head though no one can see me. 'I'm fine,' I start to say but, to the surprise of us both, a sob escapes and I find myself wailing down the phone to my little sister.

–

She arrives within the hour and I welcome her in with a mix of relief and embarrassment. We've never had the type of relationship where we bare our souls and cry together. We've not been able to be those types of sisters.

'I'm getting you some wine. Where's the fridge?' Allie says as she strolls into the kitchen and starts opening random cupboards looking for the right one. I point and she pulls open the door and shouts 'ta da' as she drags out a bottle. She pours two enormous glasses.

'You shouldn't, Allie, that's too much to drive on.'

She waves away my concern. 'Don't worry about it, I can always get an Uber.'

I frown, about to tell her that there's no way she'll get an Uber to go all the way to hers tonight but decide to leave her to it. I'm not the mother here. We move into the living room where Allie sets about lighting the log burner as if she's always lived here.

'Where do you keep the firelighters?' she asks.

I shrug. 'I don't know. Mark usually…' Tears spring to my eyes.

'Don't worry, I'll just…' She pulls out the box next to the TV and rummages through, eventually finding what she's looking for. After a few moments, the fire is lit with a dramatic whoosh of the flames.

'Ha! I wasn't sure I knew how to do that,' she says, turning to grin at me, the flames burning in her eyes. 'Now, let's sort your marriage out.'

Part of me wants to close up. To tell Allie to mind her own business so I can go back to pretending everything is absolutely fine and retain my position as the dependable and sorted older sister. But it's so nice to have someone here, someone real to talk to that I end up telling her everything.

When I'm done she screws her face up. 'But why would he take the girls to meet this woman?' she asks. 'And why would she give them a book?'

I shake my head. 'I've no fucking clue. The whole thing just seems so totally out of the realms of possibility but...' I tail off, not knowing how to rationalise things.

'What did he say when you asked him?'

'That he couldn't believe I'd think that about him,' I say, rolling my eyes.

'Mmm... that one.'

'Yeah, exactly.'

She pulls a cushion on top of her lap and hugs it to her, like she used to as a kid. 'They always say that. Like by playing the victim it will get them out of having to admit what they've really done.'

'Sounds like you're talking from experience.'

She looks down and laughs. 'Yeah... well. Men are fucking scum, aren't they?'

I'm taken aback by her harsh words and wonder once again what's happened in Allie's life that I've no idea about.

'Even the good ones. But I never thought Mark would—'

'No. Nor did I.'

We both take gulps of our wine and stare into the fire. I was hoping Allie would tell me I was wrong, that I'd jumped to conclusions but she's right – Mark acted exactly the way you would expect a guilty man to.

'What book did she give them?' Allie asks, pulling her eyes from the flames.

I curl my lip. 'A Roald Dahl one. It wasn't even new.'

'Which one?'

I laugh. Like this is the most important part of the whole situation! Allie has always been tricky to hold conversations with, I remember now. Her mind latches onto the most irrelevant details and misses the point entirely. I wonder if it's something to do with the way we lost Beth, like somehow she shies away from the most important things and focuses just off centre instead to stop herself from falling.

'I actually took the book,' I say, laughing slightly manically as I stand to fetch it from my handbag in the hallway. 'I don't even know why.'

Allie widens her eyes and tuts. 'I'd have done the same.'

I hand her the book and sit back down.

'I can't believe he told the girls to lie to me. That's what I'm really fucking furious about. Lara looked absolutely torn to pieces at being told to keep a secret from me. I'd never have believed Mark would put the girls in that position.' Fury is building in my chest as the words escape but as I turn to look at Allie I realise she's not listening.

She's holding the book in her hands with her eyes glued to it. Her fingers stroke the cover like it's a long lost love letter. A memory hits me then.

'Do you recognise the book?'

She looks up and nods her head. 'Yeah, we read it when we were younger I think.'

'Beth read it?'

She shrugs and looks again. 'Probably, yeah.'

'No. She did. I'm sure she did. I read it to her.'

251

She shrugs again and hands me the book back; I look at it again, the memory that almost came to me earlier now rushing through my mind. Beth loved this book. My stomach twists as I run my fingers across the cover.

'You remember, right?' I press her.

She wrinkles her nose and looks as I hold the book up to her. 'I don't know, Em. Probably. There were loads of books.'

I shake my head incredulously and Allie looks away, embarrassed. Have I imagined this? Am I seeing connections where there are none?

'Will you read it to me?' Allie asks, breaking my thoughts.

'What?' I laugh, embarrassed at the idea.

Allie shrugs as if this isn't important to her, but her cheeks colour and she looks away, just like Ella does when she's embarrassed. 'Nothing. Stupid idea. No one reads to you as an adult, do they? And it's nice, I remember it being nice.'

I look at the book again and wish I had memories of being read to as a child like Allie does.

I open the book and start reading; the lick and hiss of the fire crackling between my words as Allie lies down on the sofa and rests her head in my lap.

'I miss her every day,' Allie says once I'm finished. I don't know if she's talking about Beth or Mum, but it doesn't really matter now.

'Me too,' I say.

Allie sits up and smooths her hair down. She catches my eyes and smiles tightly as if embarrassed by our sudden intimacy. 'It's weird that she'd give the girls a book, isn't it?' She chews her lip. 'It's creepy, like she's already trying to be their mum or something.'

I grip the sofa beneath me as I swallow Allie's words.

'Oh god, Emily – sorry, I didn't mean that,' Allie says, her eyes wide as she takes in the look on my face. 'It's probably just her way of getting in with them. A shitty way. But that's all it is.'

I nod. 'Yeah,' I say, trying to smile. 'I know. I know. Listen, I need to get to bed, I'm sorry, I'm just knackered.'

She chews her nails and gets out her phone, opening the Uber app. I take our wineglasses from the table and walk them into the kitchen where I leave them in the sink; I'll wash up in the morning. I take a few moments to gather myself before going back into the living room. Allie is still sitting on the couch and she crinkles her nose when I walk back in.

'So, slightly bad news. I can't actually seem to get home…' She holds up her phone as if that explains the lack of taxis. I knew this would happen. 'Do you think I could sleep on the sofa? I just don't want to risk driving.'

I wave my hand. 'Of course, that's fine. You can't drive. I'll sort the spare room out,' I tell her, suppressing a groan. All I want is to be alone, but I can hardly chuck her out after she was the only person there for me tonight. I trudge upstairs and pull a fresh sheet from the laundry cupboard, unsure when we last changed the guest bed. No one really stays with us any more so god knows when it was last done. There's washing hanging from the drying rack in the room which I really should move but I've no energy for fixing things, so call down to Allie that the room's ready.

–

I wait in my bedroom until the sounds of Allie moving around the house to get ready for bed are silenced before getting out my laptop. The book could have nothing to do with TwoIsTrouble. Allie's right; we had hundreds of books. This could be nothing more than a coincidence. I try to convince myself of that, over and over. Yet the alternative drums in my head, too horrifying to ignore. What if this woman, Vicky, this stranger, whoever she is, has got to Mark and is doing all of this not to just tell the world what I did to Beth, but to take my place? This has to end now. It has to.

Thirty-Eight

Now

MumsOnline Post By MotherOfTwins

FRIDAY 11/03/2020 11:59pm

What would you do if someone was stalking you online?

Over the last few weeks, someone from MumsOnline has been stalking me. They've found out my real name and done everything they can to ruin my life. I've let them. Why? Because they know secrets about me. We all know secrets about each other here, don't we? Think of all the things you ever wrote on this hellsite becoming public. Think of the worst thing you ever said, the nastiest words you ever wrote, and imagine them being sent to the people you love the most.

But tonight I've had enough. This stranger thinks they can bully me into silence but they can't.

I've found out who they are and I've told the police.

So, TwoIsTrouble, if you're reading this – get ready.

They're coming for you.

COMMENTS

DarcyDooLittle: Babe, is this a joke????

TwoLittleTerrors: LOL someone's been on the vino this eve!

MumsOnlineAdmin: Please be assured MumsOnline takes any reports of harassment / bullying / inappropriate behaviour very seriously.

TwoLittleTerrors: BOOO piss off admin – we know you copy and pasted that from your T&Cs

ToBeMarried22: Omg this is literally my worst nightmare. If anyone ever found out my account I think I'd die

TwoLittleTerrors: [eye roll] only a moron would tell a stranger all their dirty secrets

DarcyDooLittle: Errrm hardly?! We all do it here! It's what the sites for!

TwoLittleTerrors: LOL.

ToBeMarried22: I don't think this is funny @TwoLittleTerrors!!! This is supposed to be a safe space

DarcyDooLittle: Exactly my point @ToBeMarried22!! I can't believe any woman would come on here and tear another woman down like that.

TwoLittleTerrors: Women are the worst to each other. You all bang on about feminism and #MeToo but you LOVE a bitch on here!

DarcyDooLittle: Eurrgh. @TwoLittleTerrors your a troll. Bye!

TwoLittleTerrors: I'm not being funny but why would the police give a shit about a stupid MumsOnline spat? @MotherOfTwins do you really think they're going to stop investigating RAPES and MURDERS because someone is upsetting your perfect little life? Lol. Grow up!

ToBeMarried22: It's not just about rape and murder! Stalking is an offence too!

DarcyDooLittle: DON'T FEED THE TROLLS.

TwoIsTrouble: Are you also going to tell the police what you did to your baby? What you did to Beth?

TwoIsTrouble: You can't hide from it any more, Emily. Soon, everyone will know the truth.

[POST HAS BEEN CLOSED FOR COMMENTS]

Thirty-Nine

Then

My Daughter Is Dead

What do I do now? My very worst fears have all been proven true. How do you go on with life knowing that the worst you ever possibly imagined can and will happen to you?

I can't even bear to look at my daughter. I don't want her near me. The very smell of her makes my stomach churn. This is her fault. I always knew she was going to do something like this and now she has and I can't even tell anyone.

I've done the only thing I can do; I've got her out of the house and away from Alison.

Yes, I've dropped the pretence of hiding their names. There was some part of me that felt if I wrote down our true names, I was being disloyal. As if by concealing things if someone were to one day uncover these diaries they wouldn't know who we were. But how could anyone not know us? The family to avoid in the street; the careless mother who couldn't save one child from another.

I should have never tried to protect her.

I knew there was something wrong with my daughter. I knew one day she'd hurt someone, and I let it happen.

Bethany is dead.

Emily killed her.

I'll never forgive myself for what happened. Never. The police say it was just an accident; a horrible, tragic accident. Everyone says it wasn't my fault, and they rub my back and coo over me like I need to be told that it was all just some shocking mistake, like that will make me feel better, as if I blame myself.

But I am not to blame.

The reason Beth is dead, my beautiful, sweet, perfect daughter, is not my fault.

Emily is to blame. She knows that, and I know it too.

I'll never forgive her.

I'll never forgive myself and maybe I shouldn't. Maybe I don't deserve forgiveness.

But Beth deserves justice. She deserves the world to know what happened to her. But I can never tell anyone the truth, can I? What sort of mother does it make me if I tell them my child is a killer? Even now, I am guided by shame. Plagued with it.

But perhaps one day someone will find these diaries and be braver than me. Brave enough to bring my little girl the justice she deserves.

I just hope it happens before Emily has a chance to hurt anyone else.

Forty

Now

I sit back in my bed, heart pounding as I reload the page. Will she take the bait? I don't know if what I've done is reckless and totally stupid, or brilliant. Her whole campaign against me has been based on the assumption that I won't go to the police because of my guilt over Beth's death and the car accident, and she was right.

But seeing her write Beth's name like that, along with the accusation that I caused my miscarriage, is the final straw. This whole time I've doubted myself over whether she was really out to get me and whether, if she was, it could really be about my sister's death. But it is. She knows what happened and she's going to punish me for it. If I'd trusted myself more before, maybe it would have never got to this stage. It's too late to get help from the police, or anyone now. But if she believes I might, that I already have, maybe that'll be enough to draw her out. I reload the page again, though as I've turned the comments off there's nothing new to see. Maybe that was a bad idea but I had to stop her typing any more about Beth. At least reloading shows me the post view count. 1,003 so far. I imagine all the women logging in and seeing this post on the top of their feeds tonight; safe and secure in their beds, probably with their husbands by their sides, snoring away totally unaware of what their wives are reading. It will scare them, I'm sure. It would have scared me. We're lulled into such a false sense of security on that site but we should all be more careful. You never know who you're talking to.

I click through the names of the other women who've commented and scour their profiles. Could they be other accounts made by TwoIsTrouble? TwoLittleTerrors seems the most likely candidate if so. A mother of twins with no post history before today. But that doesn't mean she's new. Some of the women are cleverer in their anonymity; it's usual to create new profiles to wipe clean your posting history. I never did it. I never thought that much about it, treating the site like my personal diary. Idiot.

The sound of my DM pinging turns my stomach. I rush to click on the red '1' in the corner of my screen. It's her.

> TwoIsTrouble: Don't lie, Emily. You haven't gone to the police. You wouldn't dare.
>
> MotherOfTwins: You left me with no choice.
>
> TwoIsTrouble: You're lying. As usual.
>
> MotherOfTwins: Are you sure about that?

I hold my breath as I see her typing. She stops, then starts again.

> TwoIsTrouble: Let's sort this out between us.
>
> MotherOfTwins: How?
>
> TwoIsTrouble: I think it's time for us to meet.

My forehead throbs as I read her words. This is what I wanted, isn't it? So why is the idea of meeting her so terrifying?

> TwoIsTrouble: Or, I could just go tell Mark that you killed your own baby then tried to crash the car with your daughters inside. I think he'd LOVE to hear it.
>
> MotherOfTwins: Where do we meet?
>
> TwoIsTrouble: Regency Square. Tomorrow. 1pm. Come on your own or I promise you'll regret it.
>
> TwoIsTrouble: Oh, and Emily? If you have called the police, I suggest you retract your statement. We both know you'll lose more than I will if the truth comes out.
>
> *TwoIsTrouble is Offline. Your messages will not be sent.*

—

The next morning, I wake with a pounding headache and scratchy throat. It's a surprise to me that I can wake at all because I'm sure I got no sleep last night, and when I did TwoIsTrouble plagued my dreams. But today it will all be over. I pick up my phone then jump when I hear a bang downstairs. My heart leaps; is Mark back? But then I remember. It's just Allie. Guilt washes over me as I wish more than anything she wasn't still here, but I swing my legs from beneath the duvet and pull on a dressing gown to go downstairs and see her.

'Morning,' she calls as I walk into the kitchen. She's already dressed and I pull my dressing gown around me tighter, embarrassed at the intimacy of her seeing me like

262

this. Allie, in comparison, is glowing. In place of her usual baggy hoody is a royal-blue fitted jumper that hugs her curves, showing off her small waist.

'Morning,' I say, unable to avoid a double-take. 'You look great.'

'I borrowed this from the wardrobe, hope you don't mind?' It's only then that I realise the jumper she's wearing is one I discarded years ago after the twins were born and none of my clothes fitted me any more. Mark must have packed it in the move, hoping I'd one day wear it again.

'Coffee?' She moves around the kitchen like I'm the guest but I tell her yes and am thankful that someone is here looking after me, even though I wish I were alone.

'Bad night's sleep?' she asks as she places the cup in front of me, her face the picture of concern and I duck my head to avoid her looking too closely at my puffy eyes.

'Mmm,' I murmur. 'Just hard to sleep, you know, with everything going on. Can't switch my mind off.'

'Yeah, I know that feeling,' she says with a smile. Her face, by comparison, is glowing with a well-rested shine despite the wine we consumed last night. 'I picked up some croissants from the deli around the corner, do you want one?'

Before I can even answer, she's taking one out of the brown paper bag and placing it in the oven to warm, humming as she goes. She seems genuinely delighted to be here and I wonder again how lonely my sister's life is and feel the familiar guilt creeping into the pit of my stomach. But I can't give her what she wants today. I need her gone.

'Sorry, Allie, I don't want to be rude but I think I'm getting a migraine. I just need to go back to bed, I think. Are you okay to drive back now, do you think?'

Her smile falters and two pink spots appear on her cheeks. 'Oh. Yeah, course. I didn't drink that much,' she laughs tightly. 'I can get off now.' She immediately starts picking up her things from around the kitchen – her phone, a book she must have brought with her – and puts them in her handbag.

'I didn't mean this second—'

'It's fine, don't worry about it. I've got loads to do today anyway...'

She tails off awkwardly and looks away, as if she can't bear to tell this obvious lie while looking at me. I follow her into the hallway where she grabs her coat from the hanger.

'I'll call you later?' I say.

She leans in for a swift hug goodbye and I catch the scent of Jo Malone Pomegranate Noir on her neck, my favourite perfume. For a moment I think we must have the same one, but then realise she's probably sprayed some of mine from the bathroom onto herself this morning. The thought makes me sad. It's the sort of thing a little sister should be used to doing, but this might be the first time I can be cross at her for borrowing my stuff. A rite of passage that was taken from both of us after Beth's death.

She pulls away and smiles. 'Yes, I'm sure we'll catch up later.'

–

When she's gone, I grab the croissant from the oven and rip it open hungrily, slathering salty butter on it that drips down my chin as I eat. The stress is making me ravenous. Once my hunger is sated, I fetch my phone from the bedroom and dial Mark. The line rings and rings as I tap my fingers impatiently on the bedside table. No answer. I try again. This time it rings out twice.

'Hello?' His voice is hard, irritated.

'Hi, it's me.'

In the background I hear Ella's laughter and the sound of squealing children all around. They must be at the park by Joanne's house. My stomach dips with longing; I should be there with them, not here alone.

'You're out early with them,' I say.

He sighs down the line. 'Yeah, Mum needed some time to sort the house out…'

I laugh, knowing how Joanne gets about the girls' mess. She loves having them to stay but you can see her itching to tidy up around them as they cast their mess around the house. *A trail of destruction*, Mark's dad always calls it.

'What are you calling for?' Mark says, interrupting my thoughts. His tone is cold, uncaring, and I feel my body curling in on itself. He's never like this with me and I gulp down to keep my voice from wobbling.

'I need to see you,' I say.

'I think we just need some space right now.'

'No, that's the opposite of what we need.' I stand up and march around the room, determined that this is going to work. 'Please, Mark.'

'Em, look…' The sound of children recedes and I imagine him walking away with the phone cupped to his ear. 'I don't want to do this today. Last night was just awful. Horrible. That wasn't us. Wasn't you. I really don't think—'

'You can't just avoid me. We need to talk about things.'

'What, like my "affair"?' He snaps.

I bite my lip at the cruelty in his tone. 'Meet me. Please. We can't go on like this.'

Eventually, he relents and I arrange for him to come to Regency Square just after one o'clock. If he gets there too early, the plan will be ruined, but Mark is always a little late. He can't help it. For once, this will work to my advantage.

–

I pull up just a few streets away from the square and check my reflection in the rear view mirror. I've had hours to prepare but somehow ended up rushing around like crazy as I realised I hadn't left myself enough time if there was traffic; my make-up has slipped beneath a pool of sweat on my upper lip and my carefully applied eyeliner has smudged. I do not look like someone in control. I swear under my breath and dab at my face with the back of my hand to remove some of the shine before swiping underneath my eyes with the back of my fingers. It comes away black. I had to phone Allie as I left, delaying me further, as I noticed her phone charger still plugged in by the kettle. I didn't want her to show up announced to claim it but she was already back home when we spoke and assured me she had a spare, not to worry. As if her running her battery low was the cause of the shake in my voice.

It's 12:48 p.m. I have twelve minutes before TwoIs-Trouble arrives. Out of the car, I pound the pavement as I walk the short distance to the square. Will she already be there? Or will she wait until she spots me before revealing herself? Adrenaline pumps through me with every step as I imagine the look on her face when Mark arrives. He'll know then, as soon as he sees her, that she's not who she says she is. However she's done it, she's tricked her way into Mark's life to start their sordid affair. I think I can forgive him for that, eventually. But what I need today is for Mark to see her for who she really is. Then, she can tell him whatever she likes about me. About Beth. He won't believe her, because instead of me looking crazy, today she'll be outed as the psychopath she is.

I get to the square in a few minutes and scan the crowds for a lone woman. I take a seat on an empty bench and look around at the people who chat with coffees in hand and Pret sandwiches on their laps. It's a busy Saturday afternoon and the atmosphere is cheery as the sun beats down, the first truly warm day we've had this year. Sweat trickles from my hairline as I search for her, too hot in my winter coat. I pull out my phone. It's one o'clock. Everyone around me seems to hear a joke at the same time as the roar of their laughter invades my ears. I look around but no one is noticing me, their faces turned to each other as if this is a normal Saturday afternoon. Where is she?

'Emily?'

I jump up.

'You're early.'

'Am I?' Mark says, looking bewildered by my sharp tone.

I scan the crowds again. No one is here alone. What is she doing? Can she see us? If she sees Mark here it's all ruined.

'Can you get me a coffee?'

'What?'

'Please, just go and grab me one.' I point wildly at the coffee truck across the other side of the square at the opening of the adjoining park.

'Let's go together.'

'No, I need to just stay here a second. Please, Mark. Just go. Please?'

His eyes widen and he shakes his head then sighs as if resigned to my erratic behaviour. 'What do you want?'

'I don't care. Latte. Anything, just go quickly please.'

'Are you okay?'

'Please!' I shout. A Chinese tourist next to us taking pictures of the fountain jumps and stares.

'Okay, okay I'm going,' he says, hands up as he retreats.

My heart is pounding as I look around us. I've ruined it, haven't I? This plan was stupid. I rub at my forehead and my fingers come away slick with sweat and grease. I dab the back of my hand there again but it only makes it worse. I feel the eyes of the tourist on me as I try to settle my breathing. I check my phone again. 1:03 p.m. She might not have seen Mark. I watch him in the coffee queue amongst the happy young couples on a Saturday lunch trip. He glances back over his shoulder to me, watching. Worrying. I don't acknowledge him with a wave, though I'm sure it would reassure him, because then she might see. And she cannot see him. Everything will be ruined.

I scan the people around me again before getting out my phone and opening MumsOnline. Nothing. 1:06. She's not here. 1:08. I wander around the square, searching the faces of everyone I pass but no one is alone. No one is her, I'm sure of it. 1:11.

'Here you go,' Mark says from behind me, catching me off guard. 'Are you all right?' He grabs me by the arm and softly pulls me towards him.

'I'm fine,' I say. His eyes flit across my face, wrinkles etched into his brow as he frowns. He looks tired; his left eye is slightly drooped like it gets when he's not had enough sleep. I yearn to reach out and stroke his face, but as I lift my hand he steps back. 'Here,' he says again, pressing the latte into my hand.

I take it before spinning around again, my eyes desperately scanning around me.

'What's going on?' Mark says. 'Who are you looking for?'

'No one,' I say, turning back to face him.

'Em, you're clearly looking for someone. You have been ever since I got here.'

As he speaks, I catch sight of a blonde woman watching us from across the square. She's alone. She's beautiful. A bare, tanned shoulder peeks out from beneath a peach slouchy jumper as she holds her coffee cup in front of her. She's attractive in the kind of expensive, untouchable way I can never be. Is she Mark's type? Is that the sort of woman he wishes I were? A smile plays on her lips as she watches me watching her. As I drop the latte and run towards her, she baulks and holds her hands in front of her.

'It's you, isn't it?' I shout, grabbing her by the sleeve of her jumper.

'What?' She wrenches her arm back in horror. 'Who are you?'

'Who are *you*?' I shout back.

'Emily!' I feel Mark's grip on my shoulders as he pulls me away. 'What the fuck are you doing?'

I spin around to face him. 'Do you know her?' I snap, jabbing at the woman.

He looks between me and her with his mouth open. I imagine his tongue sliding out into her mouth and feel fury curling through my veins.

'I think you've got me confused—'

'I've never seen that woman before in my life,' Mark says, his voice flat. He pushes me aside and speaks directly to her. 'I'm so sorry. My wife's… She's not been well…'

The woman shakes her head at him and gives me a kind smile that turns my stomach. 'Yeah, women tend to get "unwell" when their husbands cheat on them.'

'That's not what—'

'Are you okay?' she says to me, ignoring Mark. 'Do you need help?'

Tears spill from my eyes as the crowd around us gets closer, all eyes on me and Mark. Mark, who has turned from caring husband to cheating monster in front of their eyes. And me, the poor, foolish wife.

'No…' I say, my words too quiet to be heard. 'No, I… I want to go home.'

Mark shakes his head and cuts in. 'We're fine, you can all go back to whatever the fuck you were doing. Okay? This is over.' He spits the words, his cheeks burning in the sunlight, as he yanks me by the arm away from the crowd.

My phone beeps and I reach to grab it.

Unknown number.

> Come on, Emily. Did you really think I was that stupid? Luckily, your husband is. The girls say hi x

'Where are the girls?' I shout. Mark whips around.

'What?'

'Where are they? Tell me!'

He shakes his head and sighs. 'Calm down. Jesus Christ, you'll end up with someone calling the police—'

'Mark! Where are the girls?' I hit him on the arm, hard, enough to shock him into silence as he gapes at me. 'Tell me, please. Where are they?'

'Are you okay?' A man appears by Mark's side, stepping between us, his body providing an unnecessary protective barrier.

'Jesus Christ,' Mark snaps from between gritted teeth. 'We're fine, can you all just leave us alone, please?' He grabs my hand and drags me from the scene, the sweater-wearing man left looking put-out at his chance to play the hero disappearing.

'You need to calm down,' Mark says to me. 'The girls are fine. Okay? They're fine.'

I swallow and bite my lip, desperate to quell the panic that claws at my skin. I ask again, this time more calmly. Rationally. Like I know Mark needs to be. 'Mark, where are they?'

By this point, he's walked me all the way to the edge of the square and he gets out his car keys, clicking the button until the familiar bleep of the door unlocking can be heard. 'They're with your sister.'

'What?'

He rubs his head and gets out his phone. 'Allie's looking after them.'

'What? Why?'

He opens his eyes wide. 'Well, someone had to! I couldn't bring them here and risk them seeing you like this.' He throws his hands up at me as if I stand in evidence of my own bad behaviour.

My feet feel on firmer ground now that Mark has given me an answer. The girls are fine, they're with Allie. Confusion claws at me though; why Allie? Why would Mark call her when they barely know each other?

'Where are your parents?'

He frowns. 'It's Saturday, Emily.'

'Oh. Of course.' Tennis. Mark's parents play every Saturday lunchtime without fail. It strikes me as comically bizarre that they would keep this arrangement today, in the midst of everything going on, but of course no one knows what's going on. No one but me.

'I need to call her.'

'My mum? She'll be—'

I shake my head as I dial Allie's number. It rings, over and over.

'Em, what's going on?'

The voicemail kicks in. I dial again. Listen to mechanic voice. 'Not your mum. I'm calling Alison. I need to speak to the girls… To make sure they're okay.'

'Why wouldn't they be?'

The phone keeps ringing.

'Emily!' Mark shouts and grabs the phone from my hand, slamming it against the roof of his car, away from me. 'Tell me what's going on. Now.' His voice is thick with fury and I take a step back.

'I don't understand why the girls are with Allie—'

'No, well, you wouldn't,' Mark snaps.

'What does that mean?'

'Why did you want me to come here today?' he asks. 'I don't understand what's happening. Why are you acting like this?'

I search his eyes as he holds my gaze. We're barely a metre apart and the urge to reach out to him, to feel the warmth of his body on mine is unbearable. My body hurts with the want; I imagine him dragging me to him, wrapping me in his arms as I breathe in the musky aftershave he wears on the weekends. But the more I look, the more

Mark transforms into someone I don't know. His shirt is new. My eyes run across his chest, desperate to recognise the creases by his collar but I can't.

'Emily?'

I take a step back and in that second I feel his arms around me, my body forced into his chest as the blare of a horn assaults my ears. 'Fucking hell!' He shouts and pushes me back, holding me by the arms, the base of his thumb pressed in deeply. 'Get in the car,' he says. 'We're not doing this on the road. You could have fucking killed yourself.'

He opens the door and pushes me in, like I'm his prisoner. My body shakes as I sit. He gets in from the other side and puts my phone and his in the cup holders, like he always does. I grab mine and dial my sister again. I tell myself everything is okay. If they're with Allie, they're safe. But TwoIsTrouble's message continues to taunt me as we drive. *The girls say hi.*

'She's been helping out,' Mark eventually says in between my redialling.

'Who has?'

He clears his throat and indicates left away from the square, towards his parents' house. 'Allie.'

I frown. 'Helping with what?'

I dial again, but barely hear the voicemail cut in as I wait for Mark to reply. His cheeks flush. 'The girls. Me.'

'You? What have you needed help with?'

He breathes deeply and shakes his head. 'I've needed someone to talk to. Since you've been... like this.'

My head swims. Allie? Allie has been helping Mark?

'She's been there for me. For all of us.'

'Since when?'

'A while,' he says and I see him swallow once, then again, a habit he has when he's nervous. 'She got in touch just after the accident,' Mark says and my mouth drops open.

'You've been speaking for over a year?'

He shakes his head. 'It's not like that. We didn't speak that much until recently. She'd just check in every now and again, to see how you were. She was worried about you. Then after all the house stuff last week, I went to see her.'

I scoff and he throws one hand up off the steering wheel.

'I couldn't trust you to sort it out and I didn't want us losing all that money just because you were...' He stops the word 'crazy' from leaving his mouth but I can hear it on the tip of his tongue. 'I needed someone to talk to,' he adds defensively, the anger leaving his chest in a puff. He knows this is a betrayal, to go to her behind my back when I've been at my lowest, treating her like some sort of surrogate wife. 'Don't make it into something it's not,' he says, snatching a look at me as we stop at traffic lights. 'I'm not getting into your paranoia again.'

'It's not paranoia, Mark. The girls told me you'd been with a woman. That she'd given them a book.'

He shakes his head and scoffs. 'That was Allie, you idiot.' Then he laughs, as if this is all a big mix-up that's about to be happily solved, but the world starts to shift beneath me.

'Allie gave you the book?'

'Not me. But yes, she gave it to the girls.'

'The Roald Dahl book?' I say, the words fat and sluggish in my mouth. 'That was from Allie?'

'Yes, I just said so.' He pulls away from the traffic lights and I hold onto the side of the car like a life raft.

'I'm going be sick.'

'What? Why? Jesus…' The car slows and then swerves to the left. I open the door as the bile rises in my throat then pours out in yellow streaks across the pavement.

It was her. All this time. It was Allie.

Forty-One

Now

'Emily, stop!'

I'm screaming at Mark to drive faster, hitting his arm with my fists as I stare at the other road users through my tears. We have to get there. We have to get to them.

'Please, Mark. Please, we have to—'

'I'm driving! Calm down, seriously! You have to stop or you're going to make me crash.'

I gulp in air as I try and quieten the voice in my head, the one screaming at me that this is all my fault.

'Tell me what's going on,' Mark says. His tone is calm but there's a slight shake at the end of his speech, as if the panic is waiting to come out.

'We need to get to them, they aren't safe with Allie.'

'Jesus, Emily,' Mark snaps. His eyes flick across to me. The lights in front of us are red and he turns back to stare at them. 'I know things have been hard, perhaps I shouldn't have left. But the girls are fine, I promise you.'

I shake my head as the lights turn green. 'You don't understand. No one understands.'

He sighs but the car jolts forward as he cuts across the crossroads at a speed that makes the other drivers honk.

'What don't I understand? Tell me. For god's sake – you're scaring me.' He yanks the car up a gear and presses his foot flat to the floor.

'Allie's been… She's been pretending to be someone else, online. She's been threatening me.'

'What?'

We spin around the corner as another car blares their horn again; sweat drips down my back as I grip the door handle. Mark slams his foot on the brake and we come to a screeching halt. I scream at him to keep going but he stares at me resolutely.

'I'm not taking you to see the girls like this. We promised each other that.'

Though I want to scream at him and my former self for being stupid enough to make that ridiculous promise, I force myself to take a breath and calm down enough to convince Mark that this is not some kind of psychotic break.

'I met someone online last year, on the parenting forum—'

'MumsOnline,' Mark says and I flinch, as if the very knowledge of the site could be hidden from him. I nod and carry on.

'I told her a lot about us. About me, my mental health. The miscarriage, the accident with the girls…'

Mark looks at me, his expression confused but not unkind, the anger in his eyes waning.

'I shouldn't have been so open with her. I thought she was a stranger. Someone I could talk to in confidence outside of everything else. But when I left the site the other week before I went back to work, well, she followed me…'

'What?'

'She found me on Instagram, then Facebook. She started sending weird messages and making threats and I wanted to prove it to you so I brought you here today to see her for yourself, but then she texted me and you said about the book and I realise she's not a stranger at all. It's Allie, Mark. Allie is the one stalking me.'

He puffs out his cheeks and grips the steering wheel, looking straight ahead of us. My heart pounds painfully in my chest as a family walks past the car, the sound of their normal Saturday afternoon piercing the atmosphere between us. Mark sighs and finally turns to me, his eyes soft and I think, yes, this is it, he believes me.

'Em, darling… That's just… that's just not true, is it?'

Rage bubbles up inside me and I slam my hand against the dashboard, then I remember the text on my phone.

'Then explain this.' I shove the phone at him and watch as he reads, his face going from weary annoyance to disbelief in seconds.

'This is… this is ridiculous. This can't be from her. Allie would never—'

He grabs his own phone and brings it to his ear. I listen to the now familiar voicemail message. He tries again, swearing under his breath. Nothing. He looks at me, fear etched over every inch of his face. Without a word, he yanks the car into gear and slams his foot on the accelerator.

Ten minutes later, we arrive on Mark's parents' street where he says he left Allie with the girls, and I let out a breath. We're almost there. Allie won't hurt them; it's me she wants to punish, not them.

The brakes squeal as we pull into the driveway. He looks at me quickly before jumping out of the car, I run after him and try to ignore the shake in his hands as he struggles with the door key. It's hard to keep convincing myself that this is all going to be okay when Mark is visibly rattled.

'Lara? Ella? Girls?' His booming voice bounces from the walls as we enter the house. He strides from the hall to the living room to the kitchen, shouting louder as each empty room appears. He pushes past me in the hallway and runs upstairs. His shouts continue, each one piercing my heart harder than the last.

'They're not here,' he says as he stands at the top of the stairs, his face dumbfounded. 'They aren't here.'

Behind me, the sound of the front door makes us both jump and in that second I think everything will be fine. Allie will be there with the girls behind her. They've been at the park. They've had an ice-cream. My sister has been caring for them. Making them giggle as she pushes them on the swings. My daughters are safe.

'Oh, Emily! You're here!'

I cry, a feral sound, as Joanne appears in the doorway. Mark pounds down the stairs and pushes me out of the way to stand in front of his mother.

'Have you seen them? Have you seen the girls?'

She looks between Mark and me and the fear in her eyes tells me everything. Mark shakes her by the shoulders and asks her again.

'No… We haven't been here; we've been—'

'Fuck!' he screams at the top of his voice as his dad walks through the door.

'Ella? Lara? Girls?' Joanne ploughs past us and screeches through each room of the house, shooting looks over her shoulder at us as if this might be some sick joke we're playing. As she passes through the rooms finding them empty, her words become more strangled; desperate.

I follow her through into the kitchen which she scans quickly and exits back into the hallway to Mark. It's only when she's gone that I see the handwritten note on the counter.

'What has she done?' Joanne screams to Mark as I read it, hands shaking. Joanna storms back in the kitchen and spits at me, 'What have you done?'

Shame crawls over my body as she echoes the same words my mother howled at me over and over the night Beth died. I've let everyone down again. This is all my fault.

'It's my sister,' I say, my tongue fat and heavy as the words form. 'My sister has taken them.' The words fall from my mouth like lava; Mark jumps back and stares at me with his eyes so wide the red lines in his irises look fit to burst.

'But this doesn't make any sense!' Mark cries. 'Why would Allie—'

I shake my head, my tears blurring his face. How can I ever explain it to him? It strikes me for the first time how obvious this all is. Of course it would be Allie, the only person who would be so heartbroken and betrayed over the truth about Beth that they'd go to any lengths to hurt me.

'That doesn't matter now but I know it's her. She's been behind it all; the messages, the notes, and now she has the girls.'

'Emily, this is insane. If you think she's a danger to the girls, we need to call the police.'

I shake my head firmly. 'We can't.' I uncurl the note from my fist and hand it to Mark.

Mark studies the scrawled handwriting, his mouth moving with the words. 'Don't call the police. If you do, things will get worse.'

Joanna cries, the sound painful and raw. Mark pulls out his phone and I reach to stop him.

'You can't! She said things will get worse—'

He slaps my hand away, so hard that it stings.

'How the *fuck* could things get worse? She's taken the girls. Do you understand what's happening right now?' He grabs my shoulders and shakes me. 'She has our daughters.'

I open and shut my mouth, desperate to say something that will make this nightmare end but as I claw around for the words I find nothing. I see Beth's lifeless body in my mind, remember the weight of her against me as I held her on the cold kitchen floor. Was Allie watching? Does she know what really happened? Or just the parts that will make her hate me? The room spins as I think of her leaving my house this morning, the perfect little sister. She's insane, isn't she? Only an insane person could do all of this. What's coming next?

I can't breathe.

I feel Mark's hands on my back as I lurch forward, putting my head between my knees, desperate to suck in some air. The floor tiles beneath me spin in and out of focus.

After a few moments, my vision begins to still. Mark is on his knees in front of me telling me to breathe. In. Out. Control the panic. When I'm able to lift my head and breathe normally, Mark stands up and paces the room.

'Emily, just tell me what is going on. Why would Allie take them?' he asks me, feet banging against the tiles as he walks. 'Answer me!'

'Enough, Mark. That's enough,' Joanne's voice floats between us and I snap my head up; I'd forgotten she was even here. The front door is wide open and I see Mark's dad, Alan, pacing the driveway, the phone pressed to his ear.

'What's he doing?' I ask, but no one is listening to me any more. Joanne pulls Mark into the living room and sits him down as he tries to piece together what little he understands of the story so far. Alan strides through the hallway, not stopping to acknowledge me at all and the stab of pain at his dismissal makes me wince.

'They're on their way,' I hear him tell Joanne.

'Who are?' I follow him into the living room and suddenly all eyes are on me. 'Who are on their way?'

Mark looks between his parents whose eyes are glued to the floor. 'The police.'

'No!' I scream. 'She said not to tell them – how could you?' Tears blur my view as I scream at Mark; I feel his arms wrap around me as I wail. Hopeless. This is all so hopeless.

It feels like hours between Alan making the call, the two PCs arriving at Mark's parents' house and them escorting us back to our house but in reality it can't be that long; time has slowed and stretched since the girls have been gone. I try and picture where they are right now. In the back of a car? Walking through the park, Allie holding their hands? My stomach cramps painfully. She won't hurt them. She'd never hurt them. But the memory of Beth's lifeless body won't disappear from my mind and I know the women in my family are more than capable of hurting a child.

'They're here,' Mark announces as he watches from the living room window. 'They're here.' The two PCs who took our original details stand up and go outside to meet the new officers on the driveway. Detectives, we've been told, are the ones who need to deal with an 'incident of this sort'.

I stand up and smooth down my hair as he goes to the front door to let the new officers in. I stand awkwardly, not knowing what to do with my hands. I feel like I'm under inspection, like I have to present the picture of a good mother to show them this is not my fault. But the feeling of shame and guilt whirls in my stomach as they enter the room and I know they see right through me.

'This is my wife, Emily,' Mark says. The two new officers nod at me.

'I'm DS Reynolds,' the man says, 'and this is DC Sharp.' He nods at the younger female police officer beside him. She looks at me blankly. I wonder if they train them to do that. To show no feeling in their eyes. Mark hovers anxiously behind them, rubbing his hands and looking from me to them as if waiting for something to happen.

'I'll go and make some drinks, shall I?' The younger officer says, nodding towards the kitchen to confirm where to go. She strides off confidently and I hear her opening and shutting the drawers, searching for a source of comfort for us in an unfamiliar kitchen.

'Mark, would you like to take a seat and I can take down some details from you?' DS Reynolds says. Mark nods and sits down next to me. I reach out for his hand but he moves away, his eyes fixed on the officer.

'So, you believe that your sister-in-law has taken your children,' he says, looking down at his notebook. 'Lara and Ella?' He reads.

'Yes. She has them.'

'Can you tell me a bit about her, please? Name, address, that sort of thing.'

Mark looks over at me helplessly. 'We gave all of this to the other officers—' Mark starts to say but I cut him off.

'Her name is Alison Sanders,' I say. 'She still lives at our mum's house—'

'The address, please?'

I reel off the address of my childhood home, tripping over the postcode that I've not had to say out loud for so long.

'Have you contacted your mum?'

I shake my head firmly as Mark cuts in, 'She passed away last year.'

'I'm sorry to hear that. Your dad?'

Another shake as Mark tells him my dad also passed away a few years ago.

'No other siblings?'

Mark pauses for a moment, before flicking a quick look at me. 'They had another sister, but she died in an accident when she was a child.'

'I see. Okay. We'll need a description of Alison from you, Emily, and any photographs you have. The more recent, the better. We've got patrol cars ready and waiting in the local area—'

'I don't have one,' I say, panic rising in my throat. 'I don't have any photos of her.'

The words fall out in a rush, each statement compounding my fear.

DC Sharp walks back in with our drinks and places them on the coffee table in front of us.

'Have you got any photos at all, perhaps from when you last saw each other?'

I shake my head and tears cloud my vision.

'That's okay,' she tells me, as DS Reynolds walks out of the room.

'Where's he going?' I ask.

'Don't worry about him,' she tells me with a smile. She has a soothing face, now that she's let some emotion sink in. Her large hazel eyes are kind, but confident. Having her in our living room makes me feel like things are going to happen. This is a woman who gets things done.

'So, I understand from Mark's initial report that you haven't been close with your sister until very recently, and there's been a bit of an issue lately with her sending you messages online?'

I shake my head. 'Not just online,' I say. 'She's done things to me at work, and she called the girls' nursery—'

'What?' Mark cries as he recoils away from me. 'When? Why didn't you tell me?'

I close my eyes and try to ignore his outrage. 'I didn't know how. She called and pretended to be me… she made it sound like I was ill again…'

Mark puts his head in his hands and huffs in frustration. I hear him mutter 'this is insane' to himself over and over.

'Can you think of anywhere she might have gone with them?'

I shake my head.

'Any reason she might have for taking them? It can really help to try and work out where someone might have gone.'

Tears spill down my face. 'She thinks I'm a bad mother. She thinks…' I hiccup through the sobs, unable to say any more.

'Okay, Emily. It's okay.'

DS Reynolds walks back into the room and they exchange an ominous glance.

'Emily, can you come and show me a recent picture of the girls, please?' DC Sharp says, standing up. She doesn't wait for an answer and I follow her out of the room. In the hallway, she asks if I have anything printed – it's better than a phone copy, she says. I dither for a moment, wondering when I lasted printed a photo of them, suddenly feeling like a terrible mother for not printing every single image I have. I take out my phone and scroll through the endless photos of their beautiful faces, my heart in my throat.

'If you could email me a few, please,' she says, looking over my shoulder. 'They're beautiful girls, aren't they? Yes, that one is perfect.'

My hands shake as I scroll and she asks me if she can take the phone and email herself. I hand it over and watch her typing in her address then hear the whoosh of the email sending. 'We can print them at the station,' she says. 'Do you have any other photos we can take?'

I nod and take her upstairs. She follows me into our bedroom where my pyjama bottoms still lie on the floor in a pile. I kick them into the corner of the room as I enter. I remove the photo from inside the frame on our window sill; it's from their last birthday and I shake my head as I hold it in my hands. It's no good. They've already changed so much since then. I tell DC Sharp as much but she tells me not to worry; that she has the digital images too.

'Can I ask why you didn't tell your husband when this all started, Emily?' DC Sharp asks, turning over the photo in her hand.

'I was scared he wouldn't believe me,' I say. 'I've not been well… over the last few years. Post-natal depression. It made me do some strange things. I believed strange things, sometimes.'

She nods, as if she understands. My eyes fall to the curve of her stomach, hidden beneath a loose shirt, and I wonder if underneath is the sagging skin of a mother.

'Do you think your sister could be dangerous?'

I bite my lip as my stomach crunches painfully. I nod, tears clouding my vision, and tell her, yes. Yes, I think my sister could be very dangerous.

Forty-Two

Now

Allie

When I first found Mum's diaries, I couldn't work out what they were. The handwritten words inside didn't sound like Mum, not the one I remembered. Despite the familiar handwriting, at first I convinced myself that the worn notebooks weren't hers at all but rather something she found at a charity shop and took home out of interest. She was always doing things like that, wasn't she? She was obsessed with other people's lives; if we ever came across a scrap piece of paper on the pavement, she'd have to pick it up and read whatever had been scrawled on it. Do you remember? She'd dissect whatever was on there, usually a receipt or discarded shopping list, as if it held the secrets to life itself. *Look girls*, she'd say, holding the muddy piece of paper in her hand out to us, *I wonder why they were buying all of this.* I'd roll my eyes and ignore her, never understanding her fascination with the banalities of other people's lives but Beth loved it and I've since come to understand the obsession.

After I'd read a few pages of the first diary, I couldn't keep up the hope that the words weren't hers. I remember sitting in our house, the air already stale with the loss of her, and reading those pages with the same level of morbid curiosity as she'd displayed over every discarded receipt we'd ever found.

I didn't want to believe it. Any of it.

I did think about going straight to you and asking outright whether it was true. Whether you'd really done what my mum accused you of, whether everything I thought about our childhood had been a lie. But every time I picked up the phone to call you, I'd imagine saying the words and I couldn't. How do you ask someone something like that?

So I went to MumsOnline instead. I knew you used it. You'd told me before about tips you'd picked up from the other mums on there about how to manage the twins when I tried to give you my own advice. I also knew everyone on the site was anonymous; that people shared things there that they'd never say in person. That's how I got the idea. I thought if we became friends, real friends, like we'd never managed in real life, then perhaps I'd find out what really happened. Whether my own sister could have really killed my twin.

And I did.

Most days, I wish I never had.

How do you ever recover from that? How can you ever forget that your sister is a killer? A murderer. Evil.

Because that's what you are. And it wasn't enough for you to take Beth's life, to ruin mine, you went on to have two perfect girls of your own. Girls just like us. You think you'd appreciate that, right? But no. You hate those girls. I don't care what you say or do in person, I've seen the real you, laid bare on the screen. You hated Beth and me and now you hate your own children. When I read the things you would say about them, I knew that history was going to repeat itself. Unless I stopped you.

I was too late to save your baby, wasn't I? You can tell yourself what you like, but I know you took those pills on purpose. What sort of mother would double a dose without checking first? The sort of mother who wishes she wasn't one at all, that's who.

I look back at Ella and Lara in the rear view mirror and my heart pangs. They're so very like Beth and me. Indistinguishable from each other, almost. To an untrained eye, at least. But I've always been able to tell them apart. It must be a twin thing.

'How are we doing back there, girlies?' I ask in a sing-song voice.

'Where are we going?' Lara asks for the millionth time since we've been driving.

'I've told you, we're on a secret adventure! Isn't that fun?'

She eyes me suspiciously as Ella watches her from the corner of her eyes. A flare of annoyance flickers through me at the obvious lack of trust the girls are showing for me. But it's not their fault; they've been raised by a mother who doesn't care for them, who sees them as a burden, who once put them in a car and almost killed them. They're bound to have trust issues.

It won't be like that for us.

'I miss Mummy,' Ella says, lighting the fire again.

I sigh but bite back from replying. They can't help it; they've been told that you love them. That your behaviour is normal. They'll realise soon that it wasn't real love. You're incapable of love; Mum saw that years ago and because no one believed her, Beth ended up dead. Years later, you're doing the exact same thing. Pretending to be the perfect loving mother and wife, while sitting at home writing disgusting things about your family online. Sure, you can blame 'post-natal depression' and some days your pills are strong enough to fool Mark that you've changed, some days you've even appeared normal on MumsOnline, but I know the truth about you, Emily, just like Mum did. You are rotten. Evil. Incapable of love. Mark is starting to see it and soon so will everyone else.

Forty-Three

Now

After DC Sharp and DS Reynolds leave, they're replaced with another officer who tells us her name is Mo and she'll be acting as our family liaison officer. With her arrival came the return of my car by more officers; I'd discarded it at the park in Cheltenham earlier today without a thought. As they return the keys as if dropping off a hire car, Mark and I stare at each other in the hallway like we are in the midst of a war that we don't know how to escape from. But it's not long before Mo is making herself comfortable in the kitchen, supplying us both with cups of tea that we don't drink as she tells us everything the police are doing behind the scenes to find the girls. Her voice is solid, reassuring. She speaks in run-on sentences and clicks her tongue against her teeth every so often in lieu of a full-stop.

Mark has barely said a word since my confession about Alison's postcard to the house and calls to the nursery. I know what he's thinking; that she knows every element of our lives. Can reach us anywhere. Can do anything.

We are in the kitchen now, our backs pressed against the hard chairs, our hands pressed in front of us at the table. Every few seconds I take out my phone and check it for news, but nothing ever comes. Mo has told us that the patrol units have been given photos of the girls and are out looking right now. She says because the girls are identical twins, it will be harder for Alison to get anywhere unnoticed. People love twins, she tells me, and I nod, mutely.

When we've been silent for too long, Mo's mobile rings, making Mark and me jump from our seats and stare at her like anxious puppies.

'Hello?' she says, answering. I pray that they've been found, beg God in a way I didn't know I would ever do. 'Yes, that's fine. I'll show them now, thanks.'

She hangs up and all my hope evaporates.

'What is it?' Marks says.

'They think they've found a recent photo of Alison. They're sending it to me now.' Her phone beeps with the message and I hold my breath, waiting to see my sister's face.

Mo holds the phone out to me and I nod.

'That's her. That's Allie.'

The photo is horrifying in its normality; a pretty, young woman sitting at the table in a pub, a glass of wine in front of her. I wonder who took it, who made my sister smile like that? I curse myself again for not knowing a single real thing about Allie's life. Pictures of Allie as a child run through my mind, but the years between then and now are woefully blank. Other than the few days we've spent together recently, I know nothing about her at all. I look at the photo again and try to see kindness in her eyes rather than the monster I'm painting over her face.

Is she smiling like that at the girls right now? Is she being kind? Is she leading them down the street, hand-in-hand, as she tells them stories, tells them to mind their steps by the road, tells them she'll keep them safe? Or is she... No, I can't let myself go there. I won't.

'They'll find them now,' I say to Mark, dragging my eyes from the image. 'They've got her photo so she should be easy to find. They'll be back any minute.'

Mark buries his face in his hands and shakes his head. I keep going, desperate to convince him this is all going to be okay.

'She can't hide, not with the girls. Mo is right; you can't go anywhere with them without people noticing. Remember when they were babies, how much I used to moan about not being able to leave the house without answering twenty questions about what it was like to have twins?' I laugh, a hollow cackle that I don't seem to be able to control. 'It's even worse now. Everywhere I go, people stop me. You know what it's like. She'll barely be able to walk down the street without being stopped. Not with the girls. Not with them, she won't—'

'Stop!' Mark shouts, hands falling from his face and slamming against the table. 'Just stop.'

I stare at him open-mouthed, heart pumping so hard I feel he must be able to see it through the folds of my jumper. Something in Mark's face has changed. He doesn't just look scared any more. He looks angry.

'How could you keep this from me?' he snaps.

'You wouldn't have understood...'

He tosses his head back and grunts. 'You've caused this,' he says. 'You've put them in danger.'

'You were the one who left them with her!'

The colour drains from his face as the accusation sits between us. I want to take it back immediately, scrape it from the table and wash it away, but it's too late. The words are like a stain seeping into the wood. They'll never be removed. 'Why were you seeing her? What was going on?'

Mark blushes and in that instant I know that his guilt runs as deeply as mine.

'Were you two...' I can't even say the words.

'No,' he snaps, but keeps his eyes on the table. 'No. Nothing happened.'

'But you wanted it to.'

He looks up at me and shakes his head, but I'm sure I can see it in his eyes. Guilt.

'Did you *know*?' I screech. 'Did you know she was going to take them? Is this—oh my god! Are you two going to take them from me, start a new perfect family?'

'What? Jesus, Emily. No! How could you think that?'

Mo appears in the kitchen doorway and tells us to calm down. But it's too late, she's heard everything and now we aren't just one incompetent, untrustworthy parent but two.

–

They question Mark for what feels like forever about Alison. There were moments during his confession that made me want to get up and walk out, but I remained planted in my seat, rage pooling beneath me.

He liked her. He didn't say so, but it's obvious from the way he spoke about her. They spoke a lot, it turns out. Not the last few days while he's been away from me, but while he was in the house with me over the past year, after he'd shed his work suit and joined us at home, they would text all night long, me sleeping beside him like an unknowing fool, or worse, hunched over my own laptop desperately typing to her too. At first, he told them, it was just about me. Allie would check in to see how I was, how he was coping looking after the girls while I was so 'erratic'. But they soon started having their own chats about their days, what they were watching on TV, little in-jokes that the officers read on Mark's phone as I looked away, shame-faced.

She made her way into every aspect of our lives. We've both been fooled.

As the day turns to evening and the sunlight begins to fade, the sense of despair in the house grows. The idea of not putting the girls to bed, not giving them their bath, is unbearable. Every so often, there will be a noise from outside, someone pulling into their drive home from work, or walking past the house, unaware of the horror we're facing inside, and we'll both jump. Sometimes, one of us will run to the window like a child waiting for their parents to return home. But it's never them, it's never the girls. We return to the kitchen, our faces more drawn, our conviction that 'this is all going to be fine' a little weaker each time.

'I'm so sorry, Mark, Emily, but I have to go off shift now and I'm afraid we haven't got anyone to replace me. I'll be back first thing in the morning,' Mo tells us. She holds her phone tightly in her left hand as she speaks and glances at the enormous chrome clock on our mauve-painted kitchen walls. 'I'm sorry, we try not to leave the—'

She slips over the next word – parents? Victims? What are we now, if the girls aren't here? What are we if they never come back? The world falls away as I blink my eyes closed and refuse to consider the answer. That will not happen. It can't.

'It's fine,' Mark interrupts. 'We're fine on our own. Who will be in contact when... when they find them?'

The way his voice goes up at the end, the hope it contains, pulls at my heart.

Mo explains the official process to Mark: how we'll hear, what we'll hear. Everything except when. The only answer we really want. When he's done questioning her, Mo gets her things and we walk to the door together.

'Do you have kids?' I ask her as we reach the front door. She smiles tightly. 'Is that why you need to get home? To put them to bed?'

'Night, Emily. Try and get to bed yourself,' she tells me. 'I'll be back first thing tomorrow.'

She shuts the door behind her and I watch her small frame disappear down the road through the patterned glass of the door.

We are alone.

Mark appears in the hallway. 'You should eat something,' he says.

'I'm not hungry.'

He grunts and nods. We stand awkwardly, two strangers in a home we've built together.

'She won't hurt them,' he says. 'I know I don't know her like you do, but she cares about the girls, about you. Perhaps she's taken them to—'

'To what?' I snap. 'Save them? From me?'

Mark looks away, shame-faced.

Even now, in Mark's eyes, it's me who is the problem. He's barely spent any time with Allie in real life, and when he has, she's lied to him about everything. She's manipulated him, stolen his children, but still he wants to believe in her over me. How has she done this? How can my shy, nervous little sister have plotted and planned to turn the people who love me so utterly against me?

'I can see that she's had just the effect on you that she was hoping to,' I say, turning to walk up the stairs.

He grabs me from behind, his grip firm on my wrist. 'She won't hurt them,' he shouts. 'She will not hurt my daughters.'

I shake away his grip and see it then; it's not the allure of Alison that's making Mark believe she's not a danger, it's desperation. He can't bear to think that a monster has our girls. That he is, in his own way, responsible for putting them in danger. His rage quickly dissolves to despair as tears fall down his face, washing away my own anger.

I step forward and wrap my arms around his hard body; we melt into one as we cry.

'We can't let her do this,' I whisper. 'We have to do something.'

He pushes me back and wipes away his tears. 'What can we do?'

I tighten my grip on his waist. 'We can go and find her.'

Mark wrinkles his nose and sighs. 'Em, the police are out there already. What more can we do?'

Tears pool in my eyes as he pulls me back into his chest. 'We can't just sit here doing nothing,' I sob. He embraces me so tightly I can barely breathe but the relief of feeling him beside me again makes it worth it.

'It's okay,' he says. 'We'll find her. You're right. We need to do this together. Everything will be okay, I promise.'

He holds me against his warm chest and I let myself be held up by his strength before the sound of three quick thuds on the door pulls us apart.

Forty-Four

Now

'Have you found them?' Mark says as soon he opens the door.

DS Reynolds locks eyes with me from the doorstep and my blood runs cold.

'What's going on?' Mark says again.

'What's happened? Tell us!' I add as he stares. Mark clasps my hand in his as the seconds tick by.

'We have found the girls,' he finally says and I barely have time to register it before he adds, 'Emily, we need you to come with us, please.'

Mark looks at me then at him. 'What for? What's going on? Are they safe?'

DS Reynolds clears his throat. 'They're perfectly safe, I promise you. They're fine.'

'Oh my god,' I cry as my knees give way. 'Are they—'

'They're safe and well. But I do need you to come with us, please. Mark, DC Sharp is going to take you in separately.' He holds his arm out as if we're going to blindly follow, but this isn't the moment of joy I was expecting. Something is very wrong.

'Why are we going separately?' Mark asks.

DC Reynolds sighs and looks at me with contempt. 'We can chat about that at the station. Emily, come on. Don't make this more difficult than it needs to be.'

Mark looks at me then and I feel his grip on my hand loosen until finally he drops me altogether. 'What's going on?' he says to me and I start to say I have no idea but something sick curls in my stomach.

'What has she said?' I snap to the officers. 'What's Allie told you?'

They look at each other and nod, then DS Reynolds steps forward and asks me again to come with him, please, to stop making a scene, but I can't. I'm shouting that she's lying, that they can't believe anything Alison says and suddenly I'm being led from my home, away from my husband, into the back of a police car, like a criminal.

–

The girls must be fine. They wouldn't keep me from them if anything was wrong. Would they? No. They're fine. They must be fine. They told us they were fine. *Perfectly safe*, that's what he said. They wouldn't lie to us. If I keep telling myself that, then I might start to believe it.

The room I'm in doesn't have any windows. Who has sat on this seat before me? A shoplifter? An ASBO teen? A murderer? Laughter tickles at my throat followed by the certainty that something is very, very wrong with me. There is nothing funny here. Why do I so desperately want to laugh? It's the exhaustion, that's all. But I know I cannot for a moment let any madness out, not while they're watching me. That's why I'm here in the first place. I've no idea what Alison has done, what she's told the officers to get me here, but a horrible thought keeps playing through my mind: she has won.

DS Reynolds enters the room and smiles tightly at me. With him is a woman I haven't seen before. She looks around my age. Her blonde, wavy hair hangs loosely on her shoulders, the sheer cream blouse she's wearing making the ends static. My eyes search her body as I've become accustomed to doing, looking for the slight leftover bump in her stomach that betrays all mothers. I'm gleeful when I see it. She is like me.

'Are you okay, Emily?' DS Reynolds asks, spotting my smile. I wipe it from my face and nod. He nods back, slowly. The hum of the radiator buzzes in my ears as it pumps out unnecessary heat.

'Hi, Emily. My name's Hannah, I'm the duty solicitor—'

'Ella was going to be called Hannah. Mark didn't like it though, ex-girlfriend's name.' The fact crawls from the depths of my memory and I smile, as if I said it on purpose.

Hannah smiles back and takes the seat next to me. She lifts it before pulling it out and I like her for that; men so often don't, leaving it to squeal painfully across the floor. Some women, too. I like Hannah, she is someone I can trust, I'm sure of it.

DS Reynolds sits opposite us and pulls out a file, then a small tape recorder. I stare at it in wonder. A tape recorder. I'm in a police interview. It makes my stomach turn; all I can think about is the moment he'll turn it on and that beep will play. The long, drawn out, slightly comical never-ending beep that Mark and I have laughed about on Sunday evenings watching *Line of Duty*, a glass of wine in hand. *Do you think it's really that long in real life? I bet it's not, it can't be,* he would always say to me and we'd laugh as Hastings sat opposite some despicable criminal, glaring across the recorder, the beep blaring between them.

'I'm just going to switch this on, so we've a record of our conversation,' DS Reynolds tells me as I watch him press the button. The beep starts, then stops, almost immediately. I look up at him, as if it might be broken, but he begins talking, as if nothing is wrong. I'll have to tell Mark that he was right.

DS Reynolds does his introductions for the tape and I listen in fascination as my name is read out like someone else's entirely. I am Emily Jones. I am a mother. I am a wife. There is nothing wrong with me.

'As I said before, you are not under arrest but we are questioning you under caution today which is why you have been provided a solicitor.' He nods at Hannah who smiles at me encouragingly. 'Right, let's begin.'

'Emily, you reported your daughters, Ella and Lara Jones, missing earlier today, Saturday twelfth of March.'

I nod.

'You said you believed your sister, Alison Sanders, had taken the girls without your consent.'

'Yes,' I say. 'How did you find them? Are they okay? When can I see them?'

'As I've said, the girls are fine. They're with your husband now, and you can see them soon. We just need to clear a few things up first.'

I look at Hannah who gives me another tight smile then turns back to DS Reynolds.

'Now, Emily, what we need to do tonight is to understand what's going on here, because your sister, Alison, has told us that you were well aware that she had the girls – that you actually asked her to take them—'

'No!' I shout. 'No, I didn't. Why would I do that? Mark was the one who went to her.' I'm shaking my head so violently that the room spins when I stop and I find DS Reynolds looking at me with concern. I turn to Hannah. 'I'd never have left them with her; she's never even had them for the day! Why would I leave them with her now? She never sees the girls—'

'It's okay, Emily. Let's just talk through what happened,' DS Reynolds says, his voice kinder now. 'Alison says that after she left your house this morning, your husband called her and asked her to look after the girls so he could speak with you. Is that correct?'

I nod, then add, 'Yes, I think so. I didn't know he called her at first. I didn't know they were even in touch.'

'Okay. But she was at your house this morning?'

I nod, picturing the warm croissants in the oven as if it's a scene from another life entirely, Alison smiling at me from across the room.

'Now, later today, you made a call to Alison and she says that's when you asked her to keep the girls overnight.'

'What? No. I didn't—'

'A call was made from your phone to your sister's at 12:17 p.m. We've got your phone records.'

The recollection hits me. 'Her phone charger. She left it at my house. But that's all we talked about, I never mentioned the girls.'

'Okay,' DS Reynolds says as he writes something down on his pad. 'So you didn't talk about anything else on this call? Nothing at all?'

'No!' I sob. 'I don't think so… I don't remember.'

'DS Reynolds, can I suggest that you ask a question once and move on rather than badgering my client? As you can see, she's very distressed,' Hannah cuts in but DS Reynolds continues as if she hasn't spoken at all.

'Your husband had arranged with Alison to look after your children this afternoon – is that correct?'

'Yes, but I didn't know—'

'During the call you made, Alison says you asked her to keep the girls overnight so that you and your husband, Mark, could spend the evening sorting out your marital problems. Are you saying that is not correct?'

'Yes,' I snap, sure of myself again. 'That didn't happen. At the time, I didn't know Alison even had the girls with her, Mark will tell you that.'

DS Reynolds looks at his notes. 'Yes,' he says. 'Both Alison and Mark said you weren't aware of the arrangement before then. Mark had asked her to keep it from you.' He raises his eyebrows as if this in itself is suspicious. 'But Alison tells us that on this call she was forced to tell you the truth as the girls were already in the car with her and she was worried you'd hear.' I shake my head and say 'no' but he continues. 'She said you were upset at first that Mark hadn't told you himself that she'd been helping out, but that you calmed down quite quickly and that's when you suggested she keep the girls all evening so you could talk to your husband properly.'

I scoff, anger pulsing through me. 'That conversation just didn't happen.'

'Okay, so when did you discover that Alison had the girls?'

'At the square, when I went to meet Mark. He said she was looking after them.'

'So, the girls have been staying at Mark's parents' house, correct?'

I nod.

'Why was that?'

I bite my lip and shake my head. 'You know why,' I cry. 'The messages. Because of her messages, Allie's got between us. She made Mark think...' I swallow, unable to put the words in an order that DS Reynolds, with his stiff blazer and unsmiling face, could ever understand.

'Alison's denied sending you any messages, Emily.'

'Of course she has! She's not going to admit it, is she?'

DS Reynolds eyes me carefully, tapping his pen against the table. 'I understand this is incredibly difficult for you, I really do. Your younger, very attractive, sister has become close to your husband at a time when you're struggling – you'd just found out they'd both lied to you about it and perhaps it was too much for you to take—'

'What?' I laugh then, a spiky cackle that surprises no one more than me. 'That's not at all what's happening. Allie took the girls today without my permission. There was no conversation where I agreed to her having them. If this was all some innocent misunderstanding, why couldn't anyone get hold of her all day?'

'Alison tells us her phone died, unfortunately. Which would make sense, wouldn't it? If you're telling the truth about her charger being at your house.' He raises his eyebrows as if waiting for me to argue, then continues. 'She heard our appeal on the car radio as she was taking the girls to McDonald's and brought them straight into the station.'

'I can't believe this,' I say. 'Do you really believe that? You really believe she was just driving around with no phone and just happened to hear they were missing?'

DS Reynolds shrugs. 'I'm just telling you the facts we have, Emily.'

'Check her phone. You'll see all the messages she's been sending me.'

'We have her phone; we haven't found any evidence of threatening messages.'

'Not just her texts! You need to find her MumsOnline account. She's TwoIsTrouble on there, you'll see it all.'

DS Reynolds nods slowly and looks down at the file on the table. He opens it and my stomach churns as I see printouts of MumsOnline conversations.

'Please,' I say as I turn to Hannah. 'You have to get them to find her account. Please. She's dangerous and she'll hurt them if—'

'Emily, I promise you we are not going to let anything happen to your girls. Okay? They're with your husband and an officer right now in this station. Nobody can get to them.' DS Reynolds holds my stare until I finally nod, half believing him. I try to picture the girls cuddled up in Mark's lap, safe away from Allie.

'Is she here too?'

'Who?'

'Alison.'

DS Reynolds picks up the sheets of paper and spreads them across the table. 'I'm going to read you some of the conversations we found on your MumsOnline account—'

'But the history was wiped—' I try to say before Hannah cuts me off.

'Are those conversations really relevant here?' she asks, her voice cold and authoritative.

'I think so, don't you, Emily?'

I look at Hannah, unsure how to respond. How have they got the messages back? Did Allie restore them? My mind fuzzes, trying to be certain of my memory that they were gone.

'You wanted us to look at who's behind the messages you've received on MumsOnline, so we have.'

'You know who it is?'

'We'll come to that. Right now, I want to focus on some of the messages you sent yourself.'

Heat rises through my body, making everything stick to my skin. I close my eyes and wait for it to be over; the panic, the breath that won't come, that feels like it never will again and things spin and I wait and I tell myself that it will be over soon...

When things come back into focus, DS Reynolds is gone and has been replaced by a kind looking older woman in uniform. She asks me if I'm okay and I nod slowly, eyes scouring the room. The printouts of all the terrible things I said are gone too. I breathe out, long and slow, but I'm unable to dislodge the tightness in my lungs. A panic attack. Another one. They're back. I laugh to myself. As if I ever had any reason to have a panic attack before today.

The door opens and I brush my hand through my hair and sit up straighter. DS Reynolds walks in, followed by Hannah and they resume their places as the other woman walks out, whispering to DS Reynolds on her way. The file is placed back on the table, the sheets of paper pulled out again, the purple of the MumsOnline logo laughing at me from the top of each page.

'Are you feeling okay to continue?' DS Reynolds says.

I look at Hannah and she smiles and nods, urging me to say yes. There's something about her kind face that makes me want to please her and I hear myself telling DS Reynolds that I'm fine to carry on.

The beep of the tape recorder resumes. This time I think of nothing except my ugly words on the paper.

'The account "MotherOfTwins", is that your account?'

'Yes.'

'I'm going to read you some of the messages sent from this account, okay? And you can tell me if you wrote them.'

I nod, looking down at the table.

'On April twenty-fourth, 2019, at six p.m in a private message to an account called "TwoIsTrouble" a message from your account reads: *I just wish I could run away. Do you ever feel like that? Like things will never get better while they're around?* Do you recall sending that message, Emily?'

I nod.

'I need you to speak up, please.'

'Yes,' I say.

'Who were the "they" you referred to in the message?'

I rub my eyes until it hurts. 'You know who.'

'Were you referring to your children, Ella and Lara?'

'Yes.'

'In a message sent to the same account on July sixteenth at 1:04 a.m., you mention this again. *I don't think I can go on like this. I just want it to be over now.* What were you referring to then?'

'I don't know,' I whisper.

'Your life?'

'No!' I snap my head up. 'No.'

'It's quite an odd thing to say to a stranger, isn't it?'

I glance at Hannah but she won't return my look and that makes me feel worse than any of this. Like I've somehow let her down. 'Do you have kids?' I ask DS Reynolds. He doesn't reply. 'You don't. I can tell you don't. Hannah does,' I say and she whips around to stare at me but I don't take my eyes off DS Reynolds. 'I know what you're thinking. I'm a terrible mother. I wrote terrible things about my husband, about my children, for years. To a stranger online. You think you'd never do that, don't you? You think only a terrible person would – but you don't know what it's like. No one knows what it's like until it happens to them.'

'Is that why you wanted Alison to take the girls away?'

'What?'

'Did she know that you felt like this about them?'

'I don't feel like that about them. I love my children. I wasn't well. I'm better now. Ask my doctor, things are better. I was… that wasn't me.'

'DS Reynolds, you know from my client's health records that she struggled with post-natal depression and I don't think it's entirely appropriate to question her on that, especially given this is a voluntary interview.'

'With all due respect, what's appropriate or not is not really down to you. Your client has wasted a significant amount of police time with a false allegation of abduction. That's incredibly serious—'

'It wasn't false,' I shout, desperate to show them I'm not insane. 'What about the note? If I asked her to take them, why did she leave me a threatening note?' DS Reynolds and Hannah look at each other uncertainly and I let out a strangled laugh. 'See! You know it doesn't make any sense. You've got the note, haven't you?'

'We have,' DS Reynolds says. 'Mark said you found the note yourself. No one else saw it before then, did they? It was written on paper from his parents' kitchen—'

'Because that's where she was when she took them!' I shout.

'Or perhaps, Emily, it was where you wrote it when everyone was looking for the girls, knowing you'd need to make them believe Alison really was a danger to them.'

I shake my head so hard that the room spins. How can they think I've done this? I stop shaking and rest my head in my hands, trying to bring myself under control. 'Can't you see what she's doing?'

'All I see, Emily, is a woman who appears very unwell and who should not be in charge of two young girls.'

It's like a kick to the stomach. Everything I have always been afraid of summed up in one sentence. He does not trust me as a mother. I should not be a mother. The girls are not safe with me. My eyes fall back to the printout of my vile words, the disgusting things I thought about my family and I cry. Perhaps he's right.

'Are you charging my client with anything?'

'Charging me? For what?' I look at Hannah in horror.

'Wasting police time?' Ds Reynolds says as I turn my attention to his stony face. 'You made an accusation of kidnapping that you potentially knew to be false. That is an offence, Emily.'

'But I didn't...' I say as he clicks his tongue against his teeth.

'It depends whether your false accusation was deliberate or not, Emily. That's what I'm trying to work out. Did you *deliberately* set your sister up to look like she'd kidnapped your children as revenge for getting close to your husband? Or, did you genuinely not remember you'd asked her to keep them for the night? Your mental health history does show patches of memory loss, and I'm willing to believe that's what happened here.'

He stares at me from across the table and I feel my heart pumping so fast in my chest that it hurts. Neither option is good. Either way, I am an insane person in his eyes. But only one of these scenarios could see me charged with a crime. Allie has left me with no choice, has she?

'Perhaps I forgot,' I whisper.

'Sorry?'

I clear my throat. 'I might have forgotten,' I say again, louder this time. 'It's possible I forgot.'

DS Reynolds nods, and smiles, this time kindly at me and I wonder how a face can change so much in a matter of seconds.

'Okay, that's fine, Emily,' DS Reynolds says, pulling the sheets of paper back towards him and stacking them into a pile. I watch the MumsOnline logo as he buries it beneath other papers, the nasty words I spewed across the pages disappearing. I allow myself to breathe in deeply, as if air is now allowed in my lungs properly for the first time since I entered this horrible room.

'Just one more thing we do have to ask you about.' His head snaps up with a smile as the air stops. 'Last year, you had a conversation with this user, TwoIsTrouble, where you referred to something happening to "Bethany".' He makes air quotes around the name as if Beth was never real at all. 'What was that about?'

I look at Hannah who is glaring at DS Reynolds. 'Sorry, this seems totally irrelevant, DS Reynolds. My client struggles with mental health issues, as you know, and has just admitted that she may have forgotten the situation with her sister, therefore this is nothing more than a mix-up.'

'Quite an expensive "mix-up"!' DS Reynolds laughs. 'And quite a traumatic one for your husband, I should think—'

'Regardless, I don't see how questioning Mrs Jones about private conversations she had about personal matters is at all relevant and if you're not going to charge her for wasting police time I suggest we stop this conversation here.' Hannah sits back with her arms folded, raising her eyebrows at DS Reynolds.

He sits back, arms folded mirroring Hannah and studies me for a beat, before finally relenting. 'Let's leave it there for this evening, Emily. Thank you for coming in and explaining that little mix-up. We'll be in contact as and when we need anything more from you.'

He stands abruptly and swings open the door, the light from the hallway bleeding across the carpeted floor as if a route to freedom.

Forty-Five

Now

I tumble through the double doors out into the street, dazed by the darkness. Hannah has abandoned me; I'm no longer a case therefore I no longer need a solicitor. How must I appear to her? A desperate, pathetic woman who can't even remember who she left her kids with? Fury rises up through me. I haven't allowed myself to feel it until now, able only to focus on getting out of the police station so I can be back with the girls, but now it rumbles up from my stomach and burns through my blood. How could Alison do this to me?

I pull my phone from my pocket and dial Mark. It rings out and out as I mutter, 'Answer your bloody phone,' under my breath, surprising a man on a late night dog walk.

'Emily?'

I whip around to see Mark's dad, Alan, standing behind me.

'Hi, love. I'm going to take you back home.' He holds out his arm and I feel myself take it, leaning all my weight on him as he guides me across the road to his car.

'Where's Mark?' I ask, getting into the passenger seat. 'Where are the girls?'

'They've gone back to ours,' Alan says. 'They'll be fast asleep by now.'

'I need to see them.'

Alan nods slowly but he turns right out of the station, towards my house, not his.

'We need to go to your house, not mine,' I say. 'I need to see the girls.'

But he's not listening; he's staring intently at the road as we drive, his lips clasped together as if determined not to let any words out.

'What's going on? Alan, stop the car. Please, I don't want to go home. I need to see the girls—'

'You can't!' He finally shouts, banging his hand against the steering wheel. I sit back, shocked into silence. Alan, kind, mild-mannered, anything-to-avoid-a-conflict Alan, looks furious. 'You can't see them, don't you understand that? This has gone too far now, Emily. There are other people involved—'

'What other people?'

He glances over his shoulder and shakes his head, the look of pity in his eyes turning my stomach. 'Social services? Child protection? I don't know what they call them now but...'

Whatever he says after that is lost in the ringing of my ears.

We pull up to my house twenty minutes later in silence. I stare at it mutely as the dark windows look back at me accusingly. I don't know if I can bear going in there and feeling the empty cold rooms, hearing the silence without the girls' voices.

'Come on, love,' Alan says, undoing my seatbelt like I'm a child.

He leads me down the path and through the front door, holding onto my arm the whole time as though I'll tumble to the ground without him. Switching on the hallway lights, he leads me upstairs to our bedroom. Is it just 'my' bedroom now? Is Mark ever coming back?

'You'd have to ask him that, love,' Alan says, and I wonder if I posed that question out loud or if Alan actually read my mind. Tiredness pulls at every part of me as I'm lifted into bed, the cover pulled over me in a way that I don't remember my mother ever doing. I bury my body further below the duvet, vaguely aware of the strangeness of this situation.

'I'll lock up; don't you worry about anything. Get some rest, perhaps Joanne will pop in in the morning, I'll have to see...' Alan's voice tails off and I wonder if the reason he is here and not Joanne, who would make the more obvious choice of carer, is because she too is furious at me for what they all think I've done. I feel tears pooling on the pillow beneath my face as I hear Alan pull the door closed and thud down the stairs. At the sound of the front door slamming, I sit up and yank the duvet back.

There's absolutely no way that I'm sleeping tonight until I see my girls.

–

I pull up outside Mark's parents' house like I'm on a stakeout, feeling vaguely ridiculous in my all-black outfit of an oversized hoody and leggings. I'm not even sure what to do now I'm here; I imagine if I ring the doorbell they aren't going to just let me in, looking down at my clothes I realise on some level I must have already known a knock on the door wouldn't cut it. I picture the total humiliation of seeing Joanne's horrified face as she has to tell me to leave and decide I can't bear it. Looking at the windows, it appears everyone is already in bed. It's not like I want to get the girls up, I just need to see them, to see with my own eyes that they're safe.

I do have my own key.

I've always had one, ever since Mark and I got together. I could easily just let myself in and go in to check on the girls. No one would ever even know I'd been there.

Suddenly, it seems like the only good idea I've had in a long time.

I open the car door and finger the keys in my hand. They're on the same keychain as my own. I've needed to pop in and out of their house so often since having the girls it became second nature to simply let myself in without even considering whether they'd want me here. Now, as I walk up the dark path to the front door, I feel like a total intruder. Can I really just let myself in? I slip the key into the lock as the voice in my head screaming at me to stop is drowned out by the absolute certainty that nothing matters more to me right now than seeing that my girls are safe.

The door opens with a quiet click and I hold my breath, waiting to see if anyone is up. Closing the door behind me, I stand in the dark hallway and think about how best to creep up the stairs in front of me without making a sound.

Then, I hear the voices.

Mark.

But he's not alone.

Anger rushes through me as I hear her voice.

Alison.

I watch the sliver of light coming from beneath the kitchen door as I inch myself forward, the thudding in my ears drowning out any of their words. I stop near the closed door and breathe in as deeply as I can without making a sound, desperate to silence the pounding of my heart.

'I just don't know what to do now,' my husband says. His voice is low, almost whispered.

'I know. It's so hard.' Allie is consoling him. My jaw clenches to stop myself from screaming out. How is this happening? 'The thing is though, as hard as it is, you really do need to put the girls first…'

The sound of wine being poured turns my stomach.

'You say that like it's simple,' Mark says.

'It might not be easy, but in some ways it is, at least, simple…'

There's silence for a moment and I wonder if Mark is finally going to defend me. I imagine him telling Allie to get out, that nothing about this situation she's created is simple.

Instead, he sighs loudly and says. 'I know, you're right. But what can I do? I don't want to stop her from seeing the girls.'

'It would just be for a little while…'

'I don't think she'd cope.'

'She's not coping now.'

'Well, no. But she loves them. She'd never hurt them…'

'Mark, I say this as someone who loves her too, but I think you know that's not true.'

I dig my nails into the palm of my hand and bite down hard on my tongue to stem the fury that courses through me, urging me to scream out at this to stop.

'Come here. I know, I know.' Allie's voice is muffled as if she's buried in Mark's chest. Picturing it makes me sick.

I listen for a few moments to the sound of my husband crying and my heart breaks a million times. He loves me. I know he loves me. But he's weak and Allie has fooled him completely.

'No,' he finally says. 'No, this isn't right. I can't do it to her. I can't take the girls away. She's their mum, she loves them. We can work through this together.'

Tears fall down my face as I listen to his declaration made too late.

'Look, I wasn't going to tell you this but now I think I have to…' Allie's voice cuts through and I wonder what lies she's going to tell now. 'The girls aren't safe with her. I promise you, they're not. I thought you'd see it for yourself but perhaps I have to show you.'

'What do you mean? Show me what?'

'Mark, Emily is dangerous.'

'She's not. She's ill!'

'That's what they said last time…'

'Who said that? What do you mean?'

I lean against the wall and close my eyes as I wait for the inevitable.

'Before she killed Beth.'

'What?' I hear Mark's footsteps on the kitchen tiles and picture him jumping up from the table as the ugly words bounce off the kitchen walls. 'Your sister, Beth? Emily didn't… Beth died in an accident. Emily had nothing—'

'That's what my mum told everyone,' Allie says, her voice breaking up through tears. 'But it wasn't true. She wanted to protect her; she blamed herself for letting it get to that stage. She said she always knew there was something wrong with Emily but she didn't want to admit

it to anyone so she kept these diaries and I found them...
After Mum died, I found it all. Emily killed Beth. She
murdered...'

I don't need to listen to any more. Nothing will ever
be the same again. My very worst fear has come to life.
All I ever wanted was to keep my family; to make sure
Mark never found out the ugly truth about Beth; to keep
the girls. But Mark is lost. He'll never trust in me now.
All I can do is keep the girls safe. Keep them where they
belong, with me.

-

I sneak upstairs silently; the only sound my movements
make is a tiny creak on the board outside the girls' room.
In their bedroom, their polka-dot mushroom night lights
shine a warm glow across the floor as I gently close the
door behind me. At the sight of the girls, sleeping soundly
side-by-side in Ella's bed, I allow myself to breathe out.
They're here. They're safe. They look so peaceful I almost
can't bear to wake them but after a moment of watching
their small chests rise and fall, I gently coax them from
their dreams.

'Mummy?' Ella rubs her eyes and looks at me in confusion for a second, breaking my heart. But then her face is
covered by a huge smile and she presses herself into me.
Lara wakes seconds later and does the same.

'Shhh,' I tell them in a whisper. 'We're playing a game,
darlings. But you've got to be super-duper quiet, okay?
We're going on a little adventure.'

They look at each other, then back at me, and I realise
the last adventure they took ended up in a police station.

'A fun one, I promise. We're going to creep downstairs like tiny little mice and then we're going to get in Mummy's car and go home, okay?'

'Why can't we stay here?' Ella says in a stage whisper.

I press my fingers to her lips and wait for the sounds of Joanne being woken, but nothing comes. Downstairs, I can hear the faint noise of Mark and Alison, still deep in a conversation I dread to think about.

'Because we're going home, back to our own beds, but first I'll make you both a big hot choccie with lots of marshmallows and some yummy cream. Doesn't that sound fun?' They nod as I hold my fingers to my lips again.

We creep down the stairs hand-in-hand, my heart pounding as we get closer to the bottom steps. The sound of Mark crying makes the girls grip my hands together.

'Shh, it's okay,' I stop to whisper, fearing they'll cry out for Mark.

We reach the bottom of the stairs just at the moment that the kitchen door handle turns.

Forty-Six

Now

I push the girls back up the first stair, hiding them behind the curve of the wall.

'I'm sorry, Mark,' Allie says, her voice louder now and hoarse. 'I didn't know what to do…'

'Shh,' he snaps. 'You'll wake my parents.'

'Sit back down, please,' she begs and I pray that this time he listens to her. Does what she wants.

'I can't think straight… I just—'

'I know… I know, it's a lot.'

The sound of footsteps coming closer to the other side of kitchen door sends shivers through me and I hold my breath as I push the girls back further, silently willing them to keep quiet. The handle has been pulled down and stays there, the door opens only slightly, as if the person holding it from the other side isn't quite sure they want to leave.

'Come on.' Allie's voice is like treacle as she cajoles my husband to sit back down.

After what feels like hours but can't be more than seconds, the strip of light falling across the hallway floor disappears as the kitchen door is pulled shut as I hear them both retreat.

I don't waste any time and drag the girls to the front door, silently pulling it open and running out, leaving it swinging behind me. I throw them into the car, ignoring their cries, ignoring the voice in my head screaming, 'The car seats! They need to be in their car seats!' and jump into the driver's seat, thanking god that my electric car pulls away in near silence.

–

Only when we've been driving for ten minutes do I allow myself to take my eyes off the road and look in the rear-view mirror at my daughters. Their pale faces stare back at me in horror, their beautiful big blue eyes round with shock at the sudden drama of their evening. I smile at them.

'That was fun, wasn't it?' I say, my voice unnaturally high. 'Like a game of hide and seek!'

They eye me warily; my performance not even close to fooling them.

'Where we going?' Lara eventually says, quickly followed by, 'Why can't Daddy come?'

I chew my lip and fix my eyes back on the road. The streets are near empty as we wind through the twisty countryside lanes between Mark's parents' house and ours. Where are we going? I realise with a jolt that I have no idea. I can't simply take them home, can I? Mark will come. He'll demand them back; he won't ever let me have them. Fear lodges in my throat.

'Where we going?' Lara says, louder this time. 'Mummy! Mummy! Where we going?' Her shouts get louder and louder until Ella joins in too, their voices a cacophony of distress and anguish. So loud, so all-encompassing is their pain that I don't hear my phone at first, but when I do, the ringing won't stop. I look at the seat next to me where it lies.

Mark is calling.

Again, and again, and again.

My stomach curls; he knows. He knows I've taken them.

'Mummy!' This time, Lara's squeal pierces through me and I look up from the phone just in time to slam my foot on the brakes.

There's a moment when I relive the accident from last year all over again: the sight of the wall careering towards us; the certainty of instant death as the Cotswold stone came closer and closer; the ear-splitting crunch of the bricks crushing the bonnet of the car; the screams of the girls from the back seat rooted in my brain forever as I closed my eyes and waited for the pain. *This is karma*, I remember thinking. My mum told me one day I'd understand her pain and finally it had come.

Now, all the same thoughts rush back as the girls' screams claw at my ears. But that's the only sound. There is no crunching of metal; no smashing glass. I open my eyes. My knuckles are white and feel surgically attached to the steering wheel, but as I look up, I see the brake lights of the car in front of us lighting the bonnet of my car red. Barely a centimetre separates us. But it's enough.

A sudden tapping on my window makes me scream but as things come back into focus, I realise it's the driver of the other car.

She knocks again and makes the signal to wind down my window.

'You nearly went straight into me,' she says as soon as I do.

'I know, I'm sorry…'

'You could have crashed!'

I say nothing, silent in the face of her obvious disgust. To my dismay, tears fall down my cheeks as I continue to stare at her with my mouth open.

'Are you okay?' she says, the anger in her voice replaced with kindness. She peers into the car and gasps when she sees the girls. 'Oh! Gosh, I'm sorry for shouting, girls, I didn't see you there. Your mummy gave me a bit of a fright.'

Blood pumps in my ears as I imagine what this stranger is thinking of me.

'Are you okay?' she says again, and I'm not sure if she's asking them or me, but I finally unstick my tongue from between my teeth and answer.

'I'm really sorry, I was distracted by the girls… Do you have kids?' I ask.

She glances at the girls again then back at me and nods.

'You know what it's like, sometimes they're just a nightmare in the car. I just turned for a second…'

'They aren't strapped in.'

I turn to look at the girls as guilt crawls over me. They're sitting bunched up in the middle seat between the two car seats where I shoved them in to escape Mark.

'Oh. No, they're not. We've only driven from—'

'They need to be strapped in,' she says again, eyeing me warily. She reaches for her phone in her coat pocket and I realise that there's every chance she thinks I need help, or the girls do, and I have to stop her.

'You're right,' I say, trying a little laugh to relieve the tension. 'It's no excuse, is it? I'm only driving five minutes up the road and it takes fifteen to get them in those seats! How old are your kids?' I undo my own belt and open the car door, forcing her to step back.

'Eight and ten,' she replies as I open the back door and lift Ella up, placing her in her car seat.

'Oh, gosh, sometimes I think I can't wait for mine to be a little older. I hear there's less to worry about!' I laugh again, as if we are two mums chatting outside the school gates. I snap the latch on Ella's car seat closed and run my fingers through her hair. She looks up at me with worry. 'But then I think we should just treasure every moment, you know? They grow up so fast, don't they?'

The woman murmurs her agreement as I walk around to the other side and perform the same act with Lara. Once they're safely strapped in, I walk briskly around the front of the car, avoiding having to pass the woman who is peering through the window at the girls as if she can't quite trust me to have belted them in properly.

'I really am sorry about nearly going into the back of you,' I say. I open the car door and get in, talking to her through the open window again as I switch on the ignition. 'Hope the rest of your journey is less stressful.' I smile tightly at her as I nod, then wind up the window. She watches me through narrowed eyes, my hands shaking on the steering wheel as I turn the car to pull out around her.

I watch her silhouette in the rear-view mirror as we drive away, the light of her phone the only thing I can see.

When we're safely away, I pull the car over in a lay-by, the shaking of my hands forcing me to stop. Behind me, the girls are silent and suddenly I long for the shrieks of their voices. The idea that they feel too unsafe with me to even make a sound tears my heart into tiny pieces. We sit in silence for a few moments, long enough for me to catch my breath and slow the beat of my heart to an almost normal rate.

'I want to go back to Nanna's,' Ella's small voice says.

I clamp my eyes shut and count backwards from ten, desperate for whatever I say next to be of comfort to my daughters. As I do, my phone buzzes again. I reach for it instinctively. Twenty-four missed calls from Mark. Too many texts to read. And then, one from Alison.

> Emily, you have to stop this now. I won't let you hurt those girls. Everything I've done has been to stop that from happening. Please, please, stop. Please bring them back.

Disbelief courses through me, followed by fury. My fingers stab out a reply before I even have a chance to consider it.

> I would NEVER hurt the girls. NEVER. You're the one who has caused all of this. It's because of you that I've had to do this!

Her reply is almost instant.

> I know. I know, I'm sorry. I'll tell Mark everything; the truth. I promise. But please, bring them back.

Though I know she was behind everything, seeing it in black and white like this, makes me cry out in horror. My little sister. All of this time. Allie.

Another message pops up.

> If you won't bring them home, can we meet? Just the two of us, I promise. Then I'll tell Mark it was all me. Everything. I promise.

I drum my fingers on the steering wheel. She can't be trusted. I know she can't.

But I know how to end this.

I need to tell the truth.

Finally, it's time for the truth.

Forty-Seven

Now

As I walk up the drive to my childhood home, it strikes me that the girls have only been here a handful of times. This is not their 'nanna's' in the way Mark's parents' house is. This house is almost totally unfamiliar to them. So, it shouldn't be a surprise to me that they drag their feet as we approach the door and clutch at my hand like I'm leading them somewhere where terrible things happen. I suppose in truth though, I am. This house has always been a terrible place to me. The place where the very worst thing possible happened to all of us, all because of me.

I don't knock at the door, as if that would make this visit too sociable, too normal; instead, I push the old handle down gently and am pleased to find it unlocked.

'I don't want to go in!' Ella shouts as I step into the dark hallway. 'I'm scared!'

'It's okay, darling. It's okay.' I lift her up, her warm body as heavy as lead in my arms as she wraps herself around me. Lara clutches my thigh, burying her face into me.

The damp of the house cloys at my nostrils as I shiver from the chill. I run my hand along the radiator as I walk by, like I did so many times as a child, to find it stone cold. As I approach the kitchen door, I stop. The girls can't see her. Or more importantly, she can't see the girls. I turn on my heel and lead them upstairs where the air seems to drop in temperature further with every step. They're quiet as we walk until I finally reach what was once Alison and Bethany's bedroom but is now a spare room that never houses guests.

I kick open the door with my foot, not wanting to let go of the girls, then flick on the light with my elbow. The room is drowned in light so bright I squint to adjust my vision. As I look up, I see the lampshade has been removed, leaving a naked bulb swinging from the ceiling. In this light, the bedroom takes on a museum-like quality. Mum refused to change the room much after Beth died and if I ever tried to come in here she'd scream at me to get out, so I never really spent much time in here after she was gone. There was no reason to. This was not my home; it stopped feeling like that the day that Bethany and Alison arrived. That was the day my mum stopped loving me. The day it all started to go wrong.

'I don't like it here, Mummy,' Ella says, curling her body into my legs. Lara looks around the room with similar apprehension. She eyes the two single beds pressed against each side of the room, the oak toy box with a gold rusted padlock, the rocking horse in the corner of the room with patches of its black fake hair missing.

'It's okay, Els. Mummy just has to go and talk to Auntie Alison downstairs—'

At the sound of her name, the twins shake their heads and clutch me tighter.

'We don't like her,' Lara says. 'We want to go home.'

I grit my teeth. 'We'll go home in a minute. Please be good girls for Mummy, just for a minute, okay? Here,' I say, moving across the bedroom towards the chest. I heave it open, surprised by the weight of the heavy oak lid. 'Why don't you play with this while I'm gone?' I pull out the first thing I see, an old rag doll with huge knitted blue eyes and orange woollen hair.

As Ella takes it, I'm jolted back to my childhood. I see Beth reaching out for the same doll, her perfect blonde curls bouncing as she jumped up and down with delight that we were playing together one rainy afternoon in the summer holidays. I shake my head to banish the memory and Ella's face comes back into view, not Beth's. But my daughter isn't smiling, or laughing, she's staring at me, silently begging me to be a good mother and take her home. I wish I could explain to her that I'm trying to do that; I'm finally trying to do the right thing.

I kiss both of the girls on the head and tell them I love them before I walk out of the room, closing the door softly behind me. For the first time since we've arrived, I listen for the sounds of my sister in the house. She must be here. She said she would be. But I can't hear anything except the whoosh of my own heavy breath.

Downstairs, I hear her. The radio plays softly in the kitchen, just like it did when we were kids. My mum would never let us have any quiet. *Music! The house should be full of music!* she used to say in her sing-song voice when it was just the two of us. She'd pick me up and twirl me round as we danced to 'Penny Lane' over and over. But when the girls came, the music stopped being about dancing and instead became a permanent background noise all day and night, leaving no slice of silence for my mum's thoughts to fill. Does Alison do the same? Does she play that awful radio all day and all night to stop her losing her mind completely?

'You came.' My sister appears in the doorway before me, her body lit in silhouette from behind.

For a moment, I want to run back upstairs, grab the girls and drive a million miles away from here, from her. But as the light catches her face, I see Bethany staring back at me. My favourite little sister; who I loved more than anything. Who died because of me. And I know I owe it to her to stay. To finally tell the truth about what happened on that awful day.

I step forward, and she steps back. We take our seats at the kitchen table; hers on the side nearest the cooker, mine near the door. I glance at the empty chairs beside her: Mum's, and then the one beside me that barely had a chance to become Bethany's before she died.

'Are the girls—' Allie starts to ask but I cut her off with the raise of my hand.

'Don't.'

She stares at me, anger hardening her features. Has that resentment always been there? Hidden in the creases of her brow, disguised behind polite smiles and gritted teeth? Has Alison spent the last twenty-four years hating me? But then I remember what she told Mark about finding the diaries last year and feel a fleck of hope that the hatred has, at least, only been a recent part of our lives.

'Did Mum tell you?' I ask and her jaw hardens. 'Or did you find out from the diaries?'

She balls her hands into fists and then folds her arms in front of her. 'I read them after she died. I found them when you were supposed to come and clear out her things with me.'

I nod, remembering the day. I made an excuse to avoid the house, to avoid my mum's things. Even with her gone, the idea of being around her clothes, her books, her gold-plated hairbrush that she used to brush my hair with every night when it was the two of us… it was too much. The pain was too great. I couldn't bear it. If I'd come that day, been braver, perhaps Alison would have never read the diaries and none of this would be happening.

'What… What did they say?'

Alison glares at me across the table and I automatically dip my head to avoid her. How quickly we fall back into the patterns of our childhood. Although I lived with Mrs Green for a few years after Bethany's death, I was always made to come back here for Sunday lunches. *Go see your mammy, she does love you, you know*, Mrs Green would say as she'd shuffle me out of her door to make the short trip across the lane to this house. I hated those visits. Hated sitting across from my mum who wasn't my mum any more but a cold, terrifying woman who would glare at me over lumpy gravy and stone cold meat. I barely noticed Alison in those days. Looking at her was like seeing a ghost. I wonder for the first time if she felt that way too; if every time she looked in the mirror all she could see was her dead twin staring back at her. The idea makes me shudder.

'Allie, Mum wasn't well—'

She slams her hand on the table and shakes her head. 'Don't! Don't blame Mum for what you did.'

I bite my tongue as tears come to my eyes. 'You have to listen to me; you must realise now that the way she treated me wasn't—'

'She treated you like that because she knew what you were really like. She was terrified of you!' Alison spits the words and I recoil, the old feelings of self-disgust crawling all over my skin like I never scraped them off.

'I was a child…' I whisper. 'I didn't do anything to make her feel like that.'

'You turned everyone against her! You made her feel like a bad mum, you made people believe she was a bad mum, but she wasn't. She was the best mum and you—'

I close my eyes as the words wash over me. 'That's what you've read?' I ask, opening my eyes. 'That I was a terrible child, that I did terrible things, that I hated both of you?'

Allie nods and I bite my lip.

'Allie, I was five years old when you and Beth were born. Five. That's not much older than the twins are now. Do you really believe I was capable of those things at five?'

She looks away from me as her jaw hardens. 'Yes. I do. I think you can be born evil, and I think Mum knew you were.'

I throw my hands up. 'That's ridiculous! You know it. You know that's not right. I was a kid, that's all I was. Mum was…' I shake my head, letting myself remember the mum I had before she became someone else's mum too. 'Before you were born, Mum was different. Something happened to her after… It was like she was replaced by this person I didn't know and—'

'Because you hated us!' Allie screams. 'That's why she was different to you! You wanted her all to yourself and then we came along and she realised how fucking evil you were.'

'Oh, come on, Allie. You must realise that Mum was ill. I wish someone had seen it then; none of this would have happened. She probably had post-natal depression or' – I wave my hand – 'psychosis!'

Allie laughs. 'Right, Mum was a pyscho, and yet she was a perfectly good mum to me and Beth…'

'Was she?'

Allie narrows her eyes and sneers. 'Yes, Emily. You can't just rewrite history to suit your lies. She was the best mum; she was always the best mum to us. I didn't even know how bad things were with you until I read the diaries. She kept all of that from us to make sure we never had to know what sort of monster we were related to.'

I nod and bite the inside of my cheek. Hearing the words I've feared all my life hurts more than I could have ever imagined. My mum hated me. My mum thought I was a monster. Though I've long suspected it to be true, somewhere in the back of my mind I clung to the hope that it was all in my head; that the things my mum said to me the night Beth died weren't how she really felt but a symptom of the shock.

'That's what she wrote?' I ask. 'That I was a monster?'

'She always knew you were going to do something terrible, and you did. Didn't you?'

I shake my head.

'That's why I had to get the girls away from you,' Allie says, her voice panicked now. 'I didn't want it to be true, but then we spoke on MumsOnline and the things you said...' She screws her face up in disgust. 'I knew then that Mum was right, that deep down, the core of you is rotten! You cover it so well; no one can see the real you, can they? I knew then that I had to do something to stop you. I couldn't let what happened to Beth happen to the girls, I'd never forgive myself. Just like Mum.'

I focus on the table in front of me, my fingers tracing the grain in the wood, noticing the patches of dark where a drink has spilled into the oak and stained before Mum had a chance to stop it. I trace the lines as memories of Mum spill in. Not the woman who came home from the hospital with the twins, but Mum as she was before.

When she loved me. When she'd sit at this table and spend whole afternoons drawing pictures with ground-down crayons, laughing as I tried to capture her likeness on paper but of course, failing. Sometimes I wonder how many of my early memories of Mum are true or if they've been concocted from films I've seen: the beautiful smiling mother, doting on her adoring daughter. But I think some of them are real. I don't think my mum always hated me. I know she didn't.

But something happened to her after the twins. Something bad. Something none of us have ever talked about, until now. Perhaps the same thing that happened to me once I had the girls; a dirty shameful secret that we've all been holding for too long, as though if anyone knew the truth, we'd be tarred by each other's sins forever.

'Allie, I need to tell you what really happened that night.'

Forty-Eight

Allie grips the table and clenches her teeth. 'I don't need to hear it from you, I already know.'

'Do you? What did you read, Allie? What did she say?'

Her lip twitches, like it always used to when she was caught in a lie and I realise that whatever Mum wrote about Beth's death, somewhere deep down Allie knows it's not the whole story. 'I know everything I need to. You told me yourself, remember? *If they knew what really happened to her, they'd never let me be a mother.*' Alison sneers as she quotes my own awful words back to me.

I remember writing them in a haze of wine and too many pills. Some days the guilt of lying about Beth's death crept over me, the midnight dread I felt keeping me up at night, always there, threatening the life I had so carefully built.

'Because of Mum, though, Allie… Not me,' I whisper. 'I was terrified they'd think I was like her.'

'You're nothing like her!' Allie screeches, her cheeks turning an angry red as she grips the table and stands up, towering over me. 'She was a good mum, she loved us. She even loved you, despite what you did…'

'She was a good mum,' I say. 'But she was ill. You know that, you must know that, Allie.'

Allie shakes her head and how can I blame her? Isn't this what I've always wanted for her, to have no idea what was really going on with Mum? It's one of the reasons I kept her secrets for so long; to save Allie the pain I had to deal with every day.

'Please, Allie, sit down. Please, I want to tell you the truth. I need to tell you.'

Allie scratches at the back of her neck, leaving angry red marks across her pale skin. Upstairs, a bang makes her eyes shoot to the ceiling, as if remembering for the first time that my girls are here. A kick of panic hits me as I imagine her running upstairs and taking them from me.

'Please,' I say again. 'You deserve to know what really happened.'

Eventually, she sits back down, her arms folded across her chest.

'You probably don't remember the day it happened very well, do you? You were only five.'

'I remember it.'

I nod, allowing the memory that I've kept locked in the back of my mind for over twenty years to play like a film reel in my head.

It was the summer holidays; we'd been off school for three weeks yet it had felt like forever. I dreaded the holidays. School was my sanctuary; a place where I could pretend that I was just like all the other children. It was easy to do that because my mum was so good at showing the world the side of her that she wanted everyone to see. The mother who always had a perfectly good excuse for turning up at the school gates late again, holding the hands of her beautiful twins like a shield. I don't think anyone ever noticed that she never spoke to me. The twins were the perfect distraction. She could hide behind them so beautifully, no one ever really looked at me, or her. So, at school, everything felt fine. I would sit in class and draw pictures of my family, as if my stepdad hadn't left because he couldn't put up with my mum's insane mood swings, as if I went home every night to a mother who loved me the way she loved my perfect sisters.

But when school was over, I couldn't pretend. That summer was the worst. The twins were old enough by then to be properly fun to play with. I was ten, five years older than them. We never reached the stage where the age gap became a problem and I wanted to be rid of them, despite what my mum believed. I loved them so much. Sometimes, in the early days, I probably did blame them for the change in my mum. But they became my solace. Beth, especially. I adored everything about her. Alison could be spiky, bossy. She always wanted to come first; *A before B! Allie and Beth, not Beth and Allie*, she'd say crossly if anyone dared to reorder their names.

But Mum was getting worse. Everything I did made her angry. I spent as much time as I could out in the garden with the twins; we'd make up endless games to avoid having to go back into the house where my mum would often be upstairs in her bedroom, drinking.

'Did you notice how much she drank?' I ask Allie now.

She rolls her eyes. 'She barely drank at all.'

'Come on, Allie. You don't remember the smell of her bedroom?'

She clicks her tongue against her teeth and shakes her head.

'Sickly sweet; I can still smell it in the house. Even now. You must remember.'

Allie looks away from me, a flicker of recognition in the crease of her brow. But then her face hardens and she turns back to me. 'Tell me what happened,' she says, her voice lacking any emotion.

'Your dad had left by then, so it was just the four of us that summer. You remember?' I ask.

Allie gives a single sharp nod.

'It was so hot, we spent most of the day in the pond. You both loved paddling in the pond, didn't you?'

Allie's eyes shimmer and for a moment I think she's going to smile and recall the happy memories we shared before, say that she remembers how I dunked her and Beth under the water that day to relieve the sticky sweat that stuck to their little bodies. Surely those memories aren't lost to her? She must remember how much I loved them. But she just gives me another curt nod and tells me to go on.

'Mum was upstairs most of the day, so we played outside until dark. I think about that all the time, every summer when I get into bed and the night outside is still light I think about us, the three of us, playing in the pond at ten p.m....'

I shake my head, urging Allie to realise how strange our childhood was, how we ran around basically feral without any supervision, but she just stares at me blankly.

'You both started to get cold so we went in. I put you both to bed. You were angry that you were going to have to sleep with your hair wet, do you remember?' I smile at Allie, desperate to make her see how I cared for them back then. But she gives me nothing.

'I read you that story, I think, the Roald Dahl one you gave the girls. I've remembered now, it was Beth's favourite. Wasn't it?' Alison's lip twitches at the question but I keep going. 'I thought you were both asleep when

I left. I crept back downstairs, still in my wet swimming costume.'

I remember the feel of the cold, wet material against my skin and shiver.

'When I got into the kitchen, Mum was there. She was furious.'

Allie narrows her eyes. 'About what?'

I shrug. 'She was always furious at me, Allie. She hid it from you, we both did. But everything I did made her angry. Even when I'd done nothing at all. That night, it was because I'd got the floor wet bringing you both in. She'd slipped on it, apparently, when she came downstairs.'

You did it on purpose, that's what she screamed at me. *Didn't you? You wanted me to fall.* I cried, big salty tears that mixed with the pond water on my skin. I begged her to stop shouting. I told her I'd clean it up, grabbing tea towels from the Aga door and wiping at the floor. But it was too late. She was furious, I couldn't calm her down. I should have done something to stop her shouting; I shouldn't have got the floor wet; I should have been able to calm her down.

'Mum was so angry at me,' I tell Alison, avoiding her eyes. 'I told her I was sorry but it was like she couldn't hear me, couldn't hear anything through her rage. I'd almost got all the water up off the floor by the time Beth appeared...' My throat tightens as I close my eyes and picture it. I can still feel the too-tight, freezing wet swimming costume sticking to my skin as I turned to my little sister, shouted at her to go away, desperate for her not to witness the side to our mum that I spent so much of my life hiding from the world.

'Mum was in a frenzy by then, furious that I'd let you swim until that late. She said I must want you to get sick,

340

that I…' I choke on the words. 'That I wanted you to both drown so it could be just me and her.' I cry as the memory of her words lodge in my throat. *Is that what you were hoping? They could have drowned, Emily! But you knew that, didn't you?* 'I begged her to calm down, but then Beth appeared and it just made everything worse.'

I dream of that moment sometimes. It plays over and over in my nightmares: Beth appears in the doorway, her hair still wet, dripping down the front of her Tinkerbell nightie, her little face screwed up in horror at seeing the side of my mum usually only reserved for me.

'Mum didn't know Beth was there. She had never hit me before, but that night… I don't know why, but something just tipped her over the edge and she came at me, her hands knocking me from side to side as I begged her to stop and then I heard Beth shouting too… She was trying to make mum stop,' I say through my tears. 'I pushed her. Mum. I pushed her away as hard as I could. I didn't want her to hurt me or for Beth to see it, I just wanted her to get away from me… But Beth was… she was running towards me and I must have somehow caught her instead and the water… I hadn't got all the water up yet. She slipped.'

The deafening crack of her head against the slate tiles still haunts me.

I didn't realise how bad it was at first. Mum flung me across the kitchen to get to Beth and I balled myself up by the door.

What have you done? What have you done?

The sound of her voice pierces my ears even now. I'll never be able to rid myself of the sound of that. The heartbreak. The agony in her words. But also, the accusation. It was only when I ran out of the kitchen, past Beth's lifeless body, that I realised the liquid pooling around Beth wasn't just water from the pond. It was blood. Everywhere. Oozing from the back of her head, covering my mum's hands as she cradled her in her arms. I ran. Out of the house into the night, down the lane to Mrs Green's.

'When I told her what had happened, she called an ambulance, but it was too late,' I tell Allie. Her face is white and she grips the table as if its solidity is the only thing holding her up. 'I don't know what Mum told the police. Do you remember the police coming?'

Allie shakes her head.

'Do you remember any of it?'

'You're lying,' she says. 'Mum wouldn't ever hit you!'

'She didn't mean to.'

She stands up and paces the room. 'Why are you doing this? Why can't you just tell the truth? You did it on purpose – didn't you? You wanted us both dead so you could have Mum to yourself! That's what Mum said—'

'No. That's not true. I've lied about what happened for so long—'

'You're lying now! If that was true, why didn't you say anything then? If Mum was so awful, if she was this psychotic, evil mother like you claim, why didn't you tell anyone?'

'I did,' I whisper.

'Bullshit! If you'd told the police they'd have—'

'Not the police,' I explain. 'I told Mrs Green.' I squirm in my seat, remembering the courage it took to finally tell someone the truth about my mum, only to be faced with the crushing realisation that people did not want to hear about mothers like mine.

Don't say such wicked things, Emily. Your mother loves you. Don't you ever talk like that about her again, do you hear me? You'll get yourself in all manner of trouble.

We never talked about it again, though I lived with Mrs Green for the next four years after Beth's death. It was as if she knew what I'd told her was the truth, but it was safer for us all to pretend that my mum would never be a danger to any of us. It felt like my filthy secret to carry alone. After all, it was because of me that Beth was dead, wasn't it? I was the one who pushed her, even if I never meant to. I was the one who made Mum mad enough to scream vile words that woke Beth from her dreams and made her come downstairs. If I'd been a better daughter, been the sort of daughter my mother could love, she'd never have wanted to hurt me and Beth wouldn't have had to try and protect me.

I shake my head. I know that isn't true. After I had the girls, I tortured myself with the same feelings I realise she must have felt. The paranoia; anxiety; the utter disgust you feel for yourself for having everything you ever wanted yet taking no joy in it at all. But I never did anything to hurt my children the way she hurt me, did I? I never hated them; I only ever hated myself. I love my girls. I love them more than anything. Why have I ever let myself doubt that? I am not like my mother.

I've kept her secret for too long, as if the world knowing what my mother was really like would tar me with the same brush. I've lived in fear ever since that awful night in this very kitchen. Blamed myself for something that was in no way my fault and carried that with me for my whole life.

But enough is enough. I owe Mark the truth; to give him the full explanation behind all of this. To confess to

343

all the secrets I've kept from him: the desperate messages I shared with women I thought were my friends but actually were just as lost as me; the lies I've told to keep up the pretence of being the mother I always wanted as a child.

'Where are you going?' Allie snaps as I stand up to leave.

'I'm going home, Allie. Home to my husband.'

'No!' she screams, smashing her hands against the table. 'You don't get to do that. Don't you realise, Emily? I know the truth about you; I know that you killed Bethany on purpose and I know what you've just told me is total bullshit.'

'I know you want to believe that, but it's not true. I loved Beth. I'd never—'

'You think anyone is going to believe you when I show them Mum's diaries?' Allie spits.

'I think all those diaries will show is a woman who needed help… who—'

'And what about all of your messages on MumsOnline?' she smirks. 'Do you even remember what you said? Because I do. *I don't think I want this baby. Sometimes, I wish I'd never even had the girls. Is it normal to feel nothing when you look at your daughters?*'

I close my eyes and try to drown out the words that she screams across the room at me; all words I wrote. All things I felt. They disgust me.

'You said you were just like her! You said that was your biggest fear! Now you're telling me she was evil. So which is it, Emily? What's the truth? Tell me what you really did to Beth—'

She lunges for me and I see too late the little face in the doorway; history repeating itself with horrible clarity

344

as Ella's fragile body darts between us and I scream – the piercing sound the only thing louder than the horrifying, all too familiar crack of a skull splitting on slate.

Forty-Nine

Two Weeks Later

My hands shake as I walk down the too-bright corridor
where I've spent every waking moment in the last two
weeks. You'd think the shock would eventually go, but my
body has been on high alert ever since that night, though
surviving on a diet of caffeine and crisps from the vending
machine probably isn't helping. But what else can I do?
I can't leave until she speaks. Though they tell me there's
every chance she might never do that.

In her hospital room, I sit by the bed and stroke her
blonde curls. A well-thumbed copy of *Bridget Jones's Diary*
sits on the bedside table and I imagine a nurse has been
sitting in my seat at some point, watching over her while
I've not been able to.

'Hi, Allie,' I say tentatively. Holding one-sided conversations has yet to become comfortable. 'How are you
today?' I leave a pause, just in case. Nothing. 'I see
someone's been reading one of my favourites to you,' I
say, picking up the book. 'Though it's been years since I
read it. Watch the film every Christmas, much to Mark's
annoyance.' I force a laugh.

I stand up from the chair and walk around the room.
It's small, boxy. Impersonal. Mark packed up a few things
from her house after that night, though he did it with such

anger that it hardly felt worth the effort. But I couldn't bear Allie being in here without any home comforts at all. I pick up the framed photograph that sits on the window sill. It's one of my favourite photos of our childhood, with us three sisters standing side-by-side, smiles beaming in the sunlight. I flick a glance back to Alison and jump back.

Her eyes are open.

I try to calm my breathing as I watch her, but her eyes are firmly planted on the wall in front of her, not even acknowledging my presence.

'Allie?'

Her eyes flick away from the wall to the photo in my hands, then to my face. Her lip twitches, like she might be about to speak and my stomach twists. Am I ready for this?

'Emily,' she says.

Her voice is soft but crackles at the edges, creaky with underuse.

'Hi.' I walk across the room, the frame still in my hands, and take a seat back beside her bed. Her eyes don't leave mine but her expression is blank, like a baby that's trying to work out what it's being faced with.

'Shall I get someone?' I ask but she shakes her head. 'Water?' She nods. I pour luke-warm water from the jug beside the bed into plastic cups. How long has it been sitting here? I hand it to her and she takes it from me with caution before putting the cup to her lips.

We sit in silence and nerves prickle across my skin. Does Alison remember what happened? I think of Ella's tear-stained face as I scooped her up and ran from the kitchen, up the stairs, taking them two at a time. I grabbed Lara out of her cocoon of sleep and fled from the house. It was only a few minutes before I realised I couldn't repeat the mistakes of my past and called an ambulance, but it was enough. If I'd called them straight away, who knows what difference it would have made? Instead, I left Alison alone with a severe head injury that I caused. Again, I hurt one of my sisters. Only this time, thank god, it wasn't fatal.

But I'm making it right. I've been here every day, willing Allie to wake up, praying to God that she's okay. Mark moved back home, and we talked about what happened. I finally told him the truth about my childhood. We read my mum's diaries together once I found them in the house. We didn't reach much, just a few pages. Enough to know how unwell she was. Mark chucked it in the fire. Watching the pages burn, all the vile thoughts my mother had about me going up in smoke, was cathartic. But I can't help but think of my own vile words saved forever in digital form that can never be burned. I'll never be cleansed in that way. But I'm learning to come to terms with it all.

When I told Mark the truth, he couldn't understand why I'd go so far to cover up what my mum did to me. *I thought you'd take it as proof that there was something wrong with me. That there was obviously something in my blood… that I'd inherited it from her.* Mark looked at me with such love that night that I couldn't believe I ever thought he'd leave me if he discovered the truth.

I finally told him about the pills, too, admitting my fear that I'd caused the miscarriage that day and that I should have never got behind the wheel feeling the way I did. I saw anger burn in his eyes for a moment before it was fanned out with sadness, then love. Last week, the doctors confirmed that my guilt was misplaced. I finally got the nerve to see them about it, after Mark pushed me too, and they said there's no way the pills could have started

348

the bleeding. Losing our baby, they said, was just 'one of those things'. It doesn't absolve me of putting the girls into the car, knowing it was unsafe, but it helps to know that I did not cause the miscarriage, nor could I have stopped it.

The police had questions about Allie's head injury. Of course they did. It didn't look good for me that less than twenty-four hours after I accused her of abducting the girls, she was found unconscious on the floor after an argument between us. But after they looked into the situation, they realised she was the one behind the TwoIs-Trouble account after all and eventually I convinced them that I pushed her in self-defence.

'What happened?' Allie whispers, her eyes not quite focused on my face. 'Where am I?'

'You're in hospital… You had a fall.'

She looks around the room in a daze. 'I don't remember,' she whispers.

'That's okay,' I say, the knot of anxiety loosening in my stomach. 'I'm here now, I'm going to look after you.'

She meets my eyes and smiles vacantly. 'Good,' she says. 'You'll stay—'

She's cut off by a nurse rushing through the door. 'Goodness me! Look who's awake. You should have called for a doctor,' she chastises me.

And with that, the room fills with people and noise and the chance to have a conversation with Allie is lost. But as she's whisked from the room on a bed by a team of nurses, she catches hold of my hand and squeezes.

'Everything is going to be all right now,' I tell her. 'I promise I'm going to look after you.'

Once they've wheeled her out, I sit in her empty room in silence and cry. I call Mark and soon he arrives with the girls.

'Mummy!' they cry as they run into the room. I kiss them both on the tops of their heads as Mark pulls me into a hug.

'I think she's going to be okay,' I tell him, tears choking my words.

'Good,' he says. 'That's good.'

Mark hasn't forgiven Allie, not yet. But I know he will. I'm not sure he fully understands how I have, after she tried to ruin my life but for me, it was easy. She is a victim of mine and our mum's lies and I couldn't blame her for any of it. I just hope once she comes around properly, we can talk and she learns to understand what really happened. Perhaps she won't forgive me still, or believe me. But I have to believe that a part of Allie knows what happened, and we can become the sort of sisters we should always have been. I'm going to make sure of it; I won't let my mum take anything else from my life.

As I walk out of the hospital room holding my daughters' hands, Mark's arms wrapped around my shoulders, I finally allow myself to breathe. Everything is finally going to be okay.

Epilogue

Alison

It's late by the time you leave. The nurse had to come in and tell you that visiting time was over and I saw the relief on your face, even if you were quick to cover it. We hugged goodbye; your body felt strange against mine and you left behind the sweet scent of an expensive perfume on the cotton of my pyjamas.

I lie back down in bed, exhausted from the socialising. It's been weeks since I said more than a few words. Weeks of watching, listening silently, aware of everything around me.

I fucking hate this place.

But still, it's better than prison which could have of course been where I ended up after the stunt I pulled with the girls. You pushed me too far that day, Emily.

The nurse pops her head around the door to say goodnight and I smile sweetly like I'm expected to, rolling my eyes the second she's gone. Every moment spent here is a test of my endurance. At least when I was pretending to have lost the power of speech they didn't bother talking to me, only around me. Now, I'll have to engage in conversation. Smile on cue. Show them how much better I am.

It's exhausting.

This is how it must be for you all the time, isn't it? Pretending to be something you're not.

I did well with you today; perhaps I've picked up some of your tricks over the years. A smile creeps on my lips as I think of your flushed cheeks as you cried when I asked, 'Will you forgive me?'

'Only if you can forgive me,' you replied, like we were at the end of a Richard Curtis movie. I told you I did, of course. That all I wanted was my sister back.

But that's not what I want.

I want what you have. I want the girls. The twins. I want to walk down the street and have strangers stop me to remark on how amazing they are. To be asked ten times a day how I tell them apart. To watch people's amazed expressions when they do their twin-speak. I want to be special again. Like Beth and I were.

I can never get her back, but I don't need to.

Because I have them now.

I realised that it wasn't going to be enough to show everyone who you really were, Emily. I want the girls to be happy and safe; that's what I've always wanted. But they wouldn't be, without a mother, would they? I couldn't get rid of you without knowing they had someone waiting in your place. I didn't realise at first how I would do it. But it became so obvious once I started spending time with them and Mark that the perfect replacement for you was me.

You'll come here again tomorrow, you promised. You said you'll keep coming every day. Soon, you'll bring the girls. Then, you'll bring Mark. He'll be easy to win over. He's so desperate to make you happy that he'll trust your judgement on just about anything. And you think I'm worth saving.

Then, one day soon, I'll be discharged from here. I'll tell you I can't bear to go back to that house where so many terrible things happened. I'll have nowhere to go.

You'll offer me a home; I know you will.

And then, nothing will be able to stop me from being with the girls. Where I can make sure you can never hurt them again. And one day, when the time is right, I'll make sure you truly pay for what you've done.

A letter from Sophie

Dear Reader,

Thank you so much for picking up *Keep Them Close*, whether you did so after browsing your local bookstore, at a library, or downloading as an eBook. I'm so grateful that the book caught your eye enough to give it a chance and I hope you've enjoyed what you've read.

The idea for this book first came after reading about a 'Momfluencer' who had turned to anonymous forums to vent her frustrations at life and had since been 'outed' from behind her secret username. I was fascinated by the idea of a 'perfect' mum feeling so isolated and desperate that she would have no one to turn to except strangers on the internet and horrified at the idea of her anonymous posts becoming public.

Around the same time, I was facing my own struggles when, after years of trying unsuccessfully for a baby, my husband and I were told we would need IVF to conceive. Instead of turning immediately to friends and family, I found myself endlessly Googling for answers which quickly led me to online forums.

I was instantly captivated by the stories these spaces contained. Women not only talked about their day-to-day lives; what to have for dinner; how to approach a tricky conversation with their boss; but the parts of life that we just don't discuss. On IVF forums, women gladly share their egg counts, their partner's sperm results, and all the mysterious intricacies of making a life that usually go unseen.

Sadly, no matter how much advice I followed from these forums, I've yet to become a mum and have recently suffered multiple miscarriages. Once again, I was led back to the forums for support. If it weren't for these anonymous women sharing the details of their own losses so candidly, I would have been completely unprepared for what a miscarriage would entail and how to cope with the misplaced guilt and shame you're left with after. Like Emily, I desperately needed someone to tell me in no uncertain terms that my miscarriages were not my fault. If you are in that situation now, please know that miscarriages are almost *never* anyone's fault.

It may seem strange that I've written a book about motherhood when I've so far failed to be a mother myself, and stranger still that I've painted parenting forums as a dangerous place when I have so much admiration for them.

Even before I began this book, I knew I wasn't going to become a mother easily. Perhaps because of that, I have had so much time to consider what it means to be one, or in my case, not one. The expectation, guilt and loneliness that comes with all forms of motherhood, whether your babies are safely at home or have never made it there, is universal. That's what I hoped to explore in this book.

Sharing online does open you up to both criticism and potential harm but most people will not get stalked like Emily. I hope instead that most will experience the kindness and solidarity that I have from strangers on the internet. This book explores what would happen if you chose the wrong stranger to confide in because that makes a far better book. I believe in reality, most strangers will be the right ones.

If you enjoyed *Keep Them Close*, I would love to hear your thoughts via a review on Amazon and Goodreads which I hope will also encourage other readers to pick up the book. I read all my reviews and appreciate every single one.

If you would like to read more of my books, I'm thrilled to say there is another one coming in late 2022 with Hera and you can also read my debut, *All My Lies*, published in 2021.

I love hearing from readers; as an author you spend most of your time alone typing away, just hoping someone will one day read your words and enjoy them, so please do get in touch if you have. You can find me on social media or via my website.

Thank you again and happy reading.

Sophie x

Acknowledgments

This book is dedicated to my mum – the world's greatest – whose life I have stolen parts of for my plot. Like Emily's mother, mine is a mother to three girls. My oldest sister got our mum when she was very young and fun. My other sister and I had the more responsible mature adult version many years later. In both versions, my mum was the very best mother and does not at all resemble Emily's! But her experience as a mother, and ours as three sisters where two of us were sometimes mistaken for one, inspired this story. Thank you, Mum, Nicky and Rosie for being the backbone of my life and to so many of my stories.

I would also like to say a special thank you to my dad who has been there for me in the toughest year of my life; always with bread and brie and ham – the perfect picnic lunch for bad days. My love of reading came from you and look where we are now.

Tom, my husband and biggest supporter in every area of my life. Thank you for being you – the best parts of all my male characters are you and the worst parts I promise, are not. I can't wait for our kids one day to eat your special bolognese.

And, of course, my Dales family. Thank you for always taking interest in my writing and reading my books.

Becoming an author during a global pandemic is a tricky thing and I have yet to enjoy sashaying around literary parties with hordes of writerly types. (I am, however, also led to believe this representation of author life is not quite accurate, even pre-pandemic, but this is not something I am willing to give up hope for just yet.) This could have made writing rather solitary but despite lockdown, the last two years have brought an extraordinary number of people into my life, most of whom I cannot fit in these pages but I shall try.

Thank you to my colleagues and friends at Jericho Writers. These friendships have formed mostly online but I feel like I know the women of Jericho like sisters. (And if our Teams chats were ever made public, we would also have to take some rather drastic action to control the damage).

My writing friends and colleagues keep me going through WhatsApp and DMs. Special thanks to L.V. Matthews, S.V. Leonard, Polly Phillips, Sarah Clarke, Meera Shah, Hazel Compton, Sarah Juckes, Holly Seddon, Sophie Hannah, and all the Debut 2021 members.

My TopWrite girls: Janelle, Pearl, and Verity who were once strangers at a writing festival and are now my go-tos for all life and writing events. I adore you all and am so glad we found our way into each other's lives.

Finally, my publishing team. My agent Kate who was there for the setbacks and pulled me back up to bring this book to you. Thank you for always responding to my rather long, detailed emails with the patience of a saint.

My wonderful editor, Keshini, who got what I was trying to do with *Keep Them Close* from the very first read and helped me make the story far stronger than it ever would have been alone. This is our first book together, but I hope becomes one of many. Thank you for your understanding and care with my words. When I told you I wanted to write about 'the shame and guilt that comes with miscarriage' you thoughtfully added the word 'misplaced' in front of 'shame and guilt' at a time when I needed more than anything to see that distinction, thank you.

To the whole team at Hera who have worked on this book, thank you – you are excellent and I am very proud to be one of your authors.

And finally, to you, my readers. You could have picked up any book and you picked up mine. I hope you enjoyed what you've read and continue to read more books from me so I can keep doing this forever.